GOPHER HOCKEY by the HOCKEY GOPHER

Written, compiled and published by Ross Bernstein.
• Ross Bernstein Enterprises

• Edited by John Gilbert
• History by Don Clark
• Printed by: The Publishing Group, Minneapolis, Minnesota. USA

Photo Credits: University of Minnesota, U of M Archives. Additional photos by: (Let's Play Hockey, Media Guides, John Gilbert, George Karn and Don Clark)

ISBN   0-9634871-0-8

Library of Congress Catalog Card Number: 92-97306

CONTENTS

FOREWORD

By John Gilbert

It all started out so innocently. One day during the summer of '92, the phone rings and some guy says, "Hello, this is Ross Bernstein."

The momentary blank space where any glimmer of recognition might have exposed itself was followed by my response: "Ross *who*?"

Which led to Phase II of Ross's introduction: "...You know, Goldy Gopher."

"Oh."

Sports mascots tend to fall into various categories, most of them ranging from meaningless to annoying. But the Gopher hockey teams have been blessed with some good ones over the years, and the Goldy who Gophered from '90-'92 was something special, even if I didn't know who he really was. In fact, maybe *because* I didn't know who he really was.

While watching Gopher games in Williams/Mariucci Arena for somewhere around 30 years, back since I was a student, it was obvious that Gopher Hockey crowds were something special. They always have tended to be wonderfully inventive and clever on their own, without need of any prompting by a mascot, and certainly without the tedious kind of electronic cues, such as the "clap now" instruction on the scoreboards at pro arenas.

I had written stories about Gopher fans for the Minneapolis Tribune, back before it became the Star Tribune, newspaper of the Twin Cities. One story focused on the crowd's reaction to a bad call, which consisted of a long, drawn-out expletive that wound up being forceful enough to warrant being the basis for a story in that family newspaper. They'd build it up from a growl to a roar: "...buullllll-SHIT!" It was a novelty at the time, mainly because it was virtually unanimous as well as spontaneous, and also because nobody else had ever done anything like that. Nowadays it seems trite, because every crowd in every arena watching every sport seems to yell either that same epithet or some other crude, gratuitous vulgarism at officials and opponents.

The tendency is for fans elsewhere to try to inject themselves into the game, instead of merely watching and enjoying the game. Obtrusive behavior has, regrettably, become the norm. Wisconsin fans started yelling "Sieve" at opposing goalies, which always infuriated me. First off, the suggestion after a Badger goal that the opposing goalie is lousy mostly suggests that the Badgers scored by luck or opposing incompetence, casting more doubt on the Badgers skill than anything else.

I have always been elated that Gopher fans tend to be unable (unwilling?) to properly execute any unified performance of the hated "sieve" chant. It proves that Gopher fans have remained a cut above that. Despite, by the way, Goldy's effort. He admits trying to get the Gophers to yell "sieve," and even admits he likes it. But what does he know? Whenever you find yourself puzzled over Ross's behavior, repeat to yourself: He's only a rodent.

Still, cleverness fits far better than senseless chants on the Gopher crowd. How about the time Don (Red) Wilkie refereed a game and made a series of calls that annoyed the Gopher fans. Finally, and suddenly, a large group of fans chanted, in perfect unison:

"A horse's tail is long and silky;
lift it up and you'll see Wilkie."

When the new scoreboard was hung on the east wall, with a picture-generator and all, the attempt was made to get the whole crowd involved chanting "Minnesota," by the syllable. Not bad, except that we all pronounce it: "Min-nah-so-tah." However, spelled correctly, the northeast quadrant of fans was supposed to yell "MIN," the northwest group "NE," the southwest quadrant "SO," and southeastern fans, "TA." Too bad the southeastern fans got the wimpy part, but it was only a harmless little bit, intended to get the fans to out- yell each other when their turn came.

Now the fans in the northwest quadrant have always been the rowdiest, so they jumped on the phonetic breakdown. When the scoreboard flashed "NE," they screamed "NEEE," instead of "Nah." The crowd's chant, then, became "Min-NEE-so-ta." This group, forever more, was to be known as the "NEE" section, spelled "NE," and every once in a while, for no apparent reason, this gang would start chanting: "NEE, NEE, NEE..." Visiting players, coaches and reporters would ponder for a while, then finally ask what the heck the crowd was chanting. One paranoid visitor thought Goldy was imploring the crowd to cheer for a "knee" injury by a visiting player.

Anyhow, you take this raucous and clever group of dedicated Gopher Hockey fans and you add some lunatic in a Goldy Gopher suit who happens to be slightly off-center when it comes to being clever and creative, and you've got the makings of some truly funny antics. The Ross Bernstein Goldy was, in a word, awesome. But he was even good from the standpoint of mascot purity.

If you can believe this, there is something called mascot camp, where college mascots from all over the country gather with cheerleaders to do their thing. Ross originally had written a whole chapter about it, which I, serving as your obedient editor/servant, deep-sixed. You (maybe) and I (definitely) think of the Ross Bernstein Goldy as the ultimate rebel in the mundane world of mascots, but Bernstein not only went to (ugh) mascot camp, he *won* some preppy competition as the best mascot there. Pull-eeze!

He told me that going into his Goldy years, he was determined to become absolutely the biggest Gopher fan. I guessed that he was up to about 230, which should have been sufficient.

Back down to earth from his mascot camp award, Ross/Goldy climbed up on his ivory-tower, which began life as a photo-stand perch, anchored to the glassed-in western wall of Mariucci Arena. He brought with him a menagerie of pets and toys and signs and tricks, all aimed at giving the crowd inspiration. I enjoyed his antics, and the crowd's responses, thoroughly. So did the crowd, and so did other reporters. And Bill Butters, Gopher assistant coach, admitted that if and when a game ever bogged down, he found himself watching and being totally amused by Goldy.

Ironically, the only guys who didn't seem to know anything about Goldy, for a while, were Frank Mazzocco and Wally Shaver, the TV guys. They were so focused on watching the action, and living inside their headphone world, that they missed out on a lot of the Goldy nonsense. Unbeknown to them, Goldy was in the process of getting the crowd to alternately cheer, "FRANK," then "WALLY." When Goldy made his way up to the press box one time, sneaking up and hugging Frank and Wally, the crowd nearly went crazy at the whole thing. Ross/Goldy didn't realize that Frank and Wally didn't have a clue what was going on and why. They asked me, and I explained that Goldy had been making them more famous than any TV ratings could reflect. Once they found out, they loved it and willingly entered into a sort of long-range mutual admiration bit.

All of that brings us back to this phone call, from anonymous-person-known-as-large-rodent to reporter-at-home. Ross had this kinky idea. He was ending his term of Goldy, and wanted to express himself, so he thought of writing a humorous little book about Gopher Hockey, as seen by Goldy Gopher. Never one to put down an off-the-wall idea, I told him it could work, and it sounded like fun.

So he hauled out a tape-recorder and we raved on about hockey for an hour or so. He asked if I'd help him out by maybe editing the thing, and I said I would, and, if he needed it, I'd be glad to write a "Foreword," or something like that. He said good, and he hoped it wouldn't be too much trouble, although he was up front about his inexperience as a writer. I assured him that he needn't worry, that to me, the principle didn't matter so much as the money of the thing.

Several weeks later, my phone rang again. "Hi, it's Ross," a voice said.

Again, the Rolodex of my mind started filtering through all the possible hockey/auto racing/car-testing folks who might be named Ross, and just as it was coming up empty, Ross filled the hesitation with: "...You know, Goldy."

"Right."

Well, Ross went on to inform me that this brief, humorous, Gophers-as-seen-by-Goldy scheme had been expanded. Instead of encompassing the four of five years of Goldy's personal connection with the team and its players and fans, he had branched out. Just a bit. He had interviewed well over 100 people and was asking for more names, because he had decided to do an all-time history of Gopher hockey.

I felt like a school teacher might after anticipating a student's "What I did Last Summer" essay and finding out the student instead decided to write the History of the Western World. Complete, and, as they say, unabridged. There's a joke about asking somebody what time it is and being told how to build a watch. Ross would have gone on to describe the geography and geology of Switzerland.

I keep calling Ross a "guy." Just a slip. We must think of him as Goldy, this overstuffed rodent. Picture him, in his quest for historical tidbits, tunneling indiscriminately here and there, not unlike his cousin, the rat in a maze. It is easier on the nerves thinking of a large 13-striped critter interviewing and writing this epic, because spelling, punctuation and some semblance of journalistic flow might be expected of a "guy," but we must understand that such basic elements might only occur as random coincidences with a rodent.

Gopher Hockey is something special enough to deserve scrutiny by both man and mouse, as rodents go. People who don't understand Gopher Hockey tend to be those whose grasp of sports is limited to the mundane world of football, baseball or basketball, without appreciation for the complex wonders of hockey. They tend to criticize hockey for not being widespread nationally, without realizing it is widespread worldly. And if hockey is unique in the way it is played in Minnesota, then it reflects the lifestyle of Minnesotans. The fact that the Gophers depend on homestate talent makes it more special, and the fact that the homestate Gophers are perennially prominent nationally makes it extra-special. And those thousands (millions?) who are in the Gopher Hockey cult frankly don't give a damn about those who aren't. It's kind of like belonging to an exclusive club; you want to be selective about who else wants in.

Gopher Hockey history is filled with colorful players, coaches, people and games. They swarm in a blur of memories, over the years, in a warm and fuzzy area of my memory. Some I remember as sensational games, others I remember because they inspired me to write about them in a way I still recall.

Like when Bill Butters, the player, was separated from the on-ice brawl that was going on in the corner against Colorado College. Butters stood alone at center ice, trying to put his jersey on front wards and helping his elbow pads face the right direction. The players on the CC bench stood, screaming taunts at Butters, and Butters glared back at them. I was high up in the press box, that night 20-some years ago, but I remember it as if it were last night. I saw the duel evolving, and I read the glare in Butters' eyes. Involuntarily, I stood up and said, out loud to nobody, "Don't do it, Billy."

But he did. His feet whirling like a Roadrunner cartoon, Butters spun his wheels until he got traction, then he charged the CC bench, hurtling over it like an Olympian and triggering one of the more intriguing brawl-extensions of all time. In my restrained explanation for the paper, I wrote, "...as the CC players on the bench taunted him, Butters stood at center ice and assessed the odds. Fourteen to one. Pretty even."

There are as many memories as there were games, or players. I remember, practically as a child, seeing Lou Nanne with a crewcut that didn't require any transplants. His hair was hidden under a strange-looking Gopher helmet that looked a lot like a canned-ham can. Clint Sanborn, who wrote a column in the Minnesota Daily at the time, called Louie "The Ice God," who could swing down from the Williams Arena rafters whenever the Gophers needed a big play.

There was John Mariucci, starting it all off with his unique touch. When John was dying of cancer years later, Gus Hendrickson, former UMD coach and, as an Eveleth native, a worshipper-from-childhood of Maroosh, said it best: "John is rough, tough, hard, mean, gruff...and soft inside."

There were Glen Sonmor's teams, winning a WCHA title and almost an NCAA title with over-achieving rinkrats like Mike Antonovich and the Peltier brothers beating teams laden with top-flight Tier I Canadian juniors...There were Herb Brooks's players, having to learn how to avoid not only opposing checks, but schizophrenia from Herbie's constant mind-games as he whipped them to the absolute heights — WCHA titles and NCAA championships...There were some great years under Brad Buetow, when a turbulent undercurrent of trying to define true success seemed to prevail, while seeking — and failing — to grasp the highest rung...And there were (are) the Doug Woog years, which have been very successful, with plentiful WCHA trophies, but the nagging little footnote of being unable to capture that final challenge at NCAA time.

Mariucci set the tone, Sonmor battled as giant-killer against overwhelming odds...Brooks proved a true eccentric genius for taking over a last-place Gopher team, raising it from 10th to sixth place in his first year, and to a national championship in his second. He won two more NCAA crowns, shifting the balance of power forevermore...For Buetow and, later, Woog, the chore didn't become easy, but it became different. Instead of establishing the excellence of the Gopher Hockey Tradition, they had to maintain it.

The pursuit of excellence goes without saying in Gopher Hockey. The pursuit of the NCAA title is, however, something different. To those superficial and front-running fans and media-types who measure success *only* by the NCAA title, consider the alternatives: Is it a better measure of excellence to be among the elite teams every year without winning the NCAA, or to be up and down in the standings from year to year, but somehow snatching an NCAA title by luck and a hot hand?

Gopher Hockey fans know the answer, although they would undoubtedly settle for evidence that consistent excellence and an NCAA title, as Brooks's teams proved, needn't be mutually exclusive. Sure, expectations are high, perhaps unfairly high. But fast, hard, all-out effort is all the fans have asked, regardless of their expectations. And no matter how frustrating the failure to win the NCAA might be, it cannot be blamed on the pressure of expectations of zealous fans, or media, or the players and coaches themselves. Remember, winning it all means never having to rationalize. But the pursuit - done with honor and effort is what counts.

Meanwhile, when things get tense, we've all been able to glance up toward the rafters, where this crazed Goldy Gopher character, dangling Gumby down from his perch on a string trying to tickle someone, or hinting to the "NE" section that genealogy might indicate a kitchen utensil has a place in the opposing goaltender's family tree.

And now, we've got his compilation of comments, anecdotes, tidbits and statistics about Gopher Hockey for fans through the ages. At first it seemed like a hopeless situation, to have someone whose time-span with the Gophers is so short take on a challenge so immense. But it caused Ross to depend on others — players, coaches and observers — to relay Gopher hockey history from their own viewpoints. Some memories are better than others, but their comments all have their own credibility.

If you've ever had a single hair stand on end when the pep band plays the "Rouser," or gotten even a trace of a chill when the crowd spontaneously erupts as a long pass triggers a Gopher breakaway down on Mariucci Arena's expansive ice sheet, you will enjoy reading this book. You can read a chapter at a time. Or you can pick it up, open it to a random page, and get a bang out of what's there. But you may be compelled to go for it, cover-to-cover. And over and over.

Whatever, it is certain that you will find yourself repeating anecdotes that you will see here. Want one to look for? OK, how about the one where Wendy Anderson recalls Maroosh telling why he let Wendy play on his team? There are a lot of memorable ones, but that's my favorite.

Just remember, if you ever get a phone call from a strange character who identifies himself as a one-time rodent, don't hang up or call an exterminator. As hockey fans, as observers of Gopher Hockey, as Minnesotans who appreciate the greatest tradition in state athletics -- Pat Reusse notwithstanding-- we all owe Ross Bernstein a debt of gratitude.

And, as many Gophers as have gone on to the pros, why haven't the North

Stars tried to sign this guy? They could dress him up as any sort of mascot they want, and they could get him, easy, for a long-term contract. To him, the money doesn't matter, it's the principle of the thing.

As for any Goldy-to-come in the future, now you know the kind of pressure of high expectations that Doug Woog talks about. "Ross Who?" has left a big head to fill.

John Gilbert

Some kids are just plain scared to death of giant rodents.

ACKNOWLEDGMENTS

I would like to thank everyone I pestered for help with this project. I appreciate them taking time to talk to me, and I only wish I could have talked to a hundred more, about a subject they — and I — so dearly love...

FORMER GOPHERS:

Wendy Anderson	(D, 1952-54; former Minnesota Governor.)
Mike Antonovich	(C, 1970-72; Saints, Whalers, North Stars, Devils.)
Bill Baker	(D, 1976-79; Canadiens, Rockies, Blues, Rangers.)
Dean Blais	(W, 1970-73; Blackhawks, Coach: UND, Roseau, Int. Falls.)
Jim Boo	(D, 1976-78; North Stars.)
Dave Brooks	(C, 1961-63 Europe.)
Herb Brooks	(W, 1957-59; Head Coach, Rangers, North Stars, *Devils, '80 Olympics.)
Aaron Broten	(C, 1980-81; Rockies, Devils, Maple Leafs, Jets.)
Neal Broten	(C, 1979-81; North Stars, Europe.)
Paul Broten	(C, 1985-88; Rangers.)
Brad Buetow	(W, 1971-73; Head Coach, Colorado College.)
Bill Butters	(D, 1971-73; Assistant coach; Maple Leafs, North Stars.)
Gene Campbell	(W, 1952-54.)
Tom Chorske	(W, 1985-88; Canadiens, Devils.)
Steve Christoff	(C, 1977-79; North Stars, Flames, Kings.)
Dick Dougherty	(W, 1952-54.)
Butsy Erickson	(W, 1980-83; Capitals, Kings, Penguins, Jets, Europe.)
Gary Gambucci	(C, 1966-68; North Stars, Canadiens, Saints.)
Ben Hankinson	(W, 1988-91; Devils' minor league affiliate.)
Pete Hankinson	(W, 1987-90; Jets' minor league affiliate.)
Darby Hendrickson	(W, 1991-)
Tim Harrer	(W, 1977-80; Flames.)
Paul Holmgren	(W, 1975-76; Flyers, Stars; Coach: Flyers, *Whalers.)
Stanley S. Hubbard	(W, 1952-54; Owner of KSTP-TV, Gopher supporter.)
David Jensen	(D, 1980-83; North Stars.)
Trent Klatt	(W, 1990-92; North Stars.)
Reed Larson	(D, 1975-77; Red wings, Islanders, Oilers, North Stars.)
Cory Laylin	(W, 1989-92.)
Len Lilyholm	(W, 1961-63; Saints.)
John Mayasich	(C, 1952-55; Green Bay-Bobcats - Player/Coach/G.M.)
Jack McCartan	(G, 1956-58; Rangers, Saints, Scout-Canucks.)
Murray McLachlan	(G, 1968-70; Toronto farm system, Tulsa.)
Dick Meredith	(W, 1952-55; North Stars.)
Don Micheletti	(W, 1977-80.)
Joe Micheletti	(D, 1974-77; Flames, Oilers, Rockies, Blues.)
Pat Micheletti	(W, 1983-86; North Stars, Europe.)
Corey Millen	(C, 1983-87; Europe, Rangers, Kings.)
Lou Nanne	(D, 1961-63; North Stars.)
Todd Okerlund	(W, 1984-87; Islanders.)
Wally Olds	(D, 1969-71; Europe.)
Larry Olimb	(C/D, 1989-92; Sharks.)
Paul Ostby	(G, 1981-82; Assistant Coach.)
Dick Paradise	(D, 1966-68; Rangers, Buffalo, Red Wings, Saints.)
Doug Peltier	(W, 1970-72; Coach/A.D. Forest Lake High School.)
Ron Peltier	(C, 1969-71.)
Pat Phippen	(W, 1974-76.)
Mike Polich	(C, 1972-75; Canadiens, North Stars.)
Frank Pond	(C, 1923-25; Head Coach.)

Mike Ramsey	(D, 1979-80; Sabres.)
Larry Ross	(G, 1951-53; Coach: International Falls, Scout: Sharks)
Roger Rovick	(C, 59-60.)
Randy Skarda	(D, 1987-89; Blues farm system.)
Dave Snuggerud	(W, 1986-89; Sabres, Sharks.)
Glen Sonmor	(Head Coach, 1966-71; former Saints, North Stars coach.)
Dick Spannbauer	(D, 1973-74; Cincinnati, Atlanta.)
Robb Stauber	(G, 1987-89; Kings, Phoenix Road-Runners.)
Steve Ulseth	(W, 1978-81; Rangers.)
Tom Vannelli	(C, 1974-77; radio commentator.)
Bud Wilkinson	(G, 1935-38; Oklahoma football coach.)
Dean Williamson	(C, 1989-91.)
Murray Williamson	(W, 1957-59; Coach: '68, '72 Olympics, St. Paul Steers.)
Doug Woog	(C, 1964-66; Head Coach, Coach: South St. Paul High School.)
Ken Yackel Jr.	(W, 1975-77.)

MEDIA PERSONALITIES:

Steve Cannon	(WCCO Radio personality.)
John Gilbert	(Star Tribune sports writer.)
Tom Greenhoe	(Former Sports Information Director.)
Charley Hallman	(Pioneer Press sports writer.)
Frank Mazzocco	(KITN-TV broadcaster.)
Doug McLeod	(MSC-TV, and radio broadcaster.)
Jeff Passolt	(KARE-TV broadcaster, KQRS radio personality.)
Bob Reid	(Former Gopher announcer, WCHA statistician.)
Pat Reusse	(Star Tribune columnist.)
Don Riley	(Pioneer Press sports columnist.)
Mark Rosen	(WCCO-TV broadcaster.)
Joe Schmit	(KSTP-TV broadcaster.)
Wally Shaver	(KITN-TV broadcaster.)
Bob Utecht	(Founder of "Let's Play Hockey.")
Gregg Wong	(Pioneer Press sports writer.)

SIGNIFICANT OTHERS:

Amo Bessone	(Former Coach: Michigan State, Michigan Tech.)
Walter Bush	(Executive Director USA Hockey.)
Don Clark	(Hockey Historian, Officer: MAHA and USA Hockey.)
Governor Arne Carlson	(Minnesota Governor.)
Gretchen Colletti	(Widow of John Mariucci.)
Dave Ferroni	(Nephew of John Mariucci, 1970 team manager.)
Pat Forciea	(North Stars Vice President.)
Paul Giel	(Former Gopher A.D., football, baseball star; pro.)
Norm Green	(Owner of the North Stars.)
John/Bonnie Hankinson	(Gopher quarterback/cheerleader and hockey parents.)
Bret Hedican	(St. Cloud St. defenseman, '92 Olympian, Pro: Blues.)
Gary Heinrich	(President of the Gopher Blue-Line Club.)
Willard Ikola	(Michigan goalie; Coach: Edina; Hall of Fame inductee.)
Tom Ivan	(President of Chicago Blackhawks.)
Jimmy Johnson	(North Star defenseman, and former Duluth Bulldog.)

George Karn	(Artist, and lifelong friend of John Mariucci.)
Dave Knoblauch	(New Mariucci Arena coordinator, Gopher supporter.)
John Kundla	(Former Gopher Basketball coach, Minneapolis Lakers coach.)
Bill Mosienko	(Former Blackhawk, linemate of John Mariucci.)
Dr. V.A. Nagobads	(Gopher/USA Team Physician for over 30 years.)
Butch Nash	(Gopher football coach, teammate of John Mariucci.)
Bob Perrizo	(Lifelong friend of John Mariucci.)
Dave Peterson	(Coach: '88, '92 Olympics; and Southwest High for 27 years.)
Tim/Sue Podein	(Owners of Stub & Herb's Bar, lifelong Gopher fans.)
Bob Ridder	('56 Olympic Manager, past North Stars owner.)
Bob Scott	(United States Hockey Hall of Fame Director.)
Bobby Smith	(North Stars center.)
Bruce Telander	(1956 team manager, Blue-Line Club founder.)
Wendell Vandersluis	(University of Minnesota Athletics photographer.)

For Mike and Andy.
My two big brothers, and two best friends that I've ever had.
Thanks for always being there for me whenever I've needed
you, and for making me laugh. I love you guys more than
anything in the world.

INTRODUCTION

It was the first of April, 1989 at the Civic Center in St. Paul when it happened. I was sitting in the first row right behind the net with my buddy, Lindy, watching him skate down the ice. He made a move, then took a shot at the goalie. All you could hear was a dull plunk, that could've only meant one thing. Randy Skarda rang the pipe. Skarda had come one inch from returning the Gophers to that promised land of National Championships. One inch that would've stopped those pesky reporters from asking Coach Woog why he can't win the big one. That one inch was the closest the Gophers had come to being national champs in some 13 seasons, since the 1979 team under Herb Brooks beat North Dakota in Detroit. There have been other championship games, other final fours, and other great seasons. But, never as close as that brisk April day in 1989. That day is one I will always remember, because it forever changed my life and my involvement with Gopher Hockey. Here's what a couple people who were there that day had to say about two scoring chances in that game:

RANDY SKARDA: "It was probably the most crushing defeat of my life. Kenny Gernander set me up, and I hit the inside of the pipe. After the game I couldn't leave my house for two weeks, I was devastated."

DEAN WILLIAMSON: "I was five feet away from Skarda when he rang the pipe, and was dreaming of a rebound out front, but no dice."

As for the other shot at the other end:

ROBB STAUBER: "I don't like to think about it. I remember the shot, and I reached for the rebound but missed it. There were so many things in that game I would've done differently. Sometimes in big pressure games you tend to be more reserved, and play more conservatively than you'd like to. But, that was a great year, and we had nothing to be ashamed of that season at all."

Fortunately the occupational dreams of our childhoods don't come true — or else the world would be full of nothing but cowboys, and ballerinas. While I was merely a volunteer as Goldy, doing it only for a love of the team, and compromising an occasional slapshot to the chops to have the best seat in the house, some college mascots get full scholarships as cheerleaders, along with phy-ed credits, varsity letters, and many campus perks as student-athletes.

Of the 250 college mascots in America today, did you know that more than 70 are eagles? *(I lifted that fact from Spy magazine.)* After eagles, the most common mascots are, in descending order, tigers, cougars, bulldogs, lions, warriors, panthers, Indians, wildcats, and bears. *(I wonder why "Gophers" don't rank that high?)* These are mascots' mascots: Most of them are paid nothing, and they have to squeeze their performing and daily workouts in between trigonometry and English composition. They do their job because they have what the University of South Carolina's Gamecock, Cocky, calls "that fire within." *(At least there are as many*

"Gopher" mascots as there are "Gamecocks.")

The original mascot of all time, was The Clown Prince of Baseball, Max Patkin. He never wore a costume, he would just flip his hat sideways, pull up his pants and act like he was missing about 12 chromosomes. It wouldn't be for several years until we would see the likes of those "mega-star" mascots like the San Diego Chicken, Phillie Phanatic, and Phoenix Gorilla.

Mascots are at games to have fun. They are there to add entertainment in between the whistles, and let people escape. People come to games to see their team win, and if the crowd gets into the game, the home team increases its odds of victory. I had a blast being Goldy Gopher at the hockey games. I had been at Gopher football and basketball games as the mascot, and they are nothing compared to the crowds at Mariucci Arena. It's a true, college crowd, where the fans openly voice their opinions about the referees and the tempo of the game. Everybody in there is going crazy and the team feeds off it for a great home-ice advantage. That's the sports environment I love to be around. I'll never forget crying after my last home game, and knowing that I'd have to hang up those paws forever. It was the last time I would be able to "legally" punch anyone, slander someone or make them laugh at some childish prank on someone else's behalf. It was a chance to live vicariously, and not have a care in the world. I loved seeing crazy fans that would live and die for the Gophers, no matter what. That's why it was so awesome being Goldy Gopher.

I don't claim to be a historian, nor do I claim to be a writer. I only claim to be a rodent, and hopefully the people that read this will enjoy the compilation of quotes, stories and innuendoes from many of the heroes of Gopher Hockey past and present. So, sit back, grab some cheese-curls, pop open a cold one, and enjoy. If you're not a Gopher Hockey fan yet, hopefully this book will sell you on the greatest

college hockey tradition in the world.

HOW DID THE UNIVERSITY OF MINNESOTA GET THE NICKNAME GOLDEN GOPHERS?

(Rumor used to be that Sid Hartman wanted a football coach to fetch him a Diet Coke, and when he ordered him to "Go-for" it, the name stuck. But that's just rumor.)

History, by way of the Minneapolis Star Tribune, shows that the name goes back to 1858 (pre-dating even Sid). Minnesota was labeled the "Gopher State" by a satirical cartoon one time, referring to the $5 million loan bill that appeared in the Minnesota Legislature in February of 1858. That bill, providing a loan for the building of railroads in Minnesota, was bitterly opposed. The subject was shown in a cartoon by having a "Gopher Train" being pulled by nine 13-striped gophers with human heads. That's how we became known as the Gopher state.

Soon after, the expression appeared in songs of the period, like *"The Beauty of the West."* Here the lyrics sang: *"And now they call us Gophers, as you may understand. We're good as any badgers, or any in the land."*

In the 30's, the Gopher football teams under Bernie Bierman were often national champions. During that time, the local press described the team as a "Golden-shirted horde" and then "Golden swarm." These were simultaneous with the team's decision to change jerseys to golden colored and brought the name we know today as the "Golden Gophers."

WHAT DID IT MEAN TO BE A GOPHER?

Reed Larson, a former Gopher defenseman from Roosevelt and later a Red Wings standout, remembers. "Like most guys, I used to dream of skating in Williams arena," he said. "I remember when I was being recruited. I would come home from school, and see those big letters in the mail from the 'U' with the big letter "M" on them, and getting so pumped up that I'd rip them open. I consider the University of Minnesota to be the Montreal of college hockey. I got close to the guys, and it was innocent back then. We didn't worry about getting traded, there weren't any politics from the front office, and it was sincerely a lot of fun to be a Gopher. It helped me build character as a man, and introduced me to all my friends."

A lifelong fan of hockey is Breck grad, former Gopher and current owner of KSTP-TV, Stanley S. Hubbard. "Are you kidding? To sit next to a guy like John Mayasich on the bench, it was incredible."

For Todd Okerlund, a Burnsville native, and former Gopher winger, it was simple. "Ever since I was a kid I wanted to be a Gopher."

Corey Millen, a former Gopher center from Cloquet saw it this way: "Minnesota hockey was the best place to be. It's the elite college hockey program in the country. It was such a great honor, so many kids would've died to have played here. I grew up watching the Bulldogs, but was set on coming to the 'U' to be a Gopher. It was the best time of my life, and I miss it a lot. It was so much fun all the time, no pressure, and so many great friendships. I really miss roping down at old Fowl Play on Mondays too; that was a tradition I was sad to say good-bye to."

Former Gopher captain and Edina cake-eater Pete Hankinson has fond memories of being a Gopher. "I think it's all about being unified against your old high school enemies, and just playing with so many great guys," said Hankinson. "When I was in Indiana playing minor league hockey, I could see why they are crazy about basketball. It seemed that every garage had a hoop on it, and in Minnesota it seems that every neighborhood park has a rink. Besides that, there seems to always be kids of all ages zooming around on Roller blades throughout the neighborhoods in the summers to get ready for the season."

Joe Micheletti, a Hibbing native and former Gopher defenseman said: "There's not another school in the country with more hockey tradition and loyalty. It was so much fun to be a part of it."

Joe's younger brother, Don, was an outstanding left wing for the Gophers in the late 70's. "When you consider that every kid in the state of Minnesota wants to be an athlete at the University of Minnesota, and only a very few get an opportunity to do so, I was very proud to be a Gopher," said Don Micheletti. "It was a dream come true to play with guys like Steve Christoff and Tim Harrer. We had a great line and I don't know if I've ever seen one better at the U of M. I grew up thinking about one thing, and that was to play hockey for the Gophers. Herb Brooks gave me that opportunity."

Pat Micheletti, their little brother, was a Gopher All-American, and holds the record of having the most career penalty minutes with 403. "It was a show, and I get excited just thinking about it. I really miss the fans going crazy, and all the excitement," said Pat Micheletti. "It was unbelievable being a Gopher, I get goose-bumps just thinking about it. It made me who I am today."

Tim Harrer, a Bloomington native, set the record for the most goals in a single season with 53. "It was a lot of pride to wear a jersey there," Harrer said.

"Everyone wanted to be a Gopher growing up. It was something special all right."

One of the best Gopher goalies of all time was 1970 All-American Murray McLachlan, from Toronto. "I grew up in Canada figuring that I would play juniors, but luckily I wound up at the University of Minnesota," said McLachlan. "I met so many tremendous people, and it was just an honor to represent the school."

Another goalie, who holds numerous records at the U of M, including most wins with 71, is past Hobey Baker winner, Robb Stauber. "I remember growing up in Duluth watching the Gophers just kill the Bulldogs," said Stauber. "Being a Gopher was everything in the world to me. And I was lucky to have had such a great experience there."

Former Gopher center Roger Rovick is the president of Edina Realty. "I had always dreamt of playing under John Mariucci," said Rovick. "A lot of confidence was gained from going up against the competition there. You learned how to relate to others, hard work, how to take your knocks, how to accept defeat, and so many friendships. It shaped my life today, and I really miss it."

For Mike Polich, a 1975 All-American center who helped win the first NCAA trophy, it was a tough choice. "For me it was either Notre Dame or Minnesota," said Polich. "I went to Minnesota contrary to my family's belief that I would be just another number there. I learned, though, that once you're done with hockey it's best to enter the business world where people remember your name. It's a great education, and there are people out there who love to hire Gophers."

Burton Joseph was a 1938 grad of West High and extremely successful in the agricultural processing commodities, and exporting business with the Joseph Company. "I grew up desperately wanting to earn a letter at the University," said Joseph. "As a goal-guard, I grew up watching Bud Wilkinson. Marty Falk taught me everything I knew about being a good goal-guard as a Gopher."

Bryan Erickson, commonly referred to as Butsy, is a former Gopher right wing from Roseau. He has complemented his pro career with the Jets by buying two *Play it Again Sports* stores, in Duluth and Alexandria. He claims the name Butsy was given to him as a baby, when he apparently slept with his butt up in the air. "It was the most fun hockey I have ever played," said Erickson. "It meant a lot to me then, and still does today. When I look back on it, I feel it was the neatest thing that ever could've happened to me. It helped shape my life today."

For White Bear native, assistant coach, and former Gopher and pro great Bill Butters, it was a classic. "I've been a Gopher all of my life... and I love it," he said.

Wonder what it was like playing hockey in the 20's? Ask Frank Pond. "It was very special being a Gopher," said Pond. "Hockey was new in the state, and even though we played outdoors in the cold, it was something I will always remember very fondly."

One of the key members of the 1980 "Miracle On Ice," team was former Gopher forward and current pilot for Mesaba Airlines, Steve Christoff. "It was a dream of mine to be a Gopher, so when I got there it meant that I had achieved a life-long goal," Christoff said.

Former Gopher center Mike Antonovich from Greenway of Coleraine was one of the best players to ever wear the maroon and gold. "I was grateful that they gave me a chance to play," said Antonovich. "Glen (Sonmor) taught me so much about not only hockey, but about life. It was pretty special to me, and I'll never forget it."

Former Gopher center Dave Brooks is now a successful real-estate developer. "I loved being a Gopher, and miss it dearly," said Brooks. "I got to play hockey, hang out with John Mariucci, and have so much fun. I loved it."

Jack McCartan, an All-American goalie from St. Paul Marshall, was a star of the 1960 Olympic team. "I loved playing Gopher hockey," said McCartan. "Having the chance to play under Mariucci was one of the greatest things of my life."

New A.D. and hockey coach at International Falls, Dean Blais, recalls it too. "Playing for Glen Sonmor was a real treat," said Blais. "It was an extreme honor to put on that jersey, and something I'll always remember. It's a great school academically as well as a great sports school. It was for sure the best four years of my life." Blais has some pretty big shoes to fill up there in the north woods. When he played in high school, he played for International Falls high school coaching legend and former Gopher All-American Larry Ross. "I was older than the other guys," Ross recalled. I felt that I represented the whole state of Minnesota, and was very proud to have been an All-American at the University of Minnesota."

Dick Paradise, a former Cretin alum, played baseball and hockey for the Maroon and Gold. "The college life was the most fun, playing for Maroosh and Glen was quite a thrill, but the friendships were the most important," Paradise said.

Left wing Pat Phippen, a Ramsey High School star, played on two national championship teams, in '74 and '76. "It was pretty special," said Phippen. We learned a lot about ourselves, met a lot of great people, and got to play under Herb. It was a super experience."

Steve Ulseth was a 1981 Gopher All-American, and now owns a very successful hockey equipment distribution company called Ulseth Enterprises. "It's given me the confidence to go forward. We use it every day, and we will always have it in our back pockets," said Ulseth. "I always wanted to be a Gopher ever since I was a little boy, and it provides me my livelihood in the business I now have."

Dave Jensen is a former Gopher defenseman who later played for the North Stars. "To play in your home town, in front of your family and friends was something really special to me," he said.

One of Glen Sonmor's better players, Ron Peltier, is currently the Chief operating officer of Edina Realty. "Coming out of St. Paul Johnson High School, I viewed Minnesota as the premier hockey school in the country," Peltier said. "I had over 20 full-ride opportunities from schools like Harvard, Dartmouth, Michigan, Yale, Wisconsin, and Colorado. And the 'U' was where I wanted to be. It meant a lot to me, and for my business career today as well."

Ron's brother Doug, another forward under Sonmor, is the A.D. at Forest Lake. "I gave up a lot of chances all over the country to play in Mariucci Arena for the Gophers, it meant so much to me," Doug said.

One of the funniest people I interviewed for the book was former Mahtomedi High School grad and former owner of BooBoo's Restaurant, Jim Boo. "It was the biggest one accomplishment of my life," said Boo. "Herbie taught me that through hard work, you can accomplish anything you set your mind to. Our era was a mixture of great personalities. It was a good time, we built some great bonds, and awesome friendships along the way. "

Current New Jersey Devil and first ever "Mr. Hockey" winner was winger Tom Chorske. "It meant a lot. Growing up I always wanted to be a Gopher, and it was definitely the biggest thing on my mind," said Chorske. "I always thought I'd be a Gopher someday. My parents used to bring me to a lot of games as a kid. Even though I was a first round draft pick, I never would've turned down the chance to be a Gopher. It was a childhood dream that came true. It was so much fun, so many friends, and such a great experience in my life. I can remember once when I was 13, I snuck down to the locker room after a game and got to touch Neal Broten's skates."

One of the nicest guys you'll ever meet is Gary Gambucci, a former All-American center and owner of his own hockey equipment distribution company called Sport International. "To be honest, I wanted to get a college scholarship, and I didn't care so much about being a Gopher," said Gambucci. "I just wanted to play college hockey, and was recruited by a lot of schools to play. However, after four years there, I bleed maroon and gold. I never felt special to be a Gopher, but I felt honored to be a Gopher, and to be a part of the 'Fraternity.' It's a pretty select bond, and a tight family to be in."

Darby Hendrickson, WCHA Freshman of the Year in 19921-92, has deep feelings about the Gophers. "Besides my family, it means the most to me in my life," said Hendrickson. "There's nothing I'd rather be doing than playing Gopher Hockey. It's so great, it's the best to be a Gopher. I couldn't wait, I signed right after my junior year of high school at Richfield. I couldn't imagine my life without it. I can't say enough good things, it's just great to wear that sweater out there. It's so unique and special, I don't know how to describe the privilege of being there. I'll always remember having puck shooting contests with Larry Olimb after practices for juice. It was things like that I'll always remember."

For the all-time most assists leader and Warroad native Larry Olimb, it was pretty emotional. "It was definitely a great time, and you could feel the pride with the guys," said Olimb. "It was so exciting to play there — guys like Snuggerud, Chorske, Stauber and Richards were such good role-models. We looked up to them. They were good friends, good people, and were leaders that we learned a great deal from. Just the atmosphere in that old locker room seven months a year, six days a week, was like home. I wanted to get out of the small town and see what the big city was like. I didn't want to go to UND, I wanted to get out of Warroad and do my own thing. I've been playing hockey all my life — I played to have fun, I never played to get a scholarship, and I never played college to get a pro contract. I played for fun, and it worked out well for me. It was the best four years of my life. I made so many great friends, and I grew up so much. When you leave the U, it's like part of your life is over. I'd give anything to do it over again. I know I made the right choice coming here."

For St. Cloud native Cory Laylin, it was clear how he felt about being a Gopher. "It was a real sense of pride, and I know that every kid dreams of being a Gopher," said Laylin. "It was a big stepping stone in my life to be a Gopher, and I was really lucky to get the chance to play here. The friendships of guys like Trent Klatt and Jason Miller are so important to me. It was really cool."

Trent Klatt is a former Gopher wing who signed with the North Stars. "It meant everything in the world to me," said Klatt. "I used to have season tickets growing up, and it was something I had always dreamed of. The day I committed to play for Wooger was the happiest day of my life. I even got to get my head shaved as a freshman by Benny Hankinson."

The Broten Brothers from tradition-rich Roseau are perhaps the most famous Minnesota trio. Neal is a former Hobey Baker winner, and NHL All-Star. "It was an honor being a Gopher. There was so much tradition in that uniform, I really loved it," said Neal Broten. "I was very fortunate to have been a part of the program, and to have won the Hobey Baker as a Gopher was a thrill for me. I can remember coming down from Roseau to see a Gopher game with some friends. It was against Michigan State, and I'll never forget seeing Bill Baker wearing the Minnesota jersey, and that round Northland helmet. It was then that I knew I too would wear the maroon and gold."

Aaron Broten followed Neal and is the record-holder for the most total points in a single-season, with 106. He also played in the NHL with New Jersey, the North Stars and Winnipeg. "I grew up watching North Dakota, I never saw the Gophers play," said Aaron. "I came here to follow Neal, and make it easier on my parents to see us both in one spot. Every Wednesday and Sunday nights we would watch Hockey Night in Canada on TV, and dream of one day playing for the Boston Bruins. I guess I really only wanted to be a Roseau Ram when I think about it now. Anyway, I have nothing but great memories of being a Gopher, and it was a lot of fun going to school here."

Paul Broten, who holds the Gopher short-handed goal record with 10, became a member of the New York Rangers. "It meant a lot to me, they were the best years of my life," said Paul. "I went to the 'U' because it was a great team, with a lot of pride. Every kid wanted to play there, it was a dream for me to follow my brothers as Gophers. I remember screwing over UMD pretty bad. They recruited me pretty hard, and told me that I could be on the line with Brett Hull, but I wanted to wear the other maroon and gold in the state. The thing I miss the most though, are Big Ten Subs. You just can't get a decent sub in New York City."

Former Gopher All-American and current Gopher coach Doug Woog describes it as more than just a job. "It's been a great opportunity for me in my life today," said Woog. "It's been job opportunities, friends, and success later in life. It's meant a great deal to me and my family."

One of Woog's former players, Randy Skarda, holds the record for the most goals in a season by a defenseman with 19. "It was a great experience for me," said Skarda. "The boosters, coaches, fans and all your new friends for life was incredible, I wouldn't trade it for the world. It meant everything to me being a Gopher. I grew up here, and grew up watching guys like Neal Broten play for the Gophers. It was awesome."

Edina native and proud owner of the career penalty record, (182) is Ben Hankinson. "It was a great accomplishment in my life for me to be a part of that tradition," said Hankinson. "To play in Mariucci Arena, to put on that Gopher sweater, to play with my brother, and to play in my hometown was incredible."

Ken Yackel Jr. is a former Gopher winger and the son of legendary player/coach Ken Yackel Sr. "I grew up watching my dad play hockey," said Yackel. "He was a great athlete, and lettered in three sports at the U of M. I looked up to him, and I guess I've wanted to be a Gopher all of my life."

Former Gopher goalie, Elk River native, and current assistant coach Paul

Ostby: "As a kid that's all I ever wanted to be. To represent your town, team and country was an incredible experience. I owe my whole life to Gopher hockey. Everything I have, along with all my friends, I owe indirectly to Gopher hockey."

Dick Meredith, a former Gopher winger and Southwest High School alum, was one of five brothers to play at the University of Minnesota. "Hockey has been very good to me," said Meredith. "Without hockey, and having known John Mariucci, I don't think I'd be who I am today. I'm a better person today, and it's given me values, friendships, contacts and memories of a lifetime. To play Gopher hockey in your own state, and to play on the Olympics as a Gopher was an incredible honor. I wouldn't have much today without it. It definitely helps you in the business world. I could've played at Harvard, but instead wanted to be a Gopher."

Tom Vannelli was an SPA alum and former Gopher standout who played on two national championship teams. "It gave me the opportunity to prove to everybody that I could play college hockey, and that I wasn't too small," said Vannelli. "It was an honor, and really special to play in front of my family every game too. We helped nurture the program under Herbie, and got it where it is today. It wasn't very glamorous to play there back then like it is now. Herbie didn't always get the pick of the litter back then, and we had to work really hard for our success. People don't realize that the Gophers never have a night off. The intensity always had to be at the peak because every team wanted to beat us so badly. It was an incredible challenge day in and day out, but definitely worth it."

Mike Ramsey, a 1980 Olympic team member and Roosevelt alum, is currently with the Buffalo Sabres. "I grew up watching the Gophers, and I always wanted to play for them," said Ramsey. "They didn't need to recruit me, I would've gladly come to them. I can say now, though, that I regret only playing one season as a Gopher. It was so much fun. I think the worst was when they made me sing my high school fight song in front of the team. Being from Roosevelt High, it wasn't the most masculine thing in the world to sing about Teddy Bears in front of 30 guys."

Dick Spannbauer, former Gopher defenseman and Hill-Murray alum, is a Gopher Hockey 'assist' statistician. "It was not the hockey school to go to when I was there, but Herbie turned that all around in a hurry," said Spannbauer. "Herbie always told me that it's better to play in your hometown, because the people will remember you for a long time. That's why I'm a Gopher. We were the worst team that ever won a national championship at the U of M, but damn did we work hard. It was so much fun, and I even got to see Billy Butters' famous flying act into the Colorado bench. That was, for sure, the highlight of my career."

Dave Snuggerud, a Hopkins grad, Olympian, Buffalo Sabre and San Jose Shark, also holds the Gopher record for the fastest hat trick, when he did it in 3:48. "It was one of the greatest days of my life when I signed with the Gophers," said Snuggerud. "It's so much more than just playing there. The school and the tradition were so awesome. There were so many greats like Neal Broten and Bill Butters who played there. It was a serious honor. You also made so many friends in college that are forever. In the pros you find out quickly just who your friends are by seeing who returns your calls after you get traded."

Former Gopher center and Edina native Dean Williamson was a transfer to the "U" from Denver. "I wanted to go there because my dad was a star there, and I really look up to him," said Williamson. "I think I miss the guys most, I was so insecure that I hung around with just about everybody at one point or another. It was so much fun."

Former Gopher defenseman and past Governor of Minnesota Wendy Anderson said it like this: "The camaraderie of your teammates and coach, the laughs, and fun we had playing this game, winning and losing as a team, playing well, and making mistakes — that was what it was all about. On our team we had six starters. Four of them were All-American, the fifth was captain and the sixth was me. So, I was a very undistinguished player, and almost never scored any goals. However, it was a lot of great memories, fun, and I've made it a lifelong sport. Every Sunday we still get together to play in a senior league."

Lou Nanne, originally from Sault Ste. Marie, Ontario, was a former All-American, and past G.M. of the North Stars. "I'm very proud to be a University alum," said Nanne. "I was very proud that three of my four kids decided to go there. I was very fortunate to get the opportunity to play there, and I've had a lot of good success in my life that evolves around my opportunity to play hockey at the University of Minnesota. I've been very lucky, and I only hope I can give back as much as I got out. My life has been consumed by hockey since 1959, and I enjoy being out of it, and having more freedom to enjoy the things I want to do outside the sport."

Bill Baker, former Gopher All-American and 1980 Olympic team member, went back to the U of M Dental School. "Everyone on the team was from Minnesota, everybody wanted to go there, and a scholarship from there was the ultimate feather in your cap," said Baker. "For me, I bled Maroon and Gold, it's in my blood. I grew up watching them, and I loved it. There was a real mystique, and it was the biggest thrill to be selected for the team. I can remember being recruited by the Gophers, and coming home from school as fast as I could so I could scavenge through the mail. I remember spotting that big gold 'M' in the pile of mail, and would rip it open anxiously to find out what they had sent me about being a Gopher."

Former Gopher right wing Paul Holmgren, who had a long playing career with the Philadelphia Flyers, is the current coach of the Hartford Whalers. "It meant everything to me," said Holmgren. "Like most kids I grew up dreaming to play for the Gophers. It was a thrill, and I'm proud of the fact that I can say I was a Gopher."

Former Gopher coach and player Brad Buetow from Mounds View is currently the head coach at Colorado College. "It was a very positive and growing experience for me not only as a coach, but also as a player," said Buetow. "I grew up awfully fast there, and met a lot of great people there. I also feel that I built a lot of confidence and character in myself by being in some big pressure situations. It made me appreciate a lot of opportunities in life. I feel comfortable coming back, and I even got a standing ovation the first time I coached there, which meant a lot to me. I have to say though it was weird standing on the other side of the ice, and being in the visitor's locker room. I'm very proud of our record there as a coach. We made some final fours, league championships, our academics were good, and recruiting went well, I felt. With the exceptions of Blue, Pietrangelo, and MacSwain we stuck to all Minnesota kids, and I was proud of that too. It's a great school, I think very highly of if, and it will always be my home. It was great to be a Gopher. I wouldn't trade it for anything."

One player older fans still remember as the best ever was All American and Hall of Famer John Mayasich. "The camaraderie was the best," said Mayasich.

"The friendships go back 40 years now, and guys like Hubbard, Campbell, Meredith, Dougherty, Mattson and Wendy Anderson are still my pals today. I think the biggest benefit was the travel. I got to see the world through hockey. The purity of hockey is the bond that keeps these friendships together today. I look back and say to myself that it was hard work. Classes were tough, and it wasn't all fun and glory as some may think it was."

Mayasich's two linemates were Gene Campell and Dick Dougherty, an All-American. "It was just great. Hockey started to pick up in the state when we started to win," said Dougherty. "I still remember losing to RPI in overtime though, that was pretty tough to swallow. Gopher Hockey was a wonderful tradition, and a big part of my life."

Campbell is a former Gopher winger, and '56 Olympic team member. "It gave me a chance to enjoy the game of hockey, and gave me the opportunity to meet so many fun people in my life," said Campbell.

The 1979 national championship team

WHAT DID IT MEAN TO BE THE GOPHER?

It was the fall of 1990 when I heard the news that I was going to be the new U of M mascot. I was sitting on the porch of my fraternity, just hanging with some of the fellas at a party. I had conveniently positioned myself next to a random sorority bimbo, and was about to move in and wow her with some pathetic pick-up line. That's when it happened.

I heard my name bellowed out from the front yard like a sick cow, "ROOOOSSSSS!" I was terrified that it was some obnoxious beckoner who wanted my attention pretty badly. I remember having this vision of some old, disgruntled girlfriend straight out of Fatal Attraction coming at me with a butcher knife or something. To my relief it was three cheerleaders -- Kathy, Wendy and Julie -- who had come to give me some great news. They had a proposition for me. (Quit it!) It was a proposition for me to turn from human to rodent, in one fell swoop. I thought it was a joke. Like they were just going to ask me to be Goldy Gopher or something? I remember asking them sarcastically if a phone booth would be necessary for this stunt? But they were serious, three acquaintances I barely knew had made me a rather intriguing proposal, which I needed to think about carefully. I thought about what my idols, Ferris Beuller and David Letterman, would've done at that moment. Of course I would, I would love it, thank you, kiss, kiss, thank you, kiss, thank you! I had to decide between a sorority bimbo who was probably fascinated by bright, sparkly objects, or three babe cheerleaders who were giving me an opportunity to become the mascot of the alma mater of my entire family. I told the bimbo thanks for playing, we had some lovely parting gifts for her behind door number three...SEE YA!

I couldn't pass it up, I could be the ultimate cheerleader. A wild and crazy fan who would stop at nothing to get a laugh. A fanatic who would try his damnedest to get his team that home ice edge. A character who had poise, courage, humor and wit capable of bringing fans to their feet to help the mighty Gophers win a national championship. NAH! How about a chance to get dressed in a locker room with a dozen babes wearing spandex and mini-skirts? I knew you'd see it my way!

I asked them why they had chosen me to do this, and not a band member like in the past? They told me that the criteria they used was simple. They needed someone who could skate, and since they knew that I had been with the Gopher junior varsity for a short stint as a freshman, they figured I was qualified there. The other criteria was that the person had to be an absolute idiot, having no fear to get in front of thousands of people and make a fool of himself. So I qualified on both accounts.

It was as if fate and old lady luck had tag-teamed together to pick this horrendous combo of traits. I was indeed the golden child, or rather and more appropriately, the Golden Gopher. Like the song of the sirens, I heard them beckoning me in the dark to call me to duty. Maybe it was just the 12 pack I drank that was talking? Anyway, that's how I got the job. A lucky break came my way, and somebody recommended me, and the cheerleaders asked me to do it. I didn't have to try out or anything. I had always wondered how that lucky somebody got to be Goldy at all the home games. Now I had my chance to redefine a position that could be anything I wanted it to be. I was pumped, I tell ya!

I'll never forget hugging the girls, and telling them how excited I was before they left. Everything else seemed so trivial to me at that point, and I was once again excited about college. I told a few of my buddies at my fraternity what had just happened and they said, "Yeah, whatever, Ross buddy. Sure you're the Gopher. Pass the beer-nuts." So, I didn't have the immediate credibility or charisma of the San Diego Chicken or anything. Hell, I didn't have the charisma of the Dayton's Santa Bear, or even the Domino's Pizza Noid for that matter! But, I'd show them that I was just nuts enough to do this.

John Gilbert
One-on-one with Brent Hanus, St.Cloud State mascot.

I remember the first practice at the Bierman Football Complex. I was so nervous when I met all the girls. I remember being so terrified of not being funny when I got the suit on. We did all kinds of great stuff together in practices leading up to the first game. Pyramids, stunts, and routines were some of the things we practiced over and over. I was doing great until I had to put on this giant, 30-gallon drum for a head. I couldn't see a thing. When I got on the ice, I had second thoughts about doing this. Ice was a lot more slippery than astro-turf, and I was scared of killing myself out there. I was supposed to not only stand up on skates, but shoot pucks, play with little kids and be funny. I was terrified, but luckily I was buddies with the other Goldy Gopher, Randy Kish. He was the mascot for football and basketball. I was fortunate to have him help me out, and show me the ropes of mascoting. He had already gotten himself into a ton of trouble with the athletic department, and sort of blazed a trail for me. I'll never forget some of the crazy stuff he would do. One time he got the basketball fans in Williams Arena to start jumping up and down, and they made him quit when they realized it was causing structural damage to the arena. He's one of the funniest and most creative guys I have ever known. Without him, I never would've been able to have the confidence to go out there in front of all those people. So, Randy...thanks!

Well, the first game came and I was all ready to go out there to show my stuff. I let all the cheerleaders go ahead of me to get on the ice first, and they sort of gave me a grand introduction by waving their pom-poms at me. Everybody figured I would have some big-time entry to start off the festivities, and I didn't want to disappoint them, so I ran out and jumped over the boards waving a giant "M" flag. I took about ten strides, my head fell off, I skated over the flag, ripping it in half, and fell on my butt, ripping a gaping hole up both sides of my crotch. So, there I was. What an intro for my new job! Everybody thought it was hilarious. What a gag, he was OK, they thought. There's just one thing they didn't know. I didn't plan a thing, it just sort of happened like that. I soon figured that nobody knew who the hell I was, so why not act like an idiot? It was a great start, and a great beginning to one of the greatest adventures of my life.

Here's a good fact for trivia buffs: Cheerleading was originated at the University of Minnesota back in the early 1900s. (Rah Rah Rah for Ski-U-Mah!) The cheerleaders were like little sisters to me, and I was their big brother. The cheerleaders from 1990-1992 were: Kim Jeager, Stacy Bjorkland, Ellen Boss, Missi Manthei, Shannon Blegen, Wendy Smith, Jamie Walker, Kathy Stenhjem, Callie Kalogerson, Lauri Sumner, Julie Christensen, Debbie Shaw, Debbie Aguirre, Mary Cuskey, Jamie Walker and Tammy Werner. Our coaches were Gwen Schneider and Theresa Uram. We became really close friends over the two seasons, and had our share of good times together. In our locker room I was just one of the girls. They did so much for the program, players and fans. I just wish they would've gotten more recognition for their hard work.

There were times though, like at the '91 WCHA championship game at the Civic Center, when I almost killed them all. I used to always use the U of M rouser as my cue to come sliding in-between the cheerleaders just before the period started. They would line up parallel to each other, about five feet apart, and do a cheer to welcome the team back on the ice. So, I got a big head of steam, and came chugging up to them. I dove like usual to slide between the blue lines on my stomach, and that's when all hell broke loose. I somehow got twisted, and like dominos the girls started flying all over the place as a giant rodent came at them like an oversized bowling ball. Wow, did I ever catch it after that one! Poor Julie, she got the worst of it. When I ran over Callie, I spun her around and her skate blade flew up and carved into Julie's leg. There I was, totally helpless, in shock, as the crowd booed me. The girls were sprawled out on the ice all over, and here's me with that goofy Goldy perma-grin, unable to express any remorse toward the situation whatsoever. I made up for that one by buying them dinner and bringing bagels to practice.

Another time, when the St. Cloud State cheerleaders came down to cheer a game at Mariucci Arena, I nearly killed them as well. They were out on the ice in between periods, and they had just completed a pyramid-mount. While they were up in this geometrical masterpiece, getting "ooh's" and "ahh's" from the crowd, I came by chasing a puck. Not being able to see a damn thing, I plowed into them, knocking over their pyramid, and even giving the poor girl who was on top a mild concussion. As if this wasn't bad enough, we had to get dressed with these same girls in the same locker room after the game. I think it's safe to say that these ladies weren't too fond of me afterwards. Then, to add insult to injury, we had to go up to St. Cloud the next night, to complete the home-and-home series. I thought they were going to kill me, but luckily I made peace with them by getting them to laugh when I took on their mascot, Brent, in a game of one-on-one in-between periods.

THE EVOLUTION OF A RODENT

Goldy Gopher has changed faces quite a few times over the years, and I thought you would like to see what some of my mutated ancestors looked like. No rodent in history has been so thoroughly misrepresented and tampered with as the Minnesota Gopher. From the first realistic representations in early yearbooks, to the Rambo Goldy, we've seen it all. The Golden Gopher has gone through facelifts, tummy-tucks, plastic surgery, steroid rehabilitation and other metamorphoses that would make the average herbivore extinct.

Originally we had the cute little pocket-gopher, the kind you'd see on a golf-course. Later came an improved version of the same critter, only happier and bigger. The Gopher made famous by the hockey teams of John Mariucci, Glen Sonmor and of Herb Brooks's championship tenure was a sleek, fast-skating Gopher — obviously of Minnesota's homestate heritage. No steroids, no illegal injections, no phony imports. The actual state-critter gopher is actually a 13-striped ground squirrel, which rude detractors might suggest is a cousin of the groundhog. But it fit in well with the speedy little skaters that Gopher hockey fans came to know and love. Then in 1985, Lou Holtz came to town. They weren't paying Sweet Lou over $100,000 big ones a year to coach a cute, little, scrawny football team, so why should he have to put up with a cute, little, scrawny mascot? So Lou had "Rambo Goldy" designed. This Gopher could've taken Sir Charles Barkley to school in a game of one-on-one. It caused an uproar on campus, and people revolted to save their old rodent. The Minnesota Daily reported that in November of 1985, a group of students calling themselves SOW (Save Our Wimp) was formed to resurrect the old Goldie. SOW sources claimed that the old Goldie was kidnapped in the spring of '85 and taken to a hidden room on the St. Paul campus. There, they said, he was strapped to a chair, injected with rabies, and force-fed amphetamines and steroids.

The new Goldy came under further attack in 1986, for representing what a University Communications Committee spokesman referred to as, "an overly pugnacious and mean look that wasn't an appropriate representation of the University." They figured that the mascot looked too aggressive in light of the sexual assault charges involving three U of M basketball players in Madison. Go figure? So, they slimmed him up, cut his toe-nails, got rid of those villain looking eye-brows, and PRESTO! Out came a new-improved rodent. The new Goldy was a calmer, mellower version of the Rambo, but a bigger, stronger version of the "Wimp."

The classic is that all of the uproar and controversy over the Gopher symbol revolved around football and/or basketball, and yet the good ol' skating Gopher was swept out the side door in the process. Hockey wound up with the steroid-model football-basketball critter. Personally I'll take the speedy, little Gopher. According to legend, that's how Henry David Thoreau found him in 1861 on the shores of Lake Calhoun, or Walden Pond, or wherever that story comes from. Don't get me wrong, I enjoyed being the mutated cousin of the wimp. I would just like to see some tradition restored and a mascot chosen that is befitting of this grandiose institution.

MINNESOTA HOCKEY STATISTICS

*In 1992, there were 1,066 players in the four major conferences of college hockey. Of them, 145 were Minnesotans, Massachusetts had 142, Michigan 84, New York 59, and Connecticut 31. There were 641 total Americans in college hockey. The remaining 425 were Canadians, Europeans and others.

* College Hockey '92 was 38.4% Canadian, 60.4% American, and 1.2% European.
*The NHL in '92 was 71% Canadian, 17% American, and 12% European.
*In '92 the NHL had 134 Americans. 39 were from Massachusetts, 27 were from Minnesota, and 25 were from Michigan.

MINNESOTANS PLAYING IN THE FOUR MAJOR COLLEGE CONFERENCES

28	at MINNESOTA	2	at St. Lawrence
24	at Duluth	1	at Michigan
21	at St. Cloud	1	at Bowling Green
12	at Wisconsin	1	at Ferris State
9	at Colorado College	1	at Western Michigan
8	at Denver	1	at Boston College
6	at North Dakota	1	at Boston University
4	at Northern Michigan	1	at Brown
4	at Illinois of Chicago	1	at Colgate
3	at Vermont	1	at Dartmouth
3	at Miami of Ohio	1	at Harvard
3	at Providence	1	at Yale
2	at Maine	1	at Michigan Tech
2	at Lake Superior State		

MINNESOTANS PLAYING ON ALL OTHER COLLEGE TEAMS

Colleges located in Minnesota:	13	264
Colleges in states bordering Minnesota:	9	84
Colleges in other states:	13	24
TOTALS	35	372

WHERE THEY ARE IN COLLEGE HOCKEY

	WCHA	CCHA	ECAC	EAST	IND.	TOTALS
CANADA	85	119	159	54	68	485
MINNESOTA	113	11	9	10	42	185
MASSACHUSETTS	2	3	47	86	17	155

*SOURCES: USA Hockey, College Hockey Handbook, Minnesota Hockey Magazine and Sports Illustrated.

DOUG WOOG ERA

Doug Woog is a 1962 graduate of South St. Paul High School, where he garnered all-state hockey honors for three consecutive years and also starred in football. He then accepted a scholarship to attend the University of Minnesota and play under head coach John Mariucci. Woog had a stellar collegiate career at the U of M and was named to the All-American team his junior year when he led the team in scoring. He returned for his senior season to captain the squad to a 16-12-0 record and was named the team's MVP.

After graduating from Minnesota with honors with a B.S. degree in Education, he played for the 1967 U.S. National team and was a candidate for the 1968 Olympic team. After failing to make the '68 squad, he decided to pursue a career in education.

He began his teaching and coaching career at Hopkins West Junior High School in 1968. While there he taught geography and coached football and hockey. In the fall of 1968 he took a job at his high school alma mater, South St. Paul, where he became head soccer coach and an assistant in hockey and baseball. During his tenure there, the soccer program won six conference championships and reached six state tournaments. Although the Packers never won the big one, they were runner-up for the state title twice.

In 1971 his coaching career branched out to junior hockey. From 1971 through 1977 he coached the Minnesota Junior Stars, and the St. Paul Vulcans to two U.S. Junior National titles. In 1978 he was chosen as coach of the West Team in the U.S. Olympic Festival in Colorado Springs, where his squad won the gold medal. He again coached a team to the gold medal in the 1989 Olympic Festival in Oklahoma City.

In 1978 he returned to South St. Paul to take over the head hockey coaching position. From 1978 through 1985, with a 1984 leave of absence to be an assistant for the '84 Olympic team, his Packer teams won two conference titles and advanced to the state tournament four times.

Coach Woog has been involved with amateur hockey at all levels. He has been a national committee member for AHAUS. He was chairman of the National Skating Committee for USA Hockey. He was the head coach of the U.S. National Junior team in 1985 and the U.S. Select 17 team in 1989 that toured Czechoslovakia.

Woog is also an active member of the community. He is a member of the St. Paul Chamber of Commerce. He has been the chairperson for the Wakota Arena Board for the South St. Paul area. He is a past president for the South St. Paul Coaches Association. He has been instrumental in initiating and maintaining youth athletic organizations in his community. In 1973 he earned his master's degree in Guidance and Counseling from the College of St. Thomas.

From 1985 to 1992, Woog compiled 228 wins, the most of any coach in Gopher history. He made seven consecutive NCAA tournament appearances, four NCAA final four appearances, three WCHA championships and has the highest winning percentage (.721) of any coach.

He and his wife, Janice, reside in South St. Paul. They have three children: Amy, Steve, and Dan. Steve plays at Northern Michigan, Dan came to Minnesota as a freshman in the fall of '92.

BILL BUTTERS

Bill Butters played defense for the Gophers from 1969-1973. A product of White Bear Lake, he enjoyed an extensive professional career after leaving the Gophers. He first signed with the Toronto Maple Leafs. After one year in the Toronto farm system, he moved on to the WHA where twice he played for the Minnesota Fighting Saints, with a stint at Houston in between. In 1976 he was traded to Edmonton and then to Hartford. He returned to the NHL with the Minnesota North Stars in 1977.

His first coaching experience was as player-assistant coach with the Oklahoma City Blazers. He then spent five years as assistant at Breck High School in the Twin Cities. During that time he also worked as a project manager for API Inc. in the construction industry.

In 1985 he came back to the U of M as an assistant under head coach Doug Woog. He immediately set to work on improving the play of the Gopher blue line corps. In addition to his on-the-ice duties, Butters handles many administrative duties for the staff as well as the scouting and recruiting duties necessary at the Division One level.

Butters and his wife, Debby, are the parents of three children, Ben, Anne, and Rebecca.

"I love my job," Butters said. "I get to recruit high school kids, meet interesting people and keep the tradition going. We certainly believe in Minnesota kids, and make sure that our kids get the scholarships for an education. We try to help kids grow as best as we can, and let them know it's important to have fun, be aggressive and still have values. I could be a career assistant coach here. I don't like being in the limelight. I like my relationship with the players. I enjoy screwing around with the fellas and playing tricks on them. Head coaches have to portray a different image. They have to go to fund-raisers, media things and faculty events. This way I get the best of both worlds while still being buddies with the kids. That's what's most important to me."

The other Gopher coaches of the Woog era include: Mark Mazzoleni, who came in 1991-92, Jack Blatherwick, who left in '91, plus Bob Shier, and Paul Ostby. Other important people to the program include Harry Broadfoot, the team equipment manager, Bob Broxterman, the team trainer, and graduate assistant, John Hamre. Mention must also be made to Deanne Miller, the nicest person ever to work at Mariucci Arena. Thanks Deanne for all the skate sharpenings and for your warm smile that you always have.

Being the Gopher was such a thrill for me. I have been a life-long Gopher Hockey fan, and was sincerely proud to have been a small part of the team for two seasons. As a freshman, I walked-on to try to make the team. I knew I would never make the varsity, so I tried to just make the junior varsity team. I remember talking to the coach Bob Shier, and convincing him to give me a tryout. He agreed, and in one of the greatest highlights of my life, I got to work out with the team. I didn't last long on the JV. But, I became friends with some great guys who played on the varsity. Guys like: Ben and Pete Hankinson, Grant Bischoff, Sean Fabian, Dean Williamson, Luke Johnson, Cory Laylin and Lance Werness, to name a few.

My time on the JV was limited to being a practice-dummy, as well as fostering a tight bond with assistant coach Bill Butters. "Butts" and I didn't exactly hit it off with each other at the beginning. It was all because of an incident that occured in practice one day. I was out there in a scrimmage, and Todd Richards came down on me with the puck. He was wearing a red-cross on a white jersey. I figured it was one of those fancy new jerseys city kids were wearing nowadays. I wanted to impress the coaches so I decked Todd. It was a clean hit, and I was really impressed with myself that I hit him so square. It was almost as if he didn't move out of my way or something. The next thing I remembered was seeing Butters coming at me like a raging buffalo. I wasn't sure if I was going to die at this point, or if maybe I'd just only lose a limb. When he made contact with me I went flailing across the ice like a puppy trying to run on a linoleum floor. When I gained consciousness, he was hovering over me, explaining to me what happens when walk-ons try to check his star players who are injured. I didn't realize it at the time, but the red-cross was so no one would hit him, because he was injured. I had no clue.

The next encounter I had with Butters was as his student. In my five years as a student at the U of M, I took the phy-ed class, ice-hockey, four times. I took the class so I could skate every day in Mariucci Arena for an hour. Bill was the instructor one year, and I was his student. He used to give me a hard time about everything, all in good fun. He thought he got the last laugh on me, though, when the grades came out. Everyone in the class got an A, and I got the only B. I never had the heart to tell him that I never actually registered for his class, seeing as it was my third time taking it.

I went from a part-timer on the Junior Varsity to a two-year season-ticket holder, to the team mascot in my five years at the University. I saw a lot, and gained a diverse perspective on the program from the dressing room to my perch on the west-end wall, a Gumby-throw from the infamous "NE" section at Mariucci Arena. It meant the world to me that after I got cut from the JV I could make the team again in a different capacity. A way to help have fun. I always tried to be fun, and help people enjoy the games in between the whistles. Stupid, unorthodox, crazy comedy was what I guess I did up there on that perch. I loved it, and it was great for my ego to make people laugh and have a good time.

Gopher Hockey is a constant in Minnesota. I know that I will always be a season-ticket holder for Gopher Hockey games, because I enjoy the atmosphere so much on campus. It's so fun to be around the locals from around town, and to "people-watch" at the hockey games.

WOOG TRIBUTES

JOHN MARIUCCI: was quoted in the Star Tribune as saying, "Doug Woog, he was just like Murray Williamson — two little bantam roosters, who were rats on the ice. They loved to provoke people."

Larry Olimb

PAUL BROTEN: "People take the Gophers for granted, they get there year in and year out. So, they haven't won the big one yet, they will."

ROBB STAUBER: "Wooger is such a great guy. It's tough to be a coach, but you couldn't ask for a better guy. He's so knowledgeable about hockey, and he knows everything. He'll win the big one soon enough."

JOHN GILBERT (STAR/TRIBUNE SPORTS WRITER): "It takes a lot to be a championship team, and consistently excellent play is the basis. Doug Woog provides that. He's also good at sizing up what an opponent is doing and making little tactical adjustments that may open the way for his team to find success. The Gopher program would not necessarily be better it they won the NCAA; it's excellence is shown by the regularity with which they get to the national tournament. But I don't think an excellent program and an NCAA title need to be mutually exclusive. For Woog's sake, I just wish he'd find a way to psyche his team up at NCAA time. His even-keel hold on the emotions eliminates the lows through the long season, but it seems to prevent the emotional highs that are trademarks of every championship team. There is no reason that the Gophers should be susceptible to being beaten by a team — possibly an inferior team — that is riding an emotional wave."

GOVERNOR ARNE CARLSON: "Minnesota has always won in hockey, without too many ups and downs. I think the state's gotten spoiled though. Like North Carolina and Duke Basketball, they expect a winner every year. Woog has done a remarkable job in sustaining a very powerful program. With the new arena, he can continue developing his program. He seems to do great until he gets over to that Civic Center in St. Paul, for some crazy reason he can't win in there."

WALLY SHAVER (KITN - TV): "I love Gopher Hockey. I think the world of Doug Woog. There's nothing I'd like to see more than for him to win that big one. I don't like it when the fans and media get on him. He'll get it done, and with Minnesota kids too."

DAVE SNUGGERUD: "Half the fun is getting there, and there shouldn't be pressure to win the big one. We know that Gopher Hockey is a winner, and we have to remember that championships are hard to come by. Woog has so much pressure on him off the ice as well, like making sure the kids are doing well in school."

PAT MICHELETTI: "Only one team can win it. You have to have every cylinder going, a hot goalie, everyone has to play great, and you need luck. Timing is everything, and if you get breaks at the right time you can win it all. There's nothing better than winning something as a team. It's not like being All-American, where you can't experience it with the fellas. Wooger will get it done, he's a great coach."

Robb Stauber

BRAD BUETOW: "Doug and I didn't have much contact with each other. Doug applied for the head coaching job in 1979, the same time I did. Our relationship is very competitive, but we respect each other. We both understand what it's like coaching at Minnesota, and the pressures involved. Before the games we talk and stuff, but when the game starts were opponents. It's a good relationship, and I want to keep it that way."

PAT REUSSE (STAR TRIBUNE COLUMNIST): "I think Woog is a great guy, and a classy individual. But, I think the media gives Gopher Hockey way too much publicity for what it's worth."

JOHN MAYASICH: "They don't have to win the title to be successful. I would say there are American born players out there who could help him. I wouldn't say don't go out and get them to have them contribute, but I think we can be competitive with the Minnesota kids. It takes 20 players, and a hot goalie to wIn it. Woog will get it done."

TOM VANNELLI: "It's not a knock on Woog, but I think the players are better today, however they aren't as good as a team."

CHARLEY HALLMAN (PIONEER PRESS COLUMNIST): "Wooger will get it taken care of. No other school has to deal with exams before the finals which makes it tough on the kids. They have to go to class, and play hockey too, which I'm sure is pretty stressful."

DICK PARADISE: "He's a damn nice guy, Doug Woog. I remember when he used to live with Denny Zacho when we were at the 'U'. I used to commute, and when I didn't want to drive home, I would throw Doug out of his bed and sleep over there. Doug was a tough, straight- laced kid, a good student, and a hell of a nice guy. I'm sure Wooger wouldn't want to be remembered by any wild bar stories or anything, so I won't incriminate him with any dirty stories behind his back."

BILL BAKER: "Wooger has done a fantastic job there. He is one heck of a nice guy, and a great coach as well."

Trent Klatt

REED LARSON: "In hockey you're going to have to beat someone on a one-on-one somewhere down the line. The Gophers lack a goal-scoring touch, because everyone wants defense and discipline on the team. Everybody is forgetting about imagination and individual, creative playmaking. It's gotten too conservative over there, and too much clutching and grabbing as well."

JOE SCHMIT (KSTP - TV): "Unfortunately Woog gets measured by national championships. I think you should measure the program by the number of kids that get to play there, get an education, turn pro, coach later on, and wind up doing good things for the community as better people. Wooger is a heck of a guy, and just a great guy. He has the right perspective on coaching. He's there to mold the kids into better people, and he's a great role model. When you're around him, it's hard not to have a pretty positive outlook because he's such a good guy. He respects human beings, and takes time out for them. He always has a smile or a nice thing to say about someone or something every time I see him."

DON CLARK (HOCKEY HISTORIAN): "Woog is a real good coach. It's too bad they judge teams on whether or not they've won a national championship. Woog has made the team the most international style of hockey in the country and I for one, love it."

Cory Laylin

JEFF PASSOLT (KARE - TV): "I think people make a big deal out of Wooger not winning it. I remember Bud Grant answering the same question one time, and he said 'The question shouldn't be why do they keep getting there and losing?, but how does he keep getting them there?'"

LARRY OLIMB: "Wooger is such a great coach. He's done so many great things for the program. He did as much as he could to get us ready and we came up short for him. It's such a tight group all being from Minnesota. We had a lot in common with each other and we owe that to Wooger. I did feel pressure to win though. I felt the pressure from the fans and the media to win. I have no regrets at all. It's been so many great experiences, friends and fun. I owe so much to Wooger."

STANLEY S. HUBBARD: "I think there's too much selfishness in the game today. There's too much me, me, me and people don't give back what they should to the sport. I also think scholarships should go to people who need them. If a kid comes from a family that can afford college, they should pay their own way. They should let the kids who need the scholarship money get it for an education."

COREY MILLEN: "The transition from Buetow to Woog was weird. I liked Woog's style better. Buetow was a yeller and a screamer, and Doug was pretty laid back. Woog could B.S. with the fellas, be a buddy and get the most out of his players. One thing I don't like about his current teams is the fact that he's too set on having four lines out there. It's too systematic, and he needs to be a bit more flexible to mix up the lines."

DAVE PETERSON ('88 AND '92 OLYMPIC COACH): "If Doug ever brought in a Canadian, I'd never bitch about that. We've had a lot of great Canadians play here in the past. I like the fact, though, that it's an outlet for Minnesota kids to play. It's very special to the state."

Dave Snuggerud

BEN HANKINSON: "Woog gets ripped on more by the press for getting to the final four than not winning it."

TRENT KLATT: "Look at any team in Minnesota. There's not one team that can come close to his winning percentage, he's awesome. I think he does a great job, and he'll shut 'em up someday soon.

CORY LAYLIN: "We just have to be patient, it'll come. We've beaten everybody convincingly, it just takes time, discipline, depth and luck. You never know which one of these freshmen is going to step up to be the next superstar. This past year we had so many young guys play key roles, we just got beat in the playoffs in a bad game."

PAUL OSTBY: "I believe we'll win it soon. There's so many things that have to happen when you win: timing, goaltending, attitude and luck. Doug has been very successful. He has the best job in all of hockey. He is a very consistent coach, and his teams reflect that. There's not a lot of highs and not a lot of lows either. He gives kids a chance to play and prove themselves. We've worked together for seven years now and he's a great coach, and a great guy."

GREGG WONG (PIONEER PRESS REPORTER): "If Randy Skarda's shot is one inch to the right, boom! Wooger wins the big one, and the pressure is off. He will. You know Bud Grant never won one either, but he was a great coach and a super guy."

TOM CHORSKE: "We came in together at the same time, and there was a lot of unsureness between the players and coaches. He established his rules, and he wasn't quite sure how to handle some situations. He learned a lot, but he's changed a lot as well I think. He was hard on us at first, then the next year we had a mutual respect with him, and it got a lot easier for all of us."

JIM BOO: "Woog is one of the big ones in the game today. He understands the game, and it doesn't go to his head. He's a great players coach, and he cares about his players. He cares about people. I played for him with the Vulcans, and I really respect him a great deal. He is one classy guy."

LOU NANNE: "He's a good coach. He obviously prefers to take Minnesota kids, but likes Canadians. He looks at it as the coaches job and would prefer to take the local Minnesota kids, but he'd take a Canadian. The program hasn't always been all Minnesotan you know. One time when I was scouting for the Gophers under Herb Brooks, we almost signed Doug Risebrough, who's now the G.M. at Calgary. Herb always boasted of Minnesota kids, but he almost took him for the squad.

"In 1992, Michigan State went to the final four with each kid averaging 19.4 years of age. So, we're not as young as we'd like to think we are. The other teams aren't stocking their squads with 21-year-old freshmen like they used to."

PAUL HOLMGREN: "I played for Doug with the Vulcans. He was a terrific coach as well as a tremendous player. For a small guy, he could be really intimidating. I enjoyed playing for him, and I think he's done a great job with his teams."

DEAN WILLIAMSON: "I'll always be in his debt. I was a long shot, and he made me. He let me transfer and he gave me a chance to be a Gopher when he didn't have to. I scored an overtime goal in my first game as a Gopher, and I was so happy that Woog let me play for him. Woog and my dad were the two most influential people in my life. My dad would tell me to not get upset when Woog benched me, because he said I just didn't fit into Doug's plans right now, but be patient. He supported me, and he supported Woog as well. Whatever he did as a coach, he made me focus and try harder. I will always remember the confidence I got when I saw the thumbs-up signal from my dad. It gave me the confidence to play well, and for that I owe Woog a lot. Wooger has it tougher nowadays because he has to give the five blue-chip players like Brian Bonin a scholarship or else some other team will take him. So, it's harder for Woog to get junior players to come to the 'U' on a scholarship."

DARBY HENDICKSON: "Woog is an awesome coach, and a really cool guy. It really sucked losing to Lake Superior State (in the NCAA.) The time will come though. I'm going to give it my all to win. I have a great feeling about the team. It'll be hard after we lost guys like Trent (Klatt) and Doug (Zmolek), but we'll have to try harder I guess. I guess we'll have to take it one game at a time, but for now, I'm still bummed out about the fact that Station 19 took my ID."

The 1974 national championship team

HOCKEY MOM EXTRAORDINAIRE

There is one aspect of hockey that goes unnoticed, unappreciated and is underrated. I'm talking about that person who took you to the rink at the crack of dawn, and picked you up in the middle of the night. She drove you all over the state in a car filled with smelly hockey equipment and rarely complained. I'm referring to, of course, the hockey mom. The woman who put up with all this and much, much more. She sat in those cold arenas and watched as her sons fell down, got up and learned how to play this game we've grown to love in Minnesota. She worked at those hockey refreshment stands in the freezing cold. She cooked a hot-dish for your teammates at the annual hockey banquet. She washed your equipment for you time and time again. (Although, she may have done that for herself to avoid the odor, now that I think about it...) She did all this for a mere cup of hot chocolate, or perhaps for the privilege of getting to proudly wear a hockey button with her son's picture on it. (My mom, Judi, did all that plus more. I love you Ma!)

This woman, this saint, this...mom, has gone long enough without her due credit to the game. How does that go? "Behind every good man is a woman?" Well, it should be "Behind every good mom is a hockey player who needs a ride to the rink in ten minutes, and what about dinner, ma?" I think as you're reading this right now, you should put down the book, and go out and hug your mom. Go on, thank her for all those rides, dinners, hockey camps, new skates, aluminum sticks that you just had to have, and most of all for her patience and love. She deserves it, and tell her, too, that from now on you're going to wash all your own equipment. OK, maybe just tell her that from now on you won't leave it bunched up in the bag for a week at a time, until it can crawl out by itself. Tell her that she was, in retrospect, appreciated, and tell her why.

I searched far and wide to interview the best example and I came upon a pretty good one who lives in Edina. She is "Bonnie Hankinson: Hockey Mom Extraordinaire." She is the proud mother of the Hankinson brothers, a survivor of three children in a sports-crazed household. She is, for all practical terms, the Mrs. Huckstable of hockey moms. She met her husband John while she was a Vikings cheerleader, and John was the team's ball boy. He would later become the Gophers quarterback, and she would be the boppy cheerleader standing by her man. She is the epitome of, "You can take Bonnie out of the U of M, but you just can't take the U of M out of Bonnie." Besides being a loyal U of M alumnus, she also helps out as the Gopher cheerleading advisor. She is one of the neatest ladies I have ever met. The first encounter I had with her was after my first year as Goldy. She presented me with a card signed by all of the parents of the players, along with a pretty big sum of money. I was flattered, and appreciated it so much. She didn't have to do that, but she thought I should be recognized anyway.

They have three sons: Peter, Ben and Casey. It's no wonder why they had a household full of jocks, when you see their back yard. "Brothers Field, at Hankinson's Yard" they call it, and frankly it's amazing. There's a hockey rink with lights, a basketball court, a batting cage with pitching machine, and a baseball diamond complete with fences that have advertisements on them.

Gopher fans of the late '80's have known the likes of Ben and Pete

Hankinson. They are two of the nicest guys you will ever meet, and so down to earth. I remember when I was with the junior varsity, I hung around with them occasionally. I almost pledged the two of them into my fraternity as well. It didn't work out, but we've remained friends over the years. They are great guys, and my favorite two Gophers.

HERE'S WHAT BONNIE HAD TO SAY:

"Coming from a small town, I wasn't exposed to hockey. But, now I just love it, and wouldn't trade my memories for the world. I remember the first time my parents came to a game to see me as a Gopher Hockey cheerleader. Coming from Willmar, they didn't know much about the game. They watched the first period, watched the second period, and then went home. They thought that it was half-time, and just figured the game was over." (Now my father loves to watch Gopher games, and whenever Ben gets into a fight he yells out,' Give it to him Benny!')

"We had to kid-proof our house, that was for sure. We have tough fabrics on our furniture, dark carpets for when they spill all over, and not too many breakables within reach. It's been a ball, growing up in a hockey family. I remember when we decided that we were going to have a third child, Casey. Ben and Peter said they wanted a new brother to play with, or nothing. They said that if they got a girl they were going to send it back from wherever it came from."

Peter Hankinson

"Hockey is the only sport that totally encompasses your whole life. Weekends, camps, rides to the arenas at all hours, games, it's very time consuming for you whole family. The cost of all the time, energy and money was great for us. It even got our kids scholarships for college. It can be a good return on your investment. It was a good recreational activity that kept them out of trouble. Some parents spend their money on music lessons, we bought our kids skates and sent them to hockey camps instead.

"Gopher Hockey has been wonderful to us, and we wouldn't trade it for the world. It was a wonderful honor for our kids to get the opportunity to play at the

University of Minnesota. The education and experience is second to none. I respect Doug Woog so much, and we trust our kids with him. He takes kids that he thinks have good character and stays away from the troublemakers to keep a good chemistry on his teams.

"The problem today is that there's too much pressure on the kids. There's too many special interest groups that lobby for control of things that shouldn't concern them. I've seen a change now in youth hockey. The kids are too pressured by parents to go to so many hockey schools, have this particular equipment, and go to this particular school to play. It's very political in the youth ranks. Moms are pretty strong lobbyists to get what they want for their kids, and if it's post season ice time like the Tier II tournament, then they can fight for it so their kid gets a chance to play.

"Sure there are obnoxious hockey moms, but there are only a few whiners that give us a bad name. You hear a lot of complainers in peewees and bantams, but when they get to high school, their kid has made the team and, overall, they're supportive at that point. I guess it depends on the individuals, which ones are going to be the complainers.

"It's too bad that people always want to look at the negative aspects of hockey. One time when a reporter asked our family for an interview, we agreed only if he talked about positive things, and nothing negative about hockey. It's such a wonderful sport that it just hurts the game when people badmouth it.

"Gopher parents need doers. When your son enters the team as a freshman, you too enter as a freshmen with the parents. You grow up with them over their four years, and by the time they're seniors, so are you. Your whole circle of friends becomes other hockey parents that you talk to and travel with at games.

"I think it's the values and just directing your kids to do something constructive with their time. Whether it's hockey, baseball, band, a foreign language or whatever, it's best to give your kid a lot of support in any extra curricular activity they can do."

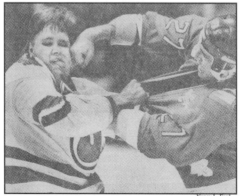

Nancy L. Ford

Ben Hankinson, demonstrating the proper technique on how to block a punch with your jaw.

OK BONNIE, WHAT'S THE DEAL WITH BEN?

"Ben was a little terror as a child. One time we were at a game when Ben was little, and he kept asking me for some gum. I said that I didn't have any gum. I turned around to watch the game, and the next thing I heard was little Ben chomping away on some gum. I asked him where he got it, and timidly he pointed to the bottom of his seat.

"One time in a game at UND, Ben got into a fight. The crowd was pretty nasty, and John Hankinson along with Ted Brill got into a scuffle in the crowd with some fans. Ben got ejected from the game and was suspended from the next game at Wisconsin as well. Just before they threw him out Ben asked the ref, 'Does my dad have to miss the Wisconsin game too?'"

(Ben said: "One time for a $5 bet, I ate three dozen eggs in 20 minutes. No one would stand within ten feet of me in practice for a week. I figured that I had enough cholesterol in my system for the next 50 years.")

ADVICE FOR ANY OF YOU FUTURE HOCKEY MOMS OUT THERE:

"It's so fun, and such a wonderful experience to grow with your kids through all of this. To be able to watch them like little birds that can't yet stand up or get over the boards by themselves, to advance to crawling out, then jumping over, and eventually flying out of there. It's so special, and you meet so many great and interesting people along the way. BUT, for any hockey moms out there who are just taking up the sport, get ready for those long road trips home from games, sitting with that horrible hockey equipment smell. It's a killer and you never can quite get used to it!"

"I'm an Edina cake-eater, and proud of it!" — **Bonnie Hankinson**

IDOLS AND FAVORITE PLAYERS

When asked who was your favorite player, idol or perhaps someone that influenced your life in hockey, there were some really interesting responses. Here's what some of the people had to say:

PAUL HOLMGREN: "Bobby Clarke."

DON CLARK: "My favorite players to watch were: Mike Pearson, John Mayasich, Ken Yackel, Reed Larson, Jack McCartan and Neal Broten."

BOB REID (FORMER GOPHER ANNOUNCER): "John Mayasich, Dick Dougherty and Gene Campbell."

ROGER ROVICK: "John Mayasich, Dick Dougherty and Gene Campbell."

TODD OKERLUND: "Bill Goldsworthy and Bobby Orr."

CORY LAYLIN: "Steve Orth."

TIM HARRER: "Bobby Hull, Bobby Orr, Stan Mikita, the Paradise Brothers, Bill Butters and Mike Antonovich."

TOM VANNELLI: "Mike Antonovich."

WILLARD IKOLA (HALL OF FAME INDUCTEE): "Frank Brimsek."

WALTER BUSH (EXECUTIVE DIRECTOR OF USA HOCKEY): "Thayer Tutt, Walter Brown and Bob Ridder."

GREGG WONG: "Pat Phippen, Tom Vannelli, Joe and Don Micheletti and Robby Harris."

DR. V.A. NAGOBADS (TEAM PHYSICIAN FOR OVER 30 YEARS): "Dave Brooks, Len Lilyholm and Craig Falkman."

MARK ROSEN (WCCO-TV ANNOUNCER): "Neal Broten, Russ Anderson, the Michelettis, Brad Shelstad, Steve Christoff, Eric Strobel and Corey Millen."

LARRY OLIMB: "Billy Christian and Cal Marvin."

BRAD BUETOW: "The Michelettis, Scott Bjugstad and Steve Jensen."

JOHN MAYASICH: "John Matchefts."

BEN HANKINSON: "Phil Verchota, Pat Micheletti, Neal Broten, Steve Christoff and Eric Strobel."

STEVE CANNON (WCCO-RADIO ANNOUNCER): "John Mayasich. He was probably the best ever. Over the years I've enjoyed watching Pat Micheletti, Corey Millen, Doug Woog, Robb Stauber, Neal Broten and Mike Polich."

FRANK MAZZOCCO (KITN-TV ANNOUNCER): "Pete and Ben Hankinson and Lance Pitlick."

MIKE ANTONOVICH: "Stan Mikita, Bobby Hull and John Lothrop."

GLEN SONMOR: "Maurice 'The Rocket' Richard and Gordie Howe."

STANLEY S. HUBBARD: "John Mayasich. He was as good as Gretzky in his day, the best player ever to come out of Minnesota. He was a brilliant skater, and puck-handler. One of his best tricks was to score quick face off goals. He would take draws on the face offs, and he was so quick that he could slap the puck out of mid-air and put it in the net. His records will be broken in time, but check out how many games we played back then compared to now. It was a lot less back then. He was the best ever. Even back when he was in high school at Eveleth, they were a dynasty up there. Eveleth was like the New York Rangers back then, and Mayasich was the heart of it all."

TIM HARRER: "Dave Harrer — my dad — he was really the biggest influence in my life. I grew up watching Bill Butters and Mike Antonovich.

HERB BROOKS: "John Mayasich."

MIKE POLICH: "Bobby Clarke."

LEN LILYHOLM: "Gordie Howe, Bobby Hull and Ken Yackel."

WENDY ANDERSON: "Jim Sedin."

STEVE CHRISTOFF: "I never really had any, I usually just looked up to the kids one level ahead of me..."

WALLY SHAVER (KITN-TV ANNOUNCER): "Pete and Ben Hankinson, Steve Orth and Lance Pitlick."

DEAN BLAIS: "Doug Woog, Herb Brooks, Peter Fichuk, Keith Bolin and Larry Ross."

COREY MILLEN: "Mark Pavelich."

BILL BAKER: "Russ Anderson, Wally Olds, Les Auge and my peewee and bantam coaches, Bob DeGrio and Dan Dilworth."

LARRY ROSS: "Doc Romnes. Doc was a great guy. He wasn't forceful enough to be a great college coach, but he was a real gentleman. He was a fine person and I enjoyed him very dearly. We were good friends, neighbors, and both enjoyed the game of hockey. He was so knowledgeable about the game of hockey too. He motivated us by making us take pride in ourselves to play well. I don't think he'd ever get on a player for not performing in a game. I patterned my coaching style after him, and I take pride in the fact that I played for him. He was a helluva guy."

MIKE RAMSEY: "Reed Larson."

MURRAY WILLIAMSON: "Gordie Howe and Ted Lindsay."

TOM CHORSKE: "Guy Lafleur, Neal Broten, Butsy Erickson, Steve Ulseth, Steve Christoff, Rob McClanahan and Tim Harrer."

DOUG WOOG: "Murray Williamson, John Mayasich, Ken Yackel, Jack McCartan and Mel Pearson."

DICK SPANNBAUER: "The Peltier Brothers and the Paradise Brothers."

BILL BUTTERS: "Lance Pitlick, Todd Richards, Dave Espe, Rob Stauber, Pete Hankinson, Paul Broten, Dave Snuggerud, Doug Zmolek and Jay Cates. I looked up to Bobby Orr and Gordie Howe growing up."

TRENT KLATT: "Steve Christoff, Neal Broten, Tom Chorske, Corey Millen and Doug Woog."

DEAN WILLIAMSON: "My dad's always been my idol. I looked up to Billy Yon, Corey Millen, Luke Johnson, Cory Laylin and Brett Strot."

MURRAY McLACHLAN: "Detroit Goalie Terry Sawchuck and Chicago's Glenn Hall."

PAUL OSTBY: "Vladislav Treitiak, the Soviet National team goalie, Larry Thayer, Jeff Tscherne, Tom Mohr, Brad Shelstad and Steve Janaszak."

DAVE SNUGGERUD: "Dean Talafous. He took me under his wing and helped me out so much, I learned everything from him."

BUTSY ERICKSON: "My two cousins, Earl Anderson and Mike Lundbohm."

PETE HANKINSON: "Wally Chapman and Dave Maley from Edina, Reed Larson, Tom Vannelli and Tom Younghans."

REED LARSON: "Mike Antonovich, Gary Gambucci, Billy Butters, Bruce McIntosh, Dean Blais, John Sheridan, Steve Hall, Dixon Shelstad, and Dick Spannbauer. In the pros I looked up to Bobby Orr, Larry Robinson and Bobby Hull."

DAVE BROOKS: "John Mariucci. When I grow up, I want to be just like him. He's been my lifelong idol. Growing up, I also idolized my neighbor, Wendy Anderson, and of course the 'Golden Jet,' Bobby Hull."

GARY GAMBUCCI: "My Father."

JOHN GILBERT: "I never saw John Mayasich play, but the most entertaining Gopher player I saw was Mike Antonovich. The most amazing Gopher teams might have been Glen Sonmor's WCHA title team and the one that went to the NCAA final the next year. They won the WCHA with Antonovich as a freshman, when they won something like 13 games in which they were tied or behind in the third period. The next year they pulled off the same sort of magic through the playoffs. Antonovich was the inspiration and catalyst for both those teams."

NEAL BROTEN: "I don't idolize anyone. But I respect guys like Robby McClanahan, Bill Baker and Eric Strobel. I respect Wayne Gretzky for all the pressures he has on him, and how well he handles it. Maybe there is one guy I do idolize — John Mariucci. He was a legend."

ROBB STAUBER: "Dale Atol. He was an influential coach that taught me to stay on my feet, and to be a stand-up goalie."

DOUG McLEOD (MSC-TV ANNOUNCER): "I've enjoyed watching the likes of guys like Ben Hankinson, Steve Orth, Gary Shopek, Steve Ulseth, and Neal Broten. My two idols were Stan Musial who was with the Cardinals, and broadcast the Game of the Week, and Dan Kelly the announcer of the St. Louis Blues. He's the best hockey announcer on the face of the earth."

DARBY HENDRICKSON: "My dad, Larry, and my grandpa, who used to be the sports editor of the Tribune. I also looked up to Neal Broten, and Steve Christoff from Richfield."

DICK DOUGHERTY: "John Mayasich and John Mariucci."

DAVE JENSEN: "My brother, Paul."

KEN YACKEL JR.: "My dad. He was the best. He lettered nine times at the U in football, baseball, and hockey. We started Ken Yackel schools, and worked together for nearly 20 years. He contributed so much to hockey in Minnesota. He opened the door for Americans in the NHL, in Canadian-prejudiced administrations. He encouraged kids to play for the fun of it, and to enjoy the game. He was a great teacher. He was famous for coaching from the bench. He was such an intense guy. He had a great vision for the game. I miss him a lot. He was the best friend I ever had."

GENE CAMPBELL: "My four brothers: Ted, Morrie, Pete and Red."

BURTON JOSEPH: "Bud Wilkinson."

"The Godfather"

THE GOPHER BLUE-LINE CLUB

The Blue-Line Club was founded in 1962, while John Mariucci was the head coach of the Gophers. The Blue-Line Club started with 59 members its first year and grew to 79 members its second. It was started by local businessmen, Bruce Telander and George Lyon, and later Bill Hurley. In October of 1992, Gopher supporters and fans alike were saddened by the death of George Lyon. Lyon was described by Bruce Telander as, "A great friend of Gopher Hockey. He believed in the Minnesota kids, and gave much of his time, support and efforts to make the program better."

The club was patterned after the Blue-Line Club that the University of Minnesota-Duluth had organized in the early '60's. The group met on Fridays of home games at Jax Cafe in Minneapolis. It was started to assist in the recruiting of kids for the U of M. The supporters of the program felt it was necessary to help Mariucci in any way possible to assure competitve Gopher Hockey teams for the future. They wanted to promote an interest in the program, give direction to the kids and assist them in their academics. The group also recognized the top metro high school players in the state at banquets to get them thinking about the University of Minnesota. In the early years, the club was emceed by Steve Cannon, of WCCO Radio.

Presently, the Blue-Line Club still meets at Jax Cafe. The club gets together before selected home series throughout the season and rallies support for the team. Coaches, fans, dignitaries, visiting coaches, local celebrities, media-types, former Gophers and Blue-Line Club members meet for luncheons to talk hockey and to support the team. The club has many contributers today who give much of their time and energy to the program. Most recent president is Gary Heinrich.

BRAD BUETOW ERA

Brad played hockey with his brother Bart in the late 1960's and early 1970's for the University of Minnesota. He came out of Mounds View High School, where he was All-State in football, track and hockey. He coached at the University of Minnesota from 1979-1980 to 1984-85. His record was 175-100-20 for a very respectable winning percentage of .689, twice bringing his teams to the NCAA finals, in 1981 and 1982. After his seven-year tenure at the University of Minnesota, he was fired by A.D. Paul Giel. He went on to coach for three years at U.S. International University in San Diego. He was very proud of beating UND the year they won the national championship.

Currently he is the head coach at Colorado College in Colorado Springs, where he resides with his wife, Cecelia, who is a psychologist. The total enrollment of the school is only 1,800 kids and he is proud of the school's rich academic history. CC has won the NCAA championship twice in its history, in 1950 and 1957. He has installed a wide-open style of hockey, and was very proud of his fourth-place finish in the league in 1991-92. He has had 13 players go into the NHL, and is very proud of the fact that 100% of his players, in his four-year tenure, graduated. He is still committed to recruiting Minnesota kids, and in 1992 there were nine Minnesotans on the CC roster.

"It's very rewarding when past players call me for advice, and it's so fun to be a teacher at the college level. However, I have coached now for almost 20 years, and am considering coaching in the NHL, or even the Olympics for the future. Recruiting is a lot of work down here, and I would maybe enjoy a change of scenery. I enjoy the college level, and it has been great for me. The pro level is big money, but there's too many situations in the pros that you can't control. It's a very unstable job, and the front offices want instant success or you're out in a hurry. It's difficult in the NHL as well with the Canadian front offices that tend to take care of their own."

On leaving: "It was an unfortunate decision made by some people who weren't given all the facts, and I hope to God it never happens to any other coaches for whatever reasons. I wasn't bitter towards the school, I loved the school, worked very hard there, and my wife had a great job there. Our roots were very deep in Minnesota. It's always tough to make changes, but we moved forward and we're very happy now. Hopefully it'll never happen to any other people in that situation. It was very unfortunate, and unfair."

BUETOW TRIBUTES

PAUL BROTEN: "He's a great coach. Sometimes we didn't touch pucks all week during practices, but we respected him. I learned a lot from him, he's a good guy."

TODD OKERLUND: "The transition from Buetow to Woog was a hard transition to move into. Buetow had a physical, pro-style of hockey that was physically tough. Woog was more into heavier skating, less emphasis on toughness, and a more European style of hockey. He stressed the speed over the toughness. It was hard for me because I wanted to turn pro, and I liked the physical style of hockey better. I saw Buetow's style of physical hockey better for helping me make it in the NHL."

PAT MICHELETTI: "Brad was a good coach. He almost got it done; we made a hell of a run at it. I think it was a different style of hockey back then, he was pretty physical in his approach to coaching. I learned a lot from him, and the transition to Woog was interesting, to say the least."

Pat Micheletti

JOHN GILBERT: "Brad had a hopeless task, to follow Herb Brooks's magic act as coach of the Gophers. Away from the game, talking about nonhockey things, Brad is a really different person, warm and easy-going. But he was driven almost as if by obsession to succeed as Gopher coach and he always pushed himself and his players. He feels bitter about his dismissal, and always will. He may not have been the man Paul Giel wanted as coach, but as assistant, he was the logical interim coach when Brooks took the Olympic team, and his success made him Giel's reluctant choice as replacement. Coaching the Gophers is a tough place to learn how to coach. None of the little disputes and hassles he had along the way were justifiable reason for his firing taken singly, but they were a bunch of little molehills that accumulated into a mountain."

DAVE JENSEN: "While you were there, you kind of hated the guy. But after you got done, you realize that he was a great coach, and a really nice guy."

BUTSY ERICKSON: "He could coach, there's no doubt about it. I liked his approach to coaching. It was different than Herbie's style of coaching, but it was effective. He tried to get the most out of his players so we could win."

Corey Millen

PAUL OSTBY: "I liked playing under him. He gave me a chance to play, when I was a longshot. I think we had some really good teams under him, and we came close to winning it a few times."
DOUG McLEOD: "He's a good friend. He just wanted to coach hockey. Woog loves to yuck it up, but Brad was more reserved and didn't enjoy the spotlight."

COREY MILLEN: "I liked Brad. He was a good coach, and he took us to some big

Butsy Erickson

games, we just came up a little bit short. It was too bad that he had to leave as he did, I remember it pretty vividly. We got swept in a series, and the next week was the hardest week of hockey in my life. We didn't see a puck all week. We skated, did push-ups, guys were puking, and it was a nightmare. He bitched at everyone, and was trying to get us ready for the CC game that weekend. We won the first game, but then lost the second night. Brad said to us that since we had lost again, he was going to make the next week of practice even tougher than the last week's. We said screw this. So we called a meeting together. We all felt he handled it poorly, and he was being unreasonable to us. So we sort of had a strike to not play if he was going to treat us like that. We had our talk, guys spoke their minds, and heads rolled. It's not to say that he was a bad coach or anything, he just got out of control that time. He's a really nice guy, and a really knowledgeable coach about hockey."

Steve Ulseth

GOPHERS IN THE HALL OF FAME:
(From the U.S. Hall of Fame Handbook)

John Mariucci

John Mariucci, an Eveleth native, played on the 1939-40 undefeated team at the University of Minnesota. He was also an outstanding football player at the U of M as well. Mariucci played briefly for Providence before joining the Blackhawks where he played until 1948. Before retiring after the 1951 season, he played for the Coast Guard Team in the Eastern League. Returning to his almamater as varsity head coach in 1952, he remained until 1966. There he made it to two NCAA finals and several final fours. He also coached the 1956 Olympic team to a silver medal in Cortina, Italy, and the 1977 National team. He later served as Assistant G.M. of the North Stars for several years. In 1977 he was awarded the Lester Patrick Award for his contributions to American hockey. He will long be remembered for being a champion of the American player, and promoting amateur hockey in Minnesota.

Elwyn (Doc) Romnes

Doc Romnes played high school hockey in White Bear Lake and St. Paul, as well as a year at St. Thomas College, before joining the professional St. Paul Saints in 1927. It was after three years with the Saints that he made the jump to the big time. Romnes played in the Stanley Cup finals on four different occasions: 1931, 1934, and 1938, all with Chicago, and 1939 with the Maple Leafs. In all of Romnes's regular and playoff career he drew 46 penalty minutes in 403 games. In 1935-36 he won the Lady Byng Trophy scoring 13 goals and 25 assists along with 6 penalty minutes in the then full 48-game schedule. The Lady Byng Trophy is awarded to the player adjudged to have exhibited the best sportsmanship and gentlemanly conduct combined with a high standard of playing ability. After the 1940 season Romnes retired and coached Michigan Tech until 1945. He led the Kansas City Pla-Mors to the United States Hockey League Championship and playoff title in 1945-46, and then coached the University of Minnesota varsity from 1947 until 1952.

John Mayasich

A product of the Hall of Fame's native city, John Mayasich has long been regarded as one of the finest amateur hockey players ever produced in the United States. From the days when Eveleth High School was the perennial Minnesota high school champion, 1948-51, his name was linked with hockey. A member of four state championship teams, the smooth skater went on to three great years at Minnesota being named an All-American in 1952-53, 1953-54, and 1954-55. His 29-49-78 and 41-39--80 scoring logs were good enough to win WCHA scoring titles in 1953-54 and 1954-55. Following college, Mayasich was a performer with eight U.S. Olympic/National teams. Declining professional hockey opportunities, Mayasich devoted his remaining hockey career to the Green Bay Bobcats. He currently is G.M. of KSTP-FM Radio in the Twin Cities.

Jack McCartan

Jack McCartan graduated from St. Paul Marshall in 1953. After the 1960 Olympics McCartan embarked on a 15-year career in professional hockey. Appearing briefly in two different seasons with the New York Rangers, he was sent to Kitchener-Waterloo of the Eastern Professional League. In 1960-61, he had a sparkling 2.78 average in 52 games. The following season he led the league in shutouts with five. Over the next decade plus, the St. Paul native played primarily in the Western League. In 1968-69 and 1970-71 he captured all-league honors, all with San Diego. He concluded his professional career in 1974 with the Minnesota Fighting Saints of the World Hockey Association. He is currently scouting for the Vancouver Canucks.

Ken Yackel

Ken Yackel graduated from St. Paul Humboldt High School, in 1949, and went on to the University of Minnesota where he was selected to the All-American team. Yackel was but one of two American-developed players to appear in the NHL in the decade of the '50's when he played with Boston in 1958-59. His other professional play included service with Cleveland and Providence in the American League as well as Saskatoon/St. Paul of the Western League. In the early '60's, Yackel coached and played in the technically amateur International League for the Minneapolis Millers. In 1962-63 Yackel coached the Millers to the finals before losing to Fort Wayne, but his 100-point season was sufficient to gain second-team all-star honors at both left wing and coach. Also active in the international scene, Yackel was a member of the 1952 United States Olympic Team that won a silver medal losing only to Czechoslovakia and tying Canada. In 1965, he coached the United States National Team in the world tournament in Tampere, Finland. He answered the call of his alma mater in late 1971 and filled in as interim coach at Minnesota when Glen Sonmor left in midseason to run the Fighting Saints.

Larry Ross

Larry Ross graduated from Morgan Park High School in Duluth in 1940. He entered the Navy and played on the Navy Team in 1942-43 and went on to the University of Minnesota where he was selected All-American in 1950-51 and 1951-52. Ross, as coach of the International Falls Broncos, met with great success compiling a record of 556 wins, 169 losses and 21 ties, took the Broncos to 13 Minnesota State Tournaments, winning six Minnesota state championships. During the 1964-1966 seasons, the Broncos went undefeated in 58 straight games. While coaching at International Falls he started hockey at Rainy River Community College and coached both teams at the same time. He has been a scout for the Hartford Whalers, Minnesota North Stars and is currently scouting for the San Jose Sharks.

Herb Brooks

Herb Brooks, a St. Paul "East Sider," helped win the state tournament for St. Paul Johnson, playing from 1952-1955. He also played at the University of Minnesota from 1955-1959. He was on U.S. Olympic Teams of 1964 and 1968, and National Teams of 1962, 65, 67, and 70. As of his induction in 1990 to the Hall of Fame, Minnesota's only three NCAA titles came during Brooks's seven years as coach. In 1980, Brooks selected and singularly directed a team of collegians to the "Miracle on Ice" at Lake Placid -- the Olympic gold medal. Brooks coached the New York Rangers for 3 1/2 years, twice topping 90 points, and he later directed St. Cloud State to third place in the national small-college tournament and moved them to Division 1 status. He coached the Minnesota North Stars for the 1987-1988 season, and then dropped out of coaching until 1991, when he moved into the New Jersey minor league team coaching ranks. In 1992 he was named head coach of the New Jersey Devils.

(Badger) Bob Johnson

Bob Johnson was a 1954 graduate of the University of Minnesota. He began his coaching career in Warroad High School, in northern Minnesota, in 1956. Then he coached at Minneapolis Roosevelt High School before moving on to coach at Colorado College in 1963. He took over as the University of Wisconsin head coach where he was given the nickname "Badger Bob" and was NCAA Coach of the Year in 1977. He led the Badgers to seven NCAA tournaments, and won three NCAA championships. He guided the 1976 U.S. Olympic team to a fourth-place finish at Innsbruck, Austria. He coached the 1981,1984, and 1987 U.S. teams in the Canada Cup. He also coached the 1973, 1974, 1975 and 1981 U.S. National Teams. Perhaps his proudest moment came in 1991, when he coached the Pittsburgh Penguins to a Stanley Cup victory over the Minnesota North Stars. It was the club's first ever Patrick Division and Prince of Wales Conference Championships. He also served as Executive Director of USA Hockey for a three-year period. Bob Johnson's memory lives on from his now-famous phrase which epitomized his love for the game:

"It's a great day for hockey."

MOST MEMORABLE GAMES

What one special Gopher game do you remember most?

"Against Denver to go to the finals in Boston, where we won our first national championship. Rob and John Harris combined on the winning goal, and the arena was just jammed and rocking with excitement."

—Tom Greenhoe, sports information director.

"The national championship game where Neal Broten was falling down, and he chipped in the puck over the goalie's shoulder. It was awesome, and reassured my opinion that Neal was the best Gopher ever to play the game."

— Tim Harrer, Gopher wing, 1977-80.

"The loss to Michigan State my senior year."

— Corey Millen, Gopher center, 1983-87.

"The three-overtime thriller in 1976 against Michigan State to go to the finals. I had covered the team that entire year, and it was very special."

— Gregg Wong, sports writer, Pioneer Press.

"The overtime win against Harvard. Glen had told us his strategy -- it was going to be Antonovich's line, the Peltiers' line, then those two again, then Gambucci's line. I said it'll never get that far coach, we'll score way before Gambucci will touch the ice. And sure enough, I got the game winner on OT, on a sweet pass from my brother out front."

— Ron Peltier, Gopher center, 1969-71.

"Against Michigan to go to the final four in Denver."

— Dave Brooks, Gopher center, 1961-63.

"My most memorable game still gives me a bad feeling, it was the Harvard loss in OT at the Civic Center. We were a goal-post away, and Jon Anderson had a whale of a game that day. We were on the fourth line together, and everything he touched went in. If Skarda's shot was just an inch to the right..."

— Larry Olimb, Gopher center, 1989-92.

"The championship game against UND, when we won it all."

— Steve Ulseth, Gopher wing, 1978-81.

"My most memorable game was against Notre Dame when I was a freshman. We won 8-1, and I had a hat trick. It was that game when I came of age as a player."

— Steve Christoff, Gopher center, 1977-79.

"My most memorable game was the championship game when we won it all. I remember a lot of champagne, toasting and crying that night. It was a lot of fun."

— Tim Harrer, Gopher wing, 1977-80.

"My favorite game was sweeping Denver at home to get into the playoffs."
— *Dick Spannbauer, Gopher defenseman, 1973-74.*

"My most memorable game was beating UND at Detroit for the championship. For me it was my first championship of any kind in my life, so it was really special."
— *Neal Broten, Gopher center, 1979-81.*

"The 1975 championship game, even though we lost to Tech, I was proud to say I was a part of that team. It was a thrill for me, and I'll never forget it."
— *Paul Holmgren, Gopher wing, 1975.*

"My most memorable game was my first win against Denver. We won 4-1, and I had 39 saves. I can remember all the guys skating back to me after the game and hitting my pads with their sticks, it was an awesome feeling."
— *Paul Ostby, Gopher goalie, 1981-82.*

"My most memorable game was the Harvard loss a few years ago in overtime. I was there broadcasting the game at the Civic Center. It was a marvelous game, and so close. You know, Skarda hits the pipe... that's hockey."
— *Steve Cannon, WCCO radio personality.*

"The Harvard loss in overtime here at the Civic Center. I was torn. Being a Harvard grad I was 49% Harvard fan, and 51% Gopher fan. We just came up a little bit short, but it was a masterful game."
— *Bob Ridder, '56 'Olympic team manager, and Hall of Fame inductee..*

"The 1976 championship game in Denver against Michigan Tech. We had a real gutsy team, and just battled all season.
— *Joe Micheletti, Gopher defenseman, 1974-77.*

"When Northern Michigan beat us (1980) to go to the final four. We lost 4-3, and I scored a goal from the blue-line on a slapper. It went so fast that it ripped a hole in the net and the ref didn't call it a goal, and we lost. The red light went on, but the ref refused it because he was convinced that the puck couldn't possibly have done that. I completely schooled the Northern goalie, Steve Weeks, on it and they didn't give it to us. Later when we watched the tape of it we went crazy, and a photo in the paper the next day showed the ripped net. That was one of the toughest losses ever for me."
— *Aaron Broten, Gopher center, 1980-81.*

"Against the Gophers in 1953 for the finals. I was playing goal for Michigan, and we beat the Gophers to win it all. I remember John Mariucci coming over to our lockerroom after the game and giving me a hard time about it."
— *Willard Ikola, former Edina coach and Hall of Fame inductee.*

"Against UND in 1992. It was that game where I scored my first ever hat trick. It was awesome."

— *Darby Hendrickson, Gopher forward.*

"Beating Michigan in a two-game series in 1960-61. My best game was against UND, where I got my only hat trick ever."

— *Lou Nanne, Gopher defenseman, 1961-63.*

"In 1976, against Michigan Tech in Denver, I scored a goal and was injured at the time. I think my best game was in Madison, when I scored the overtime winner against Wisconsin."

— *Bill Baker, Gopher defenseman, 1976-79.*

"My sophomore year against UND, up in that freezing cold arena they had up there, and I let in one goal for the whole series. Of course Glen was not averse to celebration either, so after the game the bus driver took us to the nearest liquor store for the ride home."

— *Murray McLachlan, Gopher goalie, 1968-70.*

"My most memorable game was scoring a hat trick as a freshman in Maine."

— *Paul Broten, Gopher center, 1985-88.*

"The final four loss to Harvard. Johnny Blue was awesome in nets during the semifinals, but we came up short in the end."

— *Tom Chorske, Gopher wing, 1986-89.*

"The loss to Northern Michigan to go to the final four. Aaron shot a puck through the net that they wouldn't call a goal, and we lost the game. It was without a doubt the saddest game I have ever played in."

— *Butsy Erickson, Gopher wing, 1980-83.*

"My most memorable moment as a Gopher was special for me and my mom. It was my first shift ever against Denver, and I scored a goal. The next night of the series, I scored the game-winner in OT. I was so pumped about being a Gopher at that time, but it was nothing compared to my mom's excitement. She was so excited after I scored that goal that she peed her pants in the bleachers. It was her birthday too, so... I guess that was a good present, eh mom?"

— *Cory Laylin, Gopher wing,1989-92.*

"Impossible to pick out just one. There was the NCAA tournament semifinal in Syracuse, when Glen Sonmor was coaching, and the Gophers came from something like a 4-1 deficit in the third period to win in overtime. Then there was the unbelievable WCHA playoff series at Notre Dame in 1977, when Herb Brooks was coaching. The Gophers lost by four goals in the first game of a total-goal series, then gave up the first goal the next night before roaring back to win 9-2 and take the whole series. And 1976, the Gophers tied Michigan State in the first playoff game and won the second in three overtimes. The game took so long that the Gophers missed their plane home from East Lansing, but went on to win the national tournament. The NCAA final in Detroit in '79, with Neal Broten flying through the air and chipping in the winning goal over Bob Iwabucci, the North Dakota goaltender. The Gophers didn't win all their great games. They lost a St. Paul Classic tournament final at Met Center in 1969 to North Dakota in seven overtimes — the winning goal for the Sioux was scored by Buzzy Christenson, who is now a referee. But the best-played game, perhaps in the history of college hockey, was the Gophers 4-3 loss to Harvard in overtime in the NCAA final in the Civic Center; they were the two most flowing, creative teams in the country and they played a classic, where great plays were beaten by better ones on every shift. Give me a minute, and I'll think of a dozen more..."

— John Gilbert, Sportswriter for the Star Tribune.

"The 1979 national championship game. From the first day of practice that year Herbie said we were going to win it all. I remember Neal sliding across the crease scoring that goal, and the excitement of it all. After the game we ordered champagne by the truckload, and since we didn't want to go out in Detroit for fear of our lives, we had an intimate party with all the guys in the hotel, and enjoyed a successful season together."

— Don Micheletti, Gopher wing, 1977-80.

"The overtime loss to Harvard. It was the worst feeling I have ever had as a hockey player. I think it was probably the funnest game I had ever played in, but for sure the toughest game to swallow."

— Dave Snuggerud, Gopher forward, 1986-89.

"It's amazing that the last national championship was way back in 1979, but I felt like part of the team then because I covered them all year. I had a ball covering the team back then, and I remember being in awe of it all when it happened."

— Mark Rosen, WCCO TV sports broadcaster.

"Playing at UND in that cold arena. It was 20 below in there, and I'll always remember that old chicken wire fencing around the boards. It was just terrible in there, and the fans were dumping beer on us as we came in from the locker room. One lady even smacked one of our guys on the head with a chair. It was so cold that in warm-ups we damn near broke all our pucks in half from hitting the pipes. I'll always remember that game."

— Dean Blais, Gopher forward, 1970-73.

"The semifinal game against Boston University in 1976. It was a 3-3 tie with a couple minutes to go, and we let the game get away from us. Dick Spannbauer got a penalty and we thought it was all over. I went out to try and kill the penalty and got a shorthanded goal on a slapshot with 13 seconds left to win the game. That got us into the finals against Tech, where we won it all the next night. The irony of it all was that the goalie for Tech was Ed Walsh. The next year, playing for the Canadiens, Walsh was our goalie, and I razzed him about it for the entire year.

"My favorite game was the 1974 championship game. We never should've won it. Tech was a much better team, and we knew it. They were a powerhouse team, and the reverse was true the next year about us. In 1975 we lost to the same team, Tech. But, we should've killed them that year. We were awesome that year, and I guess they were getting revenge from the year before."

— *Mike Polich, Gopher center, 1972-75.*

"The 1976 national championship game against Tech. I was the MVP of the series. The game before that there was a bench-clearing brawl, and Russ Anderson and I got ejected from the game. We had a great party that night, and I vaguely remember all the furniture from our room mysteriously winding up in the pool. It was a party-hard, play-hard team."

— *Tom Vannelli, Gopher center, 1974-77.*

"I really liked that Harvard game here a couple years ago. That was an exciting and fun game to watch. I really wanted Wooger to win that one, he was so damn close."

— *Pat Reusse, Sports columnist for the Star Tribune.*

"The 1976 championship game against Michigan Tech in Denver. Russ Anderson and I saw the game from the bench the entire game. Although I never actually played a shift, I got a watch and a ring to prove that I was there."

— *Jim Boo, Gopher defenseman, 1976-78.*

"My most memorable game was against Wisconsin when I stopped six breakaways, and we won in overtime. It was a great one-on-one challenge."

— *Robb Stauber, Gopher goalie, 1987-89.*

"My favorite game was the 1979 championship when Neal Broten slid across the ice and scored that fantastic goal to win the game. My worst favorite game was the third-place game between Minnesota and Maine in Lake Placid. We have that game to thank for the fact that there is no third-place game anymore in the final four. It was the ugliest slugfest I have ever seen. I remember Stauber and the Maine goalie playing catch with a puck as the refs were breaking up the fights. They were shooting the pucks back and forth, and the refs finally had to take the puck away from them to make them stop. And of course the fans threw them more pucks to make the referees even madder. I can say that was one hell of a rotten game."

— *Doug McLeod, MSC-TV and Gopher radio broadcaster.*

"My first game I ever played in. It was against Wisconsin, and I had a goal and a couple helpers. My favorite game was the championship game in Detroit where we beat UND. It was the best team I had ever seen, so many great guys in that bunch. Eight Olympians was incredible, plus guys like Aaron Broten, Harrer, and Don Micheletti who were right on the border of making it."

--*Mike Ramsey, Gopher defenseman, 1979.*

GOLDY'S MOST MEMORABLE GAMES?

Over my two-year career as the rodent, I've had some pretty darn strange things happen to me. As you can imagine, some of the funniest things that have occurred involved little kids in one way or the other. I could really relate to the little kids because I figured out not too long ago that I too was nothing but a little kid pretending to be a big one. I would have to say that being around all the kids was probably the biggest thrill for me while being Goldy. It was like being Santa Claus at times, I guess. Who else but Santa could get peed on, puked on, spit up on, and cried on in the span of an hour or so? Oh, and let's not forget those lovable rug-rats who liked to pull on Goldy's tail, and punch the poor rodent in the ding-ding. How does that go, it's the toughest job you'll ever love? Well anyway, the truth of the matter is that I loved the job. Tail-pulling, being spit-up on, and ding-ding punching aside, I'd be lying if I said that it wasn't the funniest time of my life.

During the 1991-92 season at Mariucci Arena, I had been skating pretty hard in the intermission between periods, and was tired. I figured this would be a good time to use the facilities to clean up, and relieve myself. I went down from the perch, and straight into the bathroom.

I walked in and I checked to see if anyone was in there. I knew this had to be a quick, "stealth-pee," if you know what I mean. The coast was clear, and I could now take off my head to take care of the business at hand. No pun intended. I had to be careful that no little kids could see me. I had to make a decision now whether to just use the cozy stalls of privacy in the rear of the lavatory, or those lovely troughs up front. I decided to play it safe, and use a stall in case someone came in. But my head was too big to fit through the door, so I took off my head and placed it on the stool in the next stall over, and went about my business. There I was, safe in the back stall from any tail-tuggers, autograph seekers or Cub Scouts who wanted me to get them a puck for their sister.

That's when I heard a horrifying, blood-curdling scream. This was the kind of scream that could set off car alarms in a 12-block radius, or cause permanent ear damage to every dog in the neighborhood. I peered through a crack in the stall and saw a little kid was just standing there crying, perplexed, and pointing at the Gopher-less head while he shook his own head in disbelief. He called for his daddy to come quickly, and do some serious explaining.

When daddy came he soon realized that this explanation would be a tough one, right up there with the birds and the bees I suppose. Nowhere in the owners manual for kids did it ever talk about how to explain something like this. Imagine a little kid seeing Goldy's head sitting on the toilet, figuring that the rest of him was somewhere below. I wanted to just jump out and make it all better for the little guy, but I was trapped in silence in a stall with the Tidy Bowl Man as my only friend. The echo of a little boy screaming in horror, "Daddy, Daddy, Help, quick! Goldy's flushed down the toilet!" will forever haunt me.

Dad jumped in and I heard him say that it was too late, he was gone, and they would talk about it on the way home. He just grabbed the little goober, and I could hear his cries all the way out the door, "GOLDEEEEEEEE!"

It was at this point that I decided that: A) I'm not having kids for a very long time. B) I guess that if I was 3 years old, and saw a giant Gopher head stuck on the

Johnson, I too would assume that Goldy was now alligator bait in the sewers below Mariucci Arena. C) I wish I could've heard the conversation that took place with the little boy and his daddy in the family truckster on the way home from the game. And D) I was never going to go to the bathroom again at a Gopher game.

Another great story happened that year as well. It was around Christmas time and the Gophers were playing at home. I decided to spice things up at the game that day, so I came out dressed as "Santa-Goldy." I zoomed out on the ice with some inflatable reindeer, and started to act like an idiot. The crowd response was pretty good. There was an occasional: "Gee that Gopher is weird as hell," but all in all, it was pretty fun stuff, and Rudolph the Red-Nosed Reindeer was a big hit. I had Rudolph play goalie for me as I gave him a few slap-shots to the nose, rode him around the rink, and we horsed around for a while. Then we got into a big brawl, I dropped my gloves, and we went at it with him. It was pretty funny, until I accidentally ran over his hoof.

Of course it was very entertaining for the crowd to see the inflatable reindeer deflate on the ice. However, all the little kids who were big fans of Rudolph way before they ever knew Goldy were a bit upset. By now a trumpeter in the band had picked up on the death of Rudolph, and started to play Taps.

At this point Rudolph was all but deflated, and I was on my knees holding his lifeless body up to the sky. The crowd thought this was all planned out, and figured it was a funny ending. WRONG! I had no idea what the heck I was doing out there. I saw a couple of little kids who had come over to talk to me that were crying. I went over to play with them, and received one of the most bizarre lectures I could remember since the second grade. There were two of the cutest little critters waiting for me there. One little boy and a little girl (presumably his sister) with a Christmas dress, and Goldy earrings on. The little boy threw his glass of Coke in my face, and the little girl, who was crying, said, "Hey you big, fat, faggot Gopher, you just killed Rudolph, and now Santa won't be able to come and bring any presents to us for Christmas!" As I put my hand out to comfort her, and play with her, the little bugger wound up and punched me right in the nose. Then, with the tears rolling down her face she said, "And I was really good this year too..."

At this point I didn't know whether to laugh, cry, or just get the heck out of there before her momma came over to kick herself some Gopher butt. So, I skated away to the jeers of the crowd over to the bench where I was greeted by the arena security people. They then lectured me for 10 minutes about the dangers of inflatable animals on the ice, and how the Zamboni might get stuck on them and blow up or something. I just shook my head and once again wondered about that minivan ride home from the arena where those little kids' parents had some serious explaining to do. Even old Dr. Spock would've been stumped trying to explain that one!

HOW HAS GOPHER HOCKEY CHANGED?

Gopher hockey has seen a lot of changes over its 100-year history. Changes like the curved stick in the '50's and the addition of helmets for not only the goaltenders, but all players. Then, one of the most controversial of all changes, the face-mask. Some people want the masks to come off, or at least be optional. They claim that with the masks, the smaller players play much bigger. They claim that the addition has hurt the game by allowing the smaller players to play a rough-tough style of hockey that used to be unheard of. They talk of the players carrying their sticks dangerously high, more running, cheap-shots, more penalties and more injuries.

On the other side of the fence, the people who have either known someone, or have themselves lost eyes or teeth, aren't complaining too loud. If anything I think the Gophers have benefitted from this rule, because since we have the huge ice-sheet we have always been a sanctuary for the litte guys who want to play with a big heart. Let them go down to block shots, let them check the bigger guys, and if a big guy gets pissed off at the little guy, let him beat the hell out of him. That's hockey, and keeping our eyes should be more important than recognizing your favorite players face on the ice with his helmet off, and certainly more important than allowing the game to be dictated by the goons. Teams have altered their game-plans because of the change, but the Gopher Hockey program has remained a constant. Our ideologies have been altered from coach to coach, but the wide-open style of physical hockey has persevered through time. If the players of yesterday loved that big 'ol sheet of ice in there, then Gophers of the future will really love the new Olympic sized ice-sheet at the new Mariucci Arena. A lot of former players shared their feelings about the change in Gopher Hockey.

"I don't think it's changed that much really. However the sticks are up, and the game has gotten chippier since the masks came off. Some will argue that the stick-handling skills aren't as refined as in our day, but it's still great hockey. I also think it's become too much of a business now. I liked it better when it was just a fun game."

— *Ron Peltier, center 1969-71.*

"In 1966, John Gilbert and I were working for a Duluth newspaper, and he took me to my first ever hockey game at the Duluth Curling Club. He explained to me all the rules about offside and so forth. I found the game silly in 1966 in Duluth, and I still find it to be a silly game today. The guys skate around for 60 minutes, doing all this crap, then someone hits someone in the back of the neck with the puck. The puck goes in, and they win 2-1. Then the next day in the paper you read about all the skill involved in hockey. There's more luck involved in hockey than any other sport known to man. Hockey hasn't changed a bit, it's still as boring as ever."

— *Pat Reusse, Star Tribune sports columnist and outspoken hockey critic.*

"The players have gotten a hell of a lot better from when we played there."

— *Jim Boo, defenseman, 1976-78.*

"Gopher Hockey has remained pretty consistent over the years. The

Minnesota tradition has always been to get the best Minnesota kids, and go out to win. Minnesota hockey is always strong, and one of the best in the nation year in and out."

— Corey Millen, center, 1983-87.

"There's no better players today than in my era, I think there's just more of them."

— Dick Spannbauer, defenseman, 1973-74.

"Similar to the NHL, the players have all gotten bigger and faster, and because they're all looking at future pro hockey careers, too many players try to play NHL-style clutch-and-grab. It is difficult for a skill team to go all the way, because most coaches are pretty limited in their pursuit of bottom-line success. It's easier for a mediocre team to play a slow-down, hook and hold game and upset a good team than it is for a good team to skate through all the sticks and succeed. The joke of it is, every coach wants to recruit the 6-foot-3, 220-pounders, but every year, when you look at the top 10 scorers in the league, eight of them are 5-9, proving quickness and cleverness still prevail.

"There are also changes in what we might call intimidation. There is intimidation in every sport, whether it's a Nolan Ryan 100-mile-an-hour fastball under your chin, a guy who always hits 300-yard drives, or a solid bodycheck in open ice. Of course, the Russians showed us that speed and precision playmaking can also be intimidating. Colleges, of course, boast that they don't have fights, and it's true; you could look it up. The joke is, a lot of altercations are pretty good fights in college, but the refs call it a roughing, or double-roughing, or even triple-roughing, because they don't want to throw the player out for that game and the next one. College officials think the strict rules prevent fights, but actually, they are so harsh they cause the refs to not enforce them.

"Two things about fights: 1, rarely does anyone get hurt in a hockey fight, slip-sliding around; and 2, when you don't have fights, the little cheapshot artists get away with murder, because they know they can stab you when the ref isn't looking, and if you punch them in retaliation, you'll get tossed. And we should all remember the immortal words of Glen Sonmor, who said, "If we don't cut out all this senseless violence, we're going to have to build bigger arenas. Forget the fights. The worst change in college hockey is letting all the hooking and interference go."

— John Gilbert, Sportswriter for the Star Tribune.

"Kids go down to block shots now, they have no fear. I also think the kids are a lot faster today. I enjoy their style of hockey 'way better than the North Stars. It's much more exciting to watch."

— Mike Polich, center, 1972-75.

"Overall I think it's still the same, just different faces, and a few more people on the wall of fame. It's really a constant. Although when the masks came off, the sticks came up, and it took away from the real flavor of the game."

— Todd Okerlund, wing, 1984-87.

"The game is much faster now. I also disagree with the face masks, they should've gotten rid of them. It's turned the game into football. Without masks there's an equality to the game. A guy like Vannelli for instance, would take one or two in the face every week. He was one tough little bugger, but it gave the game a sense of equality between the big guys and the little guys."

— *Pat Phippen, wing, 1974-76.*

"The masks take away from the skills of the better players. People have no fear of getting hurt anymore, and guys are taking end-to-end rushes like missiles out there. They kill guys, block shots, and the sticks are way up. It's like a war out there. I think masks should be optional. By that age a kid is old enough to make a decision for himself."

— *Tim Harrer, wing, 1977-80.*

"The game changed when the face masks went on. People used to carry their sticks low out of respect for other players to prevent injuries, but now that respect is gone."

— *Steve Christoff, center, 1977-79.*

"I don't think the kids are having fun anymore. It's more of a business, whereas before it was just a game for fun. It was very simple back then, and today it's gotten so technical. With us, it was pretty simple. It was just put the puck in the net, and then try and stop the other team from scoring."

— *Mike Antonovich, center 1970-72.*

"Today there's more power hockey, and not much respect for each other. They run each other so much, and it's gotten out of hand I feel. Today the kids are so big and strong, it's power hockey all the way. Dump and run, run into someone, and jam it into the net. There's not too many old school players with a lot of creativity anymore. We battled, had rivalries, and focused on hard work and skills."

— *Butsy Erickson, wing, 1980-83.*

"Get rid of those stupid face masks."

— *Dave Snuggerud, wing, 1986-89.*

" Today the game is faster than when I played. They have better facilities, curved sticks, better equipment, and better coaching. I don't see much hockey down here in Arizona, in my nursing home, but I follow the team as much as I can. Good luck fellas, win one for Minnesota."

— *Frank Pond, Gopher coach, 1930-35.*

"You can't pay me enough to go watch a Stars game. The Gophers have fantastic end-to-end rushing, individual skills, passing abilities, and simplicity. There's not a better brand of hockey anywhere, and the Gopher style of hockey has remained pretty constant over the years. Not much has changed, I don't think."

— *John Hankinson, Gopher quarterback, 1964-65.*

"I don't like what the face mask has done to college hockey. People used to be afraid to come to Mariucci Arena, they knew we were big, physical, and rough. Without masks there was a sense of equality. If a little guy popped off to a big guy, it took him just one time before he ate a little lumber, or caught some elbow in the chin before he learned how we played the game up here. Now the littlest guy out there plays like he's the biggest. He has no fear of getting hurt, and can hide behind those bars. Today you see little missiles out there, flying around fearlessly, lipping off all over the ice. People used to fear a guy like Russ Anderson because he was an enforcer, today it's much different. One other point is that I feel we played hockey for fun back then. I think that if I played hockey today, with all the pressures from parents, I wouldn't last out there. I'd get sick of it."

— *Bill Baker, defenseman, 1976-79.*

"When we were in high school, we dreamed of being Gophers. Now everybody is drafted out of high school, and their goals have changed a lot. They think they can play college for two years, play in the Olympics, then sign a huge pro contract. Gopher Hockey through the years has been fast tempo, aggressive and hard checking. I don't think that has changed much. My era was also the first to really have access to all the arenas to use. We were also the first to travel a lot, and the first to be exposed to all the hockey schools as well."

— *Steve Ulseth, wing, 1978-81.*

"I don't think college hockey is any safer now with face masks. I think they should get to choose, and at most wear a half plexi-shield. The cage is terrible, they cause a lot of injuries with the sticks coming up so much now. Kids grab masks and wrench guys' necks, and they cause a lot of facial cuts too. The cage takes away from the fans as well, they used to enjoy seeing the kids' faces out there. There's more cross checking, and running from behind, and that's more dangerous than a cut in the face any day."

— *Reed Larson, defenseman, 1975-77.*

"I hope you realize that we as Minnesotans don't have the dominant position in ice-hockey that we used to have. Take the first 15 Americans drafted in the past 25 years, and see the shift of kids coming from Massachusetts and Michigan. The USA teams from the Olympics to the National teams are being made up of predominately eastern kids. Kids play 25-35 games a year in high school with 15-minute periods. A Canadian kid plays 70 games a year for 20-minute periods. They are clearly more polished at 18 years old, and even better at 20 years old. Take the 1992 Olympic team for example. It was run by all Minnesotans, Larry Johnson, Walter Bush and Dave Peterson. So, it wasn't that they hated Minnesotans, it's just that we're not producing the talent any more like we used to. A year ago the rule saying kids can play hockey all year long in leagues was changed so kids in Minnesota can compete in leagues. Massachusetts and Michigan kids compete all year long, so now hopefully the kids who want to become polished hockey players will have the opportunity to, and we'll hopefully regain our edge.

"The fighting is absolutely absurd, the trouble with the game is they need international size rinks, and take out the red line. It would speed up and spread out the game. The players are too big and too close together and are killing each other out there now. This thing with the injury to Mario Lemieux was absolutely horrifying and sad to see in the National Hockey League. I know a lot of people who won't go to games because of the fighting. They could stop the fighting in five minutes, and 90% of the players would love it."

— Bob Ridder, '56 Olympic Team Manager, & Hall of Fame inductee.

"I don't cut easy and I'm not a bleeder. In the NHL this year, I had over 100 penalty minutes with the Rangers and never got cut up. Yet, when I played for the Gophers that mask always cut my face up. They should get rid of those things, and go with the half shields."

— Paul Broten, center, 1985-88.

"The players are faster, but overall I don't think it's changed that much since I was there."

— Jack McCartan, goalie, 1956-58.

"I think the kids are bigger, faster, stronger and they all shoot the puck. They always have had the mystique they've created. Everybody wants to be a Gopher, so a lot of kids walk on nowadays. This is a drastic change from the years past, where Mariucci felt it was your duty to go to the University because you were a Minnesotan. He didn't kiss any kids' butts, because he felt it was each individual's obligation to play here. Sometimes it hurt him. For example, in 1963 Badger Bob, who was coaching at Colorado College, and was a hell of a recruiter, stole all the top recruits from under his nose to play out there."

— Gary Gambucci, center, 1966-68.

"Gopher Hockey used to be skating, skating, skating so we could compete with the bigger Canadian kids. In recent years, starting with Herb Brooks, he made it more physical and so on. I figure we can do more things with speed. We're a sophisticated market, so fans want to watch a winner. Fans are loyal to the Gophers, and pro fans are fickle.

"It maintains a high level of success, and it has a real neat aura to it. Kids want to come here to play. It's one of the only things in the world that remains unblemished and untarnished. It's very unique, and special to Minnesota."

— Doug Woog, center, 1964-66.

"I remember a funny statement that sums up fighting pretty well I think: 'Have you ever broken your nose?' 'No, but six other guys have for me.' When I'm asked if there's room for fighting in the game I say hell yes! I've never seen anybody get seriously injured from fighting. Sure the stick is bound to come up and cut you, but come on, a good old fashioned brawl is fun. I remember fighting big Russ Lowe, a bruiser from Buffalo, when I was with Cleveland. We had some fun out there I tell ya! But I like fighting in the NHL. This clutch and grab B.S. is so slow and boring I don't like to watch it. I can't stand to watch the Scandinavians play the game.

There's no action, just passing and skating. I think that's for pussies, I like to mix it up and have fun out there."

— *Glen Sonmor, Gopher coach, 1966-71.*

"I think Gopher Hockey has improved. The teaching is better, coaching is better, and it is much more of a centralized game all the way from the mighty mites to college. It's improved a great deal. There's higher individual skills now, and it's faster as well. I think the NHL should get rid of that redline. It would tire out the defensemen, but it would make the game better.

"I personally like the face masks. It makes the game safer. I realize that if also gives little guys a lot of adrenaline, and they get courageous like Superman out there. They know they can't get hurt, and the sticks come way up. The officials don't call a damn thing when the sticks come up. They can't fight, so they use their sticks. It just simply has to stop, or we'll lose the game altogether."

— *Tom Greenhoe, former Gopher Sports Information Director.*

"The big sheet of ice opens it up a little more. But, I don't like all that hooking, grabbing, slashing and clutching. If we continue on our present course, where we're not enforcing this, we could just butcher this game to death. It wouldn't be the first time that a sport has fallen by the wayside because we didn't correct the rules the right way to make sure the game was going on the right track. People don't like fighting in hockey. It's going to wreck the game eventually. Injuries are the key issue. Eye injuries like Glen Sonmor's, and of course injuries. The most eye-opening of course was the late Bill Masterton's of the North Stars. He got checked, fell and hit his head. He wasn't wearing a helmet, and it cost him his life. That triggered the start of helmets in hockey."

— *Bob Utecht, Creator/writer for* <u>*Let's Play Hockey.*</u>

"Fighting doesn't really bother me. It hurts your knuckles more than anything else. I've never seen a guy get hurt too badly in a fight. I figure that if two guys want to go, it's their business. Hell, let 'em go, and get it out of their systems so the game can go on."

— *Neal Broten, center, 1979-81.*

"There used to be a level of 'This is what it takes to be a Gopher' and now kids aren't intimidated by that. I was in awe when I came here. I had to earn respect and credibility from the guys, it didn't just happen. I think the kids may be taking that for granted now. Freshman hot-shots can't just come in and be prima-donnas, they have to earn it. They need to take a few in the chin, work hard and earn the respect from the older guys just like they had to. Too many young kids are coming in and just fitting in. That scares me. They need to be challenged, intimidated and have to build character. You have to make kids work extra hard to earn a spot on the team, it's part of growing up in life. You have to bust your balls every night to be a part of this program. Guys that typified this work ethic to the extreme were: Gary Shopek, Jay Cates, Eric Dornfeld and Lance Pitlick."

— *Robb Stauber, goalie, 1987-89.*

74

"It was my sophomore year when the masks came off, and I immediately saw the game change at that point. The game is now much chippier. It's turned into a generic game, the skills are gone, the big players are dominating with rough play, and it's sad. We need to get rid of the masks to bring back the equality to the game. Guys who are 5-6 are running guys from behind, and then watching the refs do nothing about it. The game has to change or we're going to lose it.

"Officiating in college hockey has to change as well, or it's going to be gone. It's getting uglier and uglier each year. Officials are afraid of making calls because they don't want to determine the outcome of a game. There's 'way more shoulder and knee injuries today because the officials are letting it go and players are taking the game into their own hands. I look at some of our games, and I'm embarrassed to be a part of college hockey at times. Referees have to start calling more penalties, period. There was a referee, who — I won't say his name — I asked him why the refs don't call all the penalties they see when they see a penalty rather than making the game subjective? He said, 'Well, if we called every penalty we saw, Minnesota would never lose a game because they always have the best talent on their team.' Jesus! Is that a scary thought or what? I guess it's bring out the football uniforms, eh fellas!

"We're losing skillful hockey players because we need to recruit a different type of person. I love seeing a guy like Darby Hendrickson. He's so refreshing to see, he's a throwback to the skill and talent of guys like Mike Antonovich and Neal Broten. The skillful little guys are becoming a vanishing breed. It's disappointing as a coach to see that there were guys we couldn't consider recruiting at the 'U' that were skillful, masterful little hockey players, but simply weren't big enough. In Gopher Hockey history, who are the best guys? The little guys like Woog, Antonovich, Polich, Broten, Ulseth, Gambucci, Erickson, Millen, Micheletti, and Olimb. Those are all little guys playing hockey in that big rink where it's all spread out on that huge sheet of ice. That's Gopher Hockey." -
— *Paul Ostby, goalie, 1981-82, and assistant coach.*

"I don't mind the fighting, but I hate the face masks. When a guy goes in the corner and gives you an elbow to the chops, it's OK to pop him one back in the nose. That way he'll think twice the next time he's inclined to give you an elbow. That way the game polices itself. I hate clutch and grab too by the way. I think it's terrible the Gophers wear face-masks, unless they want to. It's an impediment to the game, the sticks are way up, and there's a lot more injuries now. I think Massachusetts has better hockey players than us too, and it's a damn disgrace. They have a better system, and they play more games. We have to get our kids playing more hockey to be competitive, and that's that."
— *Stanley S. Hubbard, wing, 1952-54.*

"Now the players are more talented, but they do not let them play hockey. I think they have gone a long ways, and have come very close to spoiling a magnificent game by failing to interpret the rules as they were intended. No one ever had a vote to interpret rules to change penalties. It's detracted from the game immensely. The game we played was up and down, up and down. I'm prejudiced, but our games were much more interesting to watch. A small player wasn't at a serious disadvantage when I played. That's why I like the new Olympic size sheet of ice in the new arena.

"It's much different. We played five months a year and we didn't have summer hockey. We had to work. Now kids get more ice time. Our games were more fun to watch though. It was cleaner hockey. Today they don't call charging, boarding, hitting from behind and there's all that pushing after the whistles. Our games took less than two hours, now they go on forever. They have changed the interpretation of the rules, and they don't call hacking. We used to have great breakaways, and guys would make end-to-end rushes. Today the guys without the pucks are being interfered with all the time so they can't break out. College hockey 15 years ago was the fastest, most entertaining sport in America. Gradually, college hockey has tried to emulate the pros, for reasons I do not understand. Now the game is less interesting, there's less action, more pushing and shoving after the whistles, and frankly...IT'S BORING, FOLKS!

"Oh, and there's one more thing that bugs me about today's college hockey —face-offs. When I played, you had to put your stick on the ice behind a line painted in the face-off circle for your stick blade. Both centers did this, the puck was dropped, and it took all of two seconds to have a face-off. Now, it takes forever to get a face-off. What the hell are they doing out there anyway? We never had the centerman kicked out of a face-off for anything, but the crowd seems to like it or something I guess. It's just no longer fun to watch, that's all."

— *Wendy Anderson, defenseman, 1953-54.*

"My era of hockey under coach Romnes was considerably different than it is today. The emphasis wasn't on the skating, it was on the skills of passing and shooting. The slap-shot wasn't around until Mayasich got very good at it in the '50s. Our sticks were straight. Curved sticks changed the game greatly. As a goalie, we never needed masks because goals were set up, and shot low.

"I also don't mind a good fight every now and then either. But these goons with very little skill don't add a thing to the game in my opinion. The clutching and grabbing is out of hand, and the games take forever to play now. The 'enforcers' as they are called, have to be on each team I suppose, to protect their star players. I have to question though, what good they add to the game. I'd like to slow down the hockey now, and bring back the skills to the game."

— *Larry Ross, goalie, 1951-53.*

"I want to change the image of Minnesota Hockey players. They're perceived as real wild type kids, and I was one of those guys. But, I want to say that you can have fun, screw around, and get an education while playing tough hockey and winning hockey at the same time. You can do all of this, and be a quality person as well, without being the type of person that I was when I was a player. I was a real derelict in some cases and there were some funny but bad stories that I did that I thought were fun at the time. Now my personal faith in God won't let me share those stories because they're not something I'm proud of. I had fun when I did it. I look back and thought it was harmless. I harmed some people, including my wife and kids at the time. My image, I'm perceived as a guy who is tough, abrasive and an aggressive person. I don't mind that image, but I also want people to know that there's a softer side of me that can have some real fun and do some things without being a total screw off.

"I'm all for the fan. I think they should come and cheer on their team, but I don't think that a person who buys a ticket has the right to verbally abuse someone. To call someone a choker, loser, bum, scum, or other choice words, or to pee in a beer cup and throw it at somebody is absolutely unnecessary. I think that if you come to watch a game, you have a responsibility to be a decent person as a fan. I also don't like it when the fans count out a player who's hurt, 1-10, or swear at a player in the penalty box. The game has changed, and the fans need to act responsibly at games. We need all the support we can get at home games, and we don't want a couple bad eggs ruining the game for everyone else."

— *Bill Butters, defenseman, 1971-73.*

"I'll go to a Gopher game or a high school game way before I'd go to a Stars game. That's not a good style of hockey, and I don't like the fighting. I like a good scrap every once in a while, but I hate all the time it takes with the penalties. The games are so damn long now to watch. I was 0-5 fighting in my career, so maybe that's why I hate it."

— *Dean Williamson, center, 1989-90.*

"The Canadian mentality is to fight, that's how they were brought up to play hockey. I think all the fighting hurts the game though. For instance I have to get in fights to make the minor league team I'm on now. It would take away from the excitement if they eliminated fighting, but if they wanted to get rid of it, they could in a second. Maybe it's because I didn't win a fight all year up there, and got sick of getting my head pounded in every night."

— *Ben Hankinson, wing, 1988-91.*

GOALIE RECORDS

MOST GAMES PLAYED: 98, ROBB STAUBER 1986-89.

MOST MINUTES PLAYED: 5,717, ROBB STAUBER 1986-89.

MOST WINS: 73, ROBB STAUBER 1986-89.

BEST GOALS AGAINST AVG.: 2.48 (61 GP), JIM MATTSON 1951-54.

MOST SHUTOUTS: 7, JIM MATTSON 1951-54.

MOST SAVES: 2,639, STEVE JANASZAK 1975-79.

BEST SAVE PERCENTAGE: .906 (61 GP), JIM MATTSON 1951-54.

SINGLE SEASON RECORDS

MOST GAMES PLAYED — 44 (ROBB STAUBER - 1987-88)

MOST MINUTES PLAYED — 2,621 (ROBB STAUBER - 1987-88)

BEST GOALS ALLOWED AVG. — 2.36 (JIM MATTSON - 1952-53) 27 GP

MOST SAVES — 1,711 (ROBB STAUBER - 1987-88)

BEST SAVE PERCENTAGE — .920 (JACK McCARTAN - 1956-57) 15 GP

MOST SHUTOUTS — 5 (ROBB STAUBER - 1987-88)

THE HOBEY BAKER AWARD

(From the 1991-92 Gopher media guide)

The Hobey Baker award is given annually to the college hockey player who best exemplifies the qualities that Hobey Baker demonstrated as an athlete in the early 1900's. He was viewed as a pure sportsman and despised foul play, picking up only two penalties in his entire college career at Princeton.

As a player, he opened up the game of hockey with his speed and stick-handling, setting new standards for the way the game was played. His habit of insisting upon visiting the opponents locker room to shake their hands after every contest is a model for today's players. His dedication to what he believed in was demonstrated in the deepest way when he gave his life in defense of his country as an American pilot in World War I.

Since the inception of the Hobey Baker Award in 1981, two Gopher players have won the award. Center Neal Broten won in the award's first year (1981) and goalie Robb Stauber became the first goalie to win the Hobey (1988).

NEAL BROTEN

Neal Broten was the first recipient of the Hobey Baker Award, winning it as a sophomore. He set the University of Minnesota freshman scoring record with 50 assists in one season. He then departed from the Gophers for one year, serving as a center and the fourth-leading scorer on the heralded 1980 gold medal-winning U.S. Olympic Team. He returned to the Gophers for his sophomore season and earned All-America honors for his efforts, leading the Gophers to the NCAA championship game for the second time in his collegiate career.

The end of that season marked the end of Broten's collegiate career. But for Minnesota hockey fans that was only the beginning. Since then, Broten has gone on to entertain the fans of his home state as a member of the Minnesota North Stars where he was the first American player to score 100 points in an NHL season in 1985-86.

ROBB STAUBER

Stauber was the backbone of the Golden Gopher team in 1987-88 and '88-89 and was named first-team All-American and the team MVP as well as being a first-team All-WCHA selection. Stauber set numerous goaltending records at Minnesota, including career records for games played, minutes played, best save percentage and most shutouts in one season.

During Stauber's three-year career at Minnesota, the team posted a 102-34-4 record, including back-to-back WCHA championships in 1988 and 1989. He also led the team to three straight NCAA final four appearances. His career record during that period was a sterling 73-23-0. He signed with the Los Angeles Kings after his junior year.

HERB BROOKS ERA

Herb Brooks helped win a Minnesota High School tournament for St. Paul Johnson, then played at the University of Minnesota from 1955-1959. He was on U.S. Olympic Teams of 1964, and 1968, and played on five National teams. He took over a last-place Minnesota team in 1972 and won the 1974 NCAA title. It was the first ever for Minnesota, and the first ever for a team of all U.S. players. the Gophers won the WCHA title (and NCAA runner-up) in 1975, and NCAA titles in 1976 and 1979. Minnesota's only three NCAA titles came during Brooks's seven years as coach.

In 1979 he coached the U.S. National team, and in 1980 he selected and singularly directed a team of collegians to the "Miracle on Ice" at Lake Placid -- the Olympic gold medal.

Brooks coached the New York Rangers for 3 1/2 years, twice topping 90 points, and becoming NHL Coach of the Year in 1982. He later directed St. Cloud State to third place in the national small-college tournament and moved them to Division 1 status. He coached the Minnesota North Stars for the 1987-1988 season, went into private business before being hired in 1991 to coach Utica in the New Jersey minor league system. In 1992 he was named head coach of the New Jersey Devils.

Some of his numerous awards and achievements include: Sports Illustrated Sportsman of the Year; AP and ABC Sports Athlete of the Year; Life Magazine Sports Achievement of the Decade; enshrined in the U.S. Hockey and the University of Minnesota Hall of Fames.

HERB BROOKS: "Today's marketplace is entirely different with Canadian players. They're not as good, and there's not as many of them. This is because the Canadian junior teams are keeping them up there with scholarship incentives, and the promise of more games to play so they can make it in the NHL"

" Some people say that the Gophers have a tough time winning championships because of the Canadians on other teams. But Brooks termed that "a Joke. An absolute joke." He went on to say that because of the rules and regulations in college hockey today, that this may be the easiest time for the Gophers to compete in their history because, "Minnesota probably has more players than ever at their disposal."

"Winning has a lot of different connotations. They've got a great program, the coaches over there have done a fine job, they've got fine players, and they're a bounce or two away. I don't think they've got anything to be ashamed of, Brooks said. " The competition the University had to face under the past coaches is harder than it is today. Every year it gets a little easier because of NCAA rules and regulations. Of all the coaches at the U of M, John Mariucci had the toughest row to hoe. I think the best players from the '40s,' 50s, '60s and '70s were just as good as they are today, but there are more of them today."

He went on to say, "Paul Giel was able to help out with a few extra scholarships and there was a good group of boosters." We went from 10th place in the WCHA to winning the national championship in two years, and that was against tougher competition than the University plays against right now. Brooks compared the caliber of Canadian players that he coached against, and played against, with those coming to WCHA schools now. "They were much older, better and more of them," he said.

BROOKS TRIBUTES

JOHN MARIUCCI, when asked about Herb, was quoted in the Star Tribune as saying, "Herbie changes his mind more often than any woman I've ever known. If someone offered him the job as president of the United States, Herbie would want to be the Premier in Canada."

BRAD BUETOW: "Herb taught me a lot, and we remain very close today. He changed me to a better player when he made me a forward from a defenseman. I was never a great player, but I got to play in the pro ranks with Cleveland. For that I owe Herbie. He also asked me to be the first-ever, full-time paid assistant coach at the U of M. He's a great guy, and a great teacher."

PAUL GIEL: "Glen Sonmor was replaced by Ken Yackel in midseason and then I hired Herb Brooks. It was a great thrill for me, and all the loyal hockey fans of Minnesota, to win the NCAA title in 1974. I had always said to Herb if there's another Lou Nanne out there from Canada who is not only a great player but a good student athlete as well, get him. I told him to not worry about someone getting on him if he went outside the state to get some players, the bottom line was winning. But Herb was confident with the Minnesotans, and he won with them. For that I give him a lot of credit."

Tom Vannelli

DEAN BLAIS: "He's a tactician. He was the best schooled in that capacity. He used to work us to death, and we hated Mondays. He was a great coach."

JOE MICHELETTI: "He was instrumental in maturing me. He helped me along to be successful, and helped me reach new hockey plateaus in my career. He had a great hockey mind, so much knowledge, and I looked up to him more than anyone."

MIKE POLICH: "Herbie always got the best out of his players. He was a great coach. He was the type of guy that would make you mad, tear you down, then challenge you to prove him wrong. He'd be right on you if you slacked off. What you put in was what you got out with Herbie. There were reasons as to why we did things in practice. He was a strong-willed person, and had a very hard work ethic."

REED LARSON: "I was fortunate to have played under Herb. If we lost under Herb, he'd buy us a beer, and if we won we skated our pants off. He knew how to motivate us, and he was a very positive coach. He would always stand behind you no matter what."

Mike Polich

BILL BAKER: "We were together for four years at the U, one year with the Olympics, and two years in New York. We've been through a lot together. What he's done for me, I couldn't quantify it. He made me into an All-American, and taught me so much about life. How to pull it together, how to work as a team, and how to win. He would try and make you hate him enough by beating your rear-end off day after day. As a result, all of us as teammates bonded together and became better friends with each other.

"We would go to the arena for practice and get our butts whipped from 2:30-5:30 every day of the week. We were dead after practices. It was hell, I can remember falling down those stairs after practice because my legs could no longer stand Herbie's Monday boot camp practices. Our big joke was that we would get out of shape on the weekends, because we had games instead of practices.

"I don't feel like I know him though. We weren't ever buddies, and we didn't talk or anything. It was weird. I can't thank him enough for what he's done for me. He gave me an education, taught me discipline and provided me with so much opportunity. But, I don't know him."

DOUG WOOG: "We have tough games to play against a lot tougher teams today. Herb took veteran guys out of Junior A's to compete. That's OK, but it's a different style of hockey ."

TOM VANNELLI: "Herb built the foundation off junior players back then, which is quite the opposite of right now. He had a fabulous vision, and he understood the game. He knew how to motivate people differently. He knows what makes people tick, and knows what buttons to push to motivate them. He didn't use the same techniques on everybody. Consequently because of that, people may resent him later on or in the process. But ultimately, in the end they respected him."

GOVERNOR ARNE CARLSON: "Herb Brooks will succeed at anything he does. He's a natural success, He's very confident, has a great value system, and has a great ability to anticipate where events are going."

Bill Baker

DAVE BROOKS: "Herb and I were different. Herb was into coaching, and development. He was also a very good player. When he had to pick the 1980 Olympic team, I remember Herbie calling the high schools of the potential Olympians to find out their records on grades, if they got into trouble, did drugs, and what kind of people they were. When I asked him why the hell he was doing that, he said that he wanted to know what kind of player he was going to have when it comes down to the last two minutes of a game. He said he wanted to know which kids he should have on the ice come clutch time. Well, look who was on the ice during the Russian game — Pavelich, Christian and Baker. He knew all three of them.

"He had a vision, and a style. He has the greatest hockey mind in the country, and he is a student of the game. He knows the game. He's my brother, I love him you know?"

STEVE CHRISTOFF: "He was the reason I went there, he was a great coach. He was tough, but always fair. It was the best thing in my career to have him as my coach. It was hard to get used to skating that hard, but we were in great shape. It was the best thing for us. We skated when we won, and we skated when we lost. We learned so much from him, I'm very grateful for all he's done for me."

PAUL HOLMGREN: "Herbie, to me, was a tremendous influence. His willingness to work with each guy on an individual basis, and help us learn more was incredible. He always had a little tidbit about your ability that you could improve on. He had a personal touch for each guy, and wanted us to give our best. I'm excited about coaching against him now. It'll be fun when the Whalers play the Devils, and I'll enjoy seeing Herbie again. It'll be a learning experience for sure. Herbie's a great coach, and I'm excited about it."

TIM HARRER: "Herbie always said there was a fine line between having fun and

Eric Strobel

getting in trouble. He wouldn't tolerate any trouble from his boys, but he let us have fun at Stub and Herb's and get crazy once in a while."

JOHN GILBERT: "When it comes to creative practice and game tactical ideas, adjustments to gain the upper hand during a game, and the plotting and execution of psychological ploys that raise players to go above and beyond their own parameters, there isn't a coach on the face of the earth as good as Brooks. If you measure coaching by 'how they play the game,' Brooks is the best; if you measure coaching by the simple bottom line, how can you fight it? Brooks wins, whether it's the WCHA, the NCAA or the Olympics. Just give him time in the NHL, and he'll come home with the big trophy there, too."

BRET HEDICAN: "I've never met Herb Brooks, but I feel like I owe him everything. He's done so much for St. Cloud hockey, it's incredible."

DON MICHELETTI: "Herbie's practices? We used to say that if Herbie did this to a dog, the humane society would throw him in jail. But it taught us to keep pushing each other as teammates, and to be in shape that third period and win.

"Herb wanted me to go to Canada for a year of juniors in return for a half scholarship at the U. CC had offered me a full scholarship afterwards, but I told them I was committed to the U of M. I went to visit the campus one time, and I told him that even though I needed the full ride because my parents needed to save money for my other family members that wanted to go to college, I would accept the half scholarship. Herbie looked at me, smiled, and said, 'I'm proud of you for making the decision to come here on a half ride. I had a full scholarship waiting for you the entire time, but I wanted to see how badly you wanted to be a Gopher."

PAUL OSTBY: "Herb encouraged me to play Vulcans. He promised me I'd be one

Tim Harrer

of six goalies on the team behind Jetland and Janaszak. I later became the team MVP, and I owe a lot of that to him. Herb was the greatest coach I ever saw. He was such a great motivator."

GREGG WONG: "He was very aloof from his players. He was a real tyrant, a jerk, and he kept his players off balance. He always played mind games with his kids, and Herbie was always more quotable when they lost. His strength was in being a psychologist, and playing his mind games. When they won he'd pick on things they did wrong, so they didn't get too cocky. He bitched when they won more than when they lost."

TOM GREENHOE: "In 1971 at the nationals in Syracuse, Marsh Ryman (the athletic director at the time) refused to spend the money to send Herbie to the nationals, so Herbie quit. He then gave up his tenure with the Junior Stars to coach the Gophers, and Doug Woog took over the Junior Stars. In 1970, Bob Johnson beat out Herb for the head coaching job at Wisconsin. Who knows, it could've been 'Badger-Herbie' if he would've gotten the job.

"Herbie and I had to come up with a label to promote the hockey program. So I came up with the slogan 'The Fastest Game In Town' and we put it on our pamphlet, and it stuck I guess.

"Herbie and I struck up a real close friendship at the athletic department. When he came in he was totally lost. He didn't know what he was going to do and how he was going to do it, because he hadn't done it before. But, he took over and the next season he got his feet wet. His second season was one the University will never forget. It was the biggest surprise any of us could imagine, being national champs. Herbie used the Vulcans as his farm club. He liked the older, tougher, hard-grinding players, who knew how to win and were more mature. Herbie was something else. I've never known anyone who fought as hard for his program as he did. Herbie was fun to be around, a fabulous coach, fun to travel with, and a whale of a nice guy."

MIKE RAMSEY: "Everyone was intimidated by Herb. He used to call me a 17-year-old prima-donna. He would breathe down your neck, and we had the same routine every week with him:

Monday: Skate until you drop, and do Herbies forever. This is where he'd try and break you in two and a half hours.
*(A **Herbie** was a skating drill: to the blue-line, back to the goal-line, red-line, goal-line, far blue-line, goal-line, far goal-line, goal-line, and then again...)*
Tuesday: not quite as hard, but very tough.
Wednesday: slack off.
Thursday: sweats.
Friday and Saturday: go like hell in our games.
Sunday: recover, and regain consciousness.
Monday: get ready to die all over again.

"I just saw him at Brian Lawton's wedding, and we reminisced about those practices, and the Olympics. I told him I was going to tell his players in New Jersey to start getting in shape for him, or else.

MARK ROSEN: "Herbie ran drill camp practices, and the guys would have their tongues down to their knees as they did their 'Herbies' in practices. I'd never seen anything like it. But I tell you what, you could see at that point that he had a special gift for teaching the game. That was pretty special, and what he did best. We all saw that in 1980 with the miracle on ice. I'll always remember what a powerful figure he was. Kids would straighten up when he walked by, and he was a real father figure. I had a lot of respect for him. He was a godlike figure who had control over his kids. He was very accommodating in interviews as well, and he always spoke his mind on whatever the issue."

BILL BUTTERS: "Herb was like a father to me. He was a big influence in my life, and I learned a lot from him. He was a tactician, and Glen was a warrior."

JIM BOO: "I showed up the first day of practice with a full length rabbit-fur coat and an earring. I guess it's no wonder we got off on the wrong foot together. That first day he told me to go home, that there's no way I'd make the team. So, I went home and taped a picture of him on my punching bag and let him have it until my knuckles were bloody into the wee hours of the night. We put our differences aside, though, when it came time to play. Our team didn't have a lot of talent, but we won. In retrospect, I'd like to thank Herb for bringing out the best in me, and challenging

me to prove him wrong."

Steve Christoff

THE BROTEN BROTHERS

Not too far from the Canadian border lies the tiny town of Roseau, Minnesota. A town of only 3,000 people, it has three hockey arenas The tiny town has one of the richest hockey traditions of anywhere in the country, thanks to three brothers. Three brothers who used to play hockey from dusk to dawn, three brothers who helped assure that the tiny town would remain on the hockey map forever, three brothers who would forever change the face of Minnesota hockey, three brothers who played the game for fun in those north woods. Three brothers: Neal, Aaron, and Paul Broten.

They all played for the Roseau Rams, playing in the state tournament several times, and later with the Gophers at the University of Minnesota. Neal has played his entire pro career with the North Stars. Aaron has played with the Rockies, Devils, Stars, Nordiques, Maple Leafs, and Jets. Paul has been with the Rangers.

The three claim that they don't argue about the check when they get together for dinner. When the bill comes, one of them will tell another that since he just got a big playoff bonus, or since he just signed a big contract, he should pay this time. They all said that the money hasn't changed them, although Neal still remembers buying a new, light blue, 1981 Grand Prix which he described as "Sweet," when he signed his first contract for $50,000 in 1980. However, the one thing they all enjoy buying is new toys for their dad.

If you didn't know them you could get confused because they all have the same mannerisms. When I interviewed them, they were each wearing a gray hockey t-shirt of some sort, and each had his own crazy Fowl Play (bar and restaurant) stories to tell. They are three classy gentlemen, and I was flattered to have the chance to have met them. They are all married, and hope to all retire back in Minnesota. Here's what they had to say about various hockey topics:

ROSEAU

NEAL: "Roseau is such a great town, with so much hockey tradition. I grew up in Roseau playing hockey and golf. We used to always watch Hockey Night In Canada on TV. Basically all we did was go to school and play hockey. The North rink was the rink we played shinny at. Mom used to make us grilled cheese sandwiches after school, then it was off to the rink. Aaron and I were pretty close, and we played together every day."

AARON: "We grew up playing hockey in the streets. Neal, Butsy Erickson -- who lived two doors down -- and I would be out there every day playing hockey. We used to play in the streets with snow chunks as pucks when we were little kids. We would play all night under the street lights, until a car would run over the puck."

PAUL: "It was awesome growing up in Roseau, it was a fun little town. I miss it a lot. In New York it's a zoo, and I miss being able to walk into a grocery store or something where no one says a word. It's kind of fun having people recognize you, but I miss the small town atmosphere a lot."

THE HOBEY BAKER

AARON: "Neal and I were close. We don't get in each other's hair during the season, but in the summers we have a lake cabin that we share together. I never played in his shadow I don't think. We were both pretty equal, and we scored the same in high school and college, although he may have had a stride on me. He usually put up better numbers than I did, but we never had any animosity towards each other. We've always enjoyed playing together, like in high school, the Gophers, and with the Stars.

"We were sophomores together for the Gophers in 1980. Neal had 80 points or so, and I had 106 that year. I think I had something like 47 goals, and 59 assists, compared to his 22 goals, and 54 assists. He also got hurt that season, so he would've had more. After we lost the national championship (1981) we both turned pro. I went to Colorado and Neal went on to play in the Stanley Cup with the Stars. He got All-American and won the Hobey Baker. The Hobey Baker should go to the best player in college hockey, and that was Neal. He deserved it, he was a great player. I had a great season, but never got nominated to be All-American, or for the Hobey Baker Award."

NEAL: "I felt terrible winning the Hobey Baker over Aaron, he deserved it more than I did. He had 106 points compared to however many I had. He had a lot better year all the way around than I did. Aaron had always been in my shadows growing up, and he finally had a great year. He deserved the award 'way more than I did, and I still feel bad about it to this day."

PAUL: "I felt sorry for Aaron, he really had to live under Neal's shadow growing up. It was a shame that he at least didn't get nominated for the award. He should've at least gotten All-American or something his last year. That was a joke."

Aaron Broten

THE BABY BROTHER

Paul Broten

PAUL: "It was tough sometimes growing up in the shadows of my brothers. People would always tell me that I wasn't as good, and that I would never make it. Sure I got harassed by players, I had two older brothers playing in the NHL while I was playing high school hockey for a small town. It was fun to prove them wrong though, and that I could play on their level. We had never played organized hockey together until I finally got to the NHL. My brothers never got to see me play. I always watched them, but they were busy in their careers so they never saw me. I understood."

PAUL: "One time when New York was playing New Jersey, there was a big fight on the ice. I was going to reach over and sucker-punch a guy on the Devils, Kenny Daneyko when Aaron grabbed me and said, 'Whoa, little brother, you don't want to mess with that guy, he'd kill you!' So, we just stood there acting like we were tying each other up, talking, and hanging out like old times."

AARON: "People ask how come Paul doesn't play anything like me, and why is he so feisty out there? Well, it's because Neal and I picked on him so much growing up, that it's just his frustrations coming out now. We used to throw him down, sit on him, beat him up, and kick him around, it's no wonder he's a tough little bugger out there."

NEAL: "We never got to see him play that much growing up, and that was unfortunate. He's a great skater, and he'll be the best of all of us."

THE TOURNAMENT

PAUL: "I got to play in the tournament twice, and I loved beating the big-school teams like Burnsville. It was fun to come to the cities. Some of the guys had never been there before. I think the new Tier II can be a good thing, as long as it doesn't interfere with the big tournament. I guess I'm biased against the big schools. We had 30 guys try out every year for Roseau, and they have over 100 kids try out. The big schools should be better than they are."

Neal Broten

NEAL: "I don't know how I feel about the new Tier II Tournament. Our kids need more ice time, because the kids out east are catching up to us. I don't think we're declining, I just think the kids from the east coast have been improving faster. The tournament was a pretty special thing, and it amazes guys from Canada on the Stars to see 18,000 fans show up for a tournament game, when we only get 5,000 for ours. I went to the tournament, but never won it, it's a pretty special thing to be a part of.

"In Roseau, high school hockey was the biggest thing to do up there. We'd pack all 3,000 people in that arena, and the whole town would root us on. Hockey is so important to the community up there, and it showed. So many people are involved in hockey up there, it was a really special place to grow up. Our parents drove us all over the state for tournaments, and the families were so supportive. They would pack up their vans, and it was off to another town that weekend. It was fun to be involved in that, and to be raised in that environment."

AARON: "I don't like the Tier II. Put that garbage somewhere else, and never head to head with the original one. In some senses it's good for the kids, and that's what it's all about. But it's hard to see something so good get diluted, forgetting about all the tradition involved. Hockey teaches you a lot about life, and not everyone can win. For most kids the tournament is the climax of their careers, as well as the end of their careers. Most kids don't go on to college or pro, so it's a very special event that the families really enjoy.

"BROTEN BROTHERS DAY"
(ROSEAU WINS THE 1990 STATE TOURNAMENT)

NEAL: "I got a lot of grief for those damn commercials we did for that car dealership. But it was an incredible coincidence that all three of us were in town for the tournament that weekend. It was great supporting the Rams, the town, and to see them win the championship like that was incredible. That was the most important thing, to see the kids win it for Roseau. That night when the Stars played the Rangers, all of us got to play together again. It was awesome. Our parents really enjoyed it."

PAUL: "Oh, and those truck commercials we did together a few years back during the state high school hockey tournament, they were worse than any Bob Lurtzema commercial. I told them to stop playing them because they were embarrassing the family. I caught a lot of crap because of those!"

AARON: "Remember those goofy car commercials we did together a couple of years ago? Oh, God, I didn't think anyone would actually remember those things! I'll never live that one down, I really caught it after that."

WHEN I RETIRE

AARON: "When I'm done playing hockey, I don't want to coach in the NHL. Those guys are married to hockey. They watch games on tape, coach and sleep hockey all day and night. I don't want anything to do with it. I want to go back to school I think. I even went back to the U of M and met with a counselor to find out what it would take to finish my business degree. She had me take a math test to see what level I would be in, and when I was finished she looked at me and told me I had better stick to hockey."

NEAL: "I don't want to think about that yet. Hell I'm not that old. Who knows, maybe I'll move up to our lake place, and fish."

PAUL: "We're all pretty competitive, but there's no question that I'm the best barbequer and fisherman of the family. When I retire I want to be a professional fisherman, play for Bucks Unpainted Furniture Senior A Team and eat Big Ten Subs all day."

GOPHERS ON THE OLYMPIC AND U.S. NATIONAL TEAMS

Alm, Larry	1965
Anderson, Wendy	1955,56,57
Auge, Les	1979
Baker, Bill	1979,80,81
Bjorkman, Rube	1948,52,55
Bjugstad, Scott	1984
Blais, Dean	1973
Blue, John	1988,90
Branch, James	1969
Brooks, Dave	1964
Brooks, Herb	1961,62,64,65,67,68,70
Broten, Aaron	1981,82,85,86,87
Broten, Neal	1980
Burg, Richard	1959,61
Campbell, Gene	1955,56,57
Chorske, Tom	1988,89
Christoff, Steve	1979,80
Dale, Jack	1968
Dougherty, Dick	1955,56,57
Erickson, Butsy	1981
Falkman, Craig	1967,68,71
Fichuk, Pete	1971
Finnegan, Pat	1947
Frick, Bud	1950
Gambucci, Gary	1969,70,71,76
Grafstrom, Myron	1965
Graiziger, Bud	1950
Griffith, Steve	1984
Harris, Rob	1976
Hirsch, Tom	1981,84
Janaszak, Steve	1980
Jensen, Dave	1984
Johnson, Larry	1965

LaBatte, Phillip	1936
Larson, Michael	1962
Larson, Reed	1981
Lilyholm, Len	1966,67,68,70,71,74
MacSwain, Steve	1990
Mahle, Oscar	1962
Marlen, Glen	1963
Mayasich, John	1956,57,58,60,61,62,66,68
McCabe, Robert	1947
McCartan, Jack	1959,60
McClanahan, Rob	1979,80
McCoy, Tom	1964
McIntosh, Bruce	1972
Melnychuk, Jerry	1967
Meredith, Dick	1956,58,59,60
Meredith, Wayne	1964
Metzen, Dave	1967
Micheletti, Joe	1977
Millen, Corey	1984,85,88,89
Morrow, Brad	1976
Nanne, Lou	1968,76,77
Newkirk, John	1959
Norqual, Don	1963
Okerlund, Todd	1988
Olds, Wally	1972,77,79,81
Opsahl, Alan	1948
Ostby, Paul	1983
Pederson, Tom	1990
Petroske, Jack	1958
Phippen, Pat	1976
Polich, Mike	1980
Ramsey, Mike	1980
Richards, Todd	1988
Riley, Tom	1961
Rovick, Dave	1961,63
Sanders, Frank	1972
Sarner, Craig	1972,76, 79

Schmalzbauer, Gary	1964
Schneider, Buzz	1974,75,76,77,80,82
Sedin, Jim	1952
Smith, Larry	1965
Snuggerud, Dave	1988,89
Stauber, Robb	1989
Stordahl, Larry	1968
Strobel, Eric	1980
Turk, Robert	1959,61
Ulseth, Steve	1981
Vaia, Don	1958
Van, Al	1938,39,47,48,49,50,52
Vannelli, Tom	1977
Verchota, Phil	197,80,83,84
Wagnild, Spencer	1938,39
Lothrop, John	1969
Westby, Gerald	1963
Westby, Jim	1959,61,64
Woog, Doug	1967
Yackel, Ken	1952

HEAD COACHES

Brooks, Herb	1979,80
Johnson, Bob	1973,74,75,76,81
Mariucci, John	1958,76,77,78
Ryman, Marsh	1959
Williamson, Murray	1967,68,70,71,72
Yackel, Ken	1965

SHOULD THEY BE THE "ALL-MINNESOTA" GOPHERS?

I came from the hockey hot-bed town of Fairmont, in southern Minnesota. It was a nice, quaint town nestled in among five beautiful lakes. They were great for playing hockey on, because even if you fell through the ice, it was only five feet deep at the deepest point so you could jump right out. There were hazards though, like running into an ice-house, or encountering a crazy ice-fisherman who may be out for a spin around the lake in his new 4 X 4 entertaining his pals, Jack Daniels and Jim Beam. Of course there was even the chance of getting sucked up by the mighty Fairmont dredge that was a permanent fixture out there on Hall Lake. All in all though, if you stayed warm, moved pretty quick, and kept one eye peeled for snowmobiles and killer-carp, you'd be OK. It seemed like just yesterday that I was hanging out with the local hockey legends: Ryan (The Rhino) Hall, Dave (Cone-Head) Cone, Patrick (Hat-trick) Cairns, Kent (Senfer) Senf and Dayn (Dayno Ciccarelli) Hansen. Today it's changed to names like: Todd (The Toddler)ʒ Rendahl, Todd (The Dooch) Salden, Erich (The Butcher-Hog) Bertsch, Jim (The Ice-Man) Eischens, Dave (Ratz) Katzenmaier, Dennis (Sir Dennie) Winchell, Chris (shed-spread) Shed, Brian (the lizard- boy) Cepek, Eric (Snus) Snustad, Brett (Stinny) Stinson, Dave (Stans) Stansberry, Steve (Frenchie) Leguen and Mike (The Spike) Rendahl. The names have changed over the years, but my love for the game hasn't.

Like most kids in Minnesota, I grew up playing hockey. I lived on a lake, and like most lake-dwellers we had a rink behind our house that we used to have pick-up games on. That was where we got the majority of our ice-time. We didn't even have an arena until I was a senior in high school. I even remember helping to build the thing. It was something all the players helped with, so we could finally have indoor ice. The only rink in town before we got our arena was just a beast. The City of Fairmont owned it, and the city workers could never quite figure out how the boards went together every year. So, we had boards sticking out all over, and if you weren't careful you could get slivers in your butt when you got too close to them. We had the ultra-modern chicken-wire plexi-glass that was real popular back in the depression, and a sharpener that was a converted power tool of some sort that somebody picked up at a flea-market I think. We used to have to flood the rink after practices, and shovel the snow in between periods as well.

I remember as a four-year-old in the warming house, I saw a can of pop sitting there, and decided to help myself. I didn't realize that it was the container that they kept the kerosene in for the heater. Luckily, the Fairmont hospital was just up the road. A quick stomach-pump, and then it was back onto the ice.

It was fun, and the whole community got involved to help out the program. My old coach, Dr. Fred Carlson, was my favorite. He was also our team dentist. That's because he was a dentist, and his kid played on the team. We never had any organized coaches who got paid or anything, they were all just volunteers. They helped out whenever they could and I was pretty thankful that they gave us as much time as they did. I will say though, that it was a pretty grass-roots approach to coaching. We usually skated laps, shot on the goalie for a while, went and warmed up our toes, and then scrimmaged until we were too cold again.

I remember the road trips to towns like Windom, Luverne, Worthington, Albert Lea, Mankato, New Ulm, Mason City, Sleepy Eye and Sioux Falls. We would meet at the rink, pack up the vans, buy some chips and pop and take off in a convoy.

The parents would sit around the outside of the rink and stand in the snow to watch us, while they passed around thermoses of coffee to stay warm. Afterward, we would pack up the van and head for home. The rides home were full of stories about the game, "Did you see that one play..." or "Remember when I decked that guy..." and "That was such a great goal..." The worst part was laying on the hockey bags on the way home, and almost dying from the post-hockey game aroma that came from deep within them. I used to love the post-game stop at McDonald's too. We stopped after games in the small towns, not only to eat, but to get cleaned up a bit, since most of the places we played in didn't have showers. So, we would have to come home all smelly and sweaty from our games. I give those hockey moms a lot of credit for driving two hours with three or four stinky kids, plus their disgusting equipment.

All in all I had a lot of fun growing up in a small town and playing hockey. I was always so jealous of the teams like Edina, Burnsville and Bloomington in the State Tournament though. We used to look up to those kids on TV so much. We were jealous that they had great coaching, new skates and equipment, and that they had the support in their communities and high schools to take an investment in the sport. Fairmont couldn't afford hockey as a varsity sport, and because of it we had Domino's Pizza sponsor us. Yeah, we caught a lot of crap from the other teams. It was pretty humbling to play a team like Mankato, when you knew you were going to get slaughtered anyway, but had to come into the arena wearing a pizza jersey on top of it all.

But, we had fun, and made the most of it. I'm glad the arena is built there now, and am glad the program has gained success thanks to families like the Abels, who have contributed so much to the program. The town just needs more kids to get involved, and make an effort to make it successful. I think as soon as they see more kids wearing tournament patches on their hockey jacket sleeves they'll get more kids involved to play hockey down there.

In the spring of 1992, the Minnesota State High School Hockey Tournament, after much debate, altered its format to include a Tier II tournament. Of course this sent the hockey purists of Minnesota scrambling to try and save their tournament. Like "New Coke" in years past, people were concerned that another tournament would dilute the "Classic," which is long in history and tradition in Minnesota. The Minnesota State High School Hockey Tournament is the largest event of its kind in the country, and we as Minnesotans are very proud of it. Canadian players in town to play the North Stars during March can't believe that over 100,000 people show up to watch high school hockey.

While interviewing all the people for this book, I could see that the high school hockey tournament was a very hot topic. So, I conducted a very un-scientific poll about whether the people, who were close to hockey in Minnesota, liked or disliked the new Tier II tournament, and what would they do to change it. The results were very interesting to say the least. Of the 80 people surveyed, 59 said they disliked it, and 21 said they liked it. Of the people who disliked it, the consensus was that they didn't want anything to interfere with tradition of the tournament — the "If it ain't broken, then don't fix it," scenario. Of the people that did like it, they wanted to see more kids playing post-season hockey. No matter what. They want to see more kids going to college to play hockey, and more kids playing hockey in general.

It was interesting to note that for the most part, the people in the survey who were against the Tier II tournament were people who came from schools that often played in the big tournament.

The new tournament was intended for the teams in the state that never had a chance of making the big tournament, and in 1992, when Greenway of Coleraine, a past state champ, and Rosemount, a team that had won but two games all year, made it to the finals, people felt it wasn't exactly the scenario they had thought of. Some of the proposed solutions to the Tier II tournament were just as interesting. Some suggested a different location, on a different weekend might be better suited for the Tier II tournament. Or maybe a rotating Tier II Tournament that would showcase hockey all over the state in places such as Duluth, St. Cloud or Rochester.

I think they need a format that will give small programs incentive to play hockey. The Tier II tournament wasn't meant to interfere with the Tier I tournament, it was merely put there to give kids from places like, oh, Fairmont, something to shoot for in hockey. It was installed to let kids taste something that has always been unattainable in the past. I'm for saving the original tournament and revising the Tier II to cater strictly to communities with small programs that want to improve so that one day they, too, will have a shot at the Tier I tournament.

My hometown of Fairmont has less than 13,000 people in it, and a town like Roseau has about 3,000. Roseau is a quarter the size, but has such a strong tradition and commitment from the community that it can win the state title in any given year. Nowhere else in America is there such a place as Minnesota, where hockey is so consuming as a part of our fabric of life. Nowhere is this more prevalent than in the movie "Hoosiers," where the David and Goliath story comes to life. Like the Indiana "Hoosiers" basketball, and the "Friday Night Lights" of Texas football, the fastest game in town is the tradition-rich Gopher Hockey program, and its feeder program is places like Roseau, Warroad, Cloquet, Hibbing, Duluth, Greenway of Coleraine and Grand Rapids, as well as the huge Twin Cities Suburbs. It's a showcase for all our home-grown kids, and no one else's program in the country can boast of that.

Amateur hockey in our state is the key to the Gophers success. Our high school programs are second to none in the country, and insure the Gophers that there will always be a vast pool of talent for them to choose from. This luxury has allowed the Gophers to recruit only Minnesota kids. Not another college program in the country can boast of this accomplishment, and it is one that we as Minnesotans are extremely proud of. We get to watch our talent rise up through the ranks of amateur hockey, aspire to play high school hockey, and for the select few that reach the pinnacle of the game, they get to wear maroon and gold sweaters at Mariucci Arena. We take pride in our local, blue-chip players and as Minnesotans we enjoy boasting about the Gophers. Like an Olympic team of all Americans that come together for a common goal, so too is the tradition of the all-Minnesota teams at the U of M.

However a debate that goes back to the days of John Mariucci continues today -- whether we should take the older, more experienced Canadian players. Our answer has been no thank you. However, we are now seeing the kids from Massachusetts and Michigan getting more and more prevelant at the elite level. Will we lose our edge as the "amateur hockey capital" of the USA? How could this happen? I mean this is Minnesota, where kids are pulled from the womb by their skate blades. We're not losing our edge to Juniors, Massachusetts, or anyone else, but we do have to allow more ice time for our kids. Massachusetts has a developmental program called "Hockey Night in Boston," where the elite, New England prep players go to play all-year-round. Boston College has drawn well out of this program to maintain its stand on recruiting only American players. A lot of the better high school players want to play college hockey and are demanding that we give them more competition, all year-round. As a result, kids are tempted to skip their senior years of high school to play junior hockey, to get more games against older, stronger players. Our high school program has prevailed thanks to people like Glen Sonmor, Herb Brooks, Brad Buetow and Doug Woog. Of course that "Godfather" guy who started this crazy idea about making a committment to our local kids a million years ago deserves most of the credit.

JOHN MARIUCCI was often said to be anti-Canadian. However he was quoted in the Star Tribune as saying: "That's wrong. My contention was the teams we were playing were bringing down 22 and 23 year old Canadians who were playing Junior A hockey, and competing against our high school kids. That's what I was fighting, the age deal. We wanted to control the Canadian kids. I mean I brought in Louie (Nanne). I brought in Murray Williamson. I could have had my whole team Canadian, but then I would have destroyed the high school program. If I didn't have a program at the university for Minnesota kids, where were they going to go?"

He was also quoted in the Pioneer Press as saying, "I don't want to sound like a missionary because you know what happens to missionaries — they get boiled in oil. I cared about winning, I cared a lot. But when I went into coaching, winning wasn't my biggest concern. I wanted to see the day when our hockey team would be all Minnesota kids. I wanted to see these kids compete against the best. Compete and win."

DOUG WOOG: "Players from other areas of the country, especially out east and in Michigan, have progressed dramatically. Their skills and hockey developpment have been enhanced through expanded games and playing opportunities. Sometimes hockey has been enhanced and other important concerns took second place in these accelerated programs. Playing for scholarships or money indirectly has altered some of the values of sportsmanship and gamesmanship. I don't like the particular direction the game has taken. I also don't like the pros taking college players early. Obviously the money offered to them becomes very successful bait. It seems everyone is concerned about encouraging guys to move on to the next step. Let them play their four years, get their schooling and enjoy the present. Let them get the full value from a special time in their life. Doug Zmolek and Trent Klatt got great offers to turn pro. I agree, but those same offers would have been as good or better a season later. With the Olympics of 1994 coming up, plus the anticipation of Hobey Baker-type senior years, their leverage would have been outstanding. Both are great guys and we wished them the best when they decided to leave school early."

WILLARD IKOLA: "It's a great thing for the people of Minnesota. Maroosh went to bat for the Minnesota player and took great care of them."

MIKE RAMSEY: "I don't see any reason why the Minnesota product won't work, and win championships. It was something really neat for us as players to be a part of a team together as Minnesotans. It's a unique tradition that I hope they keep up."

WALTER BUSH: "It all stems from Maroosh, and I like the fact that they use Minnesota kids exclusively. It's terrific. Personally, I don't like the Canadian boys coming down here taking scholarships away from our local boys. In fact, I'd do to them what their teams up there do to us. I'd say that each team can only have a maximum of three Canadian players.

"Everybody loves hockey in Minnesota except the media, they just knock it every way they can. I spent 18 years with the North Stars, and if you win they support you, and if not they hound you to death. They also pay a lot of lip service to the high school tournament. Other than that our hockey coverage is mediocre in the state, it's so much better than we get credit for. Now I'm on the Minnesota Amateur Sports Commission, appointed by the governor. We need more guys like Herb Brooks, who started St. Cloud's program, and followed the wisdom of people like John Mariucci."

PAUL HOLMGREN: "I think it's a great tradition. Obviously there are a number of good hockey players to choose from in Minnesota, and I think the Gophers, for the most part, end up with the cream of the crop."

AMO BESSONE: (FORMER MICHIGAN STATE COACH) "Don't forget there were a lot of great Canadians that played Gopher hockey. But, back then there were only two places you could get Americans: Minnesota, and Boston. Mariucci had a gold mine of kids out there. I used to harass him about taking all the good kids and not leaving me any to choose from. So he said he would send me a list of recruits. He would keep the top ten, and I could keep the bottom ten. I tried to recruit up there, but the Minnesota kids wanted to play for John. It was incredible, they were loyal as hell to Minnesota. Nowadays, if I were still coaching, I could recruit out of Detroit. They don't have a high school program like Minnesota's, but their Junior leagues are the best in the country. I attribute that incredible high school program to Maroosh. He was committed to the people, and he just did it all up there."

MIKE ANTONOVICH: "There shouldn't be any reason why the U of M, UMD, St. Cloud and Mankato shouldn't have all Minnesota kids."

TOM GREENHOE: "It's an all-American program. Like Boston College, we only take Americans. But, unlike BC taking all New England kids, we take only Minnesota kids, and they have a lot more kids to choose from out there too. We're sitting on a gold mine. Because of Mariucci's push to promote high school hockey in Minnesota, we have an amazing resource to recruit from. However there have been scams against American kids. In 1974 the Gophers had the 'All American Team With No All-Americans.' That was the year we won the national championship, but ironically had no All-Americans on the team."

DEAN WILLIAMSON: "I think they need to go outside the high schools to get older, more experienced kids. I also think Canadian kids are good for the league. Every Canadian kid I've ever known has been a good guy, and I think they add a lot to college hockey. I think the Gophers can win it all with Minnesota kids, but it would be nice to have a blend of junior players. Guys like Scotty Bell are great role players who are great for the team chemistry."

STEVE CANNON: "There is so much talent in the state, I think it's important that the kids play for the University of Minnesota. Some say we should get some quality Canadian kids in here to bring home the big one, but I don't think it's necessary or appropriate."

DON CLARK: "Gopher Hockey is my favorite hockey in the world. They play local players, and that's why I'm a local fan. If they brought in Canadians to play here, I'd never come to another game. I think there's only been 18 or 19 Canadians total that have ever played here, let's see if my memory serves me well enough to remember them all... Frank Pietrangelo, Murray McLachlan, Murray Williamson, Lou Nanne, Lorne Grosso, Gerald Melnychuk, Ken Boyle, Mike Pearson, Gordie Watters, Bob Fleming, James Frick, Ray McDermid, John O'brien, Allan Burman, Roger Goodman, Ken Cramp, Ken Anderson, Leland Watson, Rick Yurich, Jim Ebbitt and Perry Ardito. That's all I can remember, but it's pretty incredible to have built our program to this level of success with mostly Minnesota kids."

BRET HEDICAN: (ST. CLOUD STATE AND OLYMPIC DEFENSEMAN) "Playing against the Gophers in Mariucci Arena sucked. The fans are wild in there. The visiting locker rooms are the worst possible locker rooms in history. I know they turned the heat on in there to boil us out, just to piss us off when we were good and hot in between the periods. It was miserable playing there, and I used to dread coming to play the Gophers at home. I absolutely hated it. The fans are so loyal, and it was an amazing home-ice advantage they had in there. It would've been a great feeling to have played there. Sometimes you get really jealous of all that tradition in there. Everyone grows up wanting to be a Gopher in this state, But hey, it didn't work out with Wooger recruiting me, and I was happy playing for St. Cloud. I have Herb Brooks to thank for that."

RANDY SKARDA: "I guess they say that in Minnesota they pull their kids out of the wombs by their skate blades. In California they say they pull their kids out by the surf boards. I suppose in Indiana they pull them out by the basketball too. It's a pretty unique place we live in up here. People are hockey fanatics, and I'm pretty proud to have been a part of it."

BOB UTECHT: (FOUNDER OF LET'S PLAY HOCKEY) "The Gophers have been blessed with nice people -- Doug Woog, Brad Buetow, Herb Brooks, Glen Sonmor, and of course John Mariucci. We have enjoyed immense success here, and it's something we should all be proud of. We always had great teams in football and basketball with Bierman and Kundla. But hockey never got going here until Mariucci took over and traveled around the state encouraging people to play hockey. He used to speak for free, and at town gatherings he'd encourage them to build arenas. We went from around 10 rinks in the state to over 160 today. We don't have to win titles every year, as long as we make some final fours, win the league titles, and as long we keep using our own kids to do it. We need to continue to support our kids, give them educations and send the best ones to the NHL."

DAVID JENSEN: "That was something that was really neat while you were there. It was always a great motivation for us to get psyched-up in the lockerroom together, but it wouldn't bother me now if they brought in some kids from other places."

DICK SPANNBAUER: "I love it. It's the only way it should be done. We're giving local kids a great education, and carrying on a great tradition as well. We have great players here and there's no reason we should have to recruit outside the state of Minnesota."

JOE SCHMIT: "I think it's an outstanding tradition, and one the entire state of Minnesota should be proud of. It, of course, all started with John Mariucci. He believed in the Minnesota kid, and it's rubbed off on other schools in the state now as well. I think the Gophers would be making a huge mistake if they ever went outside the state to recruit. I don't think we'll see that happening in my lifetime, there's too much pride here. Kids dream of playing for the Gophers from the time they lace up their double runners."

STEVE CHRISTOFF: "It's a touchy subject these days with the kids talking about juniors rather than the high school route, like in Canada. You don't see as many high draft picks from Minnesota in the recent years. When I played I was a hockey player, and I lived my life to be a player. It seems that more and more kids are just playing it as a hobby, for fun. That's unfortunate, because when I played we felt we had to win or else we would be letting someone down, and we'd be letting things deteriorate. Kids need to try harder, and to be more dedicated to the sport today."

JOHN GILBERT: "Minnesota high school hockey is the purest form of the game — genuinely free of fighting and most of the chippy stuff. In my opinion, a true hockey fan is someone who might be headed for a North Stars game, but stops off on the way because he finds out a good high school game is going on. The Gophers have a magic thing going by getting all Minnesotans, because not only does it give them an all-star cast of the best high schoolers, but every high school kid thinks he can come to Minnesota, either on scholarship or as a walk-on, and he'll get a chance to play. It amazes me when players turn down full scholarships at other schools to take partials at Minnesota. The Gophers don't have to take only Minnesotans; in fact if they take a few Canadians they could become another St. Cloud State."

MARK ROSEN: "There's no question, this is the best game in town. To see an end-to-end rush was fantastic. Pro hockey is all that clutch and grab BS, and college hockey is an unbridled enthusiasm for the game. The speed of Gopher hockey, you just knew during a given game that you'd see some great two-on-ones, and three-on-two's. It's so exciting to watch, I love it."

BRAD BUETOW: "This year we have 13 kids on the Colorado College team from Minnesota. I'd love to have all Minnesota kids but we have to recruit in Canada to keep up with everyone else. The major junior leagues in Canada are far superior to our amateur system. But the Minnesota kids are every bit as good, they just play less games is all."

DOUG McLEOD: "The joke with North Dakota kids is that they're so old they've all voted four times in the Canadian general elections."

DR. V.A. NAGOBADS: "It's a big, close family, and we were close to each other. Others like Lou Nanne, Murray Williamson, and Murray McLachlan were welcomed into our family as well. I am thankful that I was given a chance to take care of the University of Minnesota Gopher ice hockey team. It has given me so many wonderful opportunities to meet great people, to travel and to see the world through the eyes of hockey."

LEN LILYHOLM: "Mariucci took it pretty seriously all right. When we got off the plane in Denver, he waved a big slab of Canadian Bacon at Denver coach Murray Armstrong. It's good to have the nucleus Minnesota kids, but how can you turn away a guy like Lou Nanne from the team?"

WENDY ANDERSON: "I think it's not only appropriate, but we see states like Wisconsin and Michigan that should emulate it with their own kids as well. Wisconsin is about 40 years behind us in developing programs for young people. They relied on Minnesotans and Canadians to make teams. Mariucci went out and built high school hockey in Minnesota, and frankly Wisconsin as well. When I played, all of us but a few lived within 10 minutes of the arena."

PAT REUSSE: "Winning the ice hockey championship in Division 1 college hockey on the national level is about as significant as winning the rifle or water polo championships. But, it's not as significant as winning the men's volleyball championship.

"I have long contended that if the Gopher football, or basketball coaches were allowed to include Duluth, Denver, Colorado College and North Dakota as major rivalries, they too would have a winning percentage of .750, and could use only Minnesota boys. The connotation that somehow we're noble because we only use Minnesota boys in Gopher Hockey is the stupidest thing I've ever heard in my life. Where the hell else are you gonna get 'em from, Alabama?"

GOVERNOR ARNE CARLSON: "I always found hockey to be such a *fuddley* sport, and very frustrating to watch. All those people running around chasing that little puck, at least in basketball they sink baskets to break up the monotony. I was shocked to see my first Gopher Hockey game. The speed, the talent, you could immediately tell that this was big time hockey. Coming from the east coast, I had heard of U of M greats like Bronko Nagurski and Bernie Bierman. Hockey is unique here. You're lucky if you get one decent Division one basketball player a year here in Minnesota, but you get a bundle of Division 1 hockey players every year. It's like Indiana Basketball. Each year they get to choose the top 10 or the top 20 or so Division 1 prospects in the state to play for them. It's a tremendous advantage we have here."

PAUL GIEL: "Hockey is big at the University of Minnesota, but unfortunately it gets taken for granted. It gets hurt somewhat as far as how good it really is, because of the pro influences in town. That's not a putdown or anything, it's a reality. The North Stars finish in fourth place and they get into the playoffs where it's a huge deal in town. The Gophers have a loyal following though, and can outdraw the pros for a good game any given night.

"Even though it's down right now, because of the tradition at the U of M, the Gophers football and basketball teams are still the number one and number two sports on campus. Despite the rich tradition, hockey is number three. I had a lot of respect for hockey players, they had to be tough."

PAUL OSTBY: "I think it's the best damn thing in the world. That's what drew me to Gopher Hockey in the first place. Minnesotans love to support their own. It's Minnesota's team, and it should be Minnesota's players. It would be a gross injustice if any out-of-staters played here, in my opinion."

BOBBY SMITH: "Gopher hockey is just tremendous hockey, and a great tradition that the whole state can be proud of. It gives the Minnesota kids a chance to play hockey at the college level, and that's pretty special to the people of Minnesota."

DEAN BLAIS: "I think there's definitely enough talent in the state to do it, and follow the dreams of John Mariucci and Herb Brooks."

TOM CHORSKE: "I don't have anything against Canadian kids, but as long as the state can provide the talent, we owe it to Mariucci to keep up the tradition of taking the Minnesota kids."

NEAL BROTEN: "I liked the idea of all Minnesota kids, and I knew that there were a lot of pro scouts in the cities so I could get looked at more. I could've gone to UND, which was only two hours away, but I wanted to get the hell out of Roseau and go somewhere different. I hope they always keep that tradition going there..."

AARON BROTEN: "I think they could have a better team if they took Canadians. The Gophers have to take the five best kids in the state, and the other kids that don't get scholarships go to Duluth, St. Cloud and UND. Those kids that got passed over by the Gophers want sweet revenge on the Gophers every time they play them to prove to the coach that he made a big mistake on passing him up. Minnesota could use a 21-year-old goaltender from Ontario. A guy who's older, more mature, taken his licks, and has had experience, could make a big difference for the team."

PAUL BROTEN: "There's so many good hockey players here, why not have all Minnesota kids? There's a problem at the U of M, a lot of kids don't play there. They might make the team, but only as a fourth liner who doesn't see much ice-time. That guy sacrificed going to a smaller school to be a star for the glamour of being a Gopher. It's a real problem, and will continue to be as long as they do that to themselves. Kids will eventually want to go to smaller schools so they can get looked at by the pro scouts. There's so much talent at the U of M that a great player in high school may be just average there, and won't get a chance to shine."

JIM BOO: "It's a strong commitment to Minnesota, and I like it."

DAVE SNUGGERUD: "It holds in my mind what Minnesota Hockey is all about; quality hockey from home-grown kids."

BEN HANKINSON: "Why wreck a good thing. Woog gets labeled a 'Golden-Choker' by some clowns who know absolutely nothing about hockey, and people think we need to go get some Canadian kids to win the big one? Come on, people."

REED LARSON: "Hockey gets in your blood up here, it's in you for life, and I love it. We need to keep providing the feeder programs for the kids to get to the college level and beyond. It's ridiculous that our high school kids are only playing 20-30 games per year. What's the point? We're getting passed up by the kids out east who are getting twice and three times as many games in as us. We need to get our high school programs playing hockey all year round so we can get the University the best talent, and make hockey better in the state. We can't be complacent and watch the east pass us by.

As far as Canadians go, why were there only two teams, the Stars and a German team, the only ones interested in Neal Broten last year (1991)? You know they seem to beat some dead horses with some of the older Canadian players now. There's a lot of Canadians in the NHL right now who wouldn't even make the hack team I'm playing on in Europe right now. So what's that say about front offices and favoritism? I'm a little bitter about that, it's a lot tougher being older in the NHL, but it's even tougher being American in the NHL. I'm not prejudiced or anything, but the league is Canadian majority run, and if you really take a look, it really shows."

ROBB STAUBER: "Why not? We obviously have enough kids here to be competitive and win. I think the wave of the future will be kids playing junior hockey. In juniors they can get more ice-time, they ride the bus more, get beat up more, and are more mature to play college hockey."

STEVE CANNON: "Gopher hockey has become like Indiana Basketball, but in some ways it's not good. For instance, the parents get too involved at times as a very powerful lobbying group. When parents start living vicariously through their children, playing hockey is not good anymore."

TRENT KLATT: "I think it should always be Minnesota kids playing, every kid in the state dreams of playing here."

BILL BUTTERS: "We're not anti-Canadian, our philosophy is pro-Minnesotan. Our kids have pride, tradition, and good work ethics. It's a real boost for Minnesota to see its kids represent the University. It also helps our budget, we never have to recruit outside the state, and we don't have to pay outstate tuitions either."

PAT FORCIEA: "It's Priceless that the Gophers take only Minnesota kids. Minnesotans are among the most parochial people in the country, and it's great. It would be really fun to see what would happen if the North Stars did the same.

"Hockey is part of the fabric of life in Minnesota. It's introduced to kids at a very young age, and it tends to stay with kids for a lifetime. No other sport is followed quite as intensely. There are probably more kids participating in other sports, but the interest and support of hockey far exceeds that of other sports in the state. It's a phenomenon that's hard to find anywhere else in the country. Your entire winter revolves around hockey. It's your livelihood."

LARRY ROSS: "I'm all for it. However, I am not opposed to the Canadian kids. I have much more success scouting Canadian kids, as a scout. They're more respectful, and very nice to me. They don't act like I owe them something because of where they're from. I would never legislate against a Canadian kid playing here, they're great kids and are getting a bum rap. There's no way in hell I'd ever say anything derogatory about the Canadian kid. That's like saying something bad about Gordie Watters, Murray McLachlan, Murray Williamson, and Lou Nanne. Those guys are great people, and have done great things for the Gopher program."

HERB BROOKS: "I think today the kids are just as good as when I coached, but it's different. I think the teams were always good for the Gophers. The players from the '30's, '40's. '50's, and '60's were just as good as the players today, but there's more of them today. The kid coming through Minnesota is benefiting from a fine amateur program, and his experiences are more developed than other kids from different backgrounds. You can be successful with the kids out of high school, you don't necessarily need to take junior kids."

GREGG WONG: "I don't think it means as much today as it used to. The pro teams have taken so much of the limelight away. There's a hard-core group of hockey fans that stick with the team through thick and thin, they are some of the most loyal fans you'll find. A lot of the luster of Gopher Hockey has been lost in recent years. The way hockey has grown out east, Massachusetts kids are better than Minnesota kids now. For years East Coast colleges were dominated by Canadians, now they're mostly New England kids. Massachusetts started winning the annual series between Minnesota and Massachusetts, and the pendulum started swinging towards the east. I used to think the Gophers were the fastest game in town, but I don't anymore because there's too much clutching and grabbing going on. It takes three hours to finish a game now, it's ridiculous. It went from a fast skating, passing game to a lot of B.S. It's really too bad. I think the game was better a few years ago compared to right now."

NORM GREEN: "Gopher Hockey is phenomenal, it's a great sense of tradition. I love the excitement, action, electricity, and emotional involvement of it. Everyone I sat by at the games seemed to either be related to, or knew one of the members of the team. College hockey in Canada is not an issue, whereas in the states it's regarded very highly.

"I think it's marvelous that the University takes only Minnesota kids. I don't know what I would do in that situation, it's someone else's decision not mine. I understand the strength of Minnesota kids here with the feeder programs leading up to college hockey, and the quality of life in the state, but it's also important to build the best possible championship potential you can. In the case of Minnesota, there have been so many good hockey players, that they have had good championship potential. The Montreal Canadians, and Quebec Nordiques had the same philosophy with their teams at one point as well. They only took French Canadian players for their rosters. That sooner or later hurt them, and they have since changed their views."

DON CLARK: "Massachusetts compared to Minnesota isn't fair. They have 45 million people on the east coast, and they're being compared to our four million people. They do all kinds of things to be better than us though. They have year round hockey, they send their kids to the Canadian juniors like Michigan does as well, and they have 13th grade prep school 'ringers' who play high school hockey. They have more high school hockey programs, and more people. But, we have more youth hockey players, and more arenas than Massachusetts does. Bobby Orr created a lot of interest out there for their kids to see. They have four division one hockey schools, and Michigan has seven.

"Solution to the problem: I'd like to see a short high school schedule of about 15 games in the spring, and another 15 games in the fall. That would give the Minnesota kids that want to play hockey all year round a chance to do so. After all, a basketball player can play all year round to better himself for college, so why shouldn't a hockey player have the same opportunity? This way our kids would have 50-60 games a year to play, and we could be competitive with the Canadian kids coming down.

"What would've happened if the Minneapolis Millers had become part of the NHL 40 years earlier in the state, to create hockey interests with the kids? We'd be 40 years further ahead of the east. I'm glad we'll have Olympic size ice in the new Mariucci arena. Now Minnesota will have more than 10 Olympic sheets of ice in the state over the next few years."

MURRAY WILLIAMSON: "Hmm, Canadians. There is a very distinct -- no that's not the right word -- subtle resentment against Canadians who parade their Gopher history around. They stay very low key about it, guys like Mike Pearson, Lou Nanne and myself. There's a very subtle discrimination against Canadians around here. Mariucci had us on his teams only a few at a time to help his teams win. The Gophers pride themselves on being all American, and especially all Minnesotan."

1980 OLYMPICS
LAKE PLACID, UNITED STATES, FEBRUARY 12-24

(USA HOCKEY TEAMS RESULTS BOOK, 1920-1986)

The 1980 United States Olympic Team will forever remain etched in my memory as one of the greatest sporting events of all-time. It was an event that got people excited about hockey in America, and made them want to learn more about the game. As the USA team upset the Soviets in the medal round, the sounds of Al Michaels saying, "Do you believe in miracles?" will forever give me goose-bumps. Herb Brooks, head coach of the team, and former University of Minnesota mentor, selected 20 players to represent the USA, 12 of them were native Minnesotans.

In early September, the team began as challenging an exhibition schedule as had ever been organized for an American Olympic Team. Beginning with an initial European tour in early September, the team played a 61-game pre-Olympic schedule against foreign, college and professional teams. During the tour, Ralph Jasinski replaced Johannson as manager. The team finished the exhibition season with a 42-16-3 record. The only letdowns during the pre-Olympic schedule were four losses to National Hockey League teams in late September and early October and to the Canadian Olympic team in late November. The highlight of this period was winning the Lake Placid Invitational International tournament.

Entering the Olympic games, the team was a decided underdog, an evaluation that seemed to be confirmed by a 10-3 defeat at the hands of the Soviets in the final exhibition game in New York City. Facing Sweden in the opening game of the Olympics, Bill Baker scored with 27 seconds remaining in the third period to gain a 2-2 tie. The goal acted as a catalyst for the young U.S. team, which then upset Czechoslovakia 7-3. The inevitable letdown occurred against the less-highly regarded opponents Norway, Romania, and West Germany -- but were victorious.

This set the stage for the unexpected showdown in the medal round with the perennially powerful Soviets. The result was an historic 4-3 American victory produced byMike Eruzione's goal midway in the third period. The gold medal was won two days later when the miracle Americans scored three goals in the third period to defeat Finland 4-2.

Mark Johnson led the team in scoring in both the exhibition schedule and the Olympic Games. The line of Schneider-Pavelich-Harrington, all products of Minnesota's Iron Range, led the team's four lines in scoring with 17 goals and 20 assists in the seven Olympic tournament games. Brilliant goaltending by Jim Craig, who played all seven contests, was a big factor in the victory, as was the stellar play of defensemen Dave Christian, Ken Morrow, Mike Ramsey, and Bill Baker.

A grateful nation, depressed by the Iranian hostage crisis, hailed the team as heroes. A visit to the White House followed, as well as appearances in cities across the land. of particular importance to hockey development in the U.S. was the fact that 11 players went on to become regulars in the NHL: Bill Baker, Dave Christian, Ken Morrow, Jack O'Callahan, Mike Ramsey, Neal Broten, Mark Johnson, Mark Pavelich, Rob McClanahan, Steve Christoff, and Dave Silk.

NAME	HOMETOWN	COLLEGE
Bill Baker	Grand Rapids, MN	Minnesota
Neal Broten	Roseau, MN	Minnesota
Dave Christian	Warroad, MN	North Dakota
Steve Christoff	Richfield, MN	Minnesota
Jim Craig	North Easton, MA	Boston University
Mike Eruzione	Winthrop, MA	Boston University
John Harrington	Virginia, MN	Minnesota Duluth
Steve Janaszak	White Bear Lake, MN	Minnesota
Mark Johnson	Madison, WI	Wisconsin
Rob McClanahan	St. Paul, MN	Minnesota
Ken Morrow	Davison, MI	Bowling Green
Jack O'Callahan	Charlestown, MA	Boston University
Mark Pavelich	Eveleth, MN	Minnesota Duluth
Mike Ramsey	Minneapolis, MN	Minnesota
Buzz Schneider	Babbitt, MN	Minnesota
Dave Silk	Scituate, MA	Boston University
Eric Strobel	Rochester, MN	Minnesota
Bob Sutor	Madison, WI	Wisconsin
Phil Verchota	Duluth, MN	Minnesota
Mark Wells	St. Clair Shores, MI	Bowling Green
Herb Brooks	St. Paul, MN	*Head Coach
Ralph Jasinski	Mounds View, MN	Manager
Craig Patrick	Wellesley, MA	Assistant Coach
Warren Strelow	Mahtomedi, MN	Goalie Coach
Dr. V.G. Nagobads	Edina, MN	Physician
Gary Smith	Minneapolis, MN	Trainer
Bud Kessel	St. Paul, MN	Equipment Mgr.

Mike Ramsey: "It's hard to put into words, you have to watch the tape over and over and sort of absorb it all. I guess we realized that we were on to something big, but just didn't realize it at the time that it was going to be that big. Now whenever we get together for charity appearances with the '80 team, we tease Eruzione all the time. None of us can believe it, the guy scores one goal his whole life, and he's more famous and makes more money than all of us."

Bill Baker: "You can't describe it, it was amazing. Now the teams are under a lot of pressure because of the press, corporate sponsorships and the media. Hell, we didn't have all that crap to worry about. We had a great system, and an even better coach. If we would have had some older guys like they had on the 1992 team, they would've slowed us down. We were in Herbie shape, and that just wasn't our makeup."

Steve Christoff: "We had so many great players on the team, the talent was just incredible. It was an exciting time for all of us, and a proud time to be in hockey. It was so much fun to be around so many quality players, and to be a part of that group of winners."

Neal Broten: "What can you say about that team, eh? It was awesome. Twelve Minnesota guys on there, and to play with your buddies like that, it was great. I can remember like yesterday calling my dad from Colorado Springs to tell him that I made the team. We were both so excited, it was an awesome time in my life. We couldn't have done it though without Jim Craig, he was awesome."

Dave Peterson: (1988, 1992 USA Olympic Coach) "The 1980 team was a rich part of our history and we should never forget it. It was great for hockey in the United States. It was not, however, a shadow over every Olympic team afterwards, unlike the media who missed it, and loves to compare it to every Olympics would have you believe."

111

GOPHERS IN THE NCAA FINALS

1953 - COLORADO SPRINGS, COLORADO
MICHIGAN 7, MINNESOTA 3.

1954 - COLORADO SPRINGS, COLORADO
RPI 5, MINNESOTA 4 (OT).

1971 - SYRACUSE, NEW YORK
BOSTON UNIVERSITY 4, MINNESOTA 2.

1974 - BOSTON, MASSACHUSETTS
MINNESOTA 4, MICHIGAN TECH 2.

1975 - ST. LOUIS, MISSOURI
MICHIGAN TECH 6, MINNESOTA 1.

1976 - DENVER, COLORADO
MINNESOTA 6, NORTH DAKOTA 3.

1979 - DETROIT, MICHIGAN
MINNESOTA 4, NORTH DAKOTA 3.

1981 - DULUTH, MINNESOTA
WISCONSIN 6, MINNESOTA 3.

1989 - ST. PAUL, MINNESOTA
HARVARD 4, MINNESOTA 3 (OT).

GLEN SONMOR ERA

Glen Sonmor, a native of Moose Jaw Saskatchewan, came to the University to coach the freshman team under the order of John Mariucci. The two had once played together in the late 1940's with the Minneapolis Millers, and had become the closest of friends. Glen got his degree from the U of M in physical education, and went on to Ohio State to coach and work towards his masters degree. He took over as head coach of the Gophers in 1966, before passing the torch to Herb Brooks. In 1971 Glen got offered the coaching job with the St. Paul Saints. He took the job in mid season, and Ken Yackel filled in as interim head coach for the remainder of the 1971-72 season. Glen later became head coach of the North Stars, and was with the team for several years working in the front office. He is currently working as a scout for the Philadelphia Flyers.

Matschke, Antonovich and Blais

SONMOR TRIBUTES

BILL BUTTERS: "From Glen I learned that you can't have all great players on your team. He felt that you had to have a few tomahawkers, a few skilled guys, and a good blend of guys with grit and character. He always said though, that you need five or six brutes out there to protect your good guys, and intimidate the other team. Glen had a great vitality for life.

When I played for the Stars, Lou Nanne never liked to play me, and Glen did. Lou said to Glen, 'You have to start looking at Butters with your good eye Glen, so you can see just how bad he really is.'"

Brad Buetow

DAVE FERRONI: (1970 TEAM MANAGER) "Glen was a great guy. He showcased just what American hockey could do when given the chance."

MURRAY McLACHLAN: "Glen related well with his players, and he did a good job coaching the talent he had. He was good in developing the team concept, and in accomplishing goals. He helped my game quite a bit. Glen was like a 6-year old kid on a pond. He'd scrimmage with us, and if he missed a pass he'd say you can't pass him the puck on his blind side. He made hockey fun."

RON PELTIER: "He's a classic. He was a players coach, and he could laugh at himself. I remember he used to call our team trainer Jimmy Marshall, '*With-YOU.*' This was because he used to always ask him, 'Jimmy are you with me?' He was quite a guy, and a great coach."

DEAN BLAIS: "Glen was a super motivator, he was the type of guy who would always have fun. You'd do anything for him, because his fun attitude rubbed off on

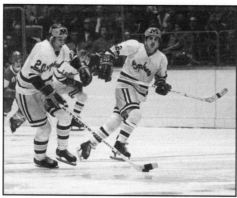
Gopher breakout

his players. He was the most motivating coach I ever played for. He motivated by pure fun. I was sad to see him leave to go coach the Saints. He brought my roommate, Mike Antonovich, with him to boot, and that was a sad day for me. But, he'd done so much for hockey in the state, it was probably good that he got more people involved with that as well."

GREGG WONG: "The most enthusiastic, upbeat, nicest guy I've ever been around, that's Glen Sonmor. He always had something good to say. Herbie could've learned a lot from Glen. Herbie was a better coach, but Glen was a much better person."
DOUG PELTIER: "Glen was a character, and one of the great hockey minds in the country."

GARY GAMBUCCI: "A character, that was Glen. He was such a nice guy, and able to laugh and have fun as well. I remember so many funny stories about Glen, he was one of a kind."

MIKE ANTONOVICH: "I loved Glen, we were from the same mold. I went to the U because of him, he taught me a lot about hockey, and about life. We got along so well, he was such a fun loving guy to be around. It was fun to play with Glen. He would let us scrimmage all practice sometimes. He'd join in too, and play with us. He was just one of the boys. He knew his hockey, and he was a great guy too."

JOHN GILBERT: "Glen didn't believe in complex systems or big tactical concepts. He'd rather get good players, put them together with the proper chemistry, then fire 'em up to the skies. And he could do it. In a one-game showdown, Glen could get his team high enough to leap tall buildings. His greatest moment of inspiration was in Duluth, when Mike Antonovich was a freshman. There was a guy who always sat near the visiting bench in Duluth to heckle the visiting team. Late in the game, Antonovich got checked near the boards, and when his stick waved up over the

116

boards, this fan grabbed the stick. It was probably only in self-defense, to avoid being hit, but the moment of contact was all Glen needed. He vaulted up over the side of the bench and beat the heck out the guy. They cleared the section and when overtime started they looked at Glen, who was trying to be calm and composed with his shirt torn to shreds and his stomach hanging out. I think Ronnie Peltier scored the winning goal, and in the dressing room, Glen was up on a table, with his fist thrust in the air and his torn shirt a symbol for paying whatever price it took. They went on to win the WCHA title that year."

Bill Butters

INDIVIDUAL CAREER RECORDS

MOST GOALS: 144 - JOHN MAYASICH 1951-55.

MOST ASSISTS: 154 - JOHN MAYASICH 1951-55.

MOST TOTAL POINTS: 298 - JOHN MAYASICH 1951-55.

MOST GOALS-DEFENSEMEN: 37 - TONY KELLIN 1982-86.

MOST ASSISTS-DEFENSEMEN: 128 - TODD RICHARDS 1985-89.

MOST POINTS-DEFENSEMEN: 158 - TODD RICHARDS 1985-89.

MOST SHORTHANDED GOALS: 10 - PAUL BROTEN 1984-88.

MOST GAMES PLAYED: 180 - GRANT BISCHOFF 1987-91.

MOST PENALTIES: 182 - BEN HANKINSON 1987-91.

MOST PENALTY MINUTES: 403 - PAT MICHELETTI 1982-86.

THE OLD BARN

Historic Mariucci Arena has been the home of Golden Gopher Hockey since February 17, 1950, when the Gophers defeated the Michigan State Spartans, 12-1, before a crowd of 3,734 in the inaugural game in the new facility. The brick and steel structure is part of the Williams Arena complex that was completed in 1928 at a cost of $650,000. The ice arena was not part of the original Williams Arena structure, so the team lived a nomadic life for the first 31 years of the program and played games at the St. Paul Auditorium, the Minneapolis Arena, Dupont Arena, the Hippodrome at the Fairgrounds, and even on outdoor sheets of ice near campus.

In 1949 the remodeling of Williams Arena was started, and a wall was erected dividing the arena into two ends — one end for basketball and the other for ice hockey. The cost was $950,000. Since that time, Mariucci Arena has been home to many historic games, including the first NCAA Championship to be played outside of Colorado Springs in 1958.

In an emotional ceremony in 1985, the structure was renamed Mariucci Arena in honor of the "Godfather of Minnesota Hockey," John Mariucci. Mariucci, a legendary former player and coach for the Golden Gophers and several U.S. Olympic Teams, passed away on March 23, 1987. (1991-92 media guide)

I'll miss that old barn something terrible. I can remember my dad taking me to games there was I was still wearing double-runner skates. I got to experience the arena from several different angles in my years at the U of M, including a two year stint as a "NE" setion resident. It has in my opinion, the most college-like atmosphere of any arena I have ever seen. I have played there, been a fan there, and even was a rodent there. It was a Minnesota Icon with all its' character and nastalgia. It's like a giant time-capsule in there with those old rafters, steam pipes, lights, trophies and bleachers. While everyone complained about their obstructed seates and horrible sight lines, I was enjoying the perfect view from my perch. It's always sad when history has to take its course, and take away our landmarks. Sure the new arena will be awesome, and it will be the finest rink in the country, but for a brief, two-year stint, that old barn was this rodent's glorious home-away-from-home.

The old barn in the '20s

WHAT ARE YOU GOING TO MISS?

"I'll miss all that mystique, tradition, and all those great pictures on the wall of All-Americans. It was just a really good feeling to walk in there and experience the arena." — *Tim Harrer*

"I'm not going to miss the bad seating, but it's a nice big sheet of ice, and a great place to play hockey. My high school team played the very first game ever played in there, in January of 1950 before a Gopher - Michigan State game. I think it'll be easy to adjust to the new one, and I'm excited for it." — *Wendy Anderson*

"There's an aura about it when you played in there. Just to think about all the sweat, and all the ups and downs of those stairs in there, there was so much tradition in there." — *Pat Micheletti*

"That ice sheet was perfect. The big corners. I just loved playing there. I'm nostalgic, and I like old things. It wasn't the locker rooms, seats, or the roof, it was that great ice. Whenever I think about the barn, I can't help but remember those afternoon games when the sun would shine in from those big windows up there. Gosh, I get shivers up my spine just thinking about it." — *Steve Christoff*

"No way, I was not in favor of the new arena. With the dollars that are so important today, I was hoping they would fix up old Mariucci arena. I think that the old arenas with character involved are very few and far between. I think the new arenas are too plastic and sterile looking. They lack that old uniqueness, like the Chicago Stadium. That was a landmark, they should've saved that one too. I wish they would've renovated the barn, but the women's athletics needed space and that's the way they went with it. A new $ 20 million facility will never recapture the feeling of old Mariucci Arena." — *Herb Brooks*

"The mystique walking in there is something I'll always remember. It was such a rush walking up those stairs, you could hear the cheerleaders and the band, it was a great feeling. Then a high-five from Goldy, the announcer welcoming us back on the ice, the fight song. I got chills every damn time I walked up those steps. I won't miss the acoustics in there though, you could never understand a word that announcer said." — *Cory Laylin*

"I think it's time for a new one, but from a players perspective I loved the old one. It was so enjoyable to play there. I think Goldy was the only one in there with a decent seat, everyone else's was obstructed. So, hopefully they'll bring new tradition into the new arena. I'll miss everything about that place: the dungeon, the locker room, and just the memories of all my friends playing hockey in there will be tough to see go." — *Larry Olimb*

"Walking down those steps thinking and thinking of all the guys before me who have done the same was intense. Everything about that old rink I loved. It'll be sad to see it go. That big ice sheet, that slope on the one end of the rink, the memories, I'll miss it all. I think the new Olympic sized ice will be a great advantage for the players though. The fans want to see passing, skating, shooting, as well as aggressive hockey. The big rink has given the Gophers two things: It allows them to have the big rough, tough guys to mix it up in the corners, to play physical hockey. Also, it gives the finesse players with speed who can stickhandle a chance to entertain the crowd with great skills. I guess we all knew that someday the barn had to be buried, and start with something new." — *Neal Broten*

"John Mariucci had the greatest influence of anyone in my life, and I'll certainly miss the old arena that was dedicated to him. I'll really miss that big old barn, I just hope they can get the tradition going in the new one. Those crowds were so supportive, they helped us so much to win games in there. It was so much fun, and there were so many great memories there, I'll be sad when it finally happens."
— *Glen Sonmor*

"I'm going to miss the ambience about it. It's obviously one of the great, classic arenas around Minnesota. Just walking in there you immediately realize that you're walking into a piece of history. So many great players, and great games in there, you hate to see it go. But, I'm glad they're getting the chance to upgrade into the new building. It says something about the program that in these hard financial times at the University, they're building a new arena for them." — *Joe Schmit*

The old barn in the '50's

"It has no nostalgic memories for me. I have a few memories on the other side of the barn, but I haven't seen enough games in there to have a real fondness for the place. I'm not going to miss the world's worst press box, if that's what you mean. I also think building a new hockey rink for the Gopher hockey team is the stupidest thing that's ever been done in this community. There's about 14 other arenas that would've done just fine. It's a waste of money for a university that's in terrible financial condition to begin with. It's just absolutely stupid, but if they want to waste their money on it, I don't care."— *Pat Reusse*

"Mariucci Arena has served the University well and will always hold a special place in my heart, but Minnesota hockey fans and the hockey program will finally get the arena they deserve. The walk up the stairs, the personal escort from Goldy, the cheerleaders, the fight song, the run up to the ice, and seeing all the fans... you bet I'll miss that arena." — *Doug Woog*

"I'll miss the old bleachers, the clomping of the skates down those wooden stairs to the locker rooms, the pictures, the smell, the familiar faces through the years, and most of all, the constant of Gopher Hockey at Mariucci Arena."
— *Charley Hallman*

"It was a warm, intimate, old arena, packed with tradition. The Minnesota hockey tradition is the richest in America, and they're capable of winning the national championship year in and year out. Mariucci was quite a legend, and his arena will be dearly missed." — *Governor Arne Carlson*

"It's definitely time for a new arena. The times have passed by old Mariucci Arena, and it's time they made a more convenient environment for the fans who support the team." — *Tom Vannelli*

"I'll miss absolutely nothing about it. Sure there were great times in there, but it's an arena way beyond its time. It's a miserable place to work. There's not enough room in there for anything, the seating is lousy, there's no backs on the seats, there's terrible sight lines, and we got so many complaints from disgruntled fans. It's way past its prime, it served its purpose for many years, and it's time to go. One time I was curious as to just how many bad seats were in there. So Ken Beuhl, the game operations manager, and I spent an afternoon counting the good seats in there. We figured that 3,000 out of 7,600 seats in there were decent. The other 4,600 were obstructed to some degree. I can't wait for the new arena, it'll be the finest college hockey arena in the country." — *Tom Greenhoe*

"As long as they bring the pictures over, I won't miss a damn thing. I'll keep getting tickets as long as they only take Minnesota kids for their teams. I'm looking forward to the new Mariucci, and I think Stanley Hubbard deserves a lot of credit for getting the new rink going." — *Don Clark*

"I say keep the ice surface, and tear down the building around it. It's the best ice in America. I'll miss the atmosphere, and tradition in there. I hope it carries over to the new building. My back won't miss the horrible seats either."
— *Dick Spannbauer*

"I won't miss the bad sight lines, or the bad seats, but I will miss the ambience of the old barn." — *Wally Shaver*

"Along with the obvious historical reasons, One of the things I'll miss will be the Channel 29 special at the concession stands. There was this one old lady who would always recognize me, and slip me a free brat. Only she would give me so many damn jalopenos I was hard to be around later in the game. I hope they bring all the concession staff to the new arena, they were great. I also won't miss the big furnace fan up in our press box. That thing shook so much I thought for sure we would either shake right off the edge, or it would blow up. I won't miss that balcony at all. The new arena will be much more accessible for the TV crews, because the designers gave us some input on the press box plans." — *Frank Mazzocco*

"I'll miss the smell, the rubber mats, and the sound of the skates clanking on the wooden stairs. That was the signal for the fans to get ready for the Gophers when they heard that noise coming from the hallway. I'll really miss that old arena, but hopefully they can build up the tradition at the new barn. The people who have supported the Gophers over the years deserve the new arena, it's for the people who have supported us over the years." — *Robb Stauber*

"The only thing I'm going to miss about the old arena is seeing John Mariucci, and as long as they take the name over to the new arena I'm fine with it. If they wouldn't have taken the name to the new arena, they wouldn't have gotten a penny from me. It's served its purpose well, and it's time for something better."
— *Bob Ridder*

"It was real special to me, I grew up in there. It's a great high walking up those stairs to the ice. Your heart is beating about a thousand times a minute, and you can feel the vibrations of the people roaring up above in the bleachers. I remember being scared of falling on my butt walking across the ice to our bench, and sure enough one time a cheerleader smashed into me, and knocked me over. I remember a guy yelling at me 'Hey Brad, nice underwear.' I soon figured out that I had split my crotch wide open in front of 7,500 laughing fans. You know, I was the one who physically hung all those pictures on the walls in there. It took me over five years to finally get all the pictures dug up from the Walter Library Archives, but I wanted to make sure it got done for tradition's sake." — *Brad Buetow*

"You were so close to the ice in there, it was great. The noise, the fans, I loved it. I'll really miss that. I had a hard time getting my wife to sit on those hard seats though. The new arena will draw better, and it'll be more comfortable as well. I don't think it'll be nearly as intimate as the old one, but it'll be good for the program over there. I always have mixed emotions about things like this, and I kind of wish they would've saved the old Brick House too." — *Steve Cannon*

"It always felt good playing there on that large ice rink. It had a certain personality to it that you can't find in arenas today. It was looked upon by all of us as something special." — *Gene Campbell*

"I remember the first time I was ever in there. It was 1961, on a Saturday morning my dad took us over to play a youth hockey game. The Gophers had come out to practice afterwards, and I'll never forget the goalie, John Lothrop, letting us score on him. He was so nice, what a thrill for me being a 5-years-old. Then I remember going downstairs to the lockerroom, and Lou Nanne gave me an autographed stick. For me, that was the coolest thing in the world. Later on as kids, I could remember sneaking by the Cub Scout security guards into games at old Williams arena. I'll miss that old barn, it gave me a lot of great memories."

— *Jeff Passolt*

"The new Olympic size sheet of ice will make hockey better all the way around for the program I think. It's had a lot of color, flavor, and it was a grand old arena for sure. It used to be considered the premier arena in college hockey in its day. My back won't miss it, but it was definitely time for the program to get a better theater to perform in." — *Walter Bush*

"I remember the great ice, it was so unique. You could set up a two-on-one behind the net there was so much room behind there. In the pros when I would play with guys that played there in college against the Gophers, they would always say that's where they most hated to play. I loved the fans, it got so damn loud in there. I'll miss it."   - - *Mike Polich*

"I'll miss the memorabilia and tradition of the old barn. But we have terrible seats, so I won't miss the old barn. As a spectator it's not nearly the thrill of playing there. It's time for a new rink, and that's a positive step in the right direction for the University of Minnesota." — *Doug Peltier*

"I'm in favor of the new arena, but I'll really miss the old one. Hopefully we can transfer the heritage and tradition to the new one. Do you think the fans in Chicago are happy about having two championship finals with the Bulls and Hawks there, and now losing the Stadium?" — *Paul Ostby*

"I'm going to miss the atmosphere. People were right on top of you in there. But, it's time for a new rink, better seats, and better sight lines. I'm gonna miss every damn little thing about that place." — *Ben Hankinson*

"The old arena was a dump, I'll miss nothing."— *Stanley S. Hubbard*

"I loved that old arena, it seemed like the crowd was right on top of you. It was the barn, what else can you say?" — *Pat Phippen*

"From a spectator's point of view I won't miss the facility, but I will miss the memories and traditions. It had tremendous ice. As a goalie I didn't always like all the room behind the nets and corners for guys to set up on me. It was a classic, but it's certainly time for a new arena." — *Murray McLachlan*

"I'll miss the character of that theater. It's a place where, when you step on the ice, you get a tingle down your spine. It's a shame to lose places like Mariucci Arena, the Chicago Stadium and Boston Garden. Those places were full of so much electricity, and it'll never be replaced." — *Joe Micheletti*

"Everybody thought Mariucci Arena was a big dump, but we loved it. To us it was home. As a player it was always a packed house, jammed with screaming fans, great ice, and a super tradition." — *Aaron Broten*

"The sheet of ice in there was gorgeous. The memories, stitches, the blood you left on the ice, the old rafters, those goofy lights hanging down over the ice, and even that crazy Gumby doll the Gopher would hold up for the crowd to scream, and the memories. God yes, I'm really gonna miss that place." — *Dave Brooks*

"The facility has had a lot to do with growth of hockey in Minnesota. I'll miss the ice sheet, and the room behind the nets though. The new rink will improve the caliber of hockey, and eliminate all this clutching and grabbing that I don't care for. I look at the Eastern Europeans and Russians, and say that's the style of hockey I'd like to see for the future of Gopher Hockey. This new rink will get us well on our way to a European style of hockey we can be proud of." — *John Mayasich*

The old barn being constructed

"They'll never replace the ice surface, it's the best in the country. We always had a full house there, and for little guys those big corners really opened it up. The important thing here is that they kept Gopher Hockey on campus, and not downtown. The new facility will be a good boost for the program." — *Len Lilyholm*

"I loved it, stepping out on the ice, people went crazy. Teams feared us at home. We were in great shape, we had our home ice, our fans, a big rink, and teams absolutely feared coming to our house to play hockey. We had so much confidence there. There's something about an old arena, so much class in there." — *Bill Baker*

"I've always watched the games in there as a kid, and I'm glad I got to play in it for a while at least. It's a great place to play at, and it's an awesome arena. I'm looking forward to the new one though, I think it should be pretty cool."

— *Darby Hendrickson*

"I'll miss the old Williams Arena. I can remember when we were laying out the plans for what they are now going to leave. It was a fine arena, we were very proud of it in Minnesota." — *Frank Pond*

"Fortunately and unfortunately I've been playing professional hockey every winter since I played there, so I haven't been back since 1979. I can't wait to come see another game there. It was a great place to play, and such great ice. I remember seeing games from behind those big beams as a kid in there. It's sad that they have to move onto something else, it had so much tradition in there."

— *Mike Ramsey*

"To just stop and think about all the people that have played in that arena, so many great players and teams, so many years of Gopher Hockey. It was a dream come true for little guys, with those big corners and huge ice sheet." — *Corey Millen*

"I'm glad the new arena will only have about 9,000 seats. That way tickets are always hard to get, and it should never be too easy to get a seat in there. The old arena was a nice place, but way past her years." — *Lou Nanne*

"I remember watching games in there when I was in high school, it was the only game in town. We need a new rink, it's deserving of the best arena in the country. After all, we're the hotbed of hockey in the country, and it's long past due. It'll go a long way to assuring fans competitive teams in the future." — *Roger Rovick*

"You go through so much there. I'll miss the memories most I think. But, as a fan I won't miss the bad back after the games. I hope a lot of the tradition will transfer over. I'll be ordering my season tickets over there for sure."

— *Dean Williamson*

"I'll miss the whole damn place, I wouldn't want to play in any other arena. There's so much tradition in there, it's the perfect rink for Gopher Hockey. It was great ice, nice and wide, and deep corners to do some damage. I loved it, and will definitely miss it big time." — *Trent Klatt*

(A big sigh...) "I'm gonna miss the entire thing. I won't miss my aching back afterwards, but it was worth it. I'd like to see more spirit in the new rink, maybe that's the U of M cheerleader talking though! Oh, and I'll really miss Goldie's perch, he made it so fun to watch in between the whistles." — *Bonnie Hankinson*

"The ice was always good in there, and it was great for little players like myself. It was a player's rink. If you had any speed you could really take off from those big corners down the sides. It's definitely time for a new one though. There's a lot of history in that arena, but I'm looking forward to the new one."

— *Dick Meredith*

"New memories will be created in the new arena. I'll always remember that big, hard, fast, beautiful sheet of ice in there, it was the best in the country in its time. There's a lot of Gopher history in there, and it's due to John Mariucci. He was the Godfather of Hockey in not only Minnesota, but in the country." — *Ron Peltier*

"I'll miss all the ghosts lurking around up there in that attic."
— *Ken Yackel Jr.*

"All the sellouts, the fans, the traditions, it was such a fun place to play hockey. I definitely won't miss the three hour skating drills-from-hell on Mondays with Jack Blatherwick." — *Randy Skarda*

"It's time for a new one. It was a great place for a couple thousand people to see a game. The deep corners, fast ice, tradition...that was where I played hockey you know? It was home." — *Steve Ulseth*

"I liked that big sheet of ice, and that one end that slanted down over the ice. I was lucky to have played there. It reminded me of the Boston Garden, and the Detroit Olympia. These were the great arenas with a lot of character, and architectural individuality." — *Reed Larson*

"I'll miss it like crazy. I remember my last day of practice when Herbie and I skated around and around the rink just talking about what lie ahead in our futures, and what we were going to do with our lives. Each of us went our separate directions, but have remained close to hockey. It was a great place to get away and think. I'll never forget that day." - - *Murray Williamson*

"Hearing the rouser start up, and stepping on that ice was the biggest thing I ever did." — *Jim Boo*

"I'll miss the mystique, tradition, and the feeling you got just looking at that rink. It had a certain smell. It was home to so many great players, and memories. I liked the big rink, and loved the deep corners." — *Tom Chorske*

"It was always so much fun playing there. There was so much tradition, that sun shining through those big windows on a day game, and the memories of a lifetime. I've been in just about every college arena in the country now, and in comparison I think it's the best ice in the world. I don't know what it was, the water up here, or just the way the arena maintenance people worked on it or what, but it was just fabulous ice." — *Dean Blais*

"It was a show. I get excited just thinking about it, and I really miss it. The fans going crazy, the excitement, it was unbelievable. Hell, I have goose bumps just thinking about it right now! I'll miss that aura it had about it when you played there. Just think about all the sweat from going up and down all those stairs before and after a game. Yeah, there's a lot of tradition in there, and it made me who I am, whatever the hell I am! That building made me somebody in life." — *Pat Micheletti*

"It was great to play there, but I'm looking forward to seeing games in the new arena. It's a real positive move for the program. Sure there's history in there, but they shouldn't try to renovate the old one for nostalgic reasons. It served its purpose for many years, and it's time to accept change. It'll be bigger and better than the old one, and more people will be able to enjoy this great game." — *Butsy Erickson*

"The heritage and tradition is rich, it's a first class organization, and it deserves a first class facility. It was a great home ice advantage playing there."
— *Todd Okerlund*

"It wasn't the greatest rink to watch a game in, but as a player, it was pretty special to play there." -- *David Jensen*

"I'm not going to miss squeezing my butt between two fat people that thought they bought two tickets on those hard benches! It's time for new rink. That

Here's what it looked like before the hockey arena was added. The football team practiced here as well.

ice surface was the best in the country, so fast, so hard, so big, and so fun to play on. I'll miss that part of it dearly. That new building is going to stimulate more interest in the game, and make it a lot more fun to watch the club play." — *Dick Paradise*

"I'm going to miss it a lot, the tradition, the memories of the barn and a lot of fun. But, tradition is winning, and fans come because you win. They don't come just to sit in Mariucci Arena, they come to see a winner. The new rink will challenge us to provide more tradition. One thing I won't miss will be walking across the ice between periods, I've wrecked more pairs of leather shoes over the years. I also won't have to worry about falling on my butt in front of all those people, or being knocked over by a flying Goldy Gopher screaming across the ice like a mad-man!"
—*Bill Butters*

129

"I am happy about the new arena, it should've been built years ago. Mariucci's ghost will live there forever in his arena. It was such a treat to sit back and watch John coach from the bench. He would yell across the ice at opposing coaches like just he and the coach were the only two in there or something. Then at the end of the game, after he had yelled at him for a couple hours, he would insist that he came to his home for wine and home-made spaghetti. I'll miss Mariucci arena, but I miss John Mariucci even more." — *Dr. V.A. Nagobads*

The original Hippodrome at the State Fair Grounds in
St. Paul. Notice the horse and buggy out front.

"I remember the first time I ever played there, it was 8:30 in the morning. St. Thomas was playing the Gopher JV team, and I think there were maybe 12 people in the crowd. But still to this day, it was one if the biggest thrills of my life to have played in there. There's an aura found in only a few venues in the country, and it's definitely in that category. The new one will be wonderful, but will never be the old one. I won't miss the seats, sightlines, and bad back though." — *Pat Forciea*

"Personally I prefer the NHL sized ice rink at 200 by 85 feet to Olympic size (200x100). There's more action with less ice, and all that extra ice leads to less confrontation. That's (international hockey) the most boring hockey I have ever seen. However, the new arena should suit the fans well. I did get to quite a few games there through the years, and it was a great place to see a hockey game. I loved the college atmosphere there." — *Bobby Smith*

"The whole atmosphere of that place was intense. I'll never forget coming up those stairs, and coming up to that ice. It's a shame that they're leaving behind such a tradition." — *Paul Holmgren*

"I'll miss the uniqueness, it was so different than any other arena I have ever seen. I used to go to games there when I was a kid, and loved playing there. I don't think you can appreciate it until you turn pro, and start playing in all the dumpy minor league arenas all over that have no character." — *Pete Hankinson*

"I loved the ice surface, it was so big we just wore opposing teams out. I also loved the atmosphere, it was so thick in there. Other guys that played against me said later that they just dreaded coming to the barn to play. It was such a great home ice advantage for us. Herbie had started an aura, and we felt it would take an incredible team to beat us at home. One thing I won't miss were those deadly long practices under Herbie. I wish they would've renovated it." — *Don Micheletti*

"It's a great place to play, it's a classic, and it has a lot of charisma. It's got great ice, and so much nostalgia in there. All the great Gophers played in there. You felt like a rat roaming around down in those tunnels to the dungeon. I'll miss getting there, the people, the campus, atmosphere, all the pictures walking in the foyer, and all the great memories. I think the saddest thing about moving into a new building is the fact that you lose a lot of the nostalgia somewhere in the move. The people who follow Gopher Hockey are something special, and are very loyal to their team. They deserve the best facility. It's just a shame to move out of something so special to so many people." — *Mike Antonovich*

"I'll miss walking into the building and seeing all the tradition. It's coming home, it's sentimentality, it's nostalgia and that's pretty special to me. The bonds you form in there, you become a man in that building. You fight together, and you cry together. You really grew up in there, and it was neat to do it with all Minnesota kids too. Selfishly I wish they would keep it because I have great seats up on the balcony. Even though my back gave out in the third period, wow did I have a great sightline up there over the ice. I am excited for the new one. It's not only a great college hockey program, but it's a great institution as well and it deserves a new arena. Today you can't sit still, you have to be on the cutting edge to stay competitive on a high level. Gosh, I'll miss the girders, and the smell too. That was my rink. I left a lot of blood on that ice, and I'd like to think that I helped to create some of that rich tradition we have here." — *Gary Gambucci*

"I think there's a lot of tradition in that rink. Like the Chicago Stadium, it's sad to see 'em come down from their glory. It was such a big sheet of ice, I loved it, it was home.. I'll remember walking down those stairs just craving a big glass of juice waiting for me in the locker room. I remember the first time I ever played there in the arena. It was a high school game, and on the way down from Roseau our bus died. They sent us another bus, but we were running late and didn't want to miss our ice time. So we got dressed on the bus coming down University Avenue. Guys were mooning people, and when we got there we all got off the bus dressed and ready to go. We must've looked like the biggest collection of dorks anyone had ever seen. But, that was the first taste of Mariucci Arena I had, and it made me want to play there more than ever." — *Paul Broten*

"The atmosphere, the big sheet of ice, the way the crowd and band noise boil around inside that big arching roof, and all the great Gopher Hockey tradition are contained inside the old arena. But have you ever tried to watch a game in there? I mean, people in the first row have to stand up to see if the puck is on their half of the rink, and then the 19 rows behind them have to stand, too. When they get 7,000 fans in there, it's one of the incredible feats in sports, because 5,000 of them will only be able to see brief snatches of play. I always hoped they'd rip out the seats and build new ones with higher risers, then add a couple of decks on the west end. The new arena plan is to try to incorporate as much tradition and history as possible, and I am convinced it will be the best hockey arena in North America, for players and fans. It's a shame to leave the old arena, but if you've got to move, it's nice to move into the best rink ever designed." — *John Gilbert*

"I'll miss walking into a game two hours before the opening face-off, and having that feeling you get in there. It's such a big cavernous barn of a place, and it reeks of tradition. I can't describe it. The game was never over in there until the fat lady sang. The Gophers could always come back in there and win at home. I did hate the TV and radio facilities up on that catwalk. The whole thing was an afterthought, and was a serious deathtrap up there. They need a modern building. It'll be good for the program. It's designed specifically for hockey, and it'll be cleaner, and more efficient as well. They even talked to our technical people to get their input about facilitating the TV and radio station needs." — *Doug McLeod*

"The balcony was the best place to be, those were the best seats in the house. The sightlines were awful in there, but the people made it fun. I feel sorry for the people who waited so long to finally get good seats. There was a great ambience in there, the fans, cheerleaders, the band, and the memories. I remember there was this lady who always yelled my name every single time I came through the hallway to the ice. Like clockwork she never forgot to yell, and I never knew her name or anything. She had a maroon and gold heart, and she gave me the confidence to play well there. I want to thank her, but don't know her. It was so reassuring to just know she was there. Gopher fans are the greatest in the world. I'm gonna miss that old place, it was something special." — *Dave Snuggerud*

"That place was some old barn. It was a part of me growing up, and we loved to play there. I remember Marsh Ryman used to divert the fire marshals from catching him getting too many people over the capacity in there. When we would play UND, there was 'way too many people in there, and Marsh, who was the ticket manager at the time, wanted to get as many fans in there as possible to see the Gophers." — *Dick Dougherty*

"I'm lucky, I get to sit in the press box when I'm there, but when I did sit in the general admission seats I had to get out the old heating pad when I got home for my back. I usually had to keep it warm for my neck which got a workout from straining to see around the girder in front of me as well. I'll miss the sights, sounds and that walk down University Avenue by the frat houses before the game. It is by far the most sacred and special walk on game-day anywhere in Minneapolis. I think the new rink is overdue, and it's great for the school. Everybody is excited about good sightlines, more seats, and the whole new package. It will be a better place to watch a hockey game, and most importantly they left it on campus where it belongs. I wish I could say the same about Gopher Football. The pride more than anything is what's most important, and to wear an M jersey is a great tradition for Minnesota.

Unlike the Dome, this new arena will have character in it. As long as we're on the topic of that eyesore, (the Dome), I have a comment about that as well. I can't stand the place, it violates everything that I stand for in sports. I could care less about taking my 6-year-old son to see a game there. I'd rather take him to County Stadium, Wrigley Field, Comiskey Field, or Camden Yards than take him to the Dome. I understand the political reasons, we don't have enough money for a retractable roof like Toronto has, but this isn't ball, it's not a ballpark by any stretch of the imagination. I mean how many other announcers call a homerun by saying 'Kirby hit one out over the Baggie in right?' What the hell is that? I'm sorry, but I'm a purist. I suppose I sound like the guy from Bull Durham talking about the designated hitter or something, but it makes me mad that we keep tearing down our sports landmarks in this town. I loved the old Met Stadium, and have to cry when I drive by now and see that Megamall in its place. The new Mariucci arena is going across the street, and it's a step up. Don't even get me started on how much I miss the old Brick House..."

— Mark Rosen

The new Mariucci Arena, scheduled for completion in
the fall of '93.

I GOT INTO A GOOD SHARE OF TROUBLE IN THAT BARN

Throughout my two-year reign as the rodent, I got in quite a bit of trouble. I figured I just wasn't doing my job if I wasn't offending someone, or getting my tail chewed by the athletic department. You see, since the Gopher mascots on ice before me were always part of the band, they had to merely answer to the mighty band director, whereas my predicament was much more interesting because I had to deal with the whole University bureaucracy. If any of you are U of M alumni, you know that red tape runs quite freely among the administrators. I was perceived by many as a "loose cannon" or perhaps "loose varmint." These people held their breath every time I took to the ice. But, in time we developed a working relationship with each other, and some even became friends.

I had many a meeting with the marketing department about who I had offended that particular series, or which letters or articles about me in the papers were the most offensive that day. I took it all in stride, and enjoyed being yelled at as much as I enjoyed being a cheerleader. It was part of the job, and what the heck, I was merely a volunteer. So, I continued to test the parameters of what was good and bad, and just how much trouble I could get into. Overall, the athletic department at the U of M is a great place. I mean the people there are top-notch, and it was really fun to be a part of the organization. Sure we had our differences about things, but we respected each other. I always had the best interests of the University in mind before I did something absolutely crazy.

Trouble, there's something I seemed to have a knack for finding at the rink. I had this bad habit of tripping referees, mocking them, and occasionally shooting pucks at them. This is all in good fun mind you, and not to discredit the University in any way. The final straw though was when I accidentally ran over a referee. Like I have any peripheral vision inside a 30-gallon drum head to see the little sucker. So what does he do? He tells the WCHA commissioner on me, and says that if I go on the ice and imitate him any more when he's out there, he'll give the Gophers a bench minor penalty. I humbly obeyed the mighty comish on that one, but got revenge back home on my perch high above the cold and frigid ice. Here I proceeded to dress up Gumby with my trusty referee's jersey that I always kept in my bag of tricks, just for emergencies like this. I held him up to the crowd, and they all proceeded to scream, "Buzzy... Buzzy... Buzzy... SUCKS!" So, what happened after this? I got another letter.

Another time I caught hell was when I de-headed myself. I decided to get cute one game and try something different. So, I got the crowd doing a cheer during a whistle, and when they all looked up at me on my perch I took my head off. I had on a gorilla mask underneath my Gopher head. People were excited to finally see that idiot in person for once and for all, and instead they got to see a big ol' ape. It was funny I thought, but the powers that be didn't think it was too cute. So, I got the gorilla mask confiscated.

One of the times I nearly got killed, and nearly killed someone else, was against Wisconsin in 1992. I nearly killed Bucky the Badger on the ice, when I decided to body slam him. Don't ask me what the heck I was thinking. I thought it would be funny if I sort of picked him up over my head, and paraded him around for the Gopher faithful. I remember telling him in our locker room that I was going to pick him up regardless of what he thought because it was my home ice. I advised him that it was best that he went along with it or he might wind up getting hurt. He was a little guy, so he just sort of gave me a nod of cautious approval. Out on the ice, we pretended to get into a fight. Then I was going to pick him up, but his head was too big to get a good grip on, and I dumped him at center ice. If there were judges there, he would've gotten ten's all the way around for artistic interpretation. Luckily he was OK, but he pleaded to me that he was plenty satisfied with my little crowd-pleasing stunt, and we could stop right there.

Now, in the same game, I nearly got myself killed. Right before the third period, I saw the Wisconsin team rallying at their own goal around their goalie. I wanted to give them a special good luck wish, so I took off full speed and dove on their pile. At first I don't think they knew what hit them. Then one guy tried to grab my head, and another one hit me. Then a couple more guys started talking trash to me, and threatened to rip my little Gopher heart out. So I punched one guy in the mask, shoved another, and decided the odds were a bit too much against me. I took off out of there victorious, as I felt the hand of a player trying to grab my tail. However, it was mission accomplished, for this proud Kamikaze varmint.

THE TOYBOX

If you'd been to a Gopher Hockey game within 1990-1992, you probable noticed a rather large critter (that's me) up on my perch holding up various signs and toys. Frank and Wally from Channel 29 referred to it on occasion as "Goldy's Toy Box," and it quickly became my signature form of slapstick comedy. Let's see if I can remember all the critters: first there was Gumby, then Pokey, Fred Flintstone, Dino Flintstone, Mr. Potato Head, Cooties, the Bull, a Pink Flamingo, (to whom the crowd would chant "Sikorski," in light of the recent congressional check-bouncing scam) The Pig, The Alligator, The Shark, The Beetlejuice Doll, (to whom which the crowd would chant "Sid" as in Sid Hartman, and then demand that I spin Sid's head) The Lobster, (to whom the crowd would chant 'Reusse' and demand that he and Sid duke it out up there) The Goldy-Gopher doll, Ken and Barbie, Godzilla, Waldo, The Pillsbury Doughboy, The Sesame Street Gang which included Ernie, Burt, Grover, Cookie Monster and Big Bird, A Cow, A Rubber Foot, A Giant Reptile creature, A Prehistoric Insect thing, and various other carnivores, herbivores, amphibians, and marsupials as well. Now you're asking yourself what is this mental-case all about? Well, basically I'm just a big kid at heart, and I like playing with toys in front of thousands of random people.

A lot of these toys got me in trouble. Like when I would drop them on the ice. Oh well, the fans loved it. Gumby used to love doing flips off the perch onto the ice, and holding up play to give the Gophers a well-needed rest.

I also used to have an alligator on a rope that I would lower down from my perch. I would try to touch someone's head with it, as sort of a game I would play when I was bored up there and everyone was looking at me. This was fun until two bad incidents happened involving the alligator. First, there was an injured player lying just below me on the ice, and I lowered the alligator over his head and touched him. This was sort of to say "Hello. Gee, I hope you're all right, can I be of any assistance to you?" You get the picture. The guy tried to grab him and missed, sending the crowd into laughter. Of course, I caught hell for it.

The other time the alligator got me in trouble was when I nearly killed an innocent bystander with it. There was a sweet, little, old lady that was a security guard at the arena. She would always stand just below me by the ice. One time I lowered the alligator just over her head, and let it sort of hover there for a while. The crowd was going nuts, and this poor lady was without a clue. Suddenly she looked up and all she saw were alligator teeth two inches in front of her eyes. She screamed, and fell over. I thought: "Great, I just killed someone with a $12 alligator from *Toys R Us.*" Luckily she just had to lie down for a while and she was OK, but I was really nervous up there.

Let's not forget about the trouble I would get in for not being a good sport. Now what constitutes being a good sport? Calling the opposing goalie a sieve? I think that's OK, but the powers that be didn't. I used to love calling the goalie a sieve after we would score a goal. I mean every college in the world has fans that call the goalie a sieve, right? Well, I was forbidden to ever use the sieve term again. So, I bought a strainer, and used that. The crowd caught on, and continued to heckle the goalie as expected, but legally. Soon I couldn't use that, so I got a colander, then a funnel, and then a big plastic bat that I pointed at him. Everything I did the crowd yelled sieve, and I was continually getting in trouble. I could point my finger at him, and the "NE" section would yell out sieve. Then I got smart and borrowed my dad's plastic water-buffalo that looked like a bull. I held it up and the crowd would yell "BULL" instead of sieve. Finally they threatened to not let me use the perch anymore if I called the goalie names. Excuse me, but I can't talk. How can I call the goalie names? I give up!

Some of these toys were more special than the others, and they had some pretty loyal followers as well. Take for instance Mr. Potato Head, this character was just as popular as Larry Olimb at times. When I first held him up, the little kids were the first to recognize him. Then a big fat guy who had clearly had his fill of Schmidt yelled, "WELLSTONE!" I couldn't hear what he'd said at first, but the crowd went nuts. I held him up again, and everyone in the "NE" section yelled out our newest freshman senator's name. This comedy went on for about three games, until this crazy looking guy tracked me down before the game and gave me a gift. I didn't know what it was at first, then I realized that it was a shiny green bus. You know, just like the one Senator Wellstone used on his 1990 campaign tour. So, I took the bus up to the perch with me to test it out. I put Mr. Potato Head on the bus and cruised him around on the railing up there. This was too much for the crowd, especially the Republicans. Then I accidentally dropped the bus with Wellstone on it over the side, and onto the ice. The crowd loved it, unfortunately the referees who had to clean up the disassembled Mr. Potato Head didn't. It was crazy how much the fans enjoyed this bit of comedy. One guy made up buttons he handed out about Wellstone and Mr. Potato Head, I couldn't believe it. Of course it eventually got me into trouble though, as this article later appeared in the St. Paul paper:

A-PEELING TO A SENATOR

Paul Wellstone, who has trying to shed an "egghead" image, now has to deal with being labeled Mr. Potato Head — whatever that means. Goldy Gopher has been having fun with the freshman Democratic U.S. Senator's image at recent hockey games. The University of Minnesota mascot holds up various stuffed animals, such as a Gumby doll, to incite the crowd. During last weekend's clash with Providence, Goldy Gopher several times held up a plastic Mr. Potato Head. To which the crowd chants: "Wellstone."

I felt sorry for the people in the athletic department, who had to take the heat and nasty letters for my little prank. But I honestly meant no harm by it. I mean, as Goldy how was I supposed to know that when I held up a Mr. Potato Head doll they were going to yell, "Wellstone?" It was intended to be funny, and a few local Democrats got a bit upset. These people would be surprised to know that Wellstone is friends with my mom, and that she helped with his campaign as senator.

Along with toys, I figured I had to find a way to speak up there. So I also had fun with signs up on my perch. Those seemed to get me into just as much, if not more trouble than the toys. The signs started as a way for me to communicate up on my perch, because of course I couldn't talk. (The signs quickly became like the old *Lite Beer* commercial, *Less Filling -Tastes Great*) So, I would hold up a sign and people on both sides would yell out whatever it read. The sides were broken down further by sections. There were the (MIN -NE - SO - TA) sections that would call out their section name in turn, by my cue up on the perch, it was great for the crowds to get involved. It made the games so much more fun I thought. Some of the more memorable ones read: "FRANK and WALLY" (The channel 29 announcers: Frank Mazzocco, and Wally Shaver), "DOUG and DICK" (The MSC announcers: Doug McLeod and Dick Bremer), "DOUG WOOG" and "LARRY OLIMB." The crowd would yell the names out loud, and would see which side of the arena could yell the names louder I guess. For those special Wisconsin fans I had: "CHEESE HEAD," "BETTER DEAD THAN RED," "94-EAST," and plenty of Kraft cheese slices to throw at them as well.

One of the funnier signs was one that read: "DR. WOOG." This was to the song "Dr. Who," you know that crazy song "Rock 'n' Roll Part II," where everyone yells "HEY!" at the North Star Games. Well, the crowd got into it, but after a couple games, the athletic department started to get letters about it. People were complaining because they didn't understand, and they wanted to know if Doug had recently received his Ph.D.

Another funny sign story occurred when I made up the "Goldy Says" signs, just like "Simon Says," only better. I would hold up signs that read: "GOLDY SAYS: PUNCH THE DUDE ON YOUR LEFT, STAND UP, JUMP, WIGGLE, SPIT, BARK, GROWL LIKE A GOPHER, SPIN, CLAP, SCREAM, VOMIT, and WHISTLE". There was even one that commanded the crowd to dance like the gopher from the movie *Caddyshack*. These were all OK, except for the "WHISTLE" sign that I used. The old barn was so big, that the noise really echoed in there something fierce. I got in trouble for it, when too many old ladies were complaining about their hearing aids going crazy.

There were other signs that got me in trouble too. Like the time I had a sign for the North Dakota game that read: "21-YEAR-OLD FRESHMEN, ARE YOU KIDDING ME?" That one didn't go over too well. Neither did the "BORN IN THE USA" sign. The truth hurts I guess. It just so happens that we're proud of the fact that our program is all Minnesota kids.

One of the funnest games I ever did was when my entire family came to see a Gopher game. I got them VIP tickets right in the "NE" section. When the game started, I went over and sprayed them with cans of silly string. I harassed them the whole game, and especially my dad, Don. I wanted to embarrass him but good, just to show him how much I loved him. So I held up a couple signs that got some good feedback. The first read: "Hey Don, Goldy Needs a New Car!" The crowd laughed, and a drunk fan even yelled at my dad, and demanded that since I was doing a good job, that he immediately buy me a new car. The other one read "Hey Don, Goldy Needs More Money!" Dad got smart on this one, and yelled back at me, "Hey kid, I already give you too much the way it is!" It was a great day, and it meant a lot to me that there was someone there that I could be funny for. I remember at the end of the game my aunt Cookie asked me why I kept calling the goalie "Butter?" I had to explain to her that the crowd was saying BUTT-HEAD, when I would point to my butt, then my head. She thought they were all yelling BUTT-ER, so she figured what the hell, and joined in to call the Bulldog goalie butter.

Sir Dennis Winchell

Crazy enough to make your head spin.

SINGLE SEASON RECORDS

MOST GOALS: 53 - TIM HARRER 1979-80.

MOST ASSISTS: 59 - AARON BROTEN 1980-81.

MOST TOTAL POINTS: 106 - AARON BROTEN 1980-81.

MOST GOALS-DEFENSEMEN: 19 - RANDY SKARDA 1987-88.

MOST ASSISTS-DEFENSEMAN: 43 - TODD RICHARDS 1986-87.

MOST TOTAL POINTS-DEFENSEMEN: 54 - BILL BAKER 1978-79.

MOST SHORTHANDED GOALS: 5 - STEVE GRIFFITH 1982-83.

MOST PENALTY MINUTES: 154 - PAT MICHELETTI 1984-85.

Here's an exerpt from a book written by Murray Williamson. The book describes what college hockey was like in the 1950's. Murray is a past Gopher All-American, two-time Olympic coach, and five-time National team coach. His book takes an in-depth look at the explosive growth of hockey in the United States, the feud between Murray Armstrong, and John Mariucci that forever changed the face of college hockey, and provides a provocative perspective into what college hockey was like for the Minnesota Gophers some 40 years ago.

The Great American Hockey Dilemma
"College Hockey in the '50's"
By Murray Williamson

College hockey in the late 1950's was booming and the Minnesota Gophers were playing to capacity houses with an average team. In 1958, Gopher Hockey, for the first time, outdrew basketball. Those were the days of Jack McCartan, Mike Pearson, Dick Burg, Herb Brooks, Bob Turk, and other Gophers who went on to make contributions to the 1960 Olympic gold medal for the United States.

The Western Intercollegiate Hockey League, prior to 1958, included Denver, Michigan, Michigan Tech, Michigan State, North Dakota, Colorado College, and Minnesota. Each year the top two teams went to the NCAA championship and usually won in convincing style over the two Eastern representatives. All seven teams in the league were thriving and the caliber of hockey was excellent.

There were no restrictions on the eligibility of Canadian juniors in those days. All teams were getting the top Canadian juniors who, under today's rules, would be ineligible. Vic Heyliger was actually using one player at Michigan with game experience in the NHL — Wally Maxwell, who had played briefly for the Toronto Maple Leafs. Maxwell was a member of a pee wee team in Winnipeg that beat us 30-1 and after the game kicked us out of the warming house. Other teams in the league had also recruited top Canadian juniors who couldn't foresee making it in the six-team NHL. Most of them were looking to the U.S. colleges for a better opportunity and as an alternative to thrashing around in the minor leagues for many years for little money just to await their chance at the NHL.

The WIHL was growing in popularity and prestige without any real signs of problems until early in the 1957-58 season when Mariucci took us on our annual Christmas trip to play four games against Colorado College and Denver. It was here that one of the most bitter feuds in college hockey history originated. It was a feud that eventually led to a breakup of the WIHL the following season and, indirectly, to the relocation of the NCAA tournament from the Broadmoor World Arena in Colorado Springs.

Our first game in Colorado was against Colorado College at the Broadmoor. Colorado College was loaded with older, experienced Canadian players. Among them were Red Hay, who later played with the Chicago Black Hawks, and Cy Whiteside, who became one of the International Hockey League's most feared fighters at the same time John Ferguson was playing in the league. Colorado was coached by Tom Bedecki, who later returned to Canada in an important government capacity as a sports advisor.

During the first period of the first game the Tigers came out and literally beat up our younger, less experienced Gopher squad. Mariucci was actually having a tough time getting the players out of the box and on to the ice. The next day the press reported that the Tigers battered the "smaller Gophers who were hardly in the game after the first 20 minutes." It was also reported that Whiteside had "flattened" two Gophers along the boards. Yet the two referees, who were from Colorado Springs, called only one penalty in the first period. It was on Minnesota's Marv Jorde, for high sticking. Jorde, the most placid player on the team, was just trying to protect himself.

Herb Brooks, the successful Gopher hockey coach, was getting his first lessons in the art of intimidation. He innocently posed a question to John between periods, asking what our young, little guys were doing playing against such an older, experienced squad. Our players were so nervous and upset that Jorde had put two contact lenses in the same eye. This wasn't discovered until the end of the next period. We had spent 10 minutes on our hands and knees in the dressing room looking for the lost contact lens before the discovery was made that they were both in the same eye.

To add to the punishment, the fans above the Gopher bench had been baiting Mariucci unmercifully. He turned and told them that they had better find a Canadian league to play in next year because he wasn't planning to bring his team back. John continued with his tirade after the game in which we were tromped 7-2.

The newspapers picked up the incident and printed it. Murray Armstrong, the Denver coach who was an innocent bystander, was apparently asked to comment on John's remarks about threatening not to schedule Colorado College the following season. Murray jokingly responded by saying that Mariucci was only a paper salesman in Minneapolis and was simply trying to explain away a bad loss.

When John read those remarks Sunday morning in the Denver airport, his wrath switched from the Colorado College hockey team to Murray Armstrong. It was the beginning of a bitter feud. If John didn't have any good reasons to get back at Murray from then on, he would think of something. The Canadian question later became the hottest issue. John's reasoning had either convinced everyone that the older Canadian must be legislated against or that it was best to be on John's side when the heavy debate started. Ultimately everybody in the league was convinced except Murray Armstrong. One by one, each member team withdrew from the WIHL. The WIHL dissolved and all the teams grouped together to form an informal league for the 1958-59 season.

The informal league was basically the same seven teams except with optional scheduling. Denver and Minnesota did not schedule each other. John had won his point, and a point for the good of the American-born player. The situation prevailed for several years before scheduling all teams became mandatory.

Murray, however, wasn't as vulnerable as some of the other teams in the league. Denver's Canadian players were somewhat younger than those on most of the other clubs. I casually mentioned to John that he shouldn't create too much a fuss because our Gopher squad had three Canadians. John responded by telling me that could be changed at any moment if I wasn't careful. John and Murray carried on the feud to the point to where it was instrumental in having the 1958 NCAA championships moved from the Broadmoor in Colorado Springs to Minneapolis.

An ironic climax came for the old WIHL in its last official game when we beat Colorado College two games in Minneapolis. That knocked CC out of the NCAA championships and put Denver in. The NCAA was scheduled for the University of Minnesota's Williams Arena with Denver and North Dakota representing the West.

Both Murray and John were great people, and no two, in my opinion, contributed more to American college hockey. Their personalities were direct opposites. John was a very gregarious Iron Ranger who liked his martinis and having a good time with his many friends in the college coaching ranks. Armstrong, on the other hand, was a conservative, reserved, non-drinking individual with the appearance of a Lutheran minister.

When Maroosh arrived on the scene, every level of hockey in Minnesota began to flourish. Within seven years the Gopher hockey team had progressed to where it out-drew the basketball team. The number of high school teams in the state expanded significantly, and the popularity of the sport began to blossom. John was a big factor in making hockey a major sport in Minnesota and at the university. These developments, along with his reputation with the Chicago Black Hawks, further enhanced his image as one of the most prestigious sport figures in Minnesota.

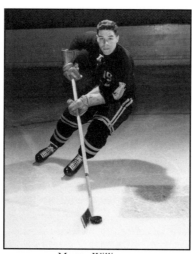

Murray Williamson

1960 WINTER OLYMPICS

SQUAW VALLEY, CALIFORNIA, FEBRUARY 19-28

(USA HOCKEY TEAMS RESULTS BOOK, 1920-1986)

The 1960 United States Olympic Team, scarcely considered as a possible Olympic winner, stunned the entire sports world by capturing the title at the Winter Games in Squaw Valley, CA. Inspirational leadership from captain Jack Kirrane, brilliant goaltending by Jack McCartan, scoring from the brother combination forwards - Christians and Cleary's, and strong defensive play by John Mayasich led the U.S. team to its first Olympic ice hockey championship.

Mayasich and McCartan, former Minnesota stars, and Harvard's Bill Cleary were late additions to the team. Their addition to the lineup proved to be the necessary talent needed to jell the team and lead it to close decisions over Canada and the Soviet Union and an undefeated record. Roger Christian, with eight goals, led Team USA in scoring, while Bill Cleary (7 goals, 7 assists for 14 points) and Mayasich (7-5--12) paced the points race.

Preliminary training camps for selection of players were held at Williams Arena, Minneapolis, and the Boston Arena. Western tryouts were under the guidance of John Mariucci, while Eastern selections were handled by Harry Cleverly. From the preliminary camps, 22 players were selected to attend the final training camp at the U.S. Military Academy at West Point, NY. Final training at the huge Army rink, under the tutelage of Jack Riley, began December 16. James Claypool managed the team.

Name	Hometown	College/Club
Roger Christian	Warroad, MN	Warroad Lakers
William Christian	Warroad, MN	Warroad Lakers
Robert Cleary	Cambridge, MA	Harvard
William Cleary	Cambridge, MA	Harvard
Eugene Grazia	W. Springfield, MA	Michigan State
Paul Johnson	W. St. Paul, MN	Rochester Mustangs
Jack Kirrane	Brookline, MA	Boston Olympics
John Mayasich	Eveleth, MN	Minnesota
Jack McCartan	St. Paul, MN	Minnesota
Robbert McVey	Hamden, CT	Harvard
Richard Meredith	Minneapolis, MN	Minnesota
Weldon Olson	Marquette, MI	Michigan State
Robert Owen	St. Louis Park, MN	Harvard
Rodney Paavola	Hancock, MI	Portage Lk Pioneers
Laurence Palmer	Wakefield, MA	Army
Richard Rodenhiser	Malden, MA	Boston University
Thomas Williams	Duluth, MN	Duluth Swans
Jack Riley	Medford, MA	*(Coach)
James Claypool	Duluth, MN	(Manager)
Ben Bertini	Lexington, MA	(Trainer)

JOHN MARIUCCI ERA

I only had the privilege of meeting Mr. Mariucci on one occasion. It was only a simple hello, and a handshake, but I remember it well. You know how it is when you meet someone famous, and you tell your friends about it later? Well, this was a different kind of experience. I didn't feel like I had to run out and tell anyone about it, I was just sort of happy that I finally got to meet the guy who started all this. This, what is this? This is one of the greatest traditions in the world of sports that we have in this country today, Minnesota Gopher Hockey. I was still in high school at the time when I met him, and had only heard about him from people who had heard of him. That one encounter, though, made me want to learn more about this man, and this institution from which he put on the map.

I can't pretend to write about a man I didn't know, but I can write about his contributions that he made to the game. I can also tell you about some of his wonderful stories, and the impressions he left upon so many people who were close to him. I didn't know how to tackle such a huge task as writing about the Godfather of Hockey. So, I just started interviewing people who knew him. One after another I learned more and more from these people about an incredible man that I wish I would've known.

I tried to talk to players, media personalities, family members, loved ones, coaches, teammates and significant people in his life who knew the real John Mariucci. I must say that it was fascinating, and I am envious of anyone that ever played with him, for him, or just got to listen to some of his famous stories. Gretchen, John's widow, let me borrow his scrapbooks and newspaper clippings about him when he passed away. From that information, along with hundreds of interviews from people close to hockey, I learned about John Mariucci. Now get ready for the feature presentation, the previews are over. This is the guy who started it all. Heeeeer'es Johnny!

In 1910, Joseph Moroni - a shoemaker, musician and the grandfather of John Mariucci, arrived in the then booming iron ore town of Eveleth, Minnesota, from the small town of Sigillo, Italy. His daughter Inez, married Edward Mariucci, whose family emigrated to Eveleth from Costacciaro - Sigillo's neighboring Italian village. Inez and Edward settled in a simple two-story house at 515 Adams Ave., a block from the fire hall. They had three children - Pauline, John, and Rose.

In the late 1920's tragedy struck. Edward Mariucci developed a mastoid in his brain, and died. His wife Inez was forced to raise the three children and several of their cousins by herself. She did so without welfare. She did so by cooking and washing clothes for people in town. She did so with John Mariucci's help. He often recalled the three-mile run he would make daily after school to the family's small farm on the outskirts of town. Here he would often gather vegetables, and poultry for his mother to cook for dinner.

He grew up on Hay Street, playing hockey with his neighbors, the Brimseks and Karakases. Some people referred to it as "Incubator Street," because it was said that there were so many nationalities living there, and every house had eight or nine kids. The kids would play hockey to stay out of trouble. They would try to emulate the Canadians who were imported there to play as entertainment for the miners. Some kids didn't even have skates, so they wore overshoes, and others used tree branches for sticks. John found his first pair of skates in a garbage can, and because he didn't have money to buy equipment, wrapped old magazines around his shins for pads.

Curt Brown wrote in the Pioneer Press that if the Iron Range was the cradle of U.S. hockey, then Mariucci was the man rocking it. Maroosh once described the Iron Range winters as a place "colder than a hooker's heart." John Mariucci, Nonny, The Old Roman, Maroosh, whatever you called him, he was a legend.

Doug Grow, a writer for the Star Tribune, summed it up well in his piece about Maroosh that came out shortly after John died. "There are those, in fact, who believe that to remember Mariucci as 'The Godfather of Minnesota Hockey' is to remember only a small part of this giant man. There was Mariucci, the man who gave so much of his time and energy to projects such as Camp Courage. There was Mariucci, the man who recited poetry and read classics. There was Mariucci, the man who could speak four languages. And there was Mariucci, the man who simply wanted others to smile. But what separated Mariucci from so many tough guys was his wit, intelligence, smile. And his heart. Mariucci wouldn't just knock you down. He'd pick you up too. And then he'd make you laugh.

"Through adversity John grew up through the depression, and aspired to great heights. He was a mans man, and often described as a Noble Roman. He was never one to shy away from a brawl, and took his share of licks. His face has often been referred to as a "Blocked punt," because it was so beat up. But underneath all those stitches, scars, and big ol' busted nose, was a teddy bear. But don't say that too loud, because that bear could really roar!"

John Mariucci

MARIUCCI'S HOCKEY CHRONOLOGY

<u>1939-40</u> - Mariucci is an All-American on the undefeated Gopher hockey team that won the national AAU title, and also played End on the Gopher football team under head coach, Bernie Bierman.

<u>1946</u> - Mariucci signs with the NHL's Chicago Blackhawks for $7,000, and turns down a $4,000 offer from the U of M to be their head hockey coach. He also takes a leave to serve in the Coast Gaurd, where he played hockey as well.

<u>Oct. 14, 1951</u> - Named coach of the Minneapolis Millers of the A.A.L.

<u>May 9, 1952</u> - Signs as the new Gopher hockey coach, replacing Doc Romnes.

<u>1953 & 1954</u> - The Gophers won WCHA titles but lost in the finals both seasons, to Michigan and RPI, respectively.

<u>Feb. 16. 1955</u> - Mariucci us named 1956 U.S. Olympic hockey coach for the games in Cortina, Italy. The team won the silver medal, losing only to the Soviet Union. Marsh Ryman, the U of M A.D., takes over the team in mid season as interim coach.

<u>May 26, 1966</u> - Mariucci ends his coaching career as Gophers coach after a long-standing personality conflict with athletic director Marsh Ryman. His Gophers record: 215-148-18 overall, and 154-125-13 in the WCHA. He is replaced by Glen Sonmor, a former teammate with the Minneapolis Millers.

<u>July 18, 1966</u> - Mariucci is named special assistant to general manager Wren Blair and chief scout of the North Stars, an NHL expansion franchise. He would later work under Lou Nanne, the North Stars GM, and a former Mariucci player.

<u>June 21, 1973</u> - Mariucci is a charter inductee to the U.S. Hockey Hall of Fame.

<u>March 8, 1977</u> - Mariucci is awarded the NHL's Lester Patrick Award for his contributions to U.S. hockey.

<u>March 2, 1985</u> - The hockey half Williams Arena is renamed Mariucci Arena in his honor, and it was declared John Mariucci Day in Minnesota by Governor Rudy Perpich.

<u>Sept. 12, 1985</u> - Mariucci is inducted into NHL's Hall of Fame.

<u>March 24, 1987</u> - John Mariucci dies at the age of 70, in a Minneapolis hospital. He is survived by his wife Gretchen, his two sisters Rose Ferroni and Paulline Ulasich, seven children, and five grandchildren.

PLAYER TRIBUTES

Maroosh in between Badger Bob and Herb Brooks

HERB BROOKS was quoted in the Star Tribune as saying, "In all social causes to better an institution, there's always got to be a rallying force, a catalyst, a glue, and a magnet, and that's what John was, for American hockey. The rest of us just filled in after him."

As coach, Mariucci also came up with good lines spontaneously. When a player played poorly, Mariucci once said: "Every day you play worse than the day before, and today you're playing like tomorrow."

Brooks, a victim of that line, reused it himself as coach. "He was like a father to me, we were very close," Brooks said. "He wasn't long on words, and didn't want to be everybody's buddy like some coaches try to be. John was an entirely different guy as a coach. You took care of yourself under John. He never called you to take care of you, or told you to go to class. His psychology of coaching was to take care of yourself, or get the hell out. You grew up pretty fast under John. He was a throwback, and was an entirely different coach than you'd see today. He was such a great guy. I remember the day they renamed the arena in his name. It was his happiest day, and such a memorable moment for him.

"At first I was scared to death of him. I was fresh out of high school at Johnson, where we had just won the state title over Southwest. I remember in practices my first year he used to call me Pete. For the longest time he never knew my name, and I was terrified of him.

"He wasn't against Canadians, he was just pro-American. This was in a day where there were no age restrictions, and very little restrictions other than they couldn't have turned pro yet.

"I patterned several aspects of my coaching after John. He was a pioneer and faced immense competition as a coach. When the '80 Olympic team won the gold, John said it was one more piece to the puzzle for American hockey. I shared these hopes, dreams and aspirations with John, and was proud of the fact that there were 12 of us from Minnesota on that team.

"St. Cloud was a very positive experience for me, and John was very influential in that endeavor as well. We felt that there were more kids in Minnesota than opportunities for them. He encouraged me to go up there for a year, get the program from division three to division one, raise money for the new rinks, and get them going in the right direction. Then I left. John was very much a visionary, and had a lot to do with my decision in going up there."

LOU NANNE was quoted once in the Star Tribune as saying, "When I first met him he asked me what I wanted to study. I told him I wanted to be a dentist. He said to me, 'You're supposed to knock people's teeth out, not put them in.'

"John was like my second father, we were very close. He treated me like his son, and was the most instrumental person in my life. John wasn't long on compliments. You knew he liked you when he gave you a lot of shit. He had fun with the guys all the time.

"I remember playing Murray Armstrong's Denver team that had all the Canadians on it. John used to hate playing them, and one time he made me carry a sign off the plane that read 'We're gonna fry Canadian bacon.'

"He would tease me about being the only Canadian on the team by saying at the banquets that he had a squad with 19 presidential candidates, and one for Prime Minister. He hated roller coasters, flying and heights. John figured it was every kid's obligation to play for the Gophers. He's done more for hockey than anyone in the country. He was a storyteller extraodinaire. He was also very special to my family, and even got my wife a green card so we could live here. I miss him a lot."

John Mayasich

ROGER ROVICK: "John was a character, and loved the Minnesota boys. He stayed in touch with all his players, and even came to my mother's funeral. That really meant a lot to me."

STANLEY S. HUBBARD: "John Mariucci was a man's man. He had a laissez faire attitude with the team. He would say, 'I don't care what you do, just don't get caught.' It was crazy. Guys wouldn't go to bed at night, they'd skip classes, smoke, and drink, but we still won. Maroosh was human. He was a dear friend, and a wonderful kind human being who was under a lot of pressure. He was a salty character, and a lot of fun, but he wasn't a Paul Bunyan above humanness. He had pressures on him from guys like Ike Armstrong, that no one knew about."

JOHN MAYASICH: "The first time I met him was in the locker room after we had won our fourth consecutive state high school hockey tournament. He was playing for the Millers at the time, and he came over to congratulate us.

"I didn't socialize with John. We respected each other as player and coach. He was a strong-willed man, and the only time I ever saw him cry was when we lost to RPI in the finals in 1954.

"He taught me a lot about defense, and helped my game a lot. He is solely responsible for the growth of hockey in Minnesota, and made it what it is today. He went with Minnesota kids, and fostered a type of nationalism against the Canadians. He typifies the state of the game of hockey. He was a great man, and I think there was a funny story every day with him.

Lou Nanne

DICK DOUGHERTY: "John was so much like Vince Lombardi. It wasn't so much losing a game under John, it was facing him afterwards. To face John after a loss was a lot worse than any loss itself. He was tough, and so intense. Our relationship lasted a long time, he was so dedicated. He got the most out of every player, and was one tough fellow. Romnes was a finesse coach, and Mariucci coached toughness and conditioning."

150

LARRY ROSS: "Everybody knew Maroosh, once you met him your life was never the same. He was brilliant. He was very bright, and never emphasized that fact about himself. He was an excellent coach for his era, and a great motivator as well. The kids really respected him a great deal."

LEN LILYHOLM: "He was a very special person in my life. He gave me the chance to play hockey where others counted me out because I was small. He was protective of me, and he was more than just a coach. He was a great motivator, and we were all over-achievers under him. There's no way we should've beaten the older junior Canadian players from other team, but we did.

"He's truly the leader of American hockey. He wouldn't let anyone know he was in pain until he died. He was tough. Underneath that big thug body of his was a kitten though. He was sensitive, intelligent, and had great wit."

MURRAY WILLIAMSON: "Every weekend was an adventure with him, he was so colorful. He was my best friend, and we were very close. He was a tough old bird, and didn't take any crap from anyone. He had a lot of clout in the league. Now it's a totally different era. The guys like Armstrong and Heyliger, which used to be the backbone of college hockey, are gone. Now the coaches are totally different, they're a bunch of pussycats."

Doug Woog

GENE CAMPBELL: "John was a person that left you alone. That's what I enjoyed about his coaching style, he gave you the liberty to play the game as well as you could. Obviously the game got a little erroneous at times with him, but generally he would let you enjoy the game. John had a sense of humor that was creative, and he made it easy for the guys to play for him."

DOUG WOOG: "Maroosh wasn't a great X - and - O guy, he just said go out and

151

work hard, and be tough. He was a promoter, but expected kids to come to the U out of obligation and respect. Nowadays we're looking at the best left-handed defenseman in the ninth grade, the size of his feet, how big his dad is, and our vision is considerably bigger than it was back then. We have to remain competitive with the other schools recruiting here. But, it all started with John, and he was a legend."

Jack McCartan

JACK McCARTAN: "John was always a big part of my life. He was the kingpin of hockey, and you just looked forward to spending that time of the day with him. Everyone looked up to him, and we had so much fun together. He was a magnetic guy to be around. I remember so many funny things about him. I remember standing in the shower with him after practices, and exchanging punches to the shoulder...God that would hurt! I can also remember fondly going to Chicago for games at the Stadium to see the Hawks. John would have tickets all lined up for us, and we would just walk in like we owned the place. Twelve years after he played there, all the fans wanted his autograph, and they would yell "Marooooosh..." as he walked by. He never wore a coat either He could never figure out why the hell people would wear coats, even in the winter time. He was a tough old bastard. He spoke 'Range', and was a real Minnesotan. He was just tougher than nails, God he was tough! He was the original architect for Minnesota hockey, and he had a vision of what he wanted to do with the Minnesota kids. I really miss him, he was quite a guy."

DICK MEREDITH: "He was the closest to me of any person in my life other than my dad. He was so personable, and so damn funny. He was off the cuff, and such a class act. He would go to bat for you, and always be there for you no matter what. He was caring, soft, but so damn rough around the edges. He loved his body, and loved to trade punches with you nude, in the showers. We were front page news back then, and his picture was in the paper at least once a week because he had an opinion on everything. He was a reporter's dream. I wish I would've kept a journal about every day of his life, there was so much incredible stuff about this guy.

"He used to say to me, 'Meredith, you're the equal of any man on that ice, as long as you hold your stick. As soon as you drop your stick, the odds really shift.' I remember the 1954 championships. We were heavily favored to beat RPI, and in overtime we lost the game. John was so upset that he actually cried. I remember after the game all the players huddling around him to shield him from the press and their cameras."

Maroosh, Shutte, Petroske, Yackel and Anderson

MEDIA TRIBUTES

BOB UTECHT: "John is gone now and at peace. The suffering is over, the mountains have been climbed and conquered. Minnesota and the entire nation is richer because this lovable guy walked and skated among us. It's a special dimension, hard to describe, but easy to feel.

"Perhaps as he rests and looks down he might well be saying, 'Pool all those tears you shed for me into a giant Zamboni and run them across the ice. The kids deserve a bit smoother surface for the stops and starts and turns and pivots. And please, no slap shots.'

"We were students together at the University way back when. We were dear friends for over 30 years, and we did over 80 speeches together. To know John Mariucci was to know someone who was always looking out for somebody else's good. He would give everything he had, including himself, to help someone in need. He was quite a man, and he would've been a great politician."

JOE SCHMIT: "You kind of knew you were talking to a legend when you spoke to him, and you could just feel the respect that he had. There was a real aura about him, and everyone just loved him."

PAT REUSSE: "He was one of the greatest guys that ever lived. He was such a character, and funnier than hell. I loved him, and loved shooting the shit with him at Stars games together. He used to always razz me about not covering hockey in the paper, he was a classic."

JOHN GILBERT: "When I first covered Gopher Hockey for the Minnesota Daily, Maroosh was still coaching. I remember walking up to him timidly for the first time at a Gopher practice. I was terrified because he was like a God. He welcomed me to the team, and made me feel like I belonged. We had a great rapport from that point on. There was hardly anyone covering the team at that point in the mid 60's, so he welcomed me warmly. He had a great capacity for his expression not changing. He always had that twinkle in his eye, and you always knew he had something up his sleeve."

JEFF PASSOLT: "John was like a father to a lot of guys. He set a tone that lasted beyond his tenure as coach, and people had a standard they wanted to live up to because of him. He was determined to make sure that more kids got a better opportunity than he did, and gave them a chance. I think with John gone, the state of the game is different. He was the guy you didn't dare upset about any issue of hockey. He was the Godfather, and watched over the game. I know that because of the seed he planted long ago, and the fire he started to burn in people like my father long ago, he created an aura that made the game bigger through the trickle down theory. I'm grateful for what he did for hockey in Minnesota, and it even got me through college at St. Cloud on a scholarship."

Dick Dougherty

STEVE CANNON: "As kids we looked up to John in Eveleth, and I had so much fun working with him at the North Stars. I was doing radio, and he was the assistant GM. He was like a second father to me. I was with him just days before he died. I went to see him in the hospital, and he was very sick. But, he started to tell a classic Mariucci story, and he just came to life. He battled that terrible sickness, and was in incredible pain, but yet never complained about anything until the day he died. I cried that day, as I knew it would be the last time I would see my old friend."

TOM VANNELLI: "I had an impression of a monster when I first met him, a real-life living legend. I always got the impression that if there was anything at all that would help hockey in the state, he'd do it."

CHARLEY HALLMAN: "Behind his gruff exterior, punctuated by scar tissue and a voice that sounded much like a scoop shovel scraping over a concrete floor, beat the heart of a gentle man who was not afraid to show his love for people. He also loved hockey — so much that he willingly invested as much of himself in the sport as he withdrew from it. There's never been a better guy than Maroosh. He was fabulous. His children were Herbie, Wooger, Louie, and Glen. His bastard stepchildren were Badger Bob, and Brad Buetow. He was a character."

DON RILEY: "If I ever had to walk down a dark alley in the South Bronx, and could pick one person to be with, I'd pick John Mariucci over anybody. He was fearless. I never heard a bad word about him in all my years as the Gopher beat reporter. He had a vision about hockey, and people used to think he was crazy to think that Minnesotans would play professional hockey one day. He predicted that there would be Minnesota kids in the NHL, he predicted that there would be arenas all over the state, and he forecasted that hockey would shift from the north to the metro area.

"You could be up all night with Maroosh. We had a lot of dinners that turned into breakfasts. He could tell stories like no one else, and his energy was unbelievable. I never saw him lose his sense of humor. He was a fantastic guy. There's never been anyone like him in the world. The sports community was in awe of him, and he made you want to cover hockey. He made hockey fans out of people that had hated hockey, he was magic.

"He had a football mind, and had a belief that it was a contact sport. He didn't have much to do with guys that weren't going to sacrifice their bodies. Now it's the fastest game in town. We used to see more of an emphasis on punishing the other players under Maroosh. He would make the other team pay if they dared go into the corner with a Gopher, and today it's more finesse hockey than Maroosh would've cared for."

Jim Mattson

155

GRETCHEN

"We met in a restaurant when one of John's buddies came over to me and said that there was someone that wanted to meet me. I looked over at him, and didn't know who the heck he was, but figured he must have been famous or something. I asked his friend, 'Say, that's not Gorgeous George is it?'

"He was a character, very brilliant, had an insatiable quest for knowledge, a great sense of humor, great memory, and there really wasn't anything he couldn't do. He spoiled me rotten as well. He did all the cooking, sewing, laundry, and house work. I don't think I ever cooked a meal for him. His favorite thing was garlic. He loved to cook pasta at the Mariucci Fiesta at Camp Confidence. He gave so much of himself to help get that camp going, it meant a lot to him.

"He was very intellectual. He was very impatient. He loved Europe, and we traveled there many times. He was very interested in religion. All religions fascinated him, and he was so curious about so many different things. He loved crystal, martinis, and going to see his mother. He had a great singing voice, and even sang 'Oh Danny Boy' on WCCO one time.

"A big misconception about him was that he only loved hockey. With me he never talked hockey. He'd rather talk about politics, language, government, geography, or just about anything.

"He was my teddy bear, a champion of the underdog, and I just adored him. My life was an adventure with him, we were so close. I really miss him. He used to call me 4-5 times a day, just to say Hi, and that he missed me.

"When I told him he was my best friend, he would tell me I was his only friend. He didn't really hang out with the guys that much, sure everybody in the world knew him, but he insisted on being with me all the time. We just enjoyed each other's company, and he was my mentor in life.

"He used to own a paper company called Gopher Paper Co. He wasn't the best businessman in the world, and would be the first to admit it. He used to hire all the Gophers to work for him, and eventually it led to the end of his company. He was the assistant GM with the North Stars, and did a lot of scouting there until he died.

"He loved to fight. One time in a bar he was walking to the counter, and he overheard some drunk softball players. One said to another, 'Hey, let's get rid of that old man and move in on his girl...' John heard them, and yelled out 'Who the hell called me an old man?' He then ran after the two, and chased them out into the parking lot. As they were running out she heard one of the guys yell, 'Oh my God, that's John Mariucci...We're going to die, HELP!' He caught one of them, and really let him have it. He came back in the bar where the others in the group were gathered, and said 'I don't mind you making a play at my wife, but dammit don't ever call me an old man!' Then being the character he was, he was proud of himself for having one more funny story he could tell the guys next time they were together.

"Another time John was out late, and it was really late by the time he got home. I was furious at him, and when he walked in the door I threw a vacuum at him. Only I missed and hit poor Scotty Bowman in the head. I didn't know what to do, so we all just laughed about it. I could never stay mad at him, no matter how hard I tried.

"I can remember the arena dedication well. That was without a doubt his proudest moment. He was so happy, I remember he bought a new camel hair sport coat for the occasion, and got all dressed up for the big day. He said afterwards to some people, ' Now that this is my arena, we have to clean this damn place up.' Then he went to get some ice cream, and when they told him how much it was he said, 'The hell if I'm paying for this, this is my damn arena now!'

"John grew up on the Iron Range in Eveleth. It was a really culturally diverse area, and John's family was fresh off the boat from Italy. John used to call his mother, 'Ma.' They were really poor, and John's mom used to volunteer John's services for the neighbors to help out. One time she had him dig a well, but they couldn't afford the pump so she made him fill it back up. He used to love going home to ma, and cooking and telling stories.

"He was so stubborn too. One time John Jr. was shoveling the driveway, and when he came in John said 'That's not how you shovel the driveway...' He then went out there in his bathrobe and socks and shoveled the entire thing over again.

"They threw away the mold when they made him. He was so good to me, I just miss him terribly. I miss the conversations we would have to all hours of the night. He never complained about anything, and he could read my mind about so many things. There were so many people that wanted that last piece of him when he was dying, and he never refused a guest. He was so sick, but wanted to see all his friends before he died. He used to take morphine to ease the pain of his prostate cancer so he could get up to see his old friends. He died at the age of 70. His funeral was beautiful, and they even played the Battle Hymn of the Republic for him. Afterwards the funeral procession went all around the city by hockey arenas on the way to the cemetery. Outside the arenas, kids lined up playing hockey to pay tribute to him.

"He had such a unique chiseled face, he was very handsome. I'll never get that recipe again for an Italian like that, it was one great love story ."

-- Gretchen Colletti

MARIUCCI TRIBUTES

Don Clark

Dave Brooks, Lou Nanne and Mariucci

157

MARIUCCI TRIBUTES

BOBBY DILL: The late Hall of Famer, when asked about Mariucci, was once quoted in the Star Tribune as saying, "He was simply the bravest, guttiest man in sports. I played against, or have seen all of the greatest enforcers and game breakers in the last 45 years. No question for sheer competitive ferocity, Mariucci and Eddie Shore were the two all time greats. Strong men backed down to them. They played every game like it was the seventh game of the Stanley Cup."

BRUCE TELANDER: ('56 TEAM MANAGER) "When John coached, it was always a treat to watch his press conferences. He used to invite the press into the locker room, and he would give them their interviews as he did chin ups from the steam-pipes, only in the nude.

"He set the tone for Gopher Hockey. He had a vision of playing the Minnesota kids, and Woog has followed it well. John's attitude about recruiting was simple. Kids should come to the U because they were Minnesotans, and it was their obligation. Because of that, George Lyon and I started the Blueline Club to help fund raise, and recruit kids. We were very close friends until the day he died. He was a one of a kind."

Len Lilyholm

BERNIE BIERMAN: Then Gopher football coach Bernie Bierman when asked about John, was quoted in the Star Tribune as saying, "I believe I have the only lineman in America who can extract people's teeth with his fists on the line of scrimmage."

BURTON JOSEPH: "I miss him. He was a citizen for the people, and a real legend. His work for Camp Confidence was amazing. His lovely wife Gretchen was a real strength for him as well. I think we all miss him."

RON CARON, GM of the St. Louis Blues, when asked about Mariucci, was quoted in the Star Tribune as saying, "There's sadness, not just here, but throughout the NHL, North America and the world of hockey. He had a lot of friends. He didn't hide what he had to say. He faced reality in life and in sickness and he never asked for sympathy. When he was defeated, he always said, 'I'll come back and beat you next time.' I loved that about him."

BOBBY SMITH: (NORTH STARS CENTER) "He was a great man. His great personality and great sense of humor was infectious with all the guys on the team. I'll never forget him."

PAUL GIEL: (UNIVERSITY OF MINNESOTA ATHLETIC DIRECTOR) "I always got a kick out of Mariucci. He'd tease me about not being tough enough to play hockey, but I had a great deal of respect for him. Hockey flourished in Minnesota because of him, and his vision for the Minnesota kid."

DR. V.A. NAGOBADS: "I miss his big heart. It will be a long time before we see another man of his stature. He put a lot of heart in his work, and I loved him. I spent a lot of days with him at his bedside before he died. We were very close, and I miss him very much indeed."

DAVE PETERSON: "There's no question that Mariucci's time, effort, drive, speaking, and persuasion is the reason Minnesota enjoys the successful hockey programs from mites to Gophers.

"John was also a good hockey player. As a goalie, it was refreshing to know that he was there in front of you. He was a tough, talented player, and a great skater as well. He was a tough, colorful, and loyal guy, and I miss him. He was a man's man, and just great for hockey."

DAVE FERRONI: "He told me once that you have to know when to get out of this game. He said that he could've had the chance to own a bar and restaurant downtown just for letting them use his name. But, he took the $8,000 a year to coach the Gophers at the 'U'. He said he later wound up kissing Lou Nanne's ass for peanuts with the North Stars, when he could've retired with the bar. He told me to never be a bum, to get a job, a family, and have fun doing it.

"I remember him arguing with my mother (John's sister) at my wedding rehearsal dinner over who was going to get to use their spaghetti sauce. Of course my mom won that battle.

"As his nephew, I was proud of him, he was my idol and the guy I respected most in life. John had respect, and was the team policeman. He never held a grudge, and he looked after his players. I will say though that he was the world's worst businessman. He would hire all his hockey buddies to work for him, and he practically gave everything away. But he had fun, and did a lot of great things for his friends.

"He was a great storyteller, very interesting, knowledgeable, loved history, was very proud of his ethnic heritage, was the master of sarcasm, made people laugh, was very classy, was the center of attention wherever he was, and just being around him was such a secure feeling. I miss him."

BOB RIDDER: "I miss him terribly, he was the best friend I ever had. It was a strange relationship, a kid from Harvard and another from Eveleth. We complimented each other, and had a ball together though. He was the outstanding man in the hockey world, so much optimism, greatness, and brightness of a man. He was a sincerely great man. He was a character, and had the capacity to understand who could play the game. He was wonderful for hockey in Minnesota, and anything that promoted hockey for the Americans, he would do. He was so colorful, and could get the press to absolutely eat right out of his hand."

AMO BESSONE: "We had a pretty close relationship. I knew him way back when he was in college. We had five kids from Eveleth playing on my college team at Illinois, so I'd see John from time to time. Also, the Blackhawks trained in Champaign, so I'd see John when he was in town for that as well. I used to go stay with him in Minneapolis, and I loved doing things with him. He did more for hockey in the United States than anyone in history. He was an innovator, and he could motivate his kids to play doubly hard. He had a heart of gold; he was a one of a kind.

"After every game we would get together in Minneapolis either at his house for spaghetti and wine, or we would go out to a restaurant.

"We used to yell at each other across the ice in those days. Our benches were separated by the scorer's table, and we would talk about this and that throughout the game. People couldn't believe it. We would be talking about going out after the game during the middle of the damn game. It was such fun coaching against him.

"When Maroosh was having problems with the A.D. (Marsh Ryman) up there about coaching, he handled it like a true gentleman. But he got a raw deal from that damn A.D. That son of a bitch fired the two greatest coaches in Minnesota history: John Mariucci, and John Kundla, the basketball coach.

"He was one of the toughest guys ever to play hockey, but he was just a big teddy-bear. I remember the Black Jack Stewart fight in Detroit. They would fight so often that they would set up ground rules for each other. John would say that the first person to grab a shirt, lost. The referees would just sit back and enjoy it. They let 'em go until they couldn't stand up anymore. Gordie Howe told me theirs was the most brutal fight he'd ever seen in his life."

"I used to enjoy going up to Camp Confidence with him as well. He enjoyed those kids and did so much for them."

WILLARD IKOLA: "Every day was an adventure with him. God he hated to fly, and would get drunker than hell every time we had to go up. I remember one time he told me that he hated to go into bars because everyone wanted to see just how tough the mighty John Mariucci was, and he was constantly getting into fights wherever he went. He used to say that he would have to fight his way out of another one last night. I owe him a lot, and he got me the Edina coaching job as well."

TOM IVAN (BLACKHAWKS PRESIDENT): "He was a great player, competitor, and leader. He had more ability than people gave him credit for, and he was a great guy to have on your team. He was such a colorful guy in the locker room, keeping everyone laughing all the time. He had a great sense of humor, and such a fun personality. It was pleasure to know him. When he was on the ice, everybody had to step up a notch and be a competitor. He would help the younger guys a lot, and would protect them as well. He was a credit to hockey, and to the USA. I can't say enough good things about him."

WALTER BUSH: "He used to say to his players 'Everyday you're playing a little bit worse, and already your playing like it's tomorrow...'

"I sought advice from him all the time when I was running the Stars. He could read people really well, and never took advantage of anybody. But, a lot of other people took advantage of him, and that bothered me.

"He never took care of himself, and his death was so unnecessary. He was so tough and afraid of doctors that he never said anything about his pain that he was having. Who knows, maybe it would've been prevented. I really miss him, he was a one of a kind."

DON CLARK: "I miss him, and I miss talking to him. We knew each other for over 50 years, and were close. He had an opinion on everything, and he had such a wonderful mind. He was a good defenseman, good puck-handler, and a pretty good skater, but shot off the wrong leg.

"I can remember when he would skate the puck up to the blue line, and if there weren't enough people hollering and rooting for him, he would turn around and make a big circle around the net and do it again. He would do this two or three times if necessary to get the fans excited. He would then make an end-to-end rush, usually getting a score.

"He did more for hockey than any one man in history. He was so colorful, and drew more people to him than anyone I had ever seen. Everyone wanted his autograph, and wanted to just shake his hand. He was a newspaper man's dream come true."

BUD WILKINSON (GOPHER GOALIE 1931-34): "I was at the University before John, but we played together for a time. I was a goal guard on the team, and played football and golf as well. John was a fine player, and a very nice gentleman."

BUTCH NASH: (GOPHER FOOTBALL TEAMMATE) "I played football with John in the '30's when it was $25 a quarter to go to the U. He was a great hockey player as well as football player. I remember him being a tough old son of a gun on the field. He was a tough hitter, and had a low center of balance. He was an excellent player, and really quick off the line. He was an important part of our offense in those days because we ran the single wing, and didn't pass much. Defensively, he was tough as nails on that end. You couldn't knock him down very easily. We played together, as opposite ends.

"I think the pros made a fighter out of him, because in college he was a finesse skater. Bernie Bierman really liked John, and he was one of his favorites on the team. John was like everyone's big brother on the team. He was a good, hard-nosed player, and very likable."

BRAD BUETOW: "Maroosh was like a dad to me, and steered me in the right direction. He had a great sense of humor and when he talked, people listened. He had a lot of wisdom, and saw the whole picture. I mean he was, and always will be, Mr. Hockey Minnesota.

"There's no question that John Mariucci made a dramatic statement on amateur hockey by refusing to play Denver on the basis that they had all the Canadians on their team. He stuck by his guns when it came to the Minnesota kid."

Bob Johnson, Ken Yackel and Dick Meredith

BILL MOSIENKO (BLACKHAWK TEAMMATE): "I played with Maroosh in Chicago in the 40's. John was a tremendous person, and I don't think even he knew his own strength. He loved to fight, and one time he told me that he was afraid that some time he might hit someone so hard that he'd kill them. That's how powerful he was. John was like our father, and he took great care of all of us. Whenever one of us would get in a fight, he would immediately step in to take care of us. He was a rough, tough guy, and fellas got out of his way when he came through. He'll always be a legend in Chicago, but even more so in Minnesota. He was the one Minnesota has to thank for bringing hockey there after the war. His contribution to the game was incredible, and Minnesotans should be thankful for that.

"He was quite a lady's man too, and when we'd go out for beers they would always give us free food because they liked him so much. He was so popular in Chicago, everyone just loved him. He used to do a radio show, and he was a great ambassador for the city. He used to run around with Al Capone's boys on occasion as well. I remember when he used to bring his Gopher players to watch our games after he had retired. He was so proud of them, and he would show them off to Chicago. But never for too long, as he would have to catch that late train home to Minneapolis. He had quite a following in Chicago. He had a lot of contacts, and the fans loved him. He spoke at banquets, hospitals and he was a real celebrity.

"He was also a great cook. One time he cooked spaghetti for all of us, and he got too close to the stove, and singed off most of his hair and eyebrows. Maybe that's why he was bald for so long.

"I remember one time a guy smashed his stick over Maroosh's back. John just turned around like nothing happened, smiled, then beat the living hell out of him.

"He was fun, so enjoyable to be around, caring, a great friend, and I will always remember John Mariucci for as long as I live."

JOHN KUNDLA ('U' BASKETBALL AND MINNEAPOLIS LAKERS COACH):

"We were the two Johns at the University. I first played basketball for the Gophers from 1936-1939. I coached the Minneapolis Lakers from 1947-1959, where we won six championships in 12 years. Then I was the basketball coach at the 'U' from 1959-1969. We each had our own programs in our own sports, but we both promoted the University first. We had a ball together, and often traveled around the state together to promote the University to small towns.

"Maroosh was a character, no doubt it. He was so damn funny. We would travel together around the state, and he would speak on why kids should play hockey. Then I would speak and say 'Yeah, play hockey if you love blood and violence. Come play a real man's sport, basketball instead.' He was the reason we have amateur hockey in the state, and he was so influential and supportive of hockey for all the kids here.

"He was a great cook of Italian food. He was one heck of a guy, a great athlete, and represented the U of M better than anyone. He was a great friend, and I miss him a lot. He waited two years before he told me he had cancer. He was so tough, he never complained about anything. He was so strong. I bet he could hit a golf ball 400 yards. His wrists were like rocks. He used to call Canadians, 'Canuck wetbacks.' He also said it was a mistake to put the Hall of Fame in Eveleth, because not enough people would get to see it up there.

"John and I were roommates at Lake Mille Lacs our freshman year of college together. We worked road construction together, as a lot of college kids did at that time. We used to call him 'Honest John.' He used to bring my Laker players to Blackhawks games when he was playing.

"One time Amo Bessone was in town with Michigan State, and they beat the Gophers in their game. After the game, Maroosh had him over for dinner. John got up to get Amo a scotch, and just before he handed it to him, he punched him in the nose and said 'Why the hell did you beat me tonight?'

"When he won the Big Ten Championship one year, I gave him a bedpan with horse shit in it as his trophy. He was so speechless, he just took it and threw it out the Cooke Hall window.

"For an incentive one time, he told his players that for every stitch they got, he would give them two dollars.

"He once told the great Gopher football player, Bobby Bell, that he would be a great goalie, because he had quick hands and great agility. So one day after practice he suited him up and let him play. After practice Bell was beaten up, and said 'To hell with this, I'll stick to football.' I never let my basketball players go near Mariucci after that out of fear that he would get one of them on the ice and kill him or something."

SCOTT BJUGSTAD, former Gopher, was quoted in the Star Tribune as saying: "I feel really indebted to him. I've been told he was the guy who was pushing for the Stars to draft me (in 1981). He knew Minnesota kids could compete with everyone else and he really was behind us. I don't think American players would be in the league if not for him. He was a great man."

PAT MICHELETTI: "He was friends of our family, and we just loved him. I got to present him with the game puck after the WCHA finals once. That was a real highlight for me."

Maroosh at the '56 Olympics, with Dick Meredith,
Gene Campbell and Wendy Anderson.

GARY GAMBUCCI: "John was a legend. He was such a colorful character. He was a caricature of himself. He had that old hat, that bow-legged walk, and was just a classic guy.

"I remember before and after every flight we went on he'd have his customary three martinis, because he hated to fly. He would walk up and down the aisles and give guys 'Nobbies' with his pipe.

"Silence from John meant approval he never complimented anyone. He could make you feel like two cents or a million bucks with one look. He was a character, and I miss him.

"My uncle Andre was a WCHA referee for over 20 years, and he and John used to always argue on the ice when games were going on. John would call Andre a filthy homer, and Andre would give him hell in return. Always though, after the game they would go out together for drinks together like nothing had happened."

NEAL BROTEN: "He was a character. When he walked into a room, everyone lit up. He could really turn on a crowd. He was so positive, and full of energy. I miss him, and all his antics. He would always come to the rink and say, 'How ya doing

Mrs. Broten?' He was such a joker, and would always harass all the fellas on the Stars. He was also very sincere, but a tough bastard. I mean just look at his face, that guy took a punch or two in the noggin. He did so much for Minnesota hockey. It's not only the stuff back then, it comes out every day with all of us in Minnesota today. It's like he's still working, even though he's gone."

DAVE SNUGGERUD: "I remember when he came with us on our trip to Alaska, and my stomach hurt from laughing so much at his stories. I was in awe of him."

PAUL BROTEN: "My parents just loved him. He did so much for hockey. What a guy, you can't say enough about him. Even though he was old, he was still one of the guys. He would tell us stories, and the guys were in absolute awe of him. It's incredible what he did for amateur hockey, and his name on the arena is proof. I don't think there will be anyone like him ever again. I was at the arena dedication and the celebration after, and it was incredible to see how many people looked up to him. I'll always remember that whenever he saw you, he'd shake your hand."

JOE MICHELETTI: "No one did more for the American in hockey than John. There will never be another like him."

MIKE ANTONOVICH: "He wanted only the best for Minnesota kids, and he made us realize that life isn't always fair. He never would have put up with this damn Tier II tournament we see today either. He said that not everyone deserves to get to the top. The guys who are on top deserve to be there because of hard work, and they worked a little harder than the other guy. I think John made people realize that they could be hockey players, and that they could go to the next level, whatever it was. He was about creating opportunity for Minnesota kids. If he would've been GM of the North Stars, he would've brought a lot more Minnesota kids into the NHL today than there are right now."

BILL BUTTERS: "Maroosh was like E.F. Hutton -- when he said Gopher Hockey, people listened. He had instant credibility, and respect from all the coaches too."

GLEN SONMOR: "It's so hard to believe he's gone sometimes. He was a one of a kind, all right. He seemed so indestructible. He was the toughest son of a bitch I ever knew. He liked fighters, that's why he liked me. I really miss him. He was just one hell of a guy.

"I played with Maroosh in 1949 with the Millers. He finished his career there, and I was just starting mine. It's been a Godsend, and a blessing in my life to have met John. He was always there to help me out, especially when I lost my eye. I was 26, and playing a game in Pittsburgh at the time, and John was there to help me through it. He called me in the hospital, and told me to come back to Minnesota to coach his freshman team. He said not to worry about the injury, and that everything would be fine. He literally took me by the scruff of my neck, and made me enroll at the U. He went and talked to Professor Lou Keller, and talked him into letting me enroll in his class late in the term. I will always be grateful to him.

"He used to tell me that I was the only Canadian he could find that had finished high school. He was proud of me for going to college, and I was proud of him. At the time he was in the NHL, he was the lone American playing. That says a lot about him, and he was captain of his team too.

He told me, 'Glen, If we don't give these kids a chance to play, promote the Minnesota high school tournament, and get these kids as accomplished as the Canadian players, they'll have no place to go when they're finished, and the program will die.' So he had a clause put in at the U that said the Canadians who were older and were getting paid couldn't play for Minnesota. He promoted the Minnesota kids, and he figured the Gophers would take their lumps at first, but he'd get the program on its feet."

Sonmor reminisced about the famous "Pony Line" in Chicago with Doug and Max Bentley, and Bill Mosienko. "They were all about 5-7 and 150 pounds, but Maroosh protected them like their mother. They were great little players, and the other teams picked on them. I later played with Max Bentley, and used to ask him about Maroosh. Max said it took just one time around the league until everybody knew to leave us alone, or they would have to face John. There was one guy, though, that challenged Maroosh -- Black Jack Stewart. He loved to play Chicago, and used to run over and smack around the Bentleys on purpose, just to razz John up. Sure enough, John would jump the boards, and take off after him to protect the little guys. God, the crowds used to love the Detroit-Chicago game because they knew they were in for a treat. Even the referees weren't stupid enough to break up that fight. They would fight for a good 20 minutes at a time, and I mean it was a fight. In those days you could come off the bench, throw your gloves and get dirty. It was great. That was when hockey was fun.

"I remember so many fond stories about him, and with him. He used to take us to games in Chicago at the Stadium and just walk us right in, never paying. They loved him there, and he was a legend with the fans. I remember walking downtown Chicago with Maroosh one time, and saw two cabbies walking towards us. The one turned to the other and said, 'Hey that's John Mariucci, he fights for the Hawks...' Yes sir, he was one hell of a bruiser, and they loved him. I miss that old son of a bitch."

Maroosh was an "Iron-Man," playing offensive and defensive end for Bernie Bierman.

MARIUCCI MEMORIES

Maroosh battling Black Jack Stewart in the famous Chicago brawl that was the NHL's longest fight, lasting nearly a half an hour.

AMO BESSONE, FORMER MICHIGAN STATE COACH AND LIFE TIME FRIEND OF MAROOSH: "One time when I was coaching at Michigan State, we were leading Minnesota 5-0 in the first period. John was so disgusted with his team that he pulled the goalie in the first period. He went out and had a smoke, and figured that if the team wasn't going to play in front of his goalie, he'd give him a rest. Well, it turns out they scored. So he did it again. He did this all throughout the game, and they finally tied it up. I was madder than hell that he was doing this. I mean it was unheard of to pull your goalie in the first period. I remember the game was tied 5-5 and he had his goalie pulled. Then, with about a couple seconds left, a Gopher was set up behind the net. He had nothing to do with the puck, so he flipped it up in the air. The puck bounced off my goalie's neck and plopped in the goal to win the game. I was madder than hell at him for that one. I told him that after that win, he really owed me one.

"Maroosh and I went out for dinner and drinks at a coaches convention one time. We were staying in a hotel that night, and I was rooming with Vic Heyliger. That night after we got home, the phone rang at about three in the morning. It was John, and he says 'Emil' — he always called me Emil — 'Come down here right away and bring me a kimono.' Now who the hell's got a Kimono? I didn't know what the hell he was doing. So he says, 'I'm in trouble, come help me!' So, I went down the hall and found him in an empty room that was being redecorated. He was stark naked. He said 'I think somebody rolled me.' Now in those days if you got rolled, that meant that somebody stole your money and clothes. So I asked him who the hell could roll a gorilla? I gave him a raincoat to wear, and we went back to bed. I asked him why the hell he was out there, and he said, 'I had to go to the bathroom, and I went out the wrong door. When I realized it, the door slammed shut behind me. I was too embarrassed to call the bell boy, and I couldn't remember where the hell your room was.' He was damn lucky that he found an open room, because there were people walking down the halls. It was crazy, he was bouncing from floor to floor buck naked, looking for someplace to hide.

"One time we were together at a coaching convention in Miami. We were roasting John really good. So I turned to Jimmy Selfi, the coach at RPI, and told him that when John went up to rebut our roast, we should walk out on him. Sure enough John gets up to the podium, and he sees us leaving. He got all mad because he couldn't roast us back, and he yells out 'EMIL, you son of a bitch, get your ass back here right now!' I turned to him, and I said, 'John, the name is AMO, not Emil,' and I walked out laughing hysterically. He was furious at me for weeks.

"One time I had a party at my house after a game. We always would have parties with the coaches after the games on the Saturday of the two-game series. So one night at a party, I was making a pitcher of martinis for John. I used one shot of gin and three of vermouth. John came in, tasted it, and says 'Jesus Christ Emil, you got the drink ratios all backwards!' Then he took the bottle of gin and poured it into the mix, just the way he liked it. So, he drank it, and about a hour later no one knew where John was. I got worried, so I went outside to look for him. There, down the block, was John with his empty pitcher in his hand, looking for my house. I asked him what the hell he was doing out there, and he told me he had to use the bathroom, but went out the wrong door again.

"There were these two Michigan referees that John used to just hate. You see back then, the referees were paid by the teams as employees, and they were real homers. Well, one time my referees were sick, and I had to get some replacements. So I called Vic Heyliger at Michigan and asked for the phone numbers of his referees. I got a hold of them and they agreed to officiate the game. Before the game against the Gophers, I told the referees to not come on the ice until just a few minutes before game time. So, the game is just about to start, and out come my referees. John took one look at them and screams, 'Oh no you son of a bitch Emil! You can't do this to me! You can't hire these guys to buy this game dammit!' I thought he was going to have a stroke right there. All I could do was laugh as he yelled at me across the ice. I couldn't even look at him, I was laughing so hard."

MURRAY WILLIAMSON: "Maroosh? Hell, every weekend was an adventure with him. He used to have a contract out on him by the mafia in Chicago at one point when he was with the Hawks. He used to associate with Lucky Luciano, and some of Capone's boys. Capone told them to forget about the contract because he was such a local celebrity in the Windy City."

DON RILEY: "In Chicago John used to play on the Blackhawks with two little guys named the Bentley Brothers. Their dad told Maroosh that if he protected his sons, he'd give him a nice bonus at the end of the season. At the end of the year Maroosh had kept his word by protecting the two, and was excited to see his bonus. Mr. Bentley thanked him, and cordially presented John with a big old cow. John, in amazement said 'That's great, but for all the punches I took for these two guys, I could've used $500 bucks or something.' No one ever knew what happened to the cow after that."

GARY GAMBUCCI: "The Hartmeyer Arena was where we played the first game they ever played against Wisconsin. John went down a day early to speak to their BlueLine Club, where he told them that there could conceivably be a competitive rivalry between the two neighboring colleges, as soon as the Badgers could beat the Gophers. He estimated that the task would take over five years, if they could recruit well, get a good coach, and have some good luck. That next night at the game, the Gophers were just killing the Badgers, and the shots were something like 65-15. But, the Badgers had a hot goalie named Gary Johnson out of Roseau, and somehow beat the Gophers in OT. Oh, was Maroosh mad. He was so mad that he wouldn't let us take off our equipment until everybody had left the arena. He said 'Nobody move a damn muscle until everybody is out of this arena. You're a disgrace to your mothers, fathers, U of M, yourselves, and me. Nobody touch a damn thing, just sit there and think about that poor excuse for a game you just played.' Well, since he was the toughest man any of us had ever known, we all just sat there like little kids in our sweaty uniforms. Pretty soon the janitors turned off all the lights in the arena and the building was completely empty, then he said we could take our skates off. We then had to go back to the hotel to take off our uniforms because the arena didn't even have showers. Subsequently, when I travel to Wisconsin now on business, I tell hockey fans there that I'm partially responsible for putting Badger hockey on the map for losing that silly game there some 25 years ago."

"At a dinner one time in North Dakota, my uncle Elio Gambucci was eating with John Mariucci. Someone asked John how he had gotten such a big nose. Now if you've ever seen John's nose before, you'd know that it was a giant hunk of flesh that had been busted more times than anyone could remember. People would tease him about having the map of Italy carved out on his nose. John told me was that it happened in a game one time while playing for the Minneapolis Millers against the Rochester Mustangs. John was in his 30's at this point in his career, and was getting tired of taking all the punches every game. Just the night before he had taken 20 stitches in the nose from a brawl he was in. A kid named Jack Bonner, an intern at the Mayo Clinic from Canada, was playing for the Mustangs. He referred to John as an old man during the game. Now if you knew Maroosh, you knew that calling him old was a no-no. John called him some names back, and the next thing you knew Bonner whacked Maroosh across the nose as hard as he could with his stick. He split open his stitches he got from the night before, and did some more damage as well. John was madder than hell, and hurried to the locker room to get it fixed. He said the hell with stitches, and he slapped some tape over it so he could get back out there and get the little bastard. Sure enough the next period Bonner came down on Maroosh, and John caught up to him and nailed him. He tattooed the kid so hard that he knocked him out cold, and ended the kid's hockey career on the spot. The irony of the story came 15 years later. John was called to his mother's bedside in Eveleth, because she was dying. She told him that she was feeling well, and not to worry about a thing because her doctor was such a nice, gentle, comforting man that she just adored. She called him over and introduced Dr. Bonner to John, and they met again. John, being the sport he was, laughed it off. He showed off his big nose to him, and gave him full credit for carving the map of Italy in his nose."

JEFF PASSOLT: "I played in a celebrity hockey game at Met Center a few years back with John, and it was a lot of fun. A few guys, Dennis Hull and Stan Mikita, were doing the old water bucket trick like the Globetrotters used to do on the ice. They were having fun splashing water on the crowd, and taunting the players. I thought they were kidding around, but they came full speed at our bench and hurled the bucket at us full speed. We all ducked because we saw it coming. John who was sitting at the end of the bench, was wearing his hounds tooth hat, a nice new suit, a long flannel coat, and he was just dressed to the nines. He didn't think they would dare soak him, but sure enough that five gallon pail hit him square with a wave of water. I can't tell you what he said after he was soaked, there were too many expletives. But it was a very spicy message from one hot Italian. If looks could kill, he was madder than hell, and wasn't laughing at all. He wanted to go out and kill each one of them right there. The crowd just laughed like it was all planned out, but, oh boy, if they only knew. Hull and Mikita probably used the back door to get out that night after the game."

JACK McCARTAN: "After we won the 1960 gold medal in Squaw Valley, I got a call from Muzz Patrick, the GM of the NY Rangers. He offered me a little contract for the remainder of the season. I ran down to John Mariucci's office at the paper company, and told him all about it excitedly. Maroosh asked me very sternly, 'What did they offer ya?' and I told him. He said 'They're taking advantage of you kid, let me call Muzz and fix this.' So he picked up the phone and called Muzz. 'Muzz, what the hell are you doing trying to take advantage of this kid like this? He deserves a lot more money than that, and you know it!' Muzz told Maroosh to mind his own damn business, and that he should just forget about the whole thing, because it was all called off.

"Now I was sitting in his office scared as hell, and convinced that my one shot to play in the NHL was now shot thanks to John and his big mouth. Maroosh calmly said 'Go home kid. Don't worry about a thing, if I know Muzz, he'll call you in an hour or so.' I was so mad, but sure enough, in about an hour, Muzz called me and gave me the money that John had asked for. In essence, I guess Maroosh was my first agent. He had a strange way of doing business, but hey it worked!

"I remember a parade in Eveleth with Maroosh. A big guy was popping off to him, and John calmly walked over to him and pointed to his chin. He looked up and said, 'Six. You can have the first five punches, and I'll take the last one.' The guy took one look at him, and ran away like a scared bunny."

"In Denver one time, Andre Gambucci, a referee that knew John from Eveleth, was getting under John's skin. John was harassing him by calling him a gutless homer, and begged him to throw him out of the game. He told him he didn't have the guts to toss him out, and that he was a pansy. Well, sure enough old Andre got some courage and ejected him from the game. John was madder than hell, and couldn't believe it. That night in a bar, Andre walked in. I thought John was going to run over and kill him but instead he yelled at him 'Hey Andre, you old homer! Come over here and let me buy you a beer!' We couldn't believe it, but John told us that when the game was over, it was over, and that's that. It was back to being friends again."

BARBARA McCARTAN (JACK McCARTAN'S WIFE, AND MARIUCCI'S FORMER SECRETARY): "One time when John was working for the Stars there was a new player named Randy Velischek that was called up. John introduced Randy to his wife, Gretchen. Gretchen took one look at him and said, 'Go home you handsome thing. Go home, or get another job or something, or else you'll wreck that gorgeous face of yours, and wind up looking like my husband.'"

"I used to be John's secretary, and would often dictate letters for him. One time I remember a letter that John sent to Amo Bessone at Michigan State. It was just vulgar, and full of profanities. It was terrible grammar, swear words everywhere, and just a filthy letter. I didn't know any better, so I fixed it up, rewrote it and made it presentable to be mailed to him. Well, John came in to check on it, and asked me what the hell I had just done. I told him that it wasn't fit to be mailed, and was just terrible to talk to someone like that. So, John said, 'Go ahead and mail your letter, but put my copy in there too, so he knows I haven't changed how I feel about him.'"

DICK MEREDITH: "It was the final game of our post-Olympic games tour around Europe, and we were playing in Glasgow. Maroosh, who was in his 40's at this point, decided he would play that night. He wore Bill Cleary's jersey, and it fit so snug it looked like he was wearing a swimsuit out there. The Glasgow team was all Canadians, and they wanted revenge for the Americans beating them in the Olympics in Cortina, Italy. The game got rough and Maroosh went out and just hammered their biggest goon. The goon got up and took a two-handed tomahawk chop with his stick over Maroosh's head. All hell broke loose at this point, and the game went straight to hell. John was bleeding like a stuck pig, and was just madder than hell. The referees gave John 14 penalty minutes, and the other guy none. So John was furious, and called the team off the ice out of protest. Now Bob Ridder, our general manager, was paranoid as all hell and was scared of an international incident. Maroosh slammed the locker room door, and locked it. He was laughing hysterically, and said to not worry about a thing because the officials would be there in five minutes to beg them to come back out. They didn't want to give back all the fans' money for not seeing the game, and they were desperate. They even threatened to not pay us for appearing there to play, and John told them to go to hell. He slammed the door again, and locked it. He said they'll be back, and sure enough, one minute later they were pounding on the door begging us to come out and play. After John got a good laugh about it, he reconsidered and agreed to play if they would start the game over, and he wouldn't play in return. They agreed, and we went on to win the game...as if it really mattered."

"I remember going to the 1956 Olympic games in Cortina, Italy. We flew over there on an old TWA plane, and we had to stop in Newfoundland to refuel the plane. Now, John who had been drinking all flight, decided to get off the plane and do a little gambling in the airport. He was late getting back to the plane, and everyone on board was mad at him. That was the first leg of the trip, and the second was when we arrived at the airport in Europe. We all had matching Samsonite luggage that the town of Eveleth had donated to us as a gift for the Olympics. John was just tanked when we got off the plane, and he ordered us to fall in like we were in the army or something. He yelled at us, and told us that from this point on, we would have to be responsible for our own luggage, and that he wasn't going to treat us like a bunch of babies. So, all our luggage comes in, and we all get it as we're lined up in order. The kicker here is that we had our luggage, and John had lost his. He was madder than hell, and so embarrassed. I had to fight back a smile, but knew he was fuming at all of us. For the rest of the trip we had to buy him new clothes and go to military surplus outposts to get him freebies wherever we could."

"One time we were in Colorado playing, and John took us horseback riding to give us a break from hockey. When we got back, John sent in his expense sheet for the trip to the accounting department. They sent it back, and said that they weren't going to pay for our leisure time. John sent it back to them, and said that we were late for the game, and had to take horse-taxis, and it went through."

WALTER BUSH: "On a plane one time, the Stars were traveling to a game, and there was an NBA team on board the plane as well. The stewardess asked John which team got which meals, because they had special food for the athletes. John replied 'The hockey players are the short white ones.'"

"In 1963 we got the Minneapolis Bruins in town as part of the Eastern Professional Hockey League. I spearheaded it, with my two partners Gordie Ritz and Bob McNulty. One night in McCarthy's bar, we got into an argument about hockey, and John felt that he didn't want any other teams in town competing with his Gophers. He said he was going to beat me up and I said go ahead. I said I wasn't going to run because he'd catch me, and besides I'm a lawyer. So I'll get you back even worse than your punches. Well, John knew he'd been stood up, and bought me a drink and we laughed it off."

STANLEY S. HUBBARD: "I remember when Maroosh played for the Minneapolis Millers. He was their resident tough guy, and used to get into fights with St. Paul's tough guy, Bobby Dill. They used to beat the hell out of each other to entertain the crowds. The fans loved the cross-town rivalry, but didn't know at the time that after the games those two would go out and drink beer together. They were big pals, and used to love beating each other up, and laughing about it later over some cold ones.

"One time on a train, Maroosh was telling us stories. He said that he would never let his daughter marry a hockey player, unless it was one certain guy, and just that one he knew. Everybody hung in the balance to hear who this lucky guy would be, and he said 'Hubbard. Because that kid's got cash!'"

LEN LILYHOLM: "Maroosh hated to fly, so we always took trains. We were on the train one night partying, and keeping John from sleeping. We were excited about going to the Blackhawks game the next day in Chicago, and John was furious at us for not letting him sleep. When we got to Chicago, we went to the hotel and Maroosh ordered us two rooms for the night. One for Maroosh and team trainer Jimmy Marshall, and the other for the team. It was so crowded that we practically had to tape guys to the walls to fit all 20 of us in there."

"The team was on the way home from a game at RPI and the bus was late in getting us to the airport. He was riding shotgun next to the driver, making him nervous as hell. He was yelling at him to not get lost, and he had better get us there on time. The bus driver, who was almost in tears, lit up a cigarette. John calmly grabbed it out of his mouth, and said 'Uh Uh, you drive!' We were caught up in traffic and John saw a police car up ahead. He made the driver let him out, and he ran full speed to chase down the moving car. He talked to the cop and conned him into giving us a police escort through the downtown so we could be on time to go home. When we got there, John felt so bad for the driver, who was in shambles, he gave him a $30 tip to make him feel better."

TODD OKERLUND: "My dad, 'Mean Gene' Okerlund, used to bring all-star wrestlers to Gopher games when I played. Maroosh and My dad hit it off, and would stay up all night telling stories about wrestling and hockey. There were a few choice incidents where the wrestlers got into a bit of trouble with the fans, but nothing too serious."

WILLARD IKOLA: " 'RRRRRRROBERT, do your legs always swell up like that in the winter time?' That was Maroosh, on seeing Bob Ridder's legs at a UND game in their terribly cold arena. Bob was putting on long johns, and his legs were little white bird legs."

CHARLEY HALLMAN: "I remember sitting in the lobby of the Drake Hotel in Chicago with Maroosh and Al Shaver. I asked John if he still had his little black book with him from when he used to live in Chicago? Maroosh said, 'Yeah, but unfortunately I can't call any of them, all the girls are in their seventies by now!'

DOUG WOOG: "I remember train rides out of St. Paul to Chicago. One time we were down 4-0 in the first period. In the locker room Maroosh yelled at all of us, and asked us why the hell we were losing so badly? I said 'Shit, we just drove 16 hours on a train, ate a two-pound steak, and hardly slept a wink in two days... I wonder why?'

"We liked to play tricks on each other all the time on the trains. We slept in the pullman, and one time a couple guys took a dump in his bed cabin while he was at the bar. He came back and said 'Holy Cow, what the hell happened in here?' He never found out who did it, but we all skated our butts off the next day anyway."

DAVE FERRONI: "John tried to keep things pretty simple in his game plans. I remember the 1976 National team that John was coaching. We were on our way to play in Poland, and Maroosh passed out a pad of paper to the guys to find out what position everyone wanted to play so he could make the lines. Well, Mike Eruzione was sleeping when he did this, and never signed up for what position he wanted to play. As a result, Maroosh had the lines made up before the team ever left the tarmac, and Eruzione hardly got to play the entire time because John hadn't put his name down on any line."

DON CLARK: "The most amazing thing I ever saw John do was when he was playing for the Eveleth Junior College team. They were playing the Fort Frances

Junior team, which was much better and had older kids. John was skating down the ice, and the tuuk he was wearing to keep warm fell off his head. Instead of forgetting about it, he did a big circle around everyone and came back to pick it up. He put it back on with his free hand while fending off people, all without losing a stride. Then he skated in between all the players and scored. It was incredible."

BOB UTECHT: "One of John's best friends was Sam LoPresti. They were from Eveleth, and later played together with the Blackhawks. Sam was a merchant marine in the war, and John was in the coast guard. John was stationed in Staton Island. He never went overseas, but he took the ferry to the mainland to play hockey at night. LoPresti's ship was sunk by a German submarine, and he survived for 65 days alone shipwrecked off the coast of South America. At the end of the war, Maroosh got an overseas pin for going over water, and LoPresti got nothing. He used to tease him about it all the time, and show off his pin to him."

JOE MICHELETTI: "I remember playing on the 1977 National Team, when Maroosh was the coach. In a game against Norway, Lou Nanne sucker-punched a guy in the nose, and got a five-minute major. We were losing to a team we should've been killing, and Maroosh was madder than hell. After the game Lou and John were arguing, and John challenged Lou to a fight. We had to hold the two back from each other, and it was pretty ugly. Later that night, I wound up in the elevator with the two of them. It was just us three, and I expected world war three to break out at any moment. But instead they were back to being buddies, and they were trying to fabricate a good story that they could tell the press that was waiting for them."

WENDY ANDERSON: "In 1970 I was a candidate for governor. A rival candidate said that the only reason I was endorsed for governor was because I was a good hockey player at the U of M, and that other than that, I had no qualifications whatsoever. A reporter went to follow up on the story, and came to interview John Mariucci to check me out. John said that the allegations were completely unfounded and false. 'Wendy was not a great hockey player, and the only reason Wendy was even on my team was because I thought someday he might be governor.'"

STEVE CANNON: "One time Murray Warmath, who was a USA thumb-wrestling champion, challenged Maroosh to a thumb-wrestling match. Maroosh had always declined to thumb-wrestle him, and Warmath would always egg him on because of it. So finally Maroosh agreed, and he busted Murray's thumb."

"Bill Ramsey was playing for John with the Gophers at a game. Maroosh was yelling at his players to come off the ice to take shorter shifts. He was yelling at Ramsey to come off the ice for a shift change, and finally had to grab him to sit down. He opened the door on the bench, and instead of coming in, Ramsey slammed it shut because he wanted more ice time. But, he slammed the door on John's hand. Instead of opening the door, he just calmly screamed, "THE DOOR...THE DOOR...OPEN THE DAMN DOOR!" His hand swelled up about five times it's normal size, but he acted like nothing had happened. The man was superhuman, just incredible strength."

BURTON JOSEPH: "We were playing Illinois in 1939, and we were up 9-0 in the game. Larry Armstrong put me in to replace goalie Marty Falk. I was nervous, and an Illinois player shot a puck at me from a ways away. It was going so slow I could practically read the trademark on the puck. I swept at the slow roller, and it went between my legs. The fans were silenced because they couldn't believe it, then they roared with excitement. After the game, John Mariucci came up to comfort me and put his arm around me. 'Burton, don't you worry about this. I've made mistakes far worse than that, and I've bounced back from them. So will you.' Now here's a mighty senior that I looked up to, and one of the greatest athletes ever to play at the University of Minnesota. He took time out for me, a lonely sophomore in need. It helped my confidence greatly, and really helped my game. That pep talk some 62 years ago is something I will remember for the rest of my life."

GENE CAMPBELL: "One time in the early 1950's, John told Wendy Anderson and me after a practice that his wife just had a baby. We could tell that he was excited about it, and we asked him what he was going to name it. John got real defensive, raised his voice, and said, 'What the hell do you mean what did I name it? I named it John. What the hell else could it be?'"

DAVE BROOKS: "One time in the club car of a train, John let me stay up with him, and was telling me mobster stories. Once in Chicago, Maroosh beat up three guys in a bar. That night Maroosh, who lived in the top floor of the La Salle Hotel, had a knock on his door. It was Matt Capone, and he told him he had just beaten up three of his boys. He said he found out thatt hey had a contract out on him, and wanted to come and personally clear it up with him. He told him to be good, quit beating up his boys, and he'd forget about the whole thing.

"Another time there was a woman sitting behind the Blackhawk bench heckling John all game. Finally John reached around and cold-cocked her, dropping her. It turns out that she was one of Capone's boy's dames. The next day he had another contract out on him, but Matt cleared it up again. They even became buddies, and John would often times eat at their restaurant hideout that they had in Wisconsin."

LOU NANNE: "One time when I was GM of the Stars, I had to send Maroosh over to Russia. We had a system worked out where he would call me collect from Russia, and then I would hang up and call him back. He wanted to save money on phone bills, so he would call and hang up as planned. But, he forgot to leave me the number that I didn't have. Finally after three days of getting cut off, Maroosh called and said 'God Dammit Louie, accept that damn charges from the operator. I lost my luggage, have no money, no credit cards, it's 30 below, and I'm really pissed off at you! So send me some damn money, OK?'"

"We were playing the Russians one time, and they were beating the hell out of us. We didn't hardly touch the puck the entire game. Then during a faceoff halfway through the game, Maroosh threw another puck on the ice. When the ref asked him what he was doing, Maroosh replied by telling him that we wanted to play with a puck too."

"One time at a game some fans grabbed his hat off his head and were throwing it around the crowd. The police came over and asked him if he wanted them to get it back for him. John simply said that he could handle his own problems. The next thing we saw were bodies flying all over, as John jumped the boards to get his hat back."

WILLARD IKOLA: "One time Maroosh was playing in a game against a Kansas City farm team. A rookie gave Maroosh some stitches in that big honker he had with a cheap shot. Maroosh tried to run him down, but the kid, realizing who he had whacked, jumped right over the boards and ran up the stairs. Maroosh jumped up and followed him right outside. Sparks were flying from the stairs as Maroosh was yelling at him from behind. He chased him right out into the street in front of the arena, and then calmly walked back down the stairs to the ice. He was even talking to the ladies in the stands on his way back down. He went on the ice and finished his shift like nothing had happened. The next night Maroosh was still mad, but the front office wanted the kid who hit him to get some playing time, because he was going to come up to the team shortly from the farm team in Kansas City. John agreed, but only if the kid came up to him and apologized in person. That night the kid came to John's room and apologized in fear, and Maroosh laughed it off telling him to keep his damn stick down next time. Big John, the captain, took the kid under his wing after that, and helped him out. That's the kind of guy John Mariucci was."

The 1976 national championship team, check out those costumes!

MARIUCCI GETS THE LAST WORD

(The whole state suffered along with John Mariucci through his battle with cancer. The love and support that was unanimous for Mariucci caused officials to rename the hockey arena in Mariucci's honor in 1985. Star Tribune sports writer John Gilbert, who had covered Gopher hockey since student days at the Minnesota Daily when Mariucci was Gophers coach, interviewed Maroosh shortly after that. It was a rambling conversation, ranging from Mariucci's youthful days in Eveleth to his ability to joke about the deadly cancer, which was temporarily in remission at the time. Gilbert wrote a free-lance article after the interview, and it turned out to be one of the last interviews with Mariucci. It is reproduced here...)

By John Gilbert

They finally got around to having John Mariucci Day in Minnesota, the day they officially proclaimed that the hockey half of Williams Arena at the University of Minnesota would become "Mariucci Arena."

And before the ceremony began in a packed new hall in a brand new hotel, they played the Star Spangled Banner. Maybe never, at a sporting event, has that been more fitting.

Mariucci is the Godfather of U.S. hockey. Minnesotans like to claim him for themselves, but he's bigger than that. Maroosh, as he is universally known, is fundamentally responsible for U.S. players getting the chance to play in pro hockey, in college hockey, even in their own programs.

During the John Mariucci Day ceremony, Robert Ridder, a long-time friend of Mariucci, said: "During the 1980 Olympics, a U.S. Destroyer passed a Russian ship and signaled to it: 'U.S.A. 4, Russia 3.' Probably nobody on that boat ever heard of John Mariucci, but it wouldn't have been possible without John Mariucci."

He admitted to not feeling too well that ceremonial day. He was hurting from treatment from cancer, and he was pretty choked up from the emotion of it all.

A couple months later, feeling much better and about to take an April vacation trip to Florida, Mariucci looked back over his rich history-book hockey career, back to the days he was growing up in the 1920s, on Minnesota's Iron Range.

"Back in Eveleth, they always had some hockey," said Mariucci. "My grandpa was a musician, and so were all my uncles. Sports just wasn't thought about; in fact, my mother detested anything that had to do with sports. She had no desire to have me play and I never got a single toy or gift that had anything to do with sports. Not even a rubber ball. I played a little basketball and track, and I was able to play some football because the school provided the equipment. But I never had skates or equipment, so I didn't play hockey as a kid.

"The story goes, if the basketball coach had given me a suit, I'd have never gotten into hockey. But my football coach was also the basketball coach in high school. He had one suit left, and there were two of us. The other guy had trouble even walking, but he got it. So I ran into the hockey coach and he said if I wanted to play I had to learn how to skate first. The only time I had ever skated was in my uncle's skates. They were so big I wore my shoes inside them. But I found some skates our landlord had thrown out."

In 1932, when Mariucci was in the 11th grade, he got a vital gift. "My uncle bought me a real good pair of skates," Mariucci recalled. "They cost $7.50, but they were real good ones. From then on, there was no stopping me. I'd skate every afternoon, night, after school, and holidays."

So Mariucci played high school hockey, then he went to the University of Minnesota and played both hockey and football. In 1936, after he had skated for four years and was a freshman at Minnesota, Mariucci turned down an offer to sign with the Chicago Blackhawks. After Minnesota, he did sign with the Blackhawks. "The 125th game of hockey in my life was with the Chicago Blackhawks," he said. "A youngster might now play 125 games by the time he's 11 or 12.

"There were some other Americans around the NHL," said Mariucci. "Mike Karakas, Frankie Brimsek, Cully Dahlstrom, Doc Romnes...A few got some mimicking, guys calling you 'Rah-Rah' and things like that. You took it for a while, until it wasn't worth taking."

Maroosh might have had a long and spectacular career in the NHL, but instead had to settle for a short spectacular career. "In those days, the four years of college set me back, and then after two years at Chicago I spent three years in the service during World War II. I went back to Chicago, but I had really lost seven years that I might have been playing pro."

He was one of the game's truly tough players, and his fights with Black Jack Stewart remain an NHL legend as the most rugged battles ever. Both played without compromise, and they fought the same way.

Mariucci then went to the U of M, where he coached from 1952-1966. "After I went to coach at the U, Ebbie Goodfellow went back to coach the Blackhawks and he offered me a playing contract in 1952 or 53," Mariucci said. "But I was in business selling for the Falk Paper Company and coaching at the U. I enjoyed it."

Mariucci became entangled in the politics that promoted U.S. hockey against the constant and easy importation of Canadian players. Some of that has been misunderstood, because Minnesota refused to play Denver's teams under Murray Armstrong. "What I was against was the junior player who played in Canada until he was 21, then, if the pros didn't sign him, he would come to this country to play college hockey as a 22-year-old freshman against our 17 or 18 year olds," Mariucci said.

"It wasn't fair to our kids, who were finishing college at the same age Canadians were freshmen. American kids were never going to do anything against guys like Red Hay, Red Berenson, Keith Magnuson and Tony Esposito. But I would never have refused to play Denver. That was Marsh Ryman, our athletic director. I was trying to put in an age rule that would start counting competition at age 19, and make players ineligible at age 23. It would still be a good rule, whether for Canadians, Americans or Swedes."

Mariucci watched an NCAA final and issued what has become a legendary statement: "It's asinine that the only two Americans on the ice for the NCAA championship game were the referees."

Mariucci still believes that American hockey needs more support, maybe even protection from exploitation in the name of winning. "College could be a developmental program for our own country, for the Olympics and for the pros," he said. "It is that now, but mostly we're training Canadians. The Winnipeg Jets have 11 players on their roster who are ex-college players. Almost 30% of the NHL players are ex-college players. But a lot of those are Canadians.

"I hate to win by legislation, but there is such a thing as fairness. In the meantime, we're taking our lickings and beatings. But now some foreign track people are coming to college here, and the same thing is happening in other sports. That could cause some legislation to happen to help U.S. athletes."

Mariucci went on to join the Minnesota North Stars in administrative capacities that ranged from scouting to assistant general manager under Lou Nanne. That prompted Mariucci's ever-sharp wit to reflect that he had coached Nanne at Minnesota, adding, "One word of advice to all you coaches. Be good to your players; you never know which one might someday be your boss."

When another Mariucci protégé, Glen Sonmor, went into coaching, Mariucci said, "If you want to coach, take my advice — buy a mobile home."

His speaking engagements always have been unpredictable and usually leave fans holding their sides from laughing.

Ridder, who managed the 1956 Olympic team, is a proper, articulate statesman. He roomed with the team's coach, Mariucci, the rugged, hard-bitten character who talked in "Eveleth-ese" but was understood just as well.

"Outside of Gretchen Mariucci, nobody else has lived with John for every moment for three months," joked Ridder, at the Mariucci ceremony. "I really deserve some kind of medal. I love my country as much as anyone, but..."

"We had this linguistic problem. I've spent a lot of my time fooling around with languages. But somehow, up in Eveleth, they all understand. John, we may not always understand the words, but we always understand the meaning.

"John had a vision, an eye to the future, where the American boy, if only given a chance, could be an excellent hockey player. By sticking to his guns here, he gave everybody the strength to stick to their guns."

Mariucci later said, "Usually I can get back at him, but I couldn't that day. It was very emotional. But I remember rooming with him. Everybody thought he was suffering. What about me? He could put away a quart of scotch without showing it. How he could drink! And it always had to be 'Mr. Ridder.' Bob was OK, but never just 'Ridder."

"After the 1956 Olympics (the U.S. won the silver medal) we came back," Mariucci said. "When he hit the States, Bob Ridder vowed to never drink again, and he hasn't touched a drop since. He said 'You spend one winter with Mariucci, and you'll never drink again.' "

Taking on cancer was a fight Mariucci hadn't counted on. Nobody does. But he fought it with typical Mariucci verve. He changed doctors, changed treatment, and he got well enough to go to Boston where he was cited by AHAUS at the Junior Olympic Tournament.

He returned to work, and his wit continued to help him feel better. "I've been able to stop the treatments," Mariucci said, during a period of remission. "Now I just hope I don't get hit by a truck. You worry about one thing and something else gets you.

"Somebody asked me, 'How are you?' I said I'm not answering that question. I've been answering it for five months and I just looked at my bill. If I wasn't sick, I could've died from seeing it. Another word of advice - - if you haven't got insurance, don't get sick."

MORE OF THE MARIUCCI FAMILY...

ROSE FERRONI (JOHN'S SISTER): "John was quite a guy, I miss him so much. He was so big-hearted, he'd do anything for you. He was full of great ideas, and loved helping people. He loved to cook and would often come home to tell me that I was going to be the guinea pig that night to try whatever he was going to prepare for dinner. He loved coming home to Eveleth and seeing all his friends for the holidays, it was part of his life. I miss his jokes, he was so funny and sarcastic. He was so good around my children -- Donald, David, Mary Rose -- and Theresa, my cousin, who lived with us. He was quite a guy, I miss him."

DONALD FERRONI (JOHN'S NEPHEW): "John came from a close family. He really enjoyed the holidays with his mother and two sisters. John's whole life was the University of Minnesota, he loved it. Also an All-American in hockey, he should've been an All-American End in football as well. He also played football with the Brooklyn Dodgers, and coached football for the University of Connecticut. Aside from being a former player and coach, he was really interested in the student athlete. He was never out for himself. He had a real vision for hockey in Minnesota and eventually a lot of his dreams came true for the American hockey player. He had a lot of compassion for his players. It meant a lot to John to see the kids progress after college and give back to the University. John encouraged them to go into business, government, teaching and to be productive people after college. Growing up in the Iron Range during the depression, John saw the value of education and really pushed kids to get their degrees.

John was my uncle and I always looked up to him. He treated me so well and took care of me. He used to bring me to places and introduce me to famous sports personalities. He used to take me to one U of M football game a year and introduce us to the players after the game. He'd take us into the lockerroom and let us shake hands with the local celebrities like Murray Warmath, Hubert Humphrey, Eugene McCarthy and Snapper Stein.

"The media loved him and he had a lot of respect for writers like: Charley Johnson, Dick Cullum, Larry Hendrickson, and Dick Gordon. That was back in the day when the reporters used to socialize with John to get a scoop. John wasn't a very complicated individual and he may have come across as having a rough exterior. But he was soft on the inside. However, you only got the opportunity for John to get mad at you once, that's all it took. He was a hero to a lot of people, but he was only mortal. He was a true missionary to the game of hockey and he'll always be remembered amongst family and friends as the *'Noblest Roman'* of them all."

PAULA HARTER (JOHN'S DAUGHTER): My father was my idol. I was always very proud to be with him and he was always very proud to be with me. My dad was a very giving person both to his family and to his friends in the community. We had a lot of great family memories in Eveleth with my sister Joanne and brother Johnny. His mother, and my grandmother, Inez, was very close to him. I remember when he used to flood our back yard in Golden Valley and skate with us, it was a lot of fun.

"He was very sensitive, very giving, very funny and very sarcastic. He loved to cook; he made the best homemade pizzas. He'd give everything he had to people, he was so generous. He also loved to promote the University. One of his favorite things was his TV show with John Kundla called the Mariucci/Kundla show, where they'd talk about Gopher sports. He was so fun to be around. He took great care of his players. I loved him and he was my idol. He was my inspiration in life."

CLASSIC HOCKEY STORIES:

ALL'S FAIR IN LOVE, WAR...AND HOCKEY PLAYERS' MEMORIES

PETE HANKINSON: "One time my brother and I were playing a game against each other in the minor leagues, and a fight broke out. We both stood by each other, and were talking on the ice. Then a goon named Bundy, skated by us and said threateningly, "Cut this pussy Minnesota B.S. right now, and get the hell out of here!" I felt like keeping my teeth, so I told Ben we'd just talk after the game."

TOM VANNELLI: During a practice one time I was feeling brave, and I squared off with Paul Holmgren. Holmgren decked me, and Russ Anderson came to my side to challenge him. It was a tense moment as the two tangled, but it got broken up. Herb came up to me afterwards and said 'Tommy, you'll live by the stick and you'll die by the stick.'

COREY MILLEN: "One time at Burger King, Steve Orth got sucker-punched by some dude. He fell and hit his head on the cement, and wound up going to the hospital because of it. Three weeks later we saw the guy in Station 19. So myself, Broten, McSwain, and Orth met up with them in the middle of the street. It was a huge brawl, and justice was served. The cops came, knew we were hockey players, and let us go. The two guys we beat up got arrested to boot."

ROBB STAUBER: "Brett Strot and I used to always get into fights with each other. We were roommates, best friends, but still got in fist fights every now and then. One time in practice we got into it, and I gave him a Three Stooges poke in the eye. He was madder than hell at me and came after me. Butters saw this, came after him, and chewed his ass for trying to injure his starting goalie."

MIKE POLICH: "One time we played in a summer tournament in Europe. After a game one night, we went to a bar. The coaches told us to be careful, and to take it easy that night. We were having fun until Russ Anderson threw a guy through a plate glass window at the bar. He and Les Auge wound up in a jail in Cortina, Italy. That was one crazy tournament.

POLICH AGAIN: "Paul Holmgren and I were roommates together in college. He was younger, but we were good buddies. He used to always get my bags at away games, and watch over me like a mother hen. He used to call me 'PEEPS' because I wore contacts. He would love it when Herbie would send him out to stir up the shit. Anyone who tried to mess with his roommate, he would take care of. One time in Duluth, Dave Langevin tried to beat me up. Paul came right over and told Langevin that unless he wanted his lips tied together, he had best let go of his roommate. He was a giant, hulking animal and I loved him."

RANDY SKARDA: "My first game was a memorable one. We were playing Wisconsin and Tony Granato was lipping off to us. So Butters sent me out there to rip his head off. There was about 15 seconds left in the game and he told me to go out. I was waiting for the whistle and he said 'NOW!' He shoved me over the boards, and said 'sic him!' I jumped up, cross-checked him in the back of the head, knocked him into the net, and got a game misconduct to start off my college career."

SKARDA AGAIN: "One time I got into a fight with Mario Lemieux. I hit him, and he called me a ——ing rookie. I called him a fat-ass in return, and smiled at him. Mario took one more look at me and said 'How much money did you say you were making?' So, I guess he got the final words in, and he shut me up!"

BEN HANKINSON: "One time in a game against Northern Michigan I got in a fight with a guy. After the game Woog wanted to know what I had said to him to make him start laughing. I told him that the guy told me that I had the fattest cheeks he had ever seen. I responded by saying 'Yeah, if you think mine are fat, you should take a good look at my coach.' Woog was pissed at me for a week!"

CORY LAYLIN: "My first fight was a doozy. It was with Davis Payne, who was a 6-3 and 210 pound thug for Michigan Tech. After the fight everyone on the bench started calling me 'Homer Hanky' because of the way he was waving and tossing me around out there so much."

BILL BUTTERS: "It was a rough game to begin with, but the Colorado College players were provoking me. Doug Palazzari drove me into the boards, and then tomahawked me. So I beat him up. The refs separated us, and the CC bench was taunting me. When the ref released his grip, I calculated my odds, and I took off full speed across the ice and hurled myself like Superman into their bench. I cross-body-blocked about six guys, and just started punching. The cops dragged me down to the lockerroom finally, and both benches cleared.

"I had to go talk to Giel about it, and he said to me, 'Bill, I heard you were a good guy, what's the problem?' I told him that I just lost control. When Giel asked Herbie about it he said 'I kept him on a pretty tight leash all year. You know some guys like that just snap once in a while.' "

BUTTERS AGAIN: "One time when I was playing with Jack Carlson for the Fighting Saints, we were losing to Hartford in the playoffs. Glen called us into the lockerroom to chew our butts. He said 'What the heck is going on out there? Look at you guys. Just look around the room. What do you think you're here for? Your good looks, and hockey ability? Heck no! I want you guys to start a brawl out there, and I don't want it to end! We're going to win this series, and when that puck drops I want this place to go crazy!' Glen thought that you had to intimidate as a coach. He wasn't into skill development for guys like me. I liked that we were on the team for one purpose. I wasn't a great player, but I knew that as long as Glen was in hockey I'd have a job, because he knew that I'd play hard and physical for him."

GLEN SONMOR: "In Duluth there was this one fan who always sat in the same spot, and gave the opposing players hell all game. Well one time this loudmouth reached over and grabbed Mike Antonovich's stick when he was checked over by the boards near him. I was looking for an excuse to nail this idiot, and figured this would be as close as I would get. So, I jumped up from the bench, and beat the snot out of him but good. I knew he wasn't a fighter because he just kept grabbing my shirt, while I bloodied his face. It was a big production, and Herbie even came down to my defense from the press-box. I guess I showed that drunk son of a bitch a thing or two about messing with a Gopher."

TODD OKERLUND: "I remember a funny story that happened after a game one night. We were at a frat party, and Dave Grannis got suckered by a frat-rat. So I cold-cocked the guy who did it. The next thing I knew I was in the back seat of a police car. Tom Rothstein told the cops that we were Gopher Hockey players, and talked our way out of it. The cops were so cool about it that they even dropped us off at Fowl Play for last call to get another beer."

DICK MEREDITH: "John always taught us how to fight, and our brawler was Dick Dougherty. The only problem was that he couldn't lick his weight. John wanted to help him out, so he gave him a new technique that was surefire to win him more brawls. He told him to take his left hand and grab the guy by the throat. Then duck your head and punch with the right. Dougherty thought this was just great. So, up at Michigan State that next series, Dougherty got into a fight. He did everything John told him to do, and he figured he'd trade a right for a left with the guy. The only problem was that the guy was a lefty, and he just pummeled poor Dick. He didn't have a chance against the big Canuck, and John couldn't help but laugh."

DEAN BLAIS: "Once at a tournament in Michigan I saw Glen go above and beyond his call of duty as our coach. We had to get dressed across the street from the arena there, and some fans were mouthing off at us outside. We were going to get into it right there in the street, but Glen came over and said he'd take care of it. He went over to the five guys and BANG-BANG. Two punches, and two guys laying on the ground. The other three ran, and he calmly walked back over to us and said smiling, 'You know, sometimes it feels good standing up for yourself!' "

TRENT KLATT: "In practices Butters and I would always have pretend fights with each other. He claims that the only person he ever beat up out of all his hundreds of people he fought was Brad Marsh. So last season I got to play with the North Stars for the first round of the playoffs against Detroit. Brad Marsh was playing for the Red Wings, and he and I got into it a little bit out there. On the first shift I knocked him down, and exchanged a few with him. On the next shift Brad was calling me a college pussy, and a punk. We were going to square off at any moment, so I looked over to him and said 'You know, Bill Butters beat the living shit out of you, FIFTEEN years ago! So shut the hell up old man!' Brad had taken about as much as he was going to take at that point, and proceeded to chase me around the rink threatening me. Butters later thanked me for giving him some long overdue respect."

JIM BOO: "I had the pleasure of skating with a picture of Bob Suter, who played for the Badgers, on my helmet all week. We were arch rivals, and I wanted to get him. So, in the pre-game warm-ups I suckered him and knocked him out cold on the ice. I got ejected for the entire series, and if that wasn't bad enough I had to get my butt chewed from my dad who had just driven six hours to see my play.
BOO AGAIN: "My best fight was out of retaliation for my buddy Robin Larson.

Don Dufek, who was also an All-American linebacker for Michigan, broke Robin's wrist the year before in a game. So in our game the next year I asked him if he wanted to go, and before he could say a word I had at least a half a dozen-punches landed. I think he hit the ice before his gloves did."

REED LARSON: "I remember playing Denver one time at Mariucci Arena. We were talking trash to each other before the game, and on the way up the stairs to the ice we got into a huge fight. Like dominos, guys were falling down the stairs on top of each other. It was ugly, and after that they started to make us wait for the other team to go up first before us."

TOM GREENHOE: "Tom Vannelli was a little scooter, and he used to score goals like mad. He was an outstanding player and used to just tear up the league. Other teams tried to pound him and wear him out. Finally against Michigan Tech one time, he had had enough. On a face off, the ref dropped the puck, and Vannelli didn't even look at the puck. He just hauled off and smacked the guy right in the chops, and dropped him right on his can. Before the ref could even say anything, he just skated right over to the penalty box, opened the door to let himself in and sat down like nothing happened."

FRESHMEN INITIATIONS

COREY MILLEN: "I can remember standing in the shower hearing screams, and I was scared to death knowing I was next. Paul Butters was the doctor in charge of shaving and Pat Micheletti was the freshman victim. I was terrified of what was about to happen to me. I remember one of the guys coming in to remind me about guys that were too cocky. He told me that they didn't get shaved, they just got their hair pulled out. That's when I got real nervous."

BILL BAKER: "My freshman initiation was nothing like a rookie I saw in Montreal get. After a game, the players grabbed this rookie out of the showers. They shaved him top to bottom, duct taped him to a chair naked, and took him up to the ice. People were still filing out of the arena, and the ones that stayed got an extra bonus. They saw a flying, naked man taped to a chair flung across the ice at full speed. I saw this happen and said 'Oh God, welcome to the NHL.' "

TOM CHORSKE: "I was the first freshman in my class to be initiated. Wally Chapman was my big brother on the team and he led me to the lockerroom. In there were about 10 smiling guys, and someone yelled 'Paging Dr. Micheletti...' and Pat popped out of a laundry hamper all dressed up in a makeshift doctor's outfit, complete with the jock over the mouth and razor in his hand. I was defenseless, so I just had to drop my linen and take it like a man. I remember stopping by the store on the way home to buy Vaseline and baby powder because I got shaved from the neck down. When I got back to the dorm, all the other freshmen were waiting for me in awe, and were just scared to death. I was so embarrassed. Word spread around the dorm and I felt so stupid. In retrospect, though, it was kind of an honor because then I was accepted as one of the guys.

"It later happened again when I was a rookie with the Montreal Canadiens, only worse. There they spray painted me and shaved my entire head."

JIM BOO: "To this day I still have a coupon in my scrapbook from Eric Strobel, to shave him. We got all the freshmen that year, except Eric for some reason. So, Eric if you read this, I still have the coupon, and can redeem it at any time. Watch out!"

RANDY SKARDA: "I was in the lockerroom and Okerlund told me to get him something out of the dungeon. As a freshman I obeyed him, and got it for him. When I got back to the lockerroom the door slammed behind me. I saw five grinning guys, and they grabbed me. They told me that if I fought it, they were going to shave my eyebrows too. Then Marty Nanne popped out of a laundry hamper with a razor, and a jock over his head like a doctor. There was nothing I could do. So, I let it happen as gracefully as possible I guess. It's an initiation from hell, but afterwards I felt like I was one of the fellas."

GLEN'S GLASS EYE

GARY GAMBUCCI: "One time Glen (Sonmor) was in the men's room going to the bathroom. His glass eye fell out and rolled into the stall next to him. The guy in there was so freaked out that all Glen heard was a quick flush, and footsteps as the guy ran out of there."

DOUG PELTIER: "One time we were on a flight to a game and Glen's eye popped out and rolled down the aisle of the plane. Another time Glen was staying in a hotel room with trainer Jimmy Marshall. Jimmy came in late one night and it was dark in the room. He stepped around quietly, and suddenly he heard something pop. He had stepped on Glen's eye, that he had dropped on the floor. Jimmy hid it from him to this day, and was too embarrassed to tell him about it."

GIRLS, GIRLS, GIRLS

REED LARSON: "One time at a tournament in Europe, we snuck out one night to see the town. We had to sneak back in without being caught and that required some intuition. So, Buzzy Schneider climbed up four balconies outside the hotel to get to our window, and let us all in. Mission accomplished."

KEN YACKEL JR.: "Whenever we played Michigan we would get psyched up for our game by remembering a funny story. It happened in a hotel lobby in Michigan before a game one time. The whole team was in the lobby, and we were waiting for our bus to take us to the game. Then a really hot girl came over, got totally naked except for her boots, and sits with us until our bus came. She got arrested, and all Herbie could do was laugh. Talk about a great pre-game psyche-up!"

COREY MILLEN: "Another player who I won't mention and I were staying in the same hotel room together after a game. We had a girl in our room, and we heard a loud noise outside. So we opened the window to investigate, and Woog saw us from the ground. He figured that we threw something out the window, and he came right up to yell at us. Meanwhile, the girl had to hide in the closet for over a half-hour as we listened to Wooger lecture us about proper conduct and ethical behavior in hotels."

DON MICHELETTI: "One time we were staying in a hotel at Michigan State. We had girls in our rooms, and Herbie came in to check on us. We had the girls hidden behind the curtains, and all you could see were their feet. He left, and came back a few seconds later saying, 'By the way, I see the chicks behind the curtains. Get them the hell out of here!'

MICHELETTI AGAIN: "Russ Anderson and I went out a lot together. Russ was a hopeless romantic. One weekend after a big series we were supposed to go out that night, but he dogged me to go to a wedding instead. He called me the next morning and said he couldn't sleep because he had met the most beautiful woman he had ever seen. He told me he was going to marry this girl, and that he was in love. Now I thought I was speaking to a drunk in puppy love here, and that it was the alcohol doing all the talking. We gave him a pretty hard time about it, until we saw her. It turned out that it was Dorothy Benham. She was the 1977 Miss America, and it turned out that they got married a year later."

THE TOOTH FAIRY'S NIGHTMARE

TOM VANNELLI: "Herb was tough on me. One time in practice I got hit in the mouth, and lost all my front teeth. As I was laying there in pain, Herb skated over and said 'Get up you little wimp!' I responded by saying 'F— you' as I spit seven bloody teeth out of my mouth at him."

STEVE CHRISTOFF: "I never used to wear a mouth guard. One time at a game in Wisconsin, Mark Johnson, the centerman against me on the face-off, told on me to the ref. The ref gave me a 10-minute penalty, and there were only 10 minutes left in the game. When we got back to Minneapolis, Herbie made me, Strobel, and McClanahan skate laps after practice with big mouth guards. We skated for a half hour with Herbie lecturing us on wearing mouth guards the entire time. The next game I had gotten a Pro-form mouth guard and was all set to play. I checked a guy in the boards, and he hit me in the mouth knocking out all my front teeth. I went to the bench, and pulled out my bloody mouth guard with all my teeth still in it. I said to Herb 'Look at your damn mouth guard you made me wear, ass-hole!' The first time I ever wear a mouth guard, I lose all of them. So, after the second period, I had stitches, and I went back out to play. I couldn't wear a mouth guard after that, so I skated with my mouth closed. I was in front of the net and a guy came by and butt-ended me in the mouth, knocking out all my bottom teeth. I just said the hell with it and gave up after that."

186

LIVING TOGETHER

DICK SPANNBAUER: "I roomed with Dean Blais my freshman year. The first day we moved into the dorm, Dean walked into the room and said 'Something wasn't right in here.' So he flipped the beds over, pulled out the drawers, threw everything on the floor and messed up the place but good. Then he said 'I wanted to make it feel like home.' "

TIM HARRER: "Steve Christoff and I had a bird that lived in our apartment, but he didn't have a cage to live in or anything, he just flew around."

DEAN WILLIAMSON: "Robb Stauber lived with Scott Nelson and Brett Strot in an apartment. Robb and Scott wanted to get even with Brett for something he had done to them. So Scott faked a suicide in their apartment. He had Robb put on fake blood makeup to make it look like a gunshot, and they left a note for Brett. Then they hid a video camera in the plants to get it on tape. Brett came in with his girlfriend, and was completely freaked out. It was the funniest tape ever made, and it was the ultimate get-back when Robb woke up and scared the hell out of him. The irony of the story is that Randy Skarda recorded an episode of Cheers over the tape. Oh, and what became of Scott Nelson? He's a mortician."

TODD OKERLUND: "I lived with Wally Chapman and Pat Micheletti in what was known as the legendary 'Animal House.' We used to have great hockey parties there, and one time we had the grand-daddy of all parties. It was so big that the floor caved in. It was major structural damage, but the party went on as people merely watched their step from falling into the basement. The house got condemned after that party, and it was such a sad occasion to see the end of an era."

THE MEDIA CIRCUS

BOB REID: "I remember the days when the games were so packed in Mariucci Arena that you couldn't find a ticket. Ike Armstrong, the old A.D., used to have to cram more people in to see games because the bleachers weren't full to capacity. He wanted to get as many fans as possible in there to root on the Gophers and needed people to get closer. So he had a famous saying he would use. Like Bob Casey's famous introduction of Kirby Puckett at Twins games, Ike would say '1,2,3 EVERY-BODY SQUEEEEEZE.' "

REID AGAIN: "My worst announcing nightmare was at an exhibition against the Blackhawks in Mariucci Arena in the early '50's. Tom Ivan was coaching the Blackhawks at the time, and it was a really big deal on campus that the Gophers had this exhibition game. I had to announce the lineups, and this was quite a big occasion, so I was nervous about it. I was reading the lineups, and suddenly came across a name from hell. 'Fred Saskamoose' from Moosejaw, Saskatchewan. I panicked and paused thinking I had murdered his name. But it turned out that I said it flawlessly, and the Blackhawks were so impressed that they looked up at me and gave me a standing ovation from the bench."

FRANK MAZZOCCO: "One time I was announcing a game and the camera was focused on a couple that was just going at it in their seats. I didn't know what the hell to say, so I naturally said 'Get a room!' We got a lot of feedback over that one down at the station."

DOUG McLEOD: "Pregame shows with Buetow were funnier than hell. We would go in the lockerroom where it was quiet to do the interview and Mike Foley would follow us down there. While we were talking, he would go back and flush all the toilets at the same time. Well, you could hear it as plain as day on the air, and finally they had to run background noise to deter him from screwing us up."

TOM GREENHOE: "One time in a game at Duluth, Steve Cannon was broadcasting on the radio and called the goalie the name of the kid who played the night before. He didn't realize that he was calling him the wrong name until the third period. Finally, when he realized that he had made a mistake, he did one of the funniest things I ever heard. He said, 'And Duluth has changed goalies on the fly, it's the most amazing thing I've ever seen.' "

DICK MEREDITH: "Sid Hartman used to cover the team a lot when Mariucci was coaching. He used to always write about his buddies every day in his column. One time he asked John for an interview. John was busy, so he told Sid to talk to me instead. I was shocked that he was going to interview me so I said, 'Geez Sid, have you really got enough room in your column to squeeze me in between Paul Giel and Bob McNamara?'"

ROAD TRIPS

REED LARSON: "One time after a game at Michigan Tech, we were driving home on our bus to Minneapolis. We made a couple of beer stops along the way, and eventually had to stop and relieve ourselves in the ditch. So the driver pulled over, and the ditch was really steep. There was several feet of snow in them as well. We were all doing our thing there, and someone pushed someone, and then everyone wound up about 20 feet down into this ditch. It took over a half an hour to get everybody out of there. We were in shorts and tee-shirts as well, so it was a long ride home."

PAUL OSTBY: "One time we were swept in a weekend series at Michigan. After the game we partied anyway, and a couple guys even missed the bus to the airport the next morning. I guess we shouldn't have been so casual about it because when we got back, we put on the wet stuff and skated for three hours with no pucks."

TIM HARRER: "One time after a loss to Lake Superior State, we were screwing around after the game. Herb told us we were in for a treat when we got home. We got off the bus in Minneapolis, put on our wet skates and skated. We skated so hard that we wore the lines off the ice, because there was no water on it. The lesson I guess, was don't lose to teams you're not supposed to."

GREGG WONG: "One time the Gophers were on their way to a game at Michigan Tech and had to change planes in Green Bay. The goalie, Jeff Tscherne, made a wisecrack about a bomb to the airport security. They grabbed him and he spent the night in jail. Herbie had to fly back and get him out of jail the next day. That kid was a wacko, but then again most goalies are."

JIM BOO: "At Colorado College one time after a game, I bumped into Herbie on the dance floor a couple hours past curfew. Herbie was pissed, so when we got off the plane that next day, we went straight to the rink and put on the wet stuff to skate. And skate we did. I watched Bill Baker barf and that was Herbie's cue to call it off."

BOYS WILL BE BOYS

STEVE ULSETH: "Brad Doshan was a guy we used to pick on quite a bit. One time as a joke we emptied his locker stall, took off his name tag, and left a note that read 'Brad, something's come up. Please come see me in my office at once. Coach Buetow.' Then when he came into practice, we all asked him if it were really true that he'd been cut, and why? Well, Brad was fuming, and stormed into Buetow's office and demanded to know what was up. Of course Buetow knew nothing, but they both felt pretty stupid. We were out in the hall watching the whole thing, trying not to laugh. I guess you had to be there."

ULSETH AGAIN: "Brad had a new graphite stick he was so proud of one time. He always bragged about it, and boasted about the slapshots he could take with it. So, after practice one day, we took off the decorative tape on the shaft, and sawed it about 3/4 the way through. The next day in practice we all waited for Brad to take that patented slapshot he was so proud of with his baby. He reared back, hit the puck, the stick snapped in two, and he fell right on his butt. We all busted out laughing hysterically. Luckily Brad had a sense of humor, or we would've skated laps forever after that."

DAVE SNUGGERUD: "One time Paul Broten Scotch-taped my skate blades before a game. I went out there and fell on my ass. It was really embarrassing."

PETE HANKINSON: "In optional skating days with my minor league team, we would split up to scrimmage each other. We divided up by Canadian Juniors and American college players. The juniors would call us college pussies, and we would piss them off by calling them dummies. After a goal we would chant 'Don't be a fool, stay in school!' They used to get so upset at us, they would pick fights after that."

GLEN SONMOR: "Murray McLachlan was the only goalie I ever saw with the same demeanor as Robb Stauber. He was awesome. I remember telling our goalie coach Don Vaia that there was only one rule for him that I wanted him to follow for teaching the goalies. I told him that he could teach any of the goalies anything he wanted to, but he wasn't allowed to speak to Murray McLachlan. I told him he was perfect just the way he was, and I didn't want him screwing him up.

SONMOR AGAIN: "Marsh Ryman (the late athletic director,) took over as coach of the 1956 Gopher squad while Maroosh coached the Olympics that year. The kids were pretty creative, and used to call him 'Ruhtracm,' which was McArthur spelled backwards. This was because McArthur made the great speech saying 'I shall return.' Ryman, on the other hand was always bitter about other teams, and would say 'I'm never coming back here again.' So they figured that was a suitable name for him. Marsh tried to get me to find out what it meant one time, but I played dumb because I didn't have the heart to tell him. I finally told him 20 years later what it meant, and he was still pissed off at me for not telling him about it."

JOHN GILBERT: "One time at a game there was a heckling woman sitting behind Glen. She wouldn't shut up, and just kept taunting him all game. So finally Glen turned around in disgust and asked. 'Excuse me ma'am. How much do you charge to haunt a three-room house?' That shut her up."

JIM BOO: "Once in a game in North Dakota I managed to score a goal on our own goalie. I felt terrible, and out of frustration I hacked the guy out front that was poke-checking me. The ref gave me a quick penalty, and to add insult to injury, I got hit in the head with a dead fish on the way to the penalty box.

BOO AGAIN: "I remember seeing Paul Holmgren take out 10 trumpets of the Wisconsin band with his stick. He said 'Hey Boo, watch this.' and he came skating by the band section that had their trumpets leaned up on the glass over the ice. He raised his stick, and like dominos they came crashing down. Needless to say there were some bruised Badger-band lips on those guys after that. Paul was one guy you always wanted on your team, no matter what. He was awesome."

RON PELTIER: "I remember playing in a Christmas Big Ten Tournament in Michigan one year. We had won the tournament, and were on our way home to the Cities. Glen was up all night partying, and was still pretty looped in the morning. Because Glen was so high-strung, he was a cheap drunk. It only took him about two drinks to get him going, and then he was great for 1,001 stories. We were in O'Hare Airport that morning, and the team really wanted breakfast. But Glen, who was still feeling pretty good, wanted to skip breakfast and get a head start on the new day by buying us rounds of beer instead. He was telling us jokes, and having kids come sit in his lap like Santa Claus. He was giving us little pep talks, and he had Stevie Hall come over to him. Now Stevie was a shy, sensitive, intellectual, good kid that didn't drink, and was balding a bit. So Glen said, 'Stevie, you fuzzy little mallard, have a beer. It'll make some hair grow on your head!' I felt so bad for Stevie seeing this big drunk guy picking on him in front of everybody. But it was all in good fun, and it was probably the funniest thing I had ever seen in my entire life.

PELTIER AGAIN: "One time Glen was showing us a technique with a stick, so he asked Don Dumais -- a hilarious kid from Silver Bay, who didn't get as much playing time as he would've liked -- if he could borrow his stick. Don replied by saying 'Which one do you want Glen? The one I used as a sophomore, or the one I used as a junior?' "

TIM PODEIN (OWNER OF STUB & HERBS): "The Gophers always have their pre-game meals at our restaurant. It's always funny to see the first pre-game meal there. The upperclassmen always tell the freshmen that it's a strict coat and tie formal gathering, and to be sure that they're on time. So the freshmen show up an hour early in suits, while everyone else sleeps an extra hour, then shows up in sweats and a hat."

ON, AND OFF, THE ICE

DOUG McLEOD: "One of the craziest games I ever saw was in Grand Forks against UND. I'll never forget, they threw dead Gophers on the ice during the game. I remember rating the Gopher goals. *'There was a Three-dead-Gopher goal...'* as a judge for how great a goal was. The same game, some crazy idiot threw a live chicken on the ice, and they spent 20 minutes trying to catch the damn thing after he pooped on the ice."

DICK MEREDITH: "We were playing UMD in an exhibition game one time to get UMD some notoriety for their program. John wanted to help out their program in any way he could, so he could get them into the WCHA. We went there to promote hockey for Duluth, and we wanted to let them have a good game. We were a superior team, and by no coincidence it was 6-0 after the second period. Mariucci told us on the bench to start shooting wide, miss the net, and to not score. He didn't want a rout, and he wanted to let their program gain some confidence. He said that no one on our team was to score, period. Now the game was in Eveleth, and John went out shmoozing with his home town cronies for about 10 minutes after his little pep-talk to us, and he returned in horror. He looked at the scoreboard, and it was Gophers 11-0. Maroosh yelled 'Holy Christ, who the hell's been scoring all these goals while I left?' Everybody pointed to Badger Bob Johnson, and started to laugh. Bob said 'Cripes coach, I'm going to score when I get the chance dammit! They don't come very often!'

"Later, Mariucci was in Johnson's home in Madison, and saw a plaque that Bob had on the wall. It read 'Bob Johnson, scores a record six goals against the UMD Bulldogs in 1956.'"

GLEN SONMOR: "I remember playing Boston University, and losing a tough one 4-2 in the NCAA finals. That game our goalie Dennis Erickson was hit in the knee with a puck, and played 52 minutes with a busted knee cap. Jimmy Marshall went out to check on him, and shot him up for the pain so he could play. We lost the game, and the next day in the airport he was limping just terribly. I told him to quit faking it, and that he was slowing us up. I found out when we got home that the kid had busted his knee, and here I was yelling at him, and practically blaming him for our loss. Well, if you read this Dennis, I'm sorry about that incident, I'll never doubt your knee again."

REED LARSON: "One time in a game against Tech, I slashed Warren Young after he had chopped me up pretty good. The ref, who only saw me retaliate, gave me a major penalty. Then, in a fit of rage I got too close to the ref, and I nudged him. The ref fell back like I had decked him or something, and later suspended me. Ron Simon, my agent, as well as Herb Brooks, both told me that now might be a good time for me to turn pro. So, Warren Young, who I later played with in Detroit, credits himself for giving me my pro career."

STANLEY S. HUBBARD: "I remember one time when John Mayasich and I lived together in Pioneer Hall, Ike Armstrong came to our room. John was hurt with an injured foot at the time, and needed to rest it so it could heal. He told John that he had to play in the game that night. John was against it because he was hurting, but Ike told him that 8,000 people had bought tickets to see him play hockey. He told him that he didn't care how hurt he was, and he reminded him that he was on scholarship too. So, they shot up his foot that night to kill the pain, and by God he played. The Michigan players couldn't keep up with him because he was so good, so they hacked at his foot all night to slow him down. He was an amazing player, the best."

JIM BOO: "One of the biggest highlights of my career was playing in the movie 'Slapshot' that starred Paul Newman with the Carlson Brothers. Dave Hanson, Jeff Carlson, and Steve Carlson played the Hanson Brothers in the movie. They came from Virginia, Minnesota in 1975, and showed up for tryouts wearing those goofy horned rimmed glasses. My buddy laughed at them, and they beat the hell out of him but good. They went to the Eastern League after failing to make the Fighting Saints roster, and the movie is based on their hilarious season-ending championship run. Jeff even thought about giving up hockey, and moving to Hollywood. I was an extra playing for the Hyannesport Presidents. I wore No. 2, had a big beard with a lot of hair on my head, and got beat up a lot in the movie. It was a ball, and if you slow the movie down real slow at one point, you can even see me."

JEFF PASSOLT: "My dad's cousin was Jim Mattson, a great goalie who played with Mayasich, and he used to always tell us stories about what a great player John was. My favorite story was one that Jim called, 'The most incredible exhibition of hockey' that he had ever seen. The Gophers were playing an exhibition game against the Blackhawks farm team at Williams Arena in the early 50's. The Gophers were getting manhandled by the older and better Canadian pros throughout the game. The Gophers were a man short during the game, and Mayasich went out to help kill off the penalty. Mayasich got the puck, and single-handedly killed off the entire penalty by himself. For the entire two minutes, he said that Mayasich skated up and down the ice with the puck, keeping it away from them. By the time he was finished bobbing and weaving through everybody, he had a bloody nose and cuts all over his face from the players trying to beat the tar out of him."

BILL BAKER: "Early in my pro career, I was playing in the minors for Fort Worth. Before a game one day, the coach came in and told me that I was being traded to St. Louis. I was nervous and upset about being traded, but I told him that it was OK because one of my good friends from college, Joe Micheletti, played there. The coach then told me that I had been traded for Joe Micheletti."

HOCKEY TOMBSTONES

How would you want to be remembered? What was your contribution? Did you leave your mark on hockey? What would your hockey tombstone say?

JOE MICHELETTI: "I was a person that worked hard, left a mark to achieve his goals and showed leadership for the younger guys."

BUTSY ERICKSON: "I tried hard."

TIM HARRER: "I was always a good person to be around."

DON CLARK: "Through a lot of hard work and dedication, I have been able to promote the sport I love most."

RON PELTIER: "I'd want to be remembered as the ultimate team player."

MIKE RAMSEY: "Hell, I wasn't even there long enough to be remembered."

STEVE ULSETH: "I made the best of an opportunity and played with my heart."

MIKE POLICH: "I learned the lessons of hard work, dedication and preparation."

REED LARSON: "I want kids to see guys like me that made it in the NHL and believe that they can make it too. I hope to be a role model for kids to work hard and make it as far as they can go with it."

CORY LAYLIN: "I was an average player. I never blossomed into anything spectacular or anything, but I had a lot of fun."

JIM BOO: "I was just happy making the team, and to be a part of it."

PAT PHIPPEN: "I met the best people in the world, it was the best time of my life."

BILL BAKER: "I gave an honest effort every night. I never had blazing speed, fantastic moves or crushing checks, but I came to play and gave it my best."

TRENT KLATT: "I want to be remembered as a guy that worked hard, went hard into the corners, and loved to play Gopher Hockey."

DAVE PETERSON: "I've worked hard to make high school hockey better in Minnesota, and overall I've worked hard to make hockey better in the USA. It's such a thrill for me to see kids go on to the pros."

ROGER ROVICK: "I'm glad to have been a part of the tradition. It gave me the opportunity to play alongside my brother David, and today we're good contributors in advertising, the new rink, and to the Blue-Line Club. It's all in memory of John Mariucci."

NEAL BROTEN: "I'm proud of my accomplishments, and feel good about playing the game that's been so good to me."

DOUG PELTIER: "I'd like to be remembered as a hard worker, and one of the many who carried on the tradition as a Gopher."

TOM VANNELLI: "I want to be remembered as having the ability to carry on the tradition."

TOM CHORSKE: "I want to be remembered most for being a fast skater."

DICK PARADISE: "Every night I worked hard and gave it my best effort. I enjoyed the game, but it was more fun to see the other guys that had skills doing well. I always supported the guys I played with, and that's the best thing to be remembered by."

MIKE ANTONOVICH: "Little guys with big hearts, who give an honest effort every night, and have a good attitude, can play this game."

DAVE SNUGGERUD: "The success of Gopher Hockey was seeing the smiles on the fans, faces. My goal in life after the pros is to be a lifetime member of the Blue-Line Club."

PAUL BROTEN: "Knowing that I gave Fowl-Play more than my share of business."

KEN YACKEL JR.: "Let's hope that another person can surface in the hockey community that can give back as much as my dad did. As for me, hopefully my hockey sculptures will be around a lot longer than I am."

BOB RIDDER: "I am proud of the fact that I brought the Olympic teams out of the east and into the midwest. The eastern schools never had a shot at the Olympics, competing only with Ivy League kids, so I helped move the training facility to Duluth in the early 1950's. I was also the president of the Minnesota Amateur Hockey Association, and I take a lot of pride in that as well. I'm very grate ful for hockey in my life."

COREY MILLEN: "I'd like to be remembered as an exciting player to watch."

DOUG WOOG: "I think the thing that's most important here is to perpetuate the growth of Minnesota kids playing hockey in their own state. Without compromise, it's all Minnesota kids and I'm proud of that. We're keeping it going at a high level with only Minnesota kids. I'm committed to going with the Minnesota kid, and I'm going to stick to it as long as I'm here as coach."

STANLEY S. HUBBARD: "I have two great kids that played hockey, and I helped promote the game of hockey in Minnesota."

PAUL OSTBY: "I was a Gopher. I'd say I bled maroon and gold, and gave everything I had to the program. I made a lot of mistakes as a player, but I've learned from them. Now I have had the chance to teach kids that were in my situation. I care about Frank Pietrangelo, John Blue, Robb Stauber, Jeff Stolp, Tom Newman and Jeff Callinan. I hope that I've helped them in their lives, and to be better players."

NORM GREEN: "One million dollars. That was our contribution. We wanted to develop a strong relationship with all the amateur hockey in the state. We got the high school tournament now, and we'll have a Gopher game here once a year. We'll give the profits of that game to the University, until it reaches one million dollars. It was an indication to the community that we have a strong commitment to hockey in the state of Minnesota."

THE HISTORY OF GOPHER HOCKEY
by Donald M. Clark

Donald M. Clark

Don Clark has made the ultimate contribution to this book by donating his extensive and vast knowledge about the history of hockey in Minnesota. This is the first time the history of Gopher hockey has been extensively compiled in some 112 years, and is truly fascinating to see. Don is without a doubt, the foremost hockey historian in the United States. His knowledge and memory are unlike anything I have ever known, and he is a real-life walking encyclopedia. He is one of the nicest guys I've ever met, and I am very grateful to him for all of his contributions and expertise.

Will Rogers' quote "I never met a man I didn't like" is a bit hard for many to accept. And yet it applies so very much to Don Clark. Everyone in hockey who ever met Don liked him. He has traveled the length and breadth of his beloved Minnesota preaching the gospel of amateur hockey. In doing so, he has won countless converts to the game and made a host of friends.

During his boyhood days in Faribault, he exhibited an early aptitude for sports, competing in high school football, hockey and baseball. Later he played amateur baseball in the Southern Minnesota League and amateur hockey in the Twin Cities area.

It was in 1947 that he, along with fellow Hall of Fame enshrinees Bob Ridder and Everett "Buck" Riley, founded the Minnesota Amateur Hockey Association (MAHA) and proceeded to build it into the most successful organization of its kind in the United States. Among his accomplishments with the MAHA were founding the first Bantam level state tournament in the nation, serving as president from 1954-57 and secretary-treasurer from 1949-55 and 1958-74.

An interest in the national aspects of the game developed in Clark and in 1958 he was manager of the first U.S. National Team to ever play in the Soviet Union. Since 1958, he has served as vice president of the Amateur Hockey Association of the United States. His areas of particular interest are amateur and youth hockey. Clark was honored by the National Hockey League in 1975 when he received the Lester Patrick Award for service to hockey in the United States. In 1978 Don was enshrined into the U.S. Hockey Hall of Fame.

Considering the time, interest and travel that Clark has devoted to hockey, it is not surprising that he has become one of the foremost American Hockey historians. As such, much of what is in the United States Hockey Hall of Fame, which he served as president, comes from his impressive collection and knowledge of the records, players, participants and incidents of the game. It can truly be said: "We shall not see another like him."

"He has the most prodigious memory of any man on the face of the earth..."
Bob Ridder

196

GOPHER COACHES

I.D. MacDonald

Emil Iverson

Frank Pond

Larry Armstrong

Doc Romnes

Marsh Ryman

John Mariucci

Glen Sonmor

Ken Yackel

Herb Brooks

Brad Buetow

Doug Woog

197

Minnesota, with its thousands of lakes and ponds, was an ideal place for the newly formed game of ice hockey to prosper. Shinny, an organized game, had been played in the state since the Civil War. Ice Polo had been popular in St. Paul and Minneapolis since the early 1880's. It was a matter of time before the University of Minnesota would display an interest in the sport. Such concern manifested itself when the first University of Minnesota team, unsanctioned by the college, was organized in January of 1895 by Dr. H. A. Parkyn, who had played the game in Toronto.

It appears that Johns Hopkins University of Baltimore may have been the first college in the United States to play hockey, having tied the Baltimore Athletic Club at the dedication of the newly built North Avenue Rink in Baltimore on December 26, 1894. The University of Minnesota may have been the second college in the nation to play the game. Although students from Yale and other eastern colleges visited Canada during Christmas vacation of 1894, Yale did not play the game until January of 1896 when they met Johns Hopkins. Columbia started hockey competition during the winter of 1896, while Brown and Harvard continued to play ice-polo through the season of 1896-1897.

Prior to meeting the Winnipeg Seven, the newly formed Minnesota team played three games against the Minneapolis Hockey Club, with the collegians winning two and losing one game.

The game against Winnipeg was played at the Athletic Park in downtown Minneapolis, located at Sixth Street and First Avenue North, just north of the famous West Hotel. The park was located on the present sight of the renowned Butler Square Building, next to the recently constructed Target Center Arena. The park was the home of the professional Minneapolis Millers Baseball Club until they moved to Nicollet Park at Nicollet Avenue and Lake Street on June 19, 1896. Athletic Park was opened in 1891. For those interested in baseball lore, Athletic Park measured 275 feet in left field, and 250 feet in right field. It was a home-run hitter's delight.

The following reports are from local newspapers:

Minnesota Ariel, February 16, 1895. page 5:

The University of Minnesota hockey team will play a game for the championship of Minneapolis against the Minneapolis Hockey Club at their rink, at the corner of Fourth Avenue and Eleventh Street South.

The game is preparatory to the game to be played Monday afternoon by Winnipeg and the University of Minnesota. Winnipeg is champion of the world.* Winnipeg has returned from a rough trip through eastern Canada and has defeated without too much trouble Montreal, Toronto, Victoria, Ottawa, Quebec, and the Limestones.

The University started practice two or three weeks ago and played against a Minneapolis team, being defeated 4-1. A week and one half ago they defeated the same team 6-4. Tonight they play the tie off for the championship. Dr. H.A. Parkyn has been coaching the boys every afternoon.

He has a couple of stars in Willis Walker and Russel. Walker plays point and Russel coverpoint, with Van Campen in goal. Parkyn and Albert are center forwards. Dr. Parkyn's long experience with the Victoria team of Toronto, one of the best, makes him a fine player. Thompsen and Head, the other two forwards, are old ice polo players and skate fast and pass well. Van Campen, quarterback on last year's football team, plays goal well.

Many tickets have been sold for tonight's and also Monday's game. Tickets are 25¢, ladies come free.

The excitement of these games is intense, and surpasses that at a football game."

*"This statement is incorrect: "The Winnipeg team did not play for the Stanley Cup in 1895. In 1895 Queens University challenged the Montreal team and lost. However, the Winnipeg Victorias did win the Stanley Cup the following year, in 1896. They must have informed the St. Paul-Minneapolis press that they were the champions or the news media garbled the story."

St. Paul Pioneer Press Feb. 19, 1895. Page 6:

The first international hockey game between Winnipeg and the University of Minnesota was played yesterday, and won by the visitors 11-3. The day was perfect and 300 spectators occupied the grandstand, coeds of the University being well represented. Features of the game was the team play of the Canadians, and individual play of Parkyn, Walker, and Head for the University. Hockey promises to become as popular a sport at the University as football, baseball, and rowing.

The first attempt to organize varsity ice hockey at the University of Minnesota took place in November of 1900 when a committee composed of George Northrop, Paul Joslyn, and A.R. Gibbons was appointed to draw up a constitution for the club and look into other problems concerning playing the game at the university. A committee of S. Collins, T.B. Richards, and R. Tibbetts conferred with the Athletic Board regarding the flooding of Northrop Field. It was decided not to flood Northrop Field, and instead to play at Como Lake in St. Paul several miles distant. No scheduled games were played during the season of 1900-1901, and it was not until late in the season of 1903 that the University of Minnesota played any games on a formal basis. Only two contests were played that season, both resulting in wins for the U of M. Minneapolis Central High School was defeated 4-0 and the St. Paul Virginias 4-3. Team members were: John S. Abbott, Frank Teasdale, Gordon Wood, Fred Elston, Frank Cutter, R.S. Blitz, W.A. Ross, Arthur Toplin, and Captain Thayer Boss.

St. Paul Globe February 1, 1900:

Chicago, Illinois — To play ice hockey, universities and colleges in the west need covered buildings. A.A. Stagg of the University of Chicago says the game would be popular with covered buildings. If Chicago had facilities they would like to meet eastern colleges."

The season of 1903 proved to be the last of ice hockey on a formal basis at the University of Minnesota for a period of nearly two decades. In 1910 efforts were made to revive the sport and to interest the Universities of Chicago and Wisconsin in the sport, so as to furnish Big Ten Intercollegiate Conference competition. This move met with failure.

University of Minnesota Daily, January 13, 1914:

As its meeting Wednesday afternoon the Board of Control voted $25 to outfit a hockey team. It was just enough to outfit one man, not seven, with sticks and pucks. In this the board, with all due respect for its other admirable qualities, shows the most parsimony in the matter of financing minor sports that it has shown over the past years. This is not so evident in the matter of hockey as it is in track. If the University ever expects to develop its minor sports program, it will have to exchange its attitude somewhat."

In 1915-1916 a series of games was played by a team representing the University of Minnesota against Minneapolis and St. Paul high schools and St. Thomas College. However, the team was not recognized by the University of Minnesota Athletic Board at this time and the games played were classed as "pick-up" contests. About this time the fraternities began taking an intense interest in hockey. While in the season of 1914-1915 only two fraternities, namely Delta Tau, and Sigma Alpha Epsilon, had iced teams. By the following season 16 fraternities were playing the game. Professor O.S. Zelner worked untiringly to organize the teams and the league. These games were played on outdoor ice on Northrop Field with the finals and playoffs often being played at the indoor "Hippodrome" ice at the state fairgrounds in St. Paul. Some of the better frat players of this era were the Bros brothers (Chet and Ben), Jenswold, and Lapiere. By 1920 the number of frat and intra-mural teams playing was over 20 in number. It is interesting to note at this time the women students at the university became interested in hockey and organized teams and a league. Some of the frat players such as Bernard and the Chester Bros acted as coaches for the women's teams.

During the 1920-1921 season a few games were played as a varsity sport. Hamline and St. Thomas were defeated. St. Thomas, considered the state champion, was defeated by Minnesota 3-1 in a game played at the Coliseum Rink on Lexington Avenue near University Avenue in St. Paul. Warm weather canceled several of the scheduled games. Beaupre Eldridge of St. Paul, a student at the time, was very instrumental in organizing the team and promoting the sport at the University during this period. Team members for the 1920-21 season were: Pond, Dwyer, Langford, Strange, Worreal, Byers, Watson, DeForest, Beard, Higgens, Swenson, Graham, Taylor, Chet Bros, Ben Bros, and Eldredge.

I.D. MacDONALD ERA:
1921-1922 through 1922-1923

After much deliberation the Athletic Board of Control finally adopted ice hockey as a varsity sport for the 1921-1922 season. Under the direction of coach MacDonald and captain Chet Bros, the team played 10 games, winning seven and losing three. Among the clubs defeated were Wisconsin, Luther Seminary, Hamline and the Michigan Mines, while losses were suffered to Hamline and the Michigan Mines. Minnesota challenged the University of Michigan to play for the Big Ten title, but they would not meet the Gophers. The starting lineup for the 1921-22 team was as follows: E.G. Bergquist, Chet Bros, Addie Wyatt, Beaupre, Eldredge, Lorin Jacobsen and Lee Bartlett. Most of the home games were played continuously as a varsity sport at the University of Minnesota.

The 1922 team playing against Wisconsin

EMIL IVERSON ERA:
1923-1924 through 1929-1930

Emil Iverson, exhibition skater and skating instructor from Denmark, followed in MacDonald's footsteps as Gopher coach. During the same period his brother Kay coached the strong Marquette University teams, and a strong rivalry was established between the two schools. After leaving the Gophers Iverson coached the Chicago Blackhawks of the NHL for a short time.

During Iverson's seven-year stay the Gophers won 70, lost 20 and tied 13 games. Captain Frank Pond and goalie Fred Schade led Iverson's first team of 1923-1924 to a 13-1-0 season, while for the following season of 1924-1925 most of the home games were played at the newly constructed Minneapolis Arena. Captain Ed Olson led the 1925-1926 team to an undefeated season by winning 12 and tying four games. The 1928-29 six shared top National honors with Yale as they compiled an 11-2-1 record. Chuck McCabe, Joe Brown, John H. Peterson, Leland Watson, and goalie

Osborne Billings were selected to the All-Western team. In addition, McCabe, Brown and Peterson were accorded All-American honors during their Gopher careers. During the six seasons of 1923-1924 through 1928-29 they lost only 10 games, won 75 and tied 11. During this period Minnesota was consistently ranked among the very best in the nation.

Among the teams approached regarding sending a team to the 1928 Winter Olympics were: Harvard, Minnesota, Augsburg and Eveleth Junior College. Either for lack of finances or students missing classes, all the colleges except Augsburg declined the opportunity. The final outcome was that no team was sent to the 1928 Winter games.

1925 team composite

Teams met during the '20s included Michigan Mines, Michigan, Marquette, Notre Dame, Hibbing, Eveleth Junior College, North Dakota, North Dakota Aggies, St. Thomas, Hamline, Luther Seminary, Ramsey, Manitoba, Dallas A.C. and Tulsa A.C. Notre Dame was met during the seasons of 1924-1925, 25-26, and 26-27 after which they dropped the sport due to lack of indoor facilities. At Marquette Canadians Don McFayden and Pudge Mackenzie proved to be very popular at the Milwaukee college. In Milwaukee, crowds of 1,500 - 2,500 would stand outdoors in cold weather to view the games, while the Marquette-Minnesota games staged at the Minneapolis Arena attracted 4,000 - 5,000 fans. As was the case at Notre Dame, due to the lack of an indoor rink, Marquette dropped hockey after the 1932-33 season.

1925 team photo

During the '20s the Gophers played their games at a variety of rinks, including an outdoor facility located on the campus. Early in the decade games were played at the Coliseum, while later many games were played at the large natural ice surface at the Hippodrome at the State Fairgrounds. With the opening of the Minneapolis arena, which possessed artificial ice, in late 1924, the Gopher home games were played there or at the Hippodrome.

1927 team photo

A large number of Gopher players during this era came from Minneapolis, with fewer from St. Paul, Duluth and the Iron Range. On occasion a Canadian was on the roster. Among the leading players to compete for Minnesota during the '20s included: Chuck McCabe, Joe Brown, Osborne Billings, Frank Pond, John H. Peterson, Cliff Thompson, Ed Owen, W.B. Eldredge, Chet, Ken and Ben Bros, Don Bagley, Reuben Gustafson, Fred Schade, Walt Youngbauer, Vic Mann, Ed Olson, Phil Scott, Jack and Bill Conway, Lloyd Russ, Herb Bartholdi, Leland Watson and H.J. Kuhlman.

FRANK POND ERA:
1930-31 through 1934-35

Frank Pond, a native of Two Harbors, who had captained the 1923-24 team to a 13-1-0 record, was appointed Gopher coach in the fall of 1930. During his five-year tenure Minnesota, he iced strong teams in 1931-32, and '32-33, and '33-34. During the three-year period, the Gophers won 34, lost 8 and tied 1. They were ranked very high ever year according to the Tonnelle System.

As in the '20s, Minnesota continued to schedule Michigan, Michigan Tech, and Wisconsin, usually playing each four times during the season. Manitoba was added to the schedule, while after the 1932-33 season Marquette dropped the sport and Wisconsin followed suit after the 1934-35 campaign.

1931 team photo

The strong 1932-33 team, captained by Marsh Ryman, who later became athletic director at Minnesota, was the first Minnesota team to meet a team from the east when they lost to formidable Harvard 7-6 in Boston. The team played in the Western Olympic Playoffs defeating Eveleth Junior College and the Upper Michigan All-Stars before losing to the Eastern All-Stars in the United States final in Boston. The forward line of Ryman-Todd-Parker led the Gophers in scoring. Using the Tonnelle System of rating the 1931-32 team was ranked second in the country behind Harvard. The following were among the team members: Captain Marsh Ryman, George Todd, Howie Gibbs, Ben Constantine, Laurie Parker, Alex Mac Innes, Andy Toth, Gordon Schaeffer, Bucky Johnson, Phil La Batte, George Clausen, Harold Carlsen, Fred Gould, John Suomi and John Scanlon. Mac Innes, Toth,

Constantine and Suomi came from Eveleth, the first of many from Eveleth who would in the future wear the maroon and gold uniform. Schaeffer and Todd were from Duluth while the others were Minneapolis products.

Russ, Gray and Munns

Another strong team was iced for the 1932-33 season. Captained by Harold Carlsen, the team lost only one game during the season, that a 3-1 loss to Michigan. The fast forward line of Russ-Gray-Munns led the team's offense, while Wagnild and La Batte anchored the defense, and Clausen and Scanlon tended goal. The writer recalls attending the 1933 Wisconsin series at the Hippodrome in which the Gophers swamped the Badgers by a combined 14-1 score in the two-game series. On the large Hippodrome ice surface (119' x 270') the fast skating Gophers outclassed the Badgers as the Minnesota "Pony Line" of Russ-Gray-Munns led the Minnesota attack.

Johnson, Zieske and Gould

With the Russ-Gray-Munns line returning, the 1933-34 sextet posted another fine season with an 11-3 record. With returnees La Batte, Wagnild and Zieske at defense and Clausen in the nets, the Gophers featured a strong defense. Later La Batte was selected as a member of the 1936 U.S. Olympic team. Wagnild received the honor of being chosen for the 1937 and 1938 U.S. National teams.

Frank Pond finished his Minnesota coaching career with a winning record for his campaign of 1934-35. Pond's five-year stay resulted in a 46-21-4 record for a winning percentage of .676%. In the 14 year Minnesota-Wisconsin rivalry extending from 1921-22 through 1934-35, the Gophers dominated the series with a 36-6-2 record. In 1928, seven years into the series, the Badgers finally were able to defeat Minnesota. During this same period the Gophers record against Michigan was 26-13-5, Michigan Tech 18-3-0, Marquette 14-8-1 and North Dakota 6-0-0.

LARRY ARMSTRONG ERA
1935-36 through 1946-47

Larry Armstrong, well-known Canadian athlete and former St. Paul Saints mentor, took over the coaching duties at Minnesota for the 1935-36 season. Armstrong held the Gopher coaching spot for 12 seasons, relinquishing his reins to Doc Romnes after the 1946-47 season. Armstrong's record was 125-55-11 for a winning .681%. He suffered only one losing campaign, that of 1937-38.

1940 team photo

With Bud Wilkinson, later to become the famous Oklahoma football coach, in the nets the Gophers defeated the University of Manitoba in 1937 for the first time in 11 seasons. In 1937 the following Minnesota players were chosen on the Midwest All-Star Team: Bud Wilkinson, Dick Kroll, Jimmy Carlson, Reynard Bjork and Ed Arnold. In 1938 and 1939 the Gophers lost all four games played against the University of Southern California, probably the best college team in the country at that time. The previous three seasons prior to World War II (1938-39, 1939-40 and 1940-41) the Gophers posted a 46-9-2 record. National championship honors were accorded the 1939-40 team as they won 18 games and finished the season undefeated. Among their college victims were Michigan, Michigan Tech, Illinois and Yale. In the

National AAU Championships they defeated with ease the New England All Stars 9-4 and Connecticut's Brock Hall 9-1. During the season the team scored 138 goals to their opponents, 25. Led by such performers as Babe Paulson, John Mariucci, Frank St. Vincent, Hayden Pickering, Jim Magnus, Ken Cramp, Fred Junger, Dave Lampton, Al Eggleton, Norb Robertson and goalie Marty Falk, the 1939-40 team was the strongest at Minnesota since the sport was inaugurated at the college in the early 1920s. Ching Johnson, former Minneapolis Miller and New York Rangers star, who watched the Gophers practice and play, was amazed at their abilities. He compared them favorably with any of the great Canadian amateur teams. The 1938-39 sextet, made up of underclassmen with the exception of Captain Kenny Anderson, also posted a fine record of 15 wins and six losses. The team finished second in the National AAU finals. They won their first two games, swamping the Philadelphia Arrows 10-1, edging the St. Nicholas Club 3-2 and losing in the finals to Cleveland Legion 4-3. Had there been a 1940 U.S. Olympic team several members of the Gopher team would undoubtedly have been members of the team.

John Mariucci

Although the 1940-41 team lost seven players from the champion 1939-40 team, the team bolstered by the addition of sophomores Bill Galligan and Bob Arnold, managed to finish the season with a respectable 11-3-2 record.

During the war years the Gophers schedule was curtailed as many colleges did not ice teams and the government discouraged travel. Minnesota scheduled a few college contests against Dartmouth, Michigan and Illinois, but the bulk of their schedule was against local amateur clubs such as Honeywell, Fort Snelling, Berman's and Wold Chamberlain and Canadian Junior teams from Winnipeg, Fort William and Port Arthur. Among the leading players during the war period were Bob Graiziger, Paul Wild, Bill Klatt, Bill Galligan, Bob Carley, Allan Van, Al Opsahl, Dick Kelley, Mac Thayer, Jack Behrendt, Pat Ryan, Don Nolander, Bob Arnold and Burton Joseph.

Harold (Babe) Paulson

Following the ending of World War II Coach Armstrong added several Canadian players from Winnipeg to the Gopher roster. Among them were Bob Fleming, Ray McDermid, Dennis Bergman, Jack O'Brien, Roger Goodman, Bud Frick and Allen Burman. By the season of 1946-47, Armstrong's last, the Gophers had a nucleus of a strong team. Minnesota-bred players such as Bill Hodgins, Roland DePaul, Bob Harris, Jim Alley, Ken Austin, Al Opsahl, Dennis Rolle, Jerry Lindegard, Cal Englestad, Bill Klatt, Jerry Remole, Dick Roberts and Tom Karakas

Bud Wilkinson

were welcome additions to the club. Harris, Roberts, Austin, Alley, Lindegard and Englestad were among the first players form northwestern Minnesota to play for the Gophers. They were natives of such small communities as Warroad, Roseau and Hallock. Injuries and ineligibility dogged the team, but they managed to finish the 1946-47 season with a respectable 12-5-3 record. Goalie Tom Karakas, from Eveleth, proved to be one of the top goaltenders in the country. DePaul, Hodgins, Roberts, Fleming and Frick were the team's leading scorers.

Players from the Armstrong era who were members of the U.S. Olympic/National teams were Bob McCabe, Graiziger, Pat Finnegan, Van, Opsahl, and Bud Frick. Players who were coached by Armstrong and turned professional include John Mariucci, Graiziger, Bill Galligan, Karakas, Ray McDermid and Allen Burman. Fleming has been the long-time Chairman of the U.S. Olympic Hockey Committee.

ELWYN "DOC" ROMNES ERA:
1947-48 through 1951-52

Elwyn "Doc" Romnes, a native of White Bear Lake and former Chicago Blackhawk star, followed Armstrong as Minnesota coach for the 1947-48 season. His best season was that of 1950-51 when the Gophers compiled a 14-12 record. The team's senior line of Bjorkman-Watters-Englestad led the offense, while Jim Sedin, Frank Larson and Tom Wegleitner were the team's leading defensemen. The team lost several close early-season encounters, but managed to win their last nine games, barely missing an NCAA bid.

Larry Ross

The Gophers posted a 13-13 record during Romnes' last season of 1951-52. The Duluth line of Bodin-Strom-Nyhus led the Minnesota team to a fifth-place finish in the newly formed Midwest Collegiate Hockey League.

During Romnes' tenure the newly remodeled Williams Arena was opened for play February 17, 1950 when the Gophers swamped Michigan State 12-1 before a crowd of 3,437 fans. This was the first time that the Gophers had their own arena for practice and games. No more would they have to bear the inconvenience of using the Arena in South Minneapolis or the Hippodrome in St. Paul. Thus ended the necessity of the players taking taxis from the campus to these facilities for team practice. In 1985 Williams Arena was renamed Mariucci Arena in honor of the former Gopher player and coach, John Mariucci. Gordy Watters in 1951 and Duluth's Larry Ross in 1952 were accorded All-American honors. Rube Bjorkman, Ken Yackel and Jim Sedin were members of the Silver Medal winning 1952 U.S. Olympic team. Bjorkman, from Roseau, coached high school hockey at Greenway and then advanced to college coaching at RPI, New Hampshire and North Dakota.

The University of Minnesota athletic department and Athletic Director Ike Armstrong were not satisfied with Romnes' five year record of 53 wins and 59 losses and replaced him with former Gopher football and hockey star John Mariucci for the 1952-53 season. The general feeling among Minnesota hockey followers was that with the large and talented pool of player material in the state a more successful program should be forthcoming.

Among the teams met for the first time during this period were Denver, Rochester Mustangs, Brandon Wheat Kings and the Olympic Club of San Francisco. Starting the season of 1951-52 seven Midwest colleges formed the Midwest Collegiate Hockey League. Charter members were Michigan State, Michigan Tech, Michigan, North Dakota, Colorado College, Denver and Minnesota. For the season of 1953-54 the name of the league was changed to the Western Intercollegiate Hockey League. Later the name of the league was changed to the present Western Collegiate Hockey Association.

By the early 1950's hockey in the state was growing at a fast rate with large youth programs in St. Paul, Minneapolis and Duluth, and increased interest in the newly developing Twin City suburban communities and other smaller cities in outstate Minnesota. This growth, combined with winning Gopher teams during this era, resulted in record crowds at Williams Arena. For the season of 1953-54 Minnesota led the nation in college attendance by attracting 103,000 fans for 18 home games. Season figures for other WIHL teams were as follows: Michigan State-10,000, Michigan-39,000, Michigan Tech-14,000 and North Dakota-54,000. Total league attendance for the following season of 1954-55 climbed to 312,304.

JOHN MARIUCCI ERA:
1952-53 through 1965-66. (On leave-1955-56)

Eveleth's John Mariucci replaced Romnes after the 1951-52 season. Mariucci, a colorful individual who with his remarks and views was a newspaperman's dream, decided to recruit American players for his Minnesota teams. With few exceptions the players on his teams during his 13-year stay were natives of

1958 team photo

Minnesota. At times he found the going difficult as his opponents often iced teams with mostly Canadians on their rosters. Often these Canadian players were over-age juniors, two or three years older than the Minnesota players and with many more games of experience under their belts. In March of 1958 the WIHL dissolved over charges of recruitment of over-age Canadian players. There was no league play in the 1958-59 season, but after the bad feelings had subsided the seven teams regrouped to form the newly named WCHA for the 1959-60 season.

Mariucci amassed a 215-148-18 record for a winning percentage of .587%. Under his guidance Minnesota was NCAA runner-up in 1953 and 1954, losing in the finals in 1953 to Michigan 7-3. In 1954 the Gophers swamped Boston College 14-1 in the opening game, and lost in the finals to RPI 5-4 in overtime. Mayasich and Dougherty each scored nine points in the two-game tourney. In 1961 in the NCAA

Craig Falkman

Championship was held at Denver, and they finished in third place. Minnesota captured league titles in 1953 and 1954 and placed second in 1961 and 1966, and third in 1955, 64 and 65.

John Mayasich, another Eveleth performer, led the Gophers in scoring for four consecutive seasons -- 1952, 53, 54 and 55. He led the league in scoring for the seasons of 1953,54 and 55. Jim Mattson, from St. Louis Park, was the league's leading goaltender in 1953 and 1954. The Mayasich-Campbell-Dougherty line, which played together as a unit for these seasons, was one of the leading lines in college hockey. Mayasich and goalie Jack McCartan played important roles in the success of the 1960 Gold Medal winning U.S. Olympic team. Recently, Mayasich was honored by the U.S. Hall of Fame as being the outstanding high/prep school hockey player in America during the first half of the present century. Another dominant player from the 1950's was the talented forward, Mike Pearson, from Fort Frances, Ontario, who played three seasons of standout hockey at Minnesota.

The following players who played for Mariucci were selected to the All-American team: Mayasich (1953, 54, 55), Jim Mattson (1954), Ken Yackel (1954), Dick Dougherty (1954), Jack McCartan (1957,58), Dick Burg (1958), Mike Pearson (1958), Murray Williamson (1959), Lou Nanne (1963), Craig Falkman (1964) and Doug Woog (1965).

The following players from this era were selected All-WIHL or WCHA. Mattson, Mayasich, Wegleitner, Dougherty, Yackel, McCartan, Nanne, Woog and Gary Gambucci. Mariucci coached players who were members of the U.S. National and/or U.S. Olympic teams are as follows: Campbell, Dougherty, Mayasich, Dick Meredith, Wayne Meredith, Jack Petroske, Oscar Mahle, Donald Vaia, Burg, McCartan, John Newkirk, Jim Westby, Gerald Westby, Robert Turk, Thomas Riley, David Rovick, Larry Alm, Herb Brooks, David Brooks, Gary Schmalzbauer, Tom McCoy, Larry Johnson, Larry Smith, Falkman, Len Lilyholm, David Metzen, Glen Marien, Donald Norqual, Myron Grafstrom, Woog, Jack Dale, Nanne, Larry Stordahl, Jim Stordahl, Jerry Melnychuk, Gambucci, Michael Larson, John Lothrop

Wendy Anderson

and Wendell Anderson. Mattson, McCartan, Larson and John Lothrop were goalies who saw extensive duty during the '50s and '60s.

During the period from 1950 through 1972 the following players led the Gophers in scoring:

YEAR	NAME	GP	G	A	TP
1950	Russell Strom	16	9	8	17
	Jack Bonner	16	9	8	17
1951	Cal Englestad	26	19	34	53
1952	John Mayasich	26	32	30	62
1953	John Mayasich	27	42	36	78
1954	•John Mayasich	28	29	49	78
1955	•John Mayasich	30	41	39	80
1956	Kenneth Yackel, Sr.	29	19	20	39
1957	Terry Bartholome	29	14	7	21
1958	Richard Burg	28	19	16	35
1959	Stu Anderson	25	15	19	34
1960	Jerry Melnychuk	28	15	25	40
1961	Jerry Norman	27	22	17	39
1962	Ron Constantine	22	15	13	28
1963 *	Lou Nanne	29	14	29	43
1964	Roy Nystrom	26	17	19	36
1965	Doug Woog	29	26	21	47
1966	Gary Gambucci	28	23	17	40
1967	Jack Dale	28	17	26	43
1968 *	Bill Klatt, Jr.	31	23	20	43
1969	Peter Fichuk	31	21	24	45
1970	Mike Antonovich	32	23	20	43
1971	Dean Blais	33	16	24	40
1972	Doug Peltier	32	22	14	36

* Led WCHA in scoring • Led league in scoring

It is interesting to note that in the four-year period of 1961-64 three of the scoring leaders — namely, Norman, Constantine and Nystrom — were Eveleth products.

Mention should be made of two Gopher forward lines that were an important part of the Minnesota hockey scene during the 1960's. These are the David Brooks-Len Lilyholm-Gary Schmalzbauer "Buzzsaw Line" of the 1961-63 era and the Mike Crupi - Greg Hughes - Rob Shattuck combination that played in the late '60s. It is interesting to note that of the six players only Lilyholm, who hailed from Robbinsdale, did not play high school hockey for the St. Paul Johnson Governors.

Lou Nanne won the 1963 WCHA scoring title with 14 goals and 29 assists in a 29 game schedule. He became the first defenseman in the history of the WIHL (WCHA) to accomplish the feat.

During the 1955-56 season Marsh Ryman, captain of the 1932 Gopher six, replaced Mariucci as the Minnesota mentor on an interim basis when Mariucci took over the coaching duties of the 1956 U.S. Olympic team and led them to a Silver Medal at the Winter Games in Cortina, Italy. Ryman, who later became athletic director at Minnesota, coached the team to fourth place finish in the WIHL.

League opponents scheduled regularly during this period were Colorado College, Michigan, Michigan State, Michigan Tech and North Dakota. Denver, a member of the league, was not scheduled for several years as the Gophers did not approve their use of older and more experienced Canadian players. During the Mariucci years, teams added to the schedule were: RPI, Boston College, Boston University, U.S. Nationals, U.S. Olympics, Czech Nationals, Providence, McMasters,

Woog, Lothrop and Maroosh

Northeastern and Army.

After 13 seasons, Mariucci was fired from coaching duties and took a position with the newly formed Minnesota North Stars. Known as the godfather of hockey in the State of Minnesota, he did more than any other individual to popularize the sport in the state. A much sought-after speaker, he gave freely of his time to further advance the game in Minnesota and surrounding area. He led the Gopher hockey team to national prominence. Attendance at home games increased greatly during his reign. The record crowd for a Minnesota game was set January 18, 1956 against North Dakota as 9,490 fans crowded into Williams Arena. Later the Minneapolis Fire Marshall reduced the allowable attendance in the rink to 7,600.

After their playing days, former Gophers Herb Brooks, Larry Johnson, Ken Yackel, Murray Williamson, Bob Johnson, Lou Nanne and Doug Woog continued on to successful coaching and management careers. In the 1970s Brooks led the Gophers to three NCAA Championships and one second-place finish. Following his Minnesota coaching career he led the 1980 US. Olympic team to the Gold Medal at Lake Placid, N.Y. Later his duties led him to the National Hockey League where he directed the New York Rangers and Minnesota North Stars and recently has been appointed head coach for the New Jersey Devils.

Bob Johnson, a product of Minneapolis Central High School, played for the Gophers in 1954 and 1955. Following high school coaching careers at Warroad and

Minneapolis Roosevelt, he took over the reins at Colorado College. After several years at Colorado College he moved to Wisconsin where, in a period of 11 years, he led the Badgers to three NCAA championships and one runner-up spot. In 1982 Johnson migrated to the NHL to coach the Calgary Flames for five seasons. The fall of 1990 found him at the helm of the Pittsburgh Penguins, where in his first season, that of 1990-91, he led the team to the Stanley Cup. In the fall of 1991 Johnson died of brain cancer at the age of 60.

Lou Nanne, a Gopher defenseman from Sault Ste. Marie, Ontario, after playing with the Minnesota North Stars managed the team for 11 seasons, 1977-78 through 1987-88. In addition, he coached the North Stars for a short time during the 1977-78 season.

Ken Yackel, who also played baseball and football in addition to hockey at Minnesota, coached high school hockey, the Minneapolis Millers of the International Hockey League and the 1965 U.S. Nationals. During the season of 1971-72 he replaced Sonmor as Gopher mentor on an interim basis. He died in 1991 at the age of 59.

Murray Williamson, one of the few Canadians to play for Mariucci, coached three U.S. National teams, those of 1967, '70 and '71. In addition, he coached the 1968 U.S. Olympic sextet and the Silver Medalist 1972 team. For several seasons he coached senior and junior teams in the state.

Doug Woog, another Gopher player who has had a successful coaching career at Minnesota, took over the position for the 1985-86 season. Before accepting the Gopher spot Woog had 19 years of experience coaching at South St. Paul High School, the St. Paul Vulcans, and the U.S. National Juniors. Through his first seven year's experience at Minnesota his teams had a 228-85-11 record, giving him a winning percentage of .720, the highest of any college coach in the nation. He led his teams to seven consecutive NCAA appearances and the NCAA final four four times.

Another notable figure from the Mariucci era was Wendell Anderson, a St. Paul Johnson graduate, who played defense for the Maroon and Gold in 1952, '53 and '54. He was also a member of the second place 1956 U.S. Olympic team. Anderson entered Minnesota politics at an early age and by the 1960s was a prominent Democratic Party figure in the state's politics. He was governor of Minnesota during the 1970's, and in 1978 was appointed to the U.S. Senate to fill out the vacancy caused by Walter Mondale's decision to run as Democratic Vice President.

Edina's Larry Johnson, an all-around athlete who played football and hockey at Minnesota, became active in USA Hockey activities. He managed the 1984, '88 and '92 U.S. Olympic sixes in addition to other USA Hockey teams.

GLEN SONMOR ERA:
1966-67 through 1971-72

After the 1965-66 season, Mariucci was dismissed of his coaching position by A.D. Marsh Ryman. Glen Sonmor, a former professional player and experienced coach, who at one time had been Mariucci's freshman coach, became the Gophers seventh mentor.

In five seasons plus part of another, Sonmor posted a 79-82-6 record. After he left early in the season of 1971-72 to join the newly formed Minnesota Fighting Saints of the World Hockey Association, he was replaced by interim coach Ken Yackel.

Wally Olds

With a season record of 21-12, and an 18-8 finish in the WCHA, the Gophers captured the 1969-70 season title edging out Denver and Michigan Tech. Goalie Murray McLachlan and the pint-sized Mike Antonovich from Greenway of Coleraine led the Maroon and Gold to the league championship. In the finals of the WCHA playoffs, Michigan Tech edged the Gophers 6-5 to dash any hopes that they had of going to the NCAA Tournament. In 1971 the upstart Gophers, saddled with a losing regular season of 11-16-2, advanced to the NCAA finals at Syracuse before losing to Boston University 4-2. In the semi-final game Minnesota edged Harvard 6-5. Frank Sanders, Mike Antonovich, Dennis Erickson, John Matschke, Wally Olds, Craig Sarner, Doug Peltier and Dean Blais were among the players who took a leading role in the surprising finish of the 1971 team. McIntosh and Blais were selected to the All-Tournament NCAA team.

From the Sonmor era, Wally Olds (1970), Gary Gambucci (1968) and

Murray McLachlan (1970) were chosen to the All-American team. In 1968 Bill Klatt led the WCHA in scoring with 23 goals and 20 assists in 31 games.

1968 team photo

Players from the period who became members of the U.S. Nationals or the U.S. Olympics were Peter Fichuk, Bruce McIntosh, Olds, Frank Sanders, Sarner, Dean Blais, Mike Polich, Antonovich, Gambucci and James Branch. Players from the era who turned professional include: Antonovich, Bill Butters, Blais, Brad Buetow, Klatt, McIntosh, Olds, Dick Paradise, Sarner, Sanders, Gambucci and Pat Westrum.

Teams met during this time, not played previously, were St. Lawrence, Ohio State and Colgate. Three new teams joined the WCHA during this period—

Minnesota Duluth in 1966-67, Wisconsin in 1969-70 and Notre Dame in 1972-73.

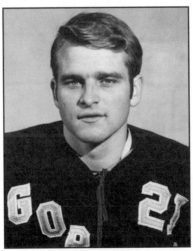
Murray McLachlan

HERB BROOKS ERA:
1972-73 through 1978-79

Herb Brooks became the eighth Minnesota coach when he replaced Glen Sonmor for the 1972-73 season. Brooks, who grew up in the hockey-happy East Side of St. Paul came from a hockey conscious family. His father had been a well known amateur player in the 1920's and his brother, David, had been a member of the Gophers in the early 1960s and the 1964 U.S. Olympic team.

In addition to his playing for Minnesota in the late 1950s, he had been a member of five U.S. National sextets and the 1964 and 1968 U.S. Olympic Teams. Prior to his appointment as Gopher mentor, Brooks had coached Minnesota junior teams and had been an assistant to Glen Sonmor.

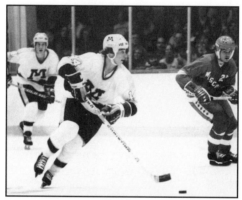

Neal Broten

Having extensive playing experience in European hockey it was only natural that he became interested in the game as played by the Russians and Czechs. He became an advocate of the Russian style of play and the coaching of Anatoli Tarasov. Brooks, who had a degree in psychology from the University of Minnesota, employed some of his learning in this field to motivate his players with the will to win.

In his second season, that of 1973-74, with a 22-12-6 overall record, the Gophers captured their first NCAA title at Boston by edging Boston University 5-4 in the first round and outlasting Michigan Tech 4-2 in the finals. Brad Shelstad, who had played at Minneapolis Southwest, was chosen as the tournament's Most Valuable Player, while Les Auge and Hibbing's Mike Polich were placed on the All-Tournament squad. During the season Minnesota had finished second in the WCHA race to Michigan Tech.

In 1975 the Gophers won the WCHA with a 24-8-0 mark. In the NCAA Tournament held in St. Louis they defeated Harvard 6-4 as Warren Miller got the first hat trick of his career. In the finals they lost 6-1 to Michigan Tech, which had finished second to them in the WCHA. Miller and defenseman Reed Larson were picked for the All-Tournament team.

The following spring of 1976 the Maroon and Gold won the NCAA crown for a second time in three seasons. In the tournament held at Denver, Boston University was Minnesota's first opponent, losing to the Gophers by a 4-2 score in a rough game. In the NCAA final game Minnesota edged arch-rival Michigan Tech 6-4. In the final game Gopher Tom Mohr, a seldom used goalie, replaced a sick Jeff Tscherne in the nets and proved to be the hero of the championship game. Minnesota's Tom Vannelli, who had amassed two goals and four assists in the two games, was chosen as the tournament's Most Valuable Player. After the win Minnesota's Pat Phippen remarked, "They called us shabby, they called us inconsistent, now they call us NCAA champions."

The Gophers had finished third in the WCHA race. To get to the NCAA final four Minnesota endured plenty of trouble from Michigan State in the league's final playoffs as the Spartans tied the Gophers in the first contest and lost to them in the second game 7-6 in three overtimes. A partial list of the 1976 team members include Jim Boo, Joe Micheletti, Russ Anderson, Warren Miller, Phil Verchota, Brad Morrow, Ton Gorence, Reed Larson, Robin Larson, Bill Baker, Joe Baker, Mark Lambert, Tom Vannelli, Joe Bonk and Pat Phippen.

Les Auge

In the 1976-77 season the Gophers with a 17-22-3 overall season lost to the Wisconsin Badgers in the WCHA playoffs. The following season with a fourth place league finish Minnesota lost in the playoffs to Colorado College.

At Detroit in 1979 Brooks led the team to their third NCAA crown in seven years of coaching at Minnesota by edging New Hampshire and North Dakota by identical 4-3 scores in Detroit. During the 1978-79 the Gophers had finished second to North Dakota in the WCHA race. Steve Janaszak, Minnesota's goalie, was named the tournament's Most Valuable Player, while Mike Ramsey, Eric Strobel and Steve Christoff were placed on the NCAA All-Tournament team. Although the Brooks-led teams did not enjoy a winning record against Wisconsin, they did post a respectable 52-34-4 effort against their three big rivals—North Dakota, UMD and Wisconsin.

After the Badgers joined the WCHA and their teams became a factor in the league races, a big rivalry built up between the two colleges. When the teams met, feelings of the fans ran high and the language employed likewise. In the book One Goal, by John Powers and Art Kaminsky, they describe Badger Bob Johnson and Brooks as follows: "They'd both graduated from the 'U' and both were driven, compulsive people. But there were important differences, too. Brooks was tight-lipped, blunt, and often critical. Johnson was hyperactive, garrulous, and unabash-edly boosterish. Brooks was mysterious and enigmatic, always keeping you off-base. With Johnson, no guessing was necessary; if you didn't know what he was doing and why, he would tell you — a dozen times."

Mike Polich led the Gophers in scoring three years in a row -- in 1973, '74 and '75. In 1976 and 1977 Tom Vannelli won the scoring title, while Steve Christoff did likewise in 1978 and 1979. Three Minnesota goalies in succession were selected as the leading goaltenders in the WCHA: Brad Shelstad in 1973-74, Larry Thayer in 1974-75 and Jeff Tscherne in 1975-76. All-WCHA selections during the Brooks era included Shelstad (1974), Polich (1975), Reed Larson(1976) and Bill Baker (1979), while Les Auge (1975), Polich (1976) and Bill Baker (1979) won All-American honors.

Nine players whom Brooks had coached at Minnesota were selected by Brooks as members of the 1980 Gold Medal U.S. Olympic team. These players were Neal Broten, Bill Baker, Steve Janaszak, Eric Strobel, Phil Verchota, Mike Ramsey, Buzz Schneider, Rob McClanahan and Steve Christoff. Gopher All-American selections who played during the Brooks reign include: Auge, Polich, Tim Harrer, Neal Broten and Steve Ulseth. Polich, Rob Harris, Brad Morrow, Auge, Phippen, Vannelli, Tom Younghans and Steve Ulseth are other Gophers who played for various U.S. Olympic/National teams.

Twenty-three former Gophers from the 1970's period have played in the NHL. With the number of years that they have played in the NHL in parenthesis they are as follows: Russ Anderson (10), Antonovich (5), Auge (1), Bob Bergloff (1), Bill Baker (3), Jim Boo (1), Neal Broten (12), Bill Butters (2), Christoff (5), Tom Gorence (6), Harrer (1), Paul Holmgren (10), Janaszak (2), Reed Larson (14), Rob McClanahan (5), Murray McLachlan (1), Pat Micheletti (1), Joe Micheletti (3), Warren Miller (4), Polich (5), Ramsey (13), Craig Sarner (7) and Younghans (6). Holmgren, a graduate of St. Paul's Harding High School, is one of the few Americans to have coached in the NHL. He was head coach for the Philadelphia Flyers for the 1988-91 seasons, and in 1992 became the head coach of the Hartford Whalers.

BRAD BUETOW ERA:
1979-80 through 1984-85

Brad Buetow, who had played under Brooks and was his assistant coach, took over head coaching duties at Minnesota on an interim basis for 1979-80 season as Brooks was at the helm of the U.S. Olympic team. Buetow was an-all around athlete at Mounds View High School and followed a similar path at Minnesota where he competed in varsity football, track and hockey. He played pro with the Cleveland Crusaders of the WHA.

With the losses of Ramsey, Neal Broten, McClanahan, Strobel and Christoff to the Olympics, all of whom had eligibility remaining at Minnesota, Buetow faced a tough job of replacing them. However, the Gophers finished with an overall record of 26-15 and surprisingly second in the league with the help of Tim Harrer, who led the WCHA in scoring and set a new school record of 45 goals for the season. Aaron Broten, one of the three brothers from Roseau who have played for the Gophers, Steve Ulseth, Peter Hayek, Bob Bergloff, David H. Jensen, Mike Knoke and goalies Jim Jetland and Paul Butters were among those who helped fill the spots left by those who departed to play for the U.S. Olympic team.

Scott Bjugstad

In the WCHA playoffs the Gophers defeated Michigan Tech and Colorado College, but lost to Northern Michigan 4-3 in a one-game playoff at Minneapolis, ending any chance of competing in the NCAA final four at Providence, R.I.

With an overall finish of 31-12 Buetow led the 1980-81 team to the WCHA title, finishing ahead of Michigan Tech and Wisconsin by six points. Neal Broten returned from the Olympics to join his brother Aaron and Butsy Erickson, to form the best line in college hockey. Both Brotens and Steve Ulseth were voted to the All-

WCHA team. Ulseth captured the WCHA scoring title, and Aaron Broten scored 106 total points for the season, leading the nation in scoring. Many old-time hockey fans compared the 1980-81 line with the best in Gopher history. For comparison they cite the Ryman-Todd-Parker and the Russ-Gray-Munns lines of the 1930's, the 1940 line of Paulson-St. Vincent-Pickering, and the early 1950's combination of Mayasich-Campbell-Dougherty. Among the players who played a prominent role in the team's success were: Paul Butters, Jetland, Jeff Teal, Mike Knoke, Kevin Hartzell, Mike Meadows, Bart Larson, Bob Bergloff, David H. Jenson and Scott Bjugstad. Teal and Butters, from Rochester, were among the first players from southern Minnesota to play for the Gophers. The team's entire roster was composed of Minnesota natives.

In the WCHA playoffs the Gophers defeated Colorado College and UMD. Minnesota then defeated the small but prestigious Colgate University of Hamilton, N.Y., by 9-4 and 5-4 scores in the NCAA Playoffs, thus allowing Minnesota to enter the NCAA final four in Duluth. The highly regarded Gophers outlasted Michigan Tech 7-2 in the opener, but were upset 6-3 in the finals by Wisconsin. The Badgers had been volted back into the NCAA tournament after having lost in the WCHA playoffs. This surprise action by the NCAA is how the monicker, "Back-Door Badgers" originated.

Defenseman Mike Knoke and Aaron Broten were selected to the NCAA final four All-Star team. Neal Broten had the honor of being chosen as the first recipient of the Hobey Baker Award. Many Gopher hockey followers considered the 1980-81 team to be among the very best to ever have represented the University of Minnesota in its 60 years of varsity hockey.

At the end of the 1980-81 season, Notre Dame, Michigan Tech, Michigan State and Michigan left the WCHA to join the more compact Central Collegiate Hockey Association. This resulted in the WCHA being reduced to a six-team circuit, which operated as such until Michigan Tech rejoined and Northern Michigan entered the league for the first time in 1984-85 to form an eight-team league.

Predicted to finish fourth or fifth in the WCHA, the 1981-82 Gophers finished third in the league to the strong North Dakota and Wisconsin sextets. Butsy Erickson led the Minnesota team in scoring with 20 goals and 25 assists for 45 total points. Other scoring leaders include forwards Hartzell, Scott Bjugstad and Rick Erdall, while Tom Hirsch and David H. Jensen led the defense, and Paul Ostby and Jim Jetland saw the most duty in goal. In the first round of the WCHA playoffs Minnesota defeated Colorado College 9-4 in a two game total goal series at Minneapolis. In the finals held at Madison the Gophers split with host Wisconsin, but lost the series on total goals, thus ending their hope for an NCAA spot.

In 1982-83 Minnesota won its second league crown in three years as they posted a 18-7-1 WCHA finish and a 33-12-1 overall season. A talented group of freshmen joined the team including goalie Frank Pietrangelo, Corey Millen, Wally Chapman, Tony Kellin and Mike Anderson.

In league playoffs the Maroon and Gold defeated UMD but lost to Wisconsin in the WCHA finals. However, both Minnesota and Wisconsin advanced to the NCAA first round where Minnesota outplayed New Hampshire 9-7 and 6-2.

The NCAA final four at Grand Forks found the Gophers losing their opening game to Harvard 5-3 and to Providence 4-3 in the consolation contest.

During the season after the first 28 games, the Gophers posted a respectable 23-4-1 record. Scott Bjugstad headed the league's scoring parade with 21 goals and 35 assists for 56 total points, while forwards Erickson, Millen, Erdall and Steve Griffith and defensemen Larson, Hirsch and Jensen were among the team's top scorers.

Gary Shopek

The Gophers, with a 16-9-1 WCHA finish, captured third place in the 1983-84 league race trailing UMD and North Dakota. UMD, under their newly appointed coach Mike Sertich, won the WCHA title with a 19-5-2 record. With the likes of Tom Kurvers, Bill Watson, Rick Kosti and Norm Maciver the Bulldogs advanced to the NCAA final four where they lost to Bowling Green 5-4 in four overtime periods.

In the WCHA playoffs Minnesota defeated Colorado College 3-1 and 4-1 and were edged by the North Dakota Sioux 4-3 and 5-4 in the finals at Grand Forks. UMD, North Dakota, Michigan State and Bowling Green advanced to the NCAA final four at Lake Placid, N.Y. Tom Rothstein, of Grand Rapids, paced the Gopher in scoring with 30 goals and 34 assists for 64 total points in 39 games. Pat Micheletti, Jeff Larson, Tony Kellin and Todd Okerlund followed in the scoring race. Frank Pietrangelo and Edina's Mike Vacanti split the goaltending duties.

Buetow posted his sixth straight winning season in 1984-85 with a 31-13-3 overall finish. With a 21-10-3 record the Gophers ended up second to UMD in the WCHA race.

The season was the first that the WCHA and Hockey East played an interlocking schedule with each WCHA team playing a two game series against each of the seven HE teams. The HE was composed of Boston University, Boston College, Providence, Maine, New Hampshire, Lowell and Northeastern. Minnesota's record against HE opponents for the initial season of competition was 10-3-1.

In the WCHA playoffs Minnesota won a two-game total series from Colorado College and Wisconsin and lost to UMD 10-8. In the NCAA playoffs in

Boston the Gophers lost to Boston College 9-8 in a two game total-goal set. The NCAA final four staged in Detroit found UMD losing to RPI 6-5 in three overtime periods in first round. RPI went on to capture the NCAA crown by edging Providence 2-1.

Pat Micheletti paced the Gopher scorers for the season with 48 goals and 48 assists for 96 total points in 44 games. Two centers, Erdall and Corey Millen, followed Micheletti in the scoring race, while two Iron Rangers, Tony Kellin and Captain Mike Guentzel, led the defense. John Blue was chosen the leading goalie in the WCHA.

Players from the Buetow era who were selected to the WCHA All-Star team include: Harrer (1980), Aaron Broten (1981), Neal Broten (1982), Ulseth (1981), Bjugstad (1983), Erickson (1983), Rothstein (1984) and Micheletti (1985). Gophers from this period who played on U.S. Olympic/National teams are as follows: Ostby, Bjugstad, Griffith, Hirsch, Jensen, Millen, John Blue, Aaron Broten, Erickson, Okerlund and Steve MacSwain. The following players have competed in the NHL: Tim Bergland, Blue, Bjugstad, Erickson, Aaron and Neal Broten, Jensen, Millen, Micheletti, Okerlund and Frank Pietrangelo. From Roseau in northwestern Minnesota, Aaron and Neal Broten, along with their younger brother Paul, all played for the Gophers and the NHL. During this period Tim Harrer (1980), Neal Broten (1981), Steve Ulseth (1981) and Pat Micheletti (1985) were accorded All-American honors.

Following the 1984-85 season Brad Buetow, who never experienced a losing season, and ended his six-year Minnesota coaching career with a 171-75-8 record, was released from his position by the University of Minnesota Athletic Department. Athletic Director Paul Giel refused to give any reason for Buetow's dismissal. Buetow finished his six-year reign with a winning percentage of .689%, highest since Emil Iverson's era of 1923-24 through 1929-30. Since leaving Buetow has coached at U.S. International in San Diego and lately at Colorado College.

DOUG WOOG ERA:
1985-86 through the present

Doug Woog, a native of South St. Paul, was named coach at Minnesota in the summer of 1985. Woog, who was a football and hockey star at South St. Paul High School, attained All-American honors while playing for John Mariucci at Minnesota. Following his college playing days he coached the St. Paul Vulcans and the Minnesota Junior Stars of the United States Hockey League to league and national titles. Following his Junior coaching career he took over the duties of head coach at South St. Paul High School for several seasons, where his teams won two league crowns and competed in the Minnesota State High School Tournament four times.

In his first Gopher season, that of 1985-86, Woog led the Maroon and Gold to a new school record of 35 wins and to a spot in the NCAA final four in Providence, R.I. From the 1984-85 team the Gophers had lost such players as Captain Guentzel, Kurt Larson, Tom Parenteau, Rick Erdall and Tom Rothstein, but returning were forwards Millen, Micheletti, Chapman, Okerlund, Bergland, Mac Swain and defensemen Tony Kellin, Gary Shopek, Craig Mack, Eric Dornfeld and goalie Frank Pietrangelo. In their interlocking schedule with HE the Gophers won 10 games and lost four. The Gophers finished second in the WCHA with a 24-10-0 finish.

Millen, with 41 goals and 42 assist for 83 total points, paced the team in scoring, followed closely by Micheletti who was only three points behind. MacSwain, Chapman, Jay Cates and Okerlund followed in that order. John Blue and Frank Pietrangelo divided goaltending chores. Blue led the WCHA goalies with a 3.08 GA average.

Ken Gernander

In the WCHA playoffs at Minneapolis the Gophers defeated Colorado College 10-4 and 4-3, Wisconsin 4-1 and 7-3 before losing to Denver at Denver 3-0 and 3-2. Both Denver and Minnesota traveled to Boston for the NCAA playoffs where the Gophers edged Boston University 6-4 and 5-3. In the NCAA final four at Providence, the Gophers lost their opener to Michigan State 4-3 and won the consolation crown from Denver 6-4.

In his second season of 1986-87 at Minnesota, Woog posted a record of 34-14-1 and a 25-9-1 finish in the WCHA, earning the Gophers a runner-up spot to the champion North Dakota Sioux.

With 12 regulars returning and the 1985-86 team's leading scorer in Corey Millen, the team got off to a fine start by winning 21 of its first 24 contests. Although later in the schedule they lost several games, they managed to make their way to the NCAA final four where they captured the consolation honors. Millen led the team in scoring, followed by Mac Swain, David Snuggerud, Todd Richards, Shopek, Tom Chorske, Jay Cates, Paul Broten and Bergland. John Blue and freshman Robb Stauber divided the goaltending duties. Defensemen were Richards, Shopek, Randy Skarda, David Espe, Eric Dornfeld, Lance Pitlick and Craig Mack.

In their schedule against HE, reduced from 14 to seven games, the Gophers recorded four wins and three losses.

225

In the first round of the WCHA playoffs the Gophers outlasted Michigan Tech 9-4 and 8-5 and in the second round split with Wisconsin but advanced to the finals on total goals of 9-6. In the WCHA finals at Grand Forks, host North Dakota defeated Minnesota in two halves by identical scores of 4-3.

The Gophers lost in the first round of the NCAA final four at Detroit to Michigan State 5-3 and overcame Harvard 6-3 in the consolation finals. In the finals North Dakota defeated Michigan State 5-3 to capture its fifth NCAA title.

With the loss of Millen, Snuggerud, Chorske, Okerlund and Blue to the 1988

Jeff Stolp

U.S. Olympic team, prognosticators predicted a third-place WCHA finish for the 1987-88 Gophers. With excellent goaltending from Duluth's Robb Stauber, unexpected performances from the returning forwards and two high scoring defensemen in Randy Skarda and Todd Richards, Minnesota won the league race by seven games. Jay Cates, from Stillwater, led the team in scoring with 48 total points in the 42 games that he played. Paul Broten, Skarda, Peter Hankinson, Richards and freshmen Grant Bischoff and Jason Miller followed in that order. Stauber, who played in all 44 games, posted a 2.72 GA average and a .913 save percentage to become the first goalie to win the coveted Hobey Baker Award. In addition, he was accorded All-American honors. Skarda set a school record of 19 goals for a defenseman. Both Skarda and Stauber were picked for the WCHA All-Star team.

In the first round of the WCHA playoffs held at Minneapolis, the Gophers shut out Colorado College 7-0 and 5-0. With St. Paul hosting the WCHA final four, Minnesota disposed of UMD 6-0 and lost to the Badgers 3-2, but moved on to the NCAA playoffs, where they defeated Michigan State 4-2 and 4-3. Continuing on to Lake Placid for the NCAA final four, the Gophers lost to St. Lawrence in the semifinals.

Continuing their dominance over HE, Minnesota won four out of their seven meetings in the fourth season of interlocking competition between the two leagues.

The return of David Snuggerud and Tom Chorske from the Olympics, seven veteran defensemen and the Hobey Baker Award recipient, Stauber in the goal, pointed to a winning season for the 1988-89 Gophers. Returning defensemen included Skarda, Richards, Sean Fabian, Brett Nelson, Pitlick, Luke Johnson and Espe in addition to two highly regarded freshmen, Tom Pederson and Travis Richards, Todds brother.

The 1988-89 team did not disappoint their loyal followers as they completed another outstanding season, winning the WCHA crown by a seven point margin over Michigan Tech, thus capturing the WCHA title two years in succession for the first time in the history of Gopher hockey. In addition, the team advanced through the WCHA and NCAA to finish runner-up to Harvard in the NCAA finals.

Chorske, playing in 37 games and Snuggerud in 45 contests, tied for the team's scoring title with 49 points each. Other forwards who placed high in the scoring parade included Peter Hankinson, freshman Larry Olimb, Bischoff, Jason Miller, and Jon Anderson while Todd Richards, Skarda and freshman Tom Pederson led the defense corps in scoring. Stauber had another outstanding season playing in 34 games and leading the WCHA goaltenders. Chorske was selected as a member of the WCHA All-Star team.

First round WCHA playoffs found the Gophers winning from Colorado College 5-4 and 7-1. The WCHA was so satisfied with the total attendance of 51,087

Ben Hankinson

for the initial four-game tournament held at the Civic Center in St. Paul in 1988 that they returned again for the 1989 playoffs. In the tournament the Gophers lost two one goal decisions, 2-1 to Denver in the first round and 4-3 to the Badgers in the consolation game.

The NCAA final four held in St. Paul found Minnesota downing Maine 7-4 in their opener and losing a close 4-3 decision in overtime to Harvard for the championship. Many in the large crowd thought it might have been the best college hockey game that they had ever viewed.

The five-year interlocking WCHA-HE schedule was terminated after the 1988-89 season. Minnesota ended their schedule with the eastern schools with an honorable 33-14-1 record and a winning percentage of .700.

The season of 1989-90 was predicted to be another good outing for the Gophers. The losses from the previous season were minimal as only three regulars, all defensemen, included Todd Richards, Brett Nelson and David Espe. The team lived up to its pre-season predictions, finishing with a 28-16-2 overall record and second to the Wisconsin Badgers in the WCHA race. The Gophers lost six of their first 13 games, but then went on a winning streak by losing only one contest in their next 16 encounters.

Peter Hankinson of Edina led the team in scoring with 25 goals and 41 assists in 46 games played. Other leading scorers were Scott Bloom, Ken Gernander, Olimb, Bischoff, Tom Pederson, Trent Klatt and Jason Miller. Freshmen who had good seasons included Klatt, John Brill, Doug Zmolek, red-shirted Travis Richards and goalie Tom Newman. Stolp, Newman and Scott Nelson divided the goalie duties with Newman seeing the most action. Peter Hankinson was selected to the WCHA All-Star team, while Ken Gernander was picked for the WCHA All-tournament team.

In the first round of the WCHA playoffs, the Gophers had little trouble from Colorado College as they ran up 9-3 and 9-2 victories. The WCHA semifinals at the St. Paul Civic Center found the Gophers edging North Dakota 5-4 in the opener and losing to Wisconsin 7-1 in the finals. An attendance of 13,704 fans viewed the Gopher-Badger game.

The Gophers met Clarkson of the ECAC at Minneapolis in the first round of the NCAA and defeated them 6-1 and 5-1. In the NCAA quarterfinals in Boston the Gophers lost two and won one from Boston College in a best two out of three series, thus ending their bid for a national crown.

During Woog's sixth season as Gopher coach Minnesota finished second to the high flying Northern Michigan Wildcats by five points. The Maroon and Gold completed the season with a 22-5-5 WCHA record, and an overall finish of 30-10-5. The Gophers had entered the 1990-91 season with a record of 13 straight winning seasons.

Losses from the 1989-90 team included top scorers Peter Hankinson and Bloom in addition to Pitlick, Brett Strot, Dean Williamson and Jon Anderson.

Several promising freshmen — Jeff Nielsen, Craig Johnson, Joe Dziedzic, Mike Muller, Chris McAlpine, Scott Bell -- added strength to both the offense and defense. Olimb, moved from defense to center, paced the team in scoring, followed by Gernander, Bischoff, Klatt and Captain Ben Hankinson. Jeff Stolp and Tom Newman divided the goalie chores with Stolp posting a respectable WCHA GA average of 2.71%.

After competing for a few seasons as a Division One independent St. Cloud State joined the WCHA in the fall of 1990 to make it a nine-team circuit. During the season Minnesota won three and tied one game with the new interstate rival Huskies.

In first round WCHA playoffs played in Minneapolis found host Minnesota outscoring Michigan Tech 5-3 and 6-5. The Gophers edged Wisconsin in their opener of the WCHA finals held in St. Paul 3-2 but lost to Northern Michigan in the finals 4-2.

Minnesota defeated Providence in the first round of the NCAA playoffs two games to one in the series played at Minneapolis. Continuing on to the NCAA quarterfinals at Orono, Maine, Minnesota lost to host Maine 4-0 and 5-3, thus missing again an opportunity to advance to the NCAA final four. Chris McAlpine and Craig Johnson were picked on the 1991 WCHA All-Rookie Team.

The 1991-92 Gophers won their third WCHA title in five years with a 26-6 league finish, 12 points ahead of second place Wisconsin. During the seven seasons that Woog had been at the Minnesota helm they had a 228-85-11 record for winning percentage of .720, the best in Division One college hockey. Woog led Minnesota to seven straight NCAA Tournaments and four NCAA final four appearances.

After losing five of their first nine contests the Gophers won 21 of their next

Grant Bischoff

23 games. A feature of the 1991-92 season was the scheduling of one of the Wisconsin games at the Met Center, with its larger seating capacity. The move proved to be a successful one as it gave an opportunity to the thousands of Wisconsin fans attending the Badger-Gopher football game a chance to view the hockey game between the two rivals. The game, won 4-1 by the Gophers, drew a full house of 15,712.

Warroad's Larry Olimb led the Minnesota scorers for the season, bringing his career total points to 200. Thus he became the seventh Gopher to score 200 points in his career as a Minnesota player. Others who have accomplished the feat include John Mayasich (298), Pat Micheletti (269), Corey Millen (241), Butsy Erickson (238), Steve Ulseth (202) and Tim Harrer (201). Other leading scorers were Trent Klatt, Craig Johnson, Darby Hendrickson, Cory Laylin, Travis Richards and Steve

Magnusson. Freshmen Hendrickson, Magnusson and Justin McHugh played a big role in the team's success. Hendrickson led the WCHA freshmen in scoring with 17 goals and 22 assists in 32 league encounters.

The Gopher defense was by far the best in the league allowing only 89 goals in the 32 game WCHA schedule. Stolp in goal had another outstanding season as he led the WCHA goal tenders with a 2.87 GA. The Gopher defensive corp of Travis Richards, Zmolek, Fabian, McAlpine, Eric Means and Mike Muller played an important part in the teams' strong defensive play.

In first round WCHA playoffs at Mariucci Arena, the Gophers won two out of three games from North Dakota to advance to the WCHA final four at St. Paul. Minnesota next defeated Colorado College 6-1 and lost to Northern Michigan 4-2 in the finals. In further competition Minnesota lost to Lake Superior State 8-3 in the NCAA quarterfinals held in Detroit. Lake Superior went on to win the NCAA crown over Wisconsin.

WCHA ATTENDANCE - 1991-92

(Reprinted from WCHA News Release 3/9/92)

College	Attendance	Games	Average
Colorado College	46,608	15	3,107
Denver	67,758	18	3,764
Michigan Tech	47,682	16	2,980
Minnesota	128,507	18	7,139
Minnesota-Duluth	87,543	17	5,150
North Dakota	93,855	19	4,940
Northern Michigan	69,784	17	4,105
St. Cloud State	69,618	18	3,868
Wisconsin	145,086	17	8,534

MINNESOTA'S RECORD AGAINST PRESENT WCHA MEMBERS THROUGH 1992

(Includes games played prior to the formation of the Midwest Collegiate Hockey League.)

MINNESOTA

OPPONENT	Won	Lost	Tied	%	1st Season Played
Colorado College	151	47	4	.757	1946-47
Denver	64	43	6	.593	1950-51
Minnesota-Duluth	84	43	8	.652	1962-63
Michigan Tech	*187	75	10	.706	1921-22
Northern Michigan	20	12	5	.608	1976-80
North Dakota	*121	96	4	.548	1927-28
St. Cloud State	9	0	2	.909	1990-91
Wisconsin	*135	65	14	.663	1921-22

Includes games played in the 1920's and 30's

GOPHER CAPTAINS

1921-22 Chet Bros
1922-23 Paul Swanson
1923-24 Frank Pond
1924-25 Vic Mann
1925-26 Ed Olson
1926-27 Phil Scott
1927-28 Jack Conway
1928-29 Joe Brown
1929-30 Charles McCabe
1930-31 William Conway
1931-32 Marsh Ryman
1932-33 Harold Carlsen
1933-34 Phil La Batte
1934-35 Spencer Wagnild
1935-36 Charles Wilkinson, Ted Mitchell
1936-37 Reynold Bjork
1937-38 Dick Kroll, Loane Randall
1938-39 Kenneth Anderson
1939-40 John Mariucci, Frank St. Vincent
1940-41 Harold Paulson
1941-42 Allan Eggleton
1942-43 Don Nolander, Robert Graiziger
1943-44 Patrick Ryan
1944-45 Allan Opsahl, Robert Carley
1945-46 Allan Opsahl, Robert Carley
1946-47 Allan Opsahl, John O'Brien
1947-48 James Frick
1948-49 Roland De Paul
1949-50 Robert Harris, Sr.
1950-51 James Sedin
1951-52 Russ Strom
1952-53 Thomas Wegleitner
1953-54 Gene Campbell
1954-55 John Mayasich, James Mattson
1955-56 George Jetty, Kenneth Yackel, Sr.
1956-57 Jack Petroske
1957-58 Jack McCarten, Mike Pearson
1958-59 Thomas Riley, Gary Alm
1959-60 Myron Grafstrom, Jerry Mylenchuk
1960-61 Jerry Norman, Larry Johnson
1961-62 Richard Young
1962-63 Lou Nanne
1963-64 David Metzen
1964-65 Craig Falkman

1965-66 Doug Woog, John Lothrop
1966-67 James Branch
1967-68 Gary Gambucci
1968-69 William Klatt Jr.
1969-70 Patrick Westrum
1970-71 Frank Sanders
1971-72 John Thoemke
1972-73 James Gambucci, William Butters
1973-74 Brad Shelstad
1974-75 Robert Harris, Jr.
1975-76 Pat Phippen
1976-77 Joe Micheletti
1977-78 Robin Larson
1978-79 William Baker
1979-80 Don Micheletti
1980-81 Steve Ulseth, Mike Knoke
1981-82 Kevin Hartzell
1982-83 David H. Jensen, Bryan Erickson
1983-84 Tom Rothstein, Jeffrey Larson
1984-85 Mike Guentzel
1985-86 Tony Kellin, Wally Chapman
1986-87 Corey Millen, Tim Bergland
1987-88 Paul Broten, Jay Gates
1988-89 Dave Snuggerud, Todd Richards
1989-90 Peter Hankinson, Lance Pitlick
1990-91 Ben Hankinson
1991-92 Larry Olimb
1992-93 Travis Richards

GOPHER BROTHERS

NAME	HOME TOWN
Arnold-Ed and Robert	Minneapolis
Alm-Gary, Rick, Mike and Larry	Minneapolis
Bros-Ben, C.W. and Kenneth	Minneapolis
Broten-Neal, Aaron and Paul	Roseau
Brooks-David and Herb	St. Paul
Buctow-Brad and Bart	Mounds View
Conway-John and William	Minneapolis
Hankinson-Peter and Ben	Edina
Harrer-Tim and Mike	Bloomington
Harris-John and Rob	Roseau
Meredith-Richard, John, Wayne and Bob	Minneapolis
Micheletti-Joe, Donald and Pat	Hibbing
Paradise-Richard and Lawrence	St. Paul
Peltier-Ron and Doug	St. Paul
Phippen-Pat and Mike	St. Paul
Richards-Todd and Travis	Crystal
Rovick-David and Roger	Minneapolis
Russ-Clyde and Lloyd	Minneapolis
Ryman-Marsh and Fred	Minneapolis
Stordahl-Jim and Larry	Roseau
Westby-James and Jerry	Minneapolis

GOPHER FATHERS AND SON (S)

FATHER	SON (S)
Harris, Robert V.	Robert B. and John
Klatt, William G., Sr.	William G., Jr.
Larson, Frank	Robb
Lundeen, Lloyd	Paul
Nanne, Louis	Marty
Ryman, Marsh	Mark
Thayer, Mack	Larry
Williamson, Murray	Dean
Yackel, Kenneth J., Sr.	Kenneth J., Jr.

Similar to their state's politics, Minnesota prides itself on being independant and self-sufficient. During the 70 seasons of hockey at the U of M, the school and the state have taken great pride in the teams' reliance on home-grown talent. Analyzing rosters going back to the early 1920's reveals that few Canadians or out-of-state players have been members of the Maroon and Gold teams. Having watched Gopher Hockey for the past 60 years, I can recall the names of only 18 Canadians and six out-of -state members dating back to 1932.

The 1974, '76 and '79 NCAA national championship Gophers sported entire lineups of Minnesota natives. During the past five seasons there has not been a Canadian or an out-of-state player on the team. During the past 20 seasons there has been a total of t hree players rostered on the Minnesota teams who were not Minnesota products. Of the Division One colleges, only Boston College rivals the Gophers in recruiting all U.S. players.

It is revealing to note where the Gopher players come from. In the by-gone days of the 1920's, '30's and early '40's, fully 70% of the players came from Minneapolis and St. Paul, with almost all the remaining coming from Duluth and the Iron Range. The post World War II period found players in greater numbers coming from the small communities in northern Minnesota.

Seven small communities in northern Minnesota -- namely Roseau, Warroad, Eveleth, Hibbing, Grand Rapids, the Coleraine area, and International Falls, total-ling less than 40,000 in population -- have sent 80 players to Minnesota over the years. Roseau and Eveleth, each with 17 players lead in numbers.

Few Gopher players have come from southern Minnesota, with the first being Winona's Roger Benson, who played for Minnesota in the early 1950's. In the past decade, Rochester, with its strong youth program, has contributed several players to the Gophers succes on the ice. Nocl Jenke, an all-around athlete from Owatonna, lettered in hockey at Minnesota. Marty Falk, Bud Wilkinson, Wally Taft and Chuck Massie, all of Minneapolis, prepped at Shattuck School in Faribault and later played at Minnesota. Eric Strobel, more recently, starred for Brooks after playing for Rochester Mayo, followed by Jake Enebak of Northfield, and Doug Zmolek and Eric Means of Rochester John Marshall.

Currently, about two-thirds of the Gopher roster is composed of players from the Minneapolis-St. Paul Metro Seven County Area. In recent years fewer players have been coming from the central cities of Minneapolis and St. Paul and more from the suburban communities, which maintain extensive youth programs and strong high school teams.

Acknowledgment should be accorded to the assistant coaches at Minne-sota for their part in the team's success during the past seasons. Glen Sonmor, Herb Brooks and Brad Buetow — all of whom became head coaches at Minnesota — spent part of their careers as assistant coaches at the Gopher institution.

Dean Talafous, Bob Shier, Jack Blatherwick, Mike Foley, Rob Larson, Bruce Lind, Mark Mazzoleni and John Perpich are others who have been assistants at Minnesota during the past decade. Assistant coaches to Woog during the past season of 1991-1992 included Bill Butters, Mark Mazzoleni, Bob Shier and Paul Ostby.

The recent NCAA reduction in the college hockey coaching staff will go into effect for the 1992-93 season. This reduction mandates that a team can have only one head coach, one full-time assistant and one part time assistant.

After 70 years of playing in several rinks — namely, the Hippodrome and Coliseum in St. Paul, Minneapolis Arena and Mariucci Arena — the Gophers at last will have a new modern facility for practice and home games.

The new $20,000,000 arena, scheduled to be opened in the fall of 1993, will be located on campus just north of the present Williams/Mariucci Arena. Seating between 8,500 and 9,500, the arena, which will have an ice surface of 200' X 100', will be the largest collegiate hockey rink in the country. It will be a single bowl design with no obstruction of sight lines. As in the case of the present Mariucci Arena, opened in 1950, no longer will devoted Gopher fans have to peek around steel posts or to endure the fans in front of them standing up to obstruct seeing the game action.

Concerning the new facility, Coach Doug Woog remarked, "Mariucci Arena has served the University well and will always hold a special place in my heart, but Minnesota hockey fans and the hockey program will finally get the arena they deserve."

Stanley S. Hubbard, a former Gopher hockey player, and Kathleen Ridder are co-chairing a fund raising campaign to raise part of the cost of the new facility.

GOPHER ALL-AMERICANS

CHARLES McCABE	1929
JOHN H. PETERSON	1930
JOE BROWN	1931
ANDY TOTH	1932
JOHN MARIUCCI	1940
HAROLD PAULSON	1940
ROLAND DePAUL	1948
GORDON WATTERS	1951
LARRY ROSS	1951
KEN YACKEL SR.	1954
JIM MATTSON	1954
DICK DOUGHERTY	1954
JOHN MAYASICH	1953,'54,'55
JACK McCARTAN	1957,'58
DICK BURG	1958
MIKE PEARSON	1958
MURRAY WILLIAMSON	1959
LOU NANNE	1963
CRAIG FALKMAN	1964
DOUG WOOG	1965
GARY GAMBUCCI	1968
MURRAY McLACHLAN	1970
WALLY OLDS	1970
LES AUGE	1975
MIKE POLICH	1975
BILL BAKER	1979
TIM HARRER	1980
NEAL BROTEN	1981
STEVE ULSETH	1981
PAT MICHELETTI	1985
ROBB STAUBER	1988

AFTERWORDS

The Gopher Hockey program is one of great history, nostalgia and tradition in Minnesota. Exceeding such traditions as basketball in Indiana or football in Texas, the hockey tradition at Minnesota is the most unique of its kind in the country. It started in the late 1800s on the frozen pond, and evolved into the great sport our state is so very proud of today. John Mariucci was the Godfather of Minnesota hockey, and without his contributions none of this would be here.

I gotta say that writing this book was a blast. I got to meet several of my childhood heroes, and learned so much about the game of hockey. Some days I would meet three or four people, and have to drive from Minneapolis to Anoka to Stillwater to Bloomington. I put some serious miles on the old Horizon this summer, but it was well worth it. It was everything from meeting Charley Hallman at J.J.'s Cafe in St. Paul where he demanded that we both eat the Meat Loaf Special, to touring the Grain Exchange with Burton Joseph. Where, when I pointed to the commodities exchange board to ask him a question, he grabbed my hand and said "Whoa boy, you have to be careful pointing around here, you almost bought yourself 10,000 bushels of September Wheat." There was dinner with Steve Cannon at his favorite Italian restaurant, and lunches with the Broten Brothers. There was laughing so hard with Glen Sonmor that my sides ached, and listening in quiet awe to Stanley S. Hubbard and Bob Ridder. There were two meetings with Frank Mazzocco and Wally Shaver. Two because we had too much fun at Stub and Herbs to remember the first one. Then there was my rendezvous with Governor Carlson, where he answered every question about hockey with a Gopher basketball response. There was Davey Brooks in a golf cart at the Mariucci Golf Classic, and the Williamsons at their "Club." There was the trek out to the Nanne home in posh Edina, where I saw some dogs walking around the neighborhood wearing sweaters worth more than my car. There were the occasional tears of Dick Meredith, when he spoke softly about an old friend named John Mariucci, and there was the sports-cluttered office of Mark Rosen. Then there were the countless meetings with my editor, John Gilbert, when we would argue about name spellings, cover designs and editorial stuff all the while comparing Al's Breakfast in Dinkytown to the various Keys Restaurants. It was a friendly chat with Jack and Barbara McCartan, and gawking at Norm Green's office, his personal shrine. It was spending an afternoon with Gretchen Colletti looking at pictures of her beau, and occasionally pausing for a Kleenex break. It was the Board of Regents meeting with Wendy Anderson, and the back yard of the Hankinsons, eating pretzels and talking chicks. All this and so much more was just part of the fun of writing this sucker. I loved it but I'd have to think real hard about doing it again. Writing a book takes a pretty hefty toll on the old social life, and I may not even have any friends left after this! Umm...Guys? Remember me? I'm the guy that blew you off all summer to write a book. Guys?

Well, I'll see you at the arena. I'll be the guy in the "NE" section unconsciously standing up in front of the crowd during the game, and expecting the crowd to yell "NEE" when I point to my knee. Don't call the security over, it's just me trying to adjust to civilian life again. It's not easy going from human to rodent and back to human again. I think a small portion of me will always be rodent. So, it's time for me to stop pretending to be an author and enter the real world. It's on to busines school for a quick MBA and then live happily ever after. (I always said that if I ever wrote a book, it would end "happily ever after.")

REFERENCES

1) Boston Herald, Jan. 28, 1898
2) Yale-Her Campus, Books & Athletes, by W Camp & L Welch, p 623-4 1899
3) Baltimore Sun, Dec. 27, 1894
4) Harper's Weekly, 1895 p 45
5) Harper's Weekly, 1896 p 313
6) St. Paul Globe, Jan. 30, 1904 p 284
7) On to Nicollet, by Thornley
8) Minnesota Ariel, Feb. 4, 1895 p 4
9) St. Paul Pioneer Press, Feb. 7, 1895
10) St. Paul Pioneer Press, Feb. 19, 1895
11) Minnesota Ariel, Feb. 16, 1895 p 5
12) St. Pioneer Press, Jan. 20, 1903
13) Spalding Ice Hockey Guide, 1904
14) Spalding Ice Hockey Guide, 1915
15) Spalding Ice Hockey Guide, 1927-28 through 1939-40
16) NCAA Ice Hockey Guide, 1940-41 through 1981-82
17) Minnesota Annuals, 1921-1950
18) Western College Hockey News, 1953-54
19) WCHA News Release, 1865-1992
20) Minnesota Hockey, 1991-92
21) NCAA Program, March 28-30, 1991
22) WCHA Program, March 10-11, 1991
23) NCAA Program, March 26-28, 1981
24) WCHA Yearbook, 40th Anniversary Edition, 1991-92
25) Minnesota Game Program, November 2, 1991
26) NHL Guide and Record Book, 1991-1992
27) Ice Hockey, U.S. Records in Olympics and World Championships 1920-86, By Donald M. Clark
28) 1991-92 Gopher Hockey Media Guides

(Correspondence and Interviews with Marsh Ryman, John Mariucci and Russell Johnson.)